**"I'm going to kiss you.
Better stop me if you don't want me to."**

It was like she'd been injected with venom that paralyzed her body but left her brain aware. She wanted to say stop, but only intellectually. Her body—and every last cell in it—wanted to feel Evan's mouth on hers.

So she said nothing.

And he kissed her, as promised.

When his lips lowered, she lifted hers and met him in the middle. The pressure increased on her neck as he adjusted the angle, and she lifted a palm and laid it on his firm chest, feeling his heart pound, feeling the earth shake, and tingling and fluttering everywhere capable of tingling and fluttering.

She lost track of hands and feet, the whole world. Everything but their mating mouths fell away as he tasted her. Their tongues speared, her head swam, and the pulse throbbing low in her belly relocated to in between her thighs...

ACCLAIM FOR JESSICA LEMMON'S LOVE IN THE BALANCE SERIES

HARD TO HANDLE

"[Aiden is] a perfect balance of sensitive, heart-on-his-sleeve guy who is as sexy and 'alpha' as they come...A real romance that's not about dominance but equality and mutual need—while not sacrificing [the] hotness factor. A rare treat."

—PolishedBookworm.com

"Lemmon's latest is a pleasant example of living in the present and celebrating second, and sometimes third, chances."

—*RT Book Reviews*

"[Aiden is] a fantastic character. He is a motorcycle-riding, tattooed, rebel kind of guy with a huge heart. What's not to love?...I really enjoyed this book and I think readers will find it entertaining and heartfelt."

—RomanceRewind.blogspot.com

"I smiled through a lot of it, but seeing Aiden and Sadie deal with all of their hurdles was also incredibly moving and had me tearing up more than once as well...I can't wait to see what Lemmon will bring to the table next."

—HerdingCats-BurningSoup.com

"Aiden has all the characteristics of a bad boy but with the heart of that perfect hero...Their gradual spark leads to some well-written steamier scenes."

—RosieReadsRomance.blogspot.com

CAN'T LET GO

TEMPTING THE BILLIONAIRE

"If you are interested in a loveable romance about two troubled souls who overcome the odds to find their own happily ever after, I would certainly recommend that you give *Tempting the Billionaire* a try. It was definitely a great Valentine's Day read, for sure!"

—ChrissyMcBookNerd.blogspot.com

"The awesome cover opened to even more awesome things inside. It was realistic! Funny! Charming! Sweet!"

—AbigailMumford.com

BRINGING HOME
THE
Bad Boy

BRINGING HOME
THE
Bad Boy

JESSICA
LEMMON

FOREVER

NEW YORK   BOSTON

Copyright © 2015 by Jessica Lemmon
Excerpt from *Rescuing the Bad Boy* copyright © 2015 by Jessica Lemmon

Forever
Hachette Book Group
1290 Avenue of the Americas
New York, NY 10104

www.HachetteBookGroup.com

Printed in the United States of America

First Edition: January 2015
10 9 8 7 6 5 4 3 2 1

OPM

Forever is an imprint of Grand Central Publishing.
The Forever name and logo are trademarks of Hachette Book Group, Inc.

The Hachette Speakers Bureau provides a wide range of authors for speaking events. To find out more, go to www.hachettespeakersbureau.com or call (866) 376-6591.

The publisher is not responsible for websites (or their content) that are not owned by the publisher.

Little Joe. Gabe. Ryan. Bob.
Too young. Gone too soon. I miss you all terribly.

ACKNOWLEDGMENTS

First and foremost, to God, for each and every day I wake up breathing. Essentially, that's what this book ended up being about—the people in life who make it worth getting up and living. For those of us who have lost loved ones, it's about learning to live without them now that we've been left behind. And like Evan and Charlie do in this book, learning to love those we lost in a new way: from afar.

Thank you to the usual suspects: family and friends who make my life worth living.

Beta readers Lauren Layne, Charissa Weaks, and Jennifer Hill, thank you for your feedback. To my Facebook friends who answer my questions about kids when I want to make sure little Lyon Downey rings true.

Nicole Resciniti, my agent and constant supporter—how you deal with my flailing and stay sane is a remarkable feat.

Lauren Plude, this book would not be what it is without you. You pulled deeper meaning and theme out of places I never would have thought to. Thank you.

Shannon Richard, who read this first—you loved Evan before anyone else did. And for that, he and I are very grateful.

Everyone at Forever and Grand Central Publishing responsible for the outside of this book. The cover is beautiful. Absolutely beautiful. Thank you to the cover model, and the artists who painstakingly put Evan's tattoos in exactly the right places.

Thank you to my publicist, Julie Paulauski—you rock! And to Leah Hultenschmidt, for your support and excitement over this series.

Fellow writers Jeannie Moon, Megan Mulry, Maisey Yates, Jennifer Probst, Diane Alberts, Katee Robert, Teri Anne Stanley, Melissa Landers, Jennifer Stark, Jules Bennett, Lexi Ryan, Rachel Van Dyken, Rachel Lacey, Erin Kern, and Audra North. What would I do without you???

Thank you to Lori Foster for the cover quote, and for welcoming me into your home and to the group book signings...being new is like being a lost lamb, but you made sure I fit right in.

Readers, you are the butter on my bread. The vegetarian ham with my eggs. The yin to my yang. Thanks for reading my books, loving them, and asking for more. I'd open a vein for you guys. Hopefully, you find proof this is true in the pages of this book.

~Jess

BRINGING HOME
THE
Bad Boy

CHAPTER ONE

*H*e'd heard the stress of moving was like dealing with death, but since Evan Downey had dealt with a lot of death, it was with a fair amount of authority he called bullshit.

There wasn't anything particularly *fun* about packing, selling, and leaving behind the house. He and his wife, Rae, had purchased the place together when they first got married—the only home their son had ever known.

The house had been a place of love and promise, but now painful memories poisoned the good ones. He would miss the door frame where he and Rae had scribbled Lyon's height each and every year. Their walk-in closet where Evan had laid Rae down and made love to her the day they moved in.

What he *wouldn't* miss was the hallway where she'd staggered, hand on her chest, and collapsed, never regaining consciousness despite his and the 911 operator's attempts to keep her heart pumping until the paramedics arrived.

Moving didn't compare to the living nightmare of losing someone he'd expected to be around when he was old and gray.

At the very least until their son entered elementary school.

As he watched the house dwindle in the side mirror of the family SUV, he calculated he should be rounding the acceptance stage of grief right about now.

About damn time.

"Bye, house," his son Lyon, age seven going on seventeen, announced from beside him. Gone was the Superman action figure he'd clung to last summer. Now his sidekick was his iPad. He had one earbud stuck in his ear and one dangled onto his chest, as per their agreement that Lyon not completely shut him out. Though the music wasn't loud enough for him to hear—another of their agreements—Evan knew it was tuned to classic rock.

Definitely his kid, he thought with a smile.

With 1417 East Level Road behind them, he turned his attention to the city that lay ahead; the city he'd called home since he'd married one beautiful, sassy woman named Rae, the curvy black girl who'd busted his balls about nearly everything since they were teenagers.

God, he missed her.

She'd built a life alongside him, settling into her nursing career while he set up his tattoo shop.

Before striking out on his own, he'd been under the tutelage of tattoo master Chris Platt; a hippie to rival all hippies, with a heart of gold and a head full of titanium. By the time Evan had packed up his things and gave notice, Chris let him know under no uncertain terms that he believed in him and his abilities. And that he'd succeed.

He had.

"Bye, Woody," Lyon piped up.

Evan turned his head as they drove by his shop where Woody had worked for years, and as of three months ago, had purchased outright. Woody had stepped in the year Rae died, when Evan's concentration revolved around breathing in and out, and keeping a three-year-old boy alive. It was no small feat and, at the time, had taken everything he had.

"Will you miss it, Dad?"

He threw a glance into the rearview, but there was no need. He knew the shop's façade as well as his own face. The crack on the sidewalk out front that sprouted dandelions every spring, the brick crumbling on the southeast corner. The black marquee done up to look like an old-fashioned apothecary that read LION'S DEN. Rae's idea, and in honor of their one and only offspring. Save for the fact their lion was a *Lyon*, which she insisted suited Evan's rebellious, go-against-the-grain demeanor.

She was right.

An image of her shining brown eyes, huge smile, and that horribly ugly sea foam green bathrobe she insisted wearing on her days off popped into his brain, and he felt his smile turn sickly.

"*Dad.*"

"Yeah, buddy," he finally answered, his throat dry as he watched Lion's Den grow tiny in the rearview. "I'm gonna miss it."

What he wouldn't miss were the memories of his late wife assaulting him everywhere he turned in this city.

"What about Leah?" his son asked as they pulled onto the highway. Evan ground his back teeth together.

Leah had been one of his, for lack of a better term, "friends with benefits" for the majority of the year. And though he arranged to keep his dates secret from his son, she'd "stopped by" unannounced last month when she saw the SOLD sign go up in the yard.

Angry tears had shimmered in her eyes while her hands gripped her purse like she might brain him with it. He hadn't understood why. A long time ago, they discussed that what they had was about the physical and nothing more. She'd insisted on arguing with him, in front of Lyon no less, and Evan had to do the unfortunate business of dumping her—when they were never really dating—on his front lawn. It was a dick move, but then, so was sleeping with a woman on a tit-for-tat basis.

No puns intended.

Speaking of tat, his eyes zeroed in on the sparrow on his right forearm, the string of hearts snapped free, the broken heart drifting. That one was for Rae. The roses on his arm were for his mom and his aunt. A lotta death. Too much, too soon. They said bad things happened in threes. For his and his son's sakes, he hoped the adage continued staying true.

"*Daaaad.*" Irritation lined his kid's voice when he didn't respond right away.

"Sorry, buddy, I was thinking. No, I won't miss Leah," he answered honestly.

Another dick thing to admit, but she hadn't meant all that much to him. Them in bed, *cordial* would be the best way to describe how he'd treated her. As awful and uninspiring as it sounded. That's what they'd both settled for, which was equally awful and uninspiring.

He bit back the grimace attempting to push forward on

his features. Rae wouldn't like who he'd become if she could see him now.

But she couldn't see him now. She hadn't been able to see him since the moment she'd collapsed four years ago and he hadn't known he'd been five minutes away from losing her forever.

He wished he could remember their last conversation, but he'd been distracted. Not listening.

"Me either," Lyon said, snapping him out of his reverie. "Leah was mean."

Evan blew a breath out of his nose, as close to a laugh as he was gonna get, and considered that Lyon was the only reason he hadn't spiraled into a whirlpool of depression.

Settling in for the drive north to the lake town they would now call home instead of Columbus, Evan once again reminded himself that this venture was a second chance. For him and his son. A place to create new memories, be closer to Rae's parents and Rae's best friend on the planet, Charlotte Harris.

"Excited to see Aunt Charlie?" he asked Lyon.

Charlie had been "Aunt Charlie" since she walked into the hospital room the day Lyon was born. Rae had held up the blue blanket Lyon was wrapped in after she'd sworn her way through eighteen hours of labor, and Charlie, with tears in her eyes, had taken him into her arms and said, *"Hi, Lionel Downey, I'm your aunt Charlie."*

She'd been a fixture in Lyon's life always.

Since Rae had passed, she'd become more of a fixture. Charlie was a dear friend. A constant, a solid person he and his son could count on. A light in a dark place.

Whenever she visited them, she dragged out photo albums, sometimes bringing new photos of her own to add to the pages, and sat Lyon down to tell him stories of his mother.

Charlie insisted on never letting him forget her. While he agreed this was best for his son, Evan did better when he wasn't confronted with Rae's smiling face as he walked down the hallway. Or her still one, a vision that woke him in a sweat more often than he cared to admit.

For that reason, he'd left the photos in the albums, had tucked the picture frames of the two of them away. But there was no escaping the spot of carpet in the hallway where she'd collapsed, or the other side of the bed, its emptiness as real a presence as Rae had been when she was alive.

Moving to Evergreen Cove would not only get them away from the house choked with her memory, but would bring Lyon closer to the things that meant most to him.

Charlie was one of those things.

"I can't wait!" Lyon said, a very real light shining in his eyes.

Kids were so resilient. Especially his kid. Through the process of packing and moving, Lyon had been both apprehensive and excited. Evan saw the sadness in his eyes when he talked about not seeing his friends at school anymore, but Malcolm and Jesse, the two boys who were his best buds, visited the Cove in the summer. Lyon had been appeased with the promise of hanging out with them.

Plus, the new house offered the attractive package of swimming in the lake, a new house with a bigger bedroom, and Charlie nearby. Evan hoped that might make up for some of what they'd all lost.

Not everything, because God knew he couldn't replace Rae, nor would he try.

But he'd sure as hell take whatever reprieve he could get.

* * *

The pain in the voice at the other end of the phone sliced through Charlotte Harris like a shard of glass. Three seconds ago, when she'd seen her best friend's name pop up on her phone, she'd answered with a chipper, "hi!"

Her greeting was met with a beat of silence, followed by a deep, male response. One hollow, broken syllable; the nickname he'd given her a year ago.

"Ace."

Her heart dropped to her stomach, her extremities going instantly cold in spite of the warm nighttime air. There was something registering in his tone that sent fear spilling into her bloodstream.

"Evan?"

A beat of silence, then, "Yeah."

She stood from the chair she'd been lounging in and paced to the three steps leading from her porch down to the inky, still surface of the lake. In the background, a pyramid of pine trees climbed the hill in the distance.

"What is it?" This from her boyfriend, Russell, who stood from the porch swing behind her.

She held out a finger to tell him to wait a minute.

"What happened?" she asked into the phone. Something. She and Evan were friends, but not call-each-other friends. If he was calling her now, it had to be because there was a problem. With Lyon, or—

"Rae." His voice cracked, a painful sob shattering the airwaves and sending an adrenaline rush through her bloodstream. He drew in an uneven breath. "Jesus, Ace."

Unable to hold herself up any longer, she sank onto a step and issued the understatement of the year. "You're scaring me."

"She's gone, Ace." His voice went hollow, into a dead tone she never wanted to hear again as long as she lived.

"Gone…" False hope she'd recognize later as denial leaped against her chest, borne of desperation to find a reason other than the obvious for this almost-midnight call.

Maybe Rae went shopping. Maybe she and Evan had a fight and Rae went to her parents' house. Maybe—

"Gone," his whisper confirmed.

That's when the tears choking her throat pulsed against her eyes. That's when Russell took the phone from her hand. And that's when she knew.

Rae Lynn Downey, her very best friend, more like a sister than her actual sister, wife to the long-ago besotted Evan Downey, and mother to a dimpled three-year-old Lyon Downey was... gone.

It took five days for that fact to settle in.

For her to see Rae's physical body in the casket, for her to notice Evan's formerly bright eyes weary and bloodshot, for her to witness firsthand the devastation of Rae's parents and the somber expressions on Evan's family's faces.

For her to accept what "gone" meant.

Gone was permanent. Gone was forever. Gone was unfair.

Standing over her body, Charlie vowed to Rae she'd watch over her family. She kissed her fingers, placed them on her best friend's cold cheek, and whispered to the woman she'd never see alive again, "Sorry, Rae."

Wheels crunched along the gravel outside her house, bringing Charlie out of the memory clouding her head and back to her living room. She dropped the open magazine she'd been staring unseeing at for the last however many minutes and swiped a single tear from her eye.

Then she cleared her throat, closed the magazine, and bucked up. Because Evan and Lyon couldn't arrive and find her mourning Rae. There was no reason to darken this occasion with melancholy. Them moving here was a good thing. The best thing for them all. Their coming here had reminded her of the promises she'd made, the pain they'd gone through. The loss they'd endured.

She peeked between the curtains and confirmed the tires on the gravel did not belong to Evan's SUV. Releasing a pent-up breath, she watched a blue pickup climb the hill and vanish into the trees.

Not them.

Evan had texted her—she checked her phone, then the clock—forty-six minutes ago, to say they were ten minutes away and since then she'd sat anxiously by the front window. Knowing him, and she did, he probably stopped at Dairy Dreem for an ice cream the moment they set foot in town.

She snapped up her iced tea, frowning at the ring on the coffee table. Where was her head today? She swiped the water ring with one hand and turned for her back porch, pausing first to slip on a pair of flats.

Charlie's house was the most modest on her street—she liked to tell herself it was because the house was built before Evergreen Cove had become a vacation destination. She and her boyfriend, Russell Hartman, had purchased the small, white clapboard because of its view of the lake and the fantastic porch. At the time, she believed that buying a vacation home as a couple was a sign of permanence.

Wrong.

But she had no regrets about the house. Since she worked from home, she'd outfitted the family room facing the lake at the back to hold her desk, computer, and a few shelves for her supplies. She'd kept the couch, and yes, the television, in the room. Her office connected to the kitchen where she had a small table and chairs, but the real prize of her home was the porch. The wide, covered expanse, befitting of a Georgia plantation five times her home's size, was where she ate most of her meals, entertained, or just sat and enjoyed the view.

Rather than stare out the window for the arrival of the Downey boys, she tracked out back to the swing hanging by a pair of chains, smoothed her dress, and sat.

Resting the tea at her feet, she sucked in a breath and took in the view. While the front of her house offered up traffic and trees, she preferred the back—the lake and the hill that rose behind it, a jagged skyline designed from pointed pine trees. This view was why she and Russell had purchased on the private beach.

When he left her two years ago, he'd kept the huge new-build with the cherry tree in the backyard. Rae had always told her a man who was unwilling to marry her was a man who would walk away. At the moment when he'd delivered her morning coffee in the enormous white kitchen with gleaming granite countertops and told her he was leaving her, Charlie thought of Rae's words first.

Sad, but true.

He let her keep the vacation house in Evergreen Cove, and the Subaru they'd recently paid off. "I'd pay alimony if we were married," he'd told her, assuaging his guilt. "The house at the Cove, the car, it's the least I can do."

The very least, she thought bitterly at the time, but now she didn't feel bitter. She considered herself blessed things had ended before she'd thrown good years after bad into a relationship doomed to fail.

Russell was a software developer, a pragmatic thinker, and ten years older than Charlie. She met him at a wedding—prior to her photography career, so rather than the photographer, she'd been the bridesmaid at this particular event. A guest of the groom, Russell had sought her out, danced with her, and practically begged her to take his phone number.

After several dates she learned he didn't want to be married, and he didn't want children. She had always wanted children and assumed children were the natural path following marriage. But when it became clear they were serious, she'd decided both marriage and children were things she could live without. With the right person, sacrifices were unavoidable. Forever would be worth it.

But her relationship didn't last forever, making the six-year compromise she'd made much harder to live with now.

After the kitchen conversation over coffee, he'd arranged for movers to extricate her from the house and then Russell had *eloped* with a woman with *three* children. One going into college and twin boys in the sixth grade. He gave no explanation for what changed his mind, but she knew. The other woman, Darian.

Darian had changed his mind.

Which had the unpleasant side effect of making Charlie feel like she hadn't been enough.

She'd taken what was behind door number two and moved on as intact as she could. Some nights, the hurt and the fear of being alone lingered. The fact she'd been unable to achieve the seemingly simple goal of having a family and settling down had haunted her enough that on those nights she became practically nocturnal.

Taking in a deep, humid breath, Charlie centered herself on the here and now. June was nearly July and the hot and sticky had both settled in at the Cove for the long haul. Sunlight danced on the surface of the lake, sending waves rippling in the wind. Behind the lake, in the sea of evergreens lining the hills, there were a few hidden homes, but that was too "deep woods" for her taste.

From her coveted porch—yes, even her fancy neighbors with their large, enviable homes admitted to coveting her porch—a patch of grass gave way to shore and led into the water. Her aquatic neighbor, Earl, stepped out onto the deck of his beaten houseboat off to the left where it was anchored in the deep, and raised a hand to wave. She could make out his pipe, handlebar white mustache, and sunglasses from here. He was tanned and brawny and made the best clam chowder she'd ever tasted.

Murmuring from the side of her house brought her to her feet as the smile spread her mouth.

Finally!

The voices grew louder as they closed in and she strode across the porch to meet them. She couldn't make out the exact words, but she knew the boy's voice as if he were her own.

"Aunt Charlie!" Lyon appeared around the corner and burst into a run. Before she had a chance to take the three steps to the grass to meet him, he bounded up them and straight into her arms. She caught him against her, savoring how small he was, knowing it was a battle with time she'd lose, and bent to kiss his head. His tight curls had grown out some since she saw him last. They tickled her nose.

Pulling away, she flattened his hair with both hands. It sprang up again, refusing to be tamed.

"You need a haircut," she teased.

"I *knoooooow.*" He rolled his green-blue eyes. Lionel Downey was a stunning kid. He had Rae's chocolate-brown skin, a touch lighter than hers had been, and her genuine, full smile. He had his father to thank for his eye color: ocean blue so striking against his dark features.

"That's a tired subject, if you can't tell."

Her eyes went to Evan, who'd crossed his bare arms over his chest and leaned a hip into the column at the bottom of the steps to watch their interaction. His presence wasn't overbearing or intimidating, but easy. Evan matched his laid-back, live-and-let-live attitude with a lazy swagger that was anything but. He'd worked hard his entire life and as a result, confidence oozed from every pore. The thinning pair of Levi's, the casual T-shirt hugging his chest, his array of tattoos, and devil-may-care smile he showed to the world were him through and through, but Charlie knew Evan ran deeper than his outer layer.

Her eyes tracked along the tattoos decorating his arms to the new one. His latest patch of artwork was a series of evergreen trees, their dark blue-black bases circling his wrist and branching up his arm, their tops almost reaching his elbow. Each tree was a different height, and knowing his attention to detail, each one had some significance. The whole of the pictorial on his arm had a big one.

His moving to Evergreen Cove.

Unable to keep it from happening, her heart reverted to the state it'd been in at age fifteen, somersaulting in the wrongest way imaginable. Before he was Rae's, oh, how Charlie had pined for Evan Downey. Must have been seeing him back here, or maybe her earlier thoughts about her life, that caused the mini-backslide.

But she couldn't backslide. She'd made a vow to herself, to Rae's silent body, to care for Lyon and Evan.

"Did you guys eat?" she asked.

"Yeah. Dairy Dreem," Lyon confirmed.

She knew it. She tilted her chin at Evan in reprimand. An accidentally sensual smirk crooked his mouth, surrounded in a one or two days' worth of stubble.

"We didn't *only* get ice cream."

"Yeah, we had French fries," Lyon added, earning a headshake from his dad.

"No loyalty." The smirk slid into a grin and if that didn't cause her heart the subtlest flutter, the wink would. And there it was, one blue eye closing and opening again—a flutter in and of itself—the blue so bright, it was nearly electric.

Was it any wonder he'd been on her radar when she was a vacationing teen visiting the Cove? There'd been three "bad boys" she and Rae had noticed whenever they sunbathed at the beach. Evan Downey, Donovan Pate, and Asher Knight. For Charlie, Evan stood out the most.

Evan only had eyes for Rae.

At first she was heartbroken, but Charlie had kept that fact to herself. Teenage crushes were a dime a dozen, and predictably, she outgrew it in a few summers. Rae and Evan had been designed for each other. By the time she stood at Rae's side as her maid of honor, there wasn't a bone in her body not overjoyed that her best friend had found the love of her life.

After Rae's death, Charlie had become a more consistent part of Evan's and Lyon's lives. Russell hadn't liked it. More than once, she wondered if her decision to care for Rae's family rather than prioritize him had ultimately led to their demise.

Staying in touch with Evan had been easy when she and Russell lived close by. After the breakup and relocation, however, her trips to Columbus became less frequent. Once she was settled and had a job, Charlie did make an overnight trip down to visit, and she ended up babysitting for Lyon.

She hadn't minded the babysitting part. Not at all. But the fact that Evan had gone on a date with an incredibly beautiful blonde, then come home around three in the morning smelling of perfume and sex, had hurt her heart in a way she hadn't known possible.

When he'd passed her in the hallway, Charlie had ducked her face into her palm to stifle a sob. Evan abruptly turned on his heel to wrap her in his arms and comfort her, and she had just lost it.

Him giving himself to a harlot who didn't appreciate the things Rae had fallen in love with: his huge heart, his bottomless love for his family, was awful to witness.

Rae and Evan were supposed to live happily ever after. Lyon was supposed to grow up, get married, and dance with his mom at the reception. And Charlie... well, her life hadn't turned out the way she'd planned, either.

Unable to voice the real reason for her crying jag, she'd blamed her emotions on her breakup with Russell, rather than the way it punched a hole in her chest to see the way she and Evan, Lyon, and Rae had all been shortchanged.

Life didn't heed plans and dates. Life went on, and left whomever it pleased behind in the wreckage.

The memory caused her heart to ache, and her gut to yearn for what could have been. She flicked her eyes heavenward and sent up a mental, *Sorry, Rae.*

"Can I go inside?" Lyon pulled away from her and grabbed the handle on her sliding door.

"Knock yourself out," she answered. "One more hug, though." He acquiesced, giving her a halfhearted squeeze. She'd take what she could get. Soon, he'd be at an age where he wouldn't snuggle with her any longer and she thought that might be the day she started crying and never stopped.

Evan pushed out of his casual lean, uncrossed his inked arms, and stomped up the three steps separating her from him. "Missed you, Ace."

Him being close made her feel better instantly. "Missed you, too."

He slid the door aside and motioned for her to go in, but when he ran a hand through his shaggy, mussed bed-head, she felt her heart kick against her chest in the slightest show of appreciation.

And for that, she should be ashamed.

Sorry, Rae.

CHAPTER TWO

One week later, Evan's new house was beginning to feel like home. No, better than home. Like the place he was supposed to be but never knew it.

Floor-to-ceiling windows offered an amazing view of the hill of evergreens on the opposite side of the lake, and the lake herself.

This house was nothing like the old one. That'd been the whole point in coming here. Its best feature being his art supplies were no longer stashed in a cramped back room barely holding his drawing desk and easel. The front room, formerly dance studio, also had floor-to-ceiling windows and was twenty times the size of his art *corner* on East Level Road. It held not only his desk, but *three* large easels, a stack of canvases—some full, some empty leaning against the wall—and a tall black shelf packed with supplies.

The space may have been designed for a dancer but transformed perfectly for a former tattooist with a bud-

ding illustration career. The "former" part was in name
only. He hadn't been able to resist setting up his chair,
table, and inks in the corner. He couldn't completely trade
out one passion for the other. Wasn't the way he was built.

The AC kicked on as he rounded the wall—the only
privacy for his open loft bedroom—and took the stairs,
laundry basket in hand. Lyon was on the floor in the living room, settled on a rug in front of a twenty-foot stone
fireplace likely responsible for keeping this room cooler
than the others.

"Laundry, buddy."

Lyon sighed over the iPad where he played some battling clan game a magazine article recently claimed was
"as addictive as meth." Evan had laughed the claim off at
first. Now he was beginning to see the signs.

"In a minute," Lyon responded in a zombie drone.

He stood over his son and toed his ribs with one shoe.
"Bud."

Lyon frowned up at him, miraculously tearing his eyes
away from the game for two seconds to argue, "I'll lose
this battle if I stop now!"

God. The look on his face. Evan's heart clutched.
Pulled brows, set mouth. He looked like Rae whenever he
did that. Which was probably why he let the kid get away
with murder.

"After this battle. But right after. Do not play another
or no more iPad today."

As a single parent, he'd dealt a lot with the issue of
being too soft or too hard. Sometimes it was best for both
of them if he rode the middle.

Lyon ignored him, the yells and hollers coming from
the game an annoying cacophony.

Evan pushed his foot into Lyon's side and rolled him over, wiggling his shoe into his son's belly. "Yeah?"

"Yeah, Dad," Lyon confirmed, smile intact, eyes returning to the screen.

Bleary-eyed from a sleepless, and artless, night, Evan headed to the washer and dryer on the opposite side of the house and loaded in towels, sorting the whites from the colors and pulling the washer button on. Unlike everyone assumed, he didn't have to learn how to do laundry after Rae died. He'd always done the laundry.

He grunted a dry chuckle as he recalled why: early on, she had dyed every last one of his whites pink. Rae Lynn Downey. Epic in the kitchen, disaster in the laundry room.

The memory of her face, smiling wide as she'd pressed his newly stained T-shirt to his chest, slammed into him, making his next breath impossible to draw.

Last night, a dream, more memory than dream, shook him awake. Rae's smiling face losing its light, his inability to bring her back. In a habit he wished he could shed, he'd reached for her side of the bed. Empty as expected, but worse because it wasn't "her" side at all. When he moved, he'd replaced their bed.

He told himself a second chance meant starting over, and bringing history into the new house wasn't good juju. So, he'd dragged the old pillow-top, queen-size bed he and Rae had conceived their son on out to the curb and ordered a new mattress to be delivered the day after he arrived. And he'd been fine with that.

Until last night.

In the barren emptiness of three a.m., the massive king bed with a black iron headboard and plain white bedding, the bed he'd told himself would be a "blank canvas" for his life in Evergreen Cove, felt . . . wrong.

Sheets soaked through with sweat, his hands shaking, and Rae's blank, open eyes flashing in the forefront of his brain, a sick realization washed over him. No longer was she merely missing from his bed. He'd erased her entirely.

Unable to sleep, he'd traipsed down to his studio, knowing what came out of his paintbrush would be the opposite of productive, but at least would get him through to morning.

Demons exorcised, the images he'd created were like the others he painted in the wee hours. Dark, broody, and having no place in a children's book.

Evan dropped the lid of the washer as Lyon marched into the laundry room, dropped off his clothes, and started out again.

"Bud. Sort."

"Daaaad."

His response was to point at the hamper.

Lyon's shoulders slumped until he resembled a melting Wicked Witch of the West, but at Evan's silent stare, he finally obeyed and began to sort.

The attitude was something he could live without, but at least the kid was doing his chore.

Good enough.

In the land of single parenthood, it was the national anthem.

"Oatmeal or eggs?"

"Eggs," Lyon answered, exasperated.

"You got it." Evan tracked to the kitchen to fix his boy eggs, and reminded himself he was raising an independent man who would eventually care for himself. Since their small family had decreased by one member, it'd been Lyon and Evan as a unit. A team.

Team Downey.

That was how this was gonna work . . . the *only way* this was gonna work. Especially as they settled in to a new town, Lyon went to a new school, and Evan adjusted to his new career.

A second chance. A fresh start.

As he put the pan on the burner, Rae's beautiful face flashed in his memory again. In the light of day it was easier to convince himself a blank canvas wasn't a bad thing.

$\mathscr{C}$HAPTER THREE

$\mathscr{S}$hit."

Propping a hand on his thigh, Evan slouched on the wheeled wooden chair in his studio and stared down the fat, blank pad of newsprint. Like the tan, soft paper in front of him might have an answer for what to try next.

Whenever he ran up against the equivalent of writer's block for painters—artist's block, if that was a thing—he refused to let it stop him. He drew through it. As a result, the floor was littered with sketches of farm animals. Fifteen, no—wait—sixteen if he counted the one he'd wadded up and tossed to the other side of the room.

He scratched the scruff on his jaw. *Defeated by a cartoon pig.* He blew out a frustrated breath.

When grief took him in the wee hours, he had no problem unleashing his creative instincts on canvas. But when it came to work—keeping food on the table, a roof over their heads—*bam!* Roadblock.

Last summer, his agent, Gloria Shields, persuaded him to attend an immersion class with her other illustrator clients in Chicago. He had, leaving Lyon in the care of his oldest brother, Landon. Evan took the break and used it to focus on his art. Surprise, surprise, he'd tuned into a muse that didn't solely lurk around in the dead of night.

He came back home and life started up again, with its monotonous schedule and repetitive requirements like trash day, dental appointments, and grocery shopping, and that fresh-faced muse grew bitchy, donned fangs, and became nocturnal once again.

If she showed up at all.

Then he got a visit from another muse entirely—a real one, by the name of Asher Knight.

Every year when he was a kid, his family vacationed in the same area of Evergreen Cove. A group of cabins lined the public beach, and though his parents hadn't succeeded in getting the same cabin every year, they did manage to go the same week.

They weren't the only ones.

The youngest in his family at age fourteen, Evan had been the rebel without a clue. Wasn't any wonder he'd sought out trouble when he came here on vacation. His brother, Aiden, had been all about the girls; their sister, Angel, busy keeping her girlfriends *away* from Aiden; and Landon—well, hell, he was out of high school by then and didn't associate with the "kids."

But that summer in particular, Evan had met two guys who had been more bad news than good. Donovan Pate was one of them, Asher Knight was the other, and arguably, both were *still* more bad news than good.

Donovan was the scrappier of the two and enjoyed a good fistfight. The day Evan met the taller boy with ink-black hair and ghostly silver-blue eyes, Evan had stood his ground and earned the bump on his nose he still sported. They were still close. Go figure.

Asher was far less intense, leaning more toward mischief than meanness. Proof in the fact they'd sneaked out one night to the library and covered the brick walls in anatomically correct graffiti. He'd never forget the newspaper headline that weekend: PENIS BANDITS STRIKE! Or the combination of terror and joy he'd felt when he heard his mother gasp, followed by the laughter she and his dad hadn't been able to repress.

Evan hadn't seen much of Ash since Ash had made something of himself, but out of nowhere, a call came from fellow Penis Bandit turned "rock god"—Asher's words—that his band, Knight Time, had an upcoming show nearby.

He hadn't hesitated inviting his buddy over.

Within thirty seconds, they were back where they were years ago, recanting the past while Evan touched up a tattoo for him. When Evan mentioned his recent foray into illustration, Asher admitted he'd been entertaining the idea of writing a children's book.

Evan's response had been, "*You*?" He'd watched Ash on stage, screaming his lungs out, and the turnstile of women he'd been seen with since his rise to fame. "Kid-friendly" didn't exactly describe his buddy. "The hell do you know about children's books?"

"What the hell do you know about illustrating?" Asher had shot back, followed by the very valid point of, "You can't write for shit. I write songs for a living."

That's when *The Adventures of Mad Cow* had started. Over the next two days, they conceptualized a story and Evan dug in on the concept. A badass bovine was born.

Mad Cow longed to break free from the farm before he became a double cheeseburger, and they'd matched him with a troupe of oddball, big-hearted animals who agreed to help.

When Gloria laid eyes on Mad Cow, his leather collar decked out with a row of cowbells, a ring through one nostril, gauged ears, tattoo of a weather vane on one bicep, she was sold.

Lucky for them, so was the publisher.

The book hit shelves in spring, surprising no one more than Evan by climbing the best-seller lists, which prompted the publisher to ask for a second book.

Asher was due to arrive in Evergreen Cove soon to help conceptualize the new book, which he'd explained to Evan was a revamped Batman and Robin situation. Mad Cow was getting a superhero sidekick.

Swine Flew.

But of course.

Unfortunately, Swine wasn't coming together as easily as his counterpart. Evan groused down at the pile of papers, unsatisfied.

Like. At all.

Well. Hell. He'd have to hit it again later. His stomach was rumbling.

Lifting from his chair, he crossed the studio and paused to look out the windows. He took in the lapping shore, sand, and trees. Gorgeous here. Peaceful, quiet, and since it was summer, had the enviable location of being close to the water.

He pulled in a breath, vowed to get back to work after lunch, and started to step away when his eyes caught sight of one very curvy blonde lying on the dock, sunbathing.

Damn.

A long, narrow staircase led down the hill to the shared dock between his and Charlie's house. The dock was supposed to be private, only used by Evan, Charlie, or their mostly absentee neighbors. Neighbors he hadn't met. Neighbors, he was told, who were in their sixties.

The chick on the dock was *not* in her sixties.

Here he'd thought there wouldn't be any hot, available women in this vacation town. Given they were on a private beach, that must mean the gorgeous creature sunning herself not far from his window lived around here.

One could hope.

Before he could head to the kitchen, an exuberant seven-year-old entered the scene outside, running out to the dock to greet her.

"Ah, shit."

His boy knew not a stranger.

Evan slipped on a pair of flip-flops before rushing out the door, down the beach, and to the dock to retrieve his kid. Lyon was jabbering away about something, his voice carrying on the wind.

A few steps on the wooden dock, Evan opened his mouth to get Lyon's attention when the blonde turned her head. His tongue stuck to the roof of his mouth for a second as his eyes traveled down her body and back up in disbelief.

Charlie?

She beamed up at him, squinting behind big, round sunglasses. "Hey."

Barely dressed in a skimpy, hot-pink string bikini, her lush breasts were on display, her slim stomach and thick thighs bare and tanned. He realized belatedly he was staring at parts of her he'd never thought to admire before—and God, there was a lot to admire. She looked like a centerfold.

Her eyebrows rose the slightest bit as her smile faded.

Forcing himself to speak and stop being a creeper, he dipped his chin in greeting. "Ace."

Her smile returned. "I was asking Lyon if he knew the names of the neighbors yet."

Again, it hit Evan that when he was in the house, he'd thought Charlie might be a neighbor he'd like to get to know. Nothing much threw him anymore, but that displaced surge of attraction had. It still rumbled beneath the surface. *Not good.*

He redirected his attention to what he could handle—his son. "Hey, bud, what'd I say about getting too close to the water?"

"*Dad.* Charlie's here."

"Yeah, I see that." She was *all* he could see at the moment. "And I'm sure she doesn't want to be bothered every time she's outside."

"He's okay." Lounging, leaning on one elbow, she put a hand on Lyon's arm.

He turned to his son, and away from Charlie's incredible body, and crossed his arms over his chest. "*Lionel.*"

"*Okaaaay.*" Exasperated, as per his usual.

"Why aren't you supposed to be down here?" Evan asked him.

"Because I haven't had swimming lessons yet. But I can swim," he insisted.

Lyon could doggie paddle. He couldn't "swim." Evan speared him with a look.

Charlie intervened. "When are your lessons?"

His kid stopped frowning at him and smiled at her instead. "Tomorrow!"

"Sounds promising," she said, lightening the mood between father and son. It was new to have the tension erased. Maybe living nearer to her would have more benefits than Evan had first imagined.

"For now, stay off the dock," he told his son. "The shore is fine, though."

"Okay," Lyon said, not sounding okay at all.

"Why don't you bring your paper and markers out to the beach?" Maybe that's what *he* should do. Despite the wall of windows letting in natural sunlight into his studio, Evan had been cooped up indoors all day. "I'll get my stuff and join you."

"I hate drawing." Lyon dragged his feet. Evan felt his head shake.

He knew this, of course, but it hadn't stopped him from trying to get his kid to show an ounce of interest in the very thing making Evan's world go round.

"I'm gonna watch TV." Lyon tromped up the dock, and Evan turned to Charlie, gesturing with an arm in the direction of his argumentative son.

"Ouch," she said, but not out of sympathy. The tilt of her lips clearly showed amusement.

"First football, then superheroes, now swimming. How did Rae give birth to a sports nut?" She'd hated sports and Evan, at best, was ambivalent.

Charlie pushed her sunglasses into her blond hair and peered up at him, her hazel eyes scrunched.

"What are you doing out here, anyway? Playing hooky?" he asked. Like him, she worked from home.

He leaned a hip on the railing running along one side of the dock. She sat up, pushing off her elbows and bending her long, long legs to one side.

Incredible.

Again, it shocked him to notice. He'd always known she was attractive—far too attractive for that toad, Russell, she used to date—but he'd never noticed as much as he was noticing now.

"I work better at night." She pushed the length of her hair off her shoulder where it slid like silk. "What about you? Shouldn't you be illustrating?"

"I work better at night, too." Not that last night had been productive by any stretch of the imagination.

"Why don't you work at night then?"

Now she was giving him hell. Back on familiar ground.

"Because my son won't let me sleep until noon."

Knowing he was needling her, her mouth dropped open. "Hey! I was up by eleven thirty today, thank you very much."

He knew. He'd spotted her on her deck, nursing a cup of coffee and staring out at the lake. He'd been in lunch mode, slapping bologna onto bread and starting load number three of laundry. In short, avoiding the studio.

"Live it up, Ace." His eyes went to a boat docked in the distance, to the guy on his deck watering a plant that looked questionably legal. Reminded him of the time the three of them—Donny, Ash, and himself—tried to steal a boat from the dock. Morons.

"I can help, you know."

His eyes snapped back to her. "Help with what?"

Inappropriate ideas popped into his head, causing a rogue smile to pull his lips, but he managed to bite his tongue.

"Lyon. He can sunbathe with me, help me develop photos, go with me to the grocery. And you can work."

"Not gonna happen, Ace." His creative mind kicked into third gear at one in the morning, but that didn't mean he'd give into the temptation.

He knew the price of getting to the zone-out stage. Locking himself in the studio at night. Music pumping into his head, the hours flying by, time ceasing to exist. In those dark hours, art became his drug, dragging him away from the real world rife with grief and responsibility and into a world where the only things that mattered were paint and canvas and color. Problem was, when he resurfaced, the real world waited to flay him, claws bared.

There was no true escape.

Didn't make her offer any less tempting, but he brushed it aside. The price was too high to give into the beast that stalked him when the moon came out.

He pushed off the railing.

"I'm coming, too. Help me up." Charlie held out a hand and he reached for her palm and pulled her up. She stood gracefully, coming to his shoulders, and tipped her head. In the breeze, her fair hair blew, and the warmth of her fingers wrapped around his made his head swim the slightest bit.

"Thanks," she breathed.

"Welcome," he said, amused when his voice came out in a growl. His next words didn't stay in his mouth. "Packing a lot of heat there, Ace."

His gaze trickled down to her breasts, bursting out of

her bikini top. When he reached her face, he saw that her eyebrows had closed in slightly.

"Thought you were some hot local chick. I came down here to ask you on a date."

She blinked at him, big hazel eyes going bigger.

Now that he considered it, he realized she *was* a hot local chick. *Charlie* and *hot* hadn't exactly been synonyms in his mind. Until now.

Her laugh didn't sound a hundred percent genuine, and he guessed the reason was shock over hearing he saw her as a hot chick. Couldn't be helped. He'd never seen her this undressed before.

More's the pity.

A strand of hair blew over her face and he reached to move it aside, skimming the piece behind her ear.

"You could send a seven-year-old straight into puberty in an outfit like that. And a full-grown man into a cold shower."

Her smile faltered slightly, but before he became sure he'd pushed her too far, she laughed, the sound more natural than before.

"I'd talk." She tipped her head toward one of his arms, then the other. "How many tickets to the gun show are you selling, anyway?"

"Enough for you and two of your friends."

She shook her head but grinned.

He grinned back.

Her eyes went to her house. "Gotta go. I'm expecting a package."

He smirked. "A 'package,' Ace?"

She rolled her eyes. "Pervert."

"You said it."

Collecting her towel and book, she shuffled into a pair of hideous pink Crocs and wiggled her amazing ass up the dock. "Talk to you later!" she called over her shoulder, looping the towel around her hips.

Shame.

Could've watched that ass a while longer.

CHAPTER FOUR

Oh! Oh, that's perfect."

Sofie Martin stood from the chair she'd been sitting in and held both hands in front of her like she was stopping traffic.

Faith Garrett turned her head, her long, plaited, light blond braid swishing against her crisp cotton shirt. "What? What did I do?"

"It's going to be so pretty!" Sofie clasped her hands in front of her face. She pinned Charlie with jade green eyes gone soft. "Tell me you're getting this."

Laughing, Charlie returned her eye to the viewfinder of her camera. "Almost," she told her, then instructed Faith. "Keep walking," followed by, "Lift the tray a little higher." She adjusted the focus. "Little bit higher...there. Right there."

She snapped a few more pictures of Faith in her waitress costume: white shirt, black pants, jaunty bow tie, holding a silver tray filled with mini-cheesecake bites from the local bakery, Sugar Hi.

Knowing the Evergreen Club had only given them an hour to use the empty reception hall, they had to hustle. Charlie had already taken the photos of Sofie and had quite a few good ones. Helping was Sofie's curvaceous body bedecked in a clingy, but professional, short black dress, and the shine coming off her shoulder-length mahogany hair.

"Can we eat these now?" Faith asked of the tray of miniature cheesecakes balanced on one hand.

"Yes, please," Charlie agreed while scrolling through the digital photos on her camera.

"I'm dieting," Sofie said, but sat at the empty round table at the same time Charlie and Faith did. Charlie plugged the camera into her laptop and pulled up the photos so they could all see. "Can you Photoshop my ass so it looks smaller?"

"Shut up." Faith shoved a mini-cheesecake in her mouth and elbowed Charlie. "Are you hearing this?"

"Sofe, how do you think you landed the USO event you planned over the spring? Because Jim Rivers thinks you're drop-dead gorgeous," Charlie supplied before she could answer.

"Jim Rivers." Sofie scrunched her face. "Ewww."

Faith reached for another cheesecake. "It's true. I'll never have your ass."

Sending a longing look at the tray, Sofie muttered, "I wish you could have it. I'd so give it to you."

Charlie met Sofie a few years ago at the furniture store where Charlie worked at that time. Sofie had just founded her party-planning company, *Make It an Event*. Charlie had just made the vacation house her permanent residence and, needing part-time work, had snapped up the sales job.

Sofie came into the shop looking to furnish her new storefront on Endless Avenue, and Charlie visited Make

It an Event to give her recommendations. She and Sofie spent as much of the afternoon yakking as they did decorating. Sofie learned Charlie took photos for fun and encouraged her to look into selling her services. And when Charlie wasn't sure she was good enough to get paid for her photography, it was Sofie who'd hired her first.

They'd been inseparable since.

"How many calories do you think are in one of these?"

"Seriously, sweetheart, if you bemoan the fat and calories one more time, I'll eat the entire tray," Faith said.

Charlie lifted a cheesecake bite and let the creamy, tart morsel melt on her tongue. "Faith is right. This is worth it."

With a quirk of her lips, Sofie reluctantly reached for one and nibbled.

Faith rolled her eyes at Charlie, making her smile. She'd met the svelte, tanned, graceful-limbed Faith Garrett at Sofie's apartment a few years ago. The woman who could double for a runway model was so easy to like, Charlie couldn't hate her for her metabolism and good genes.

Faith worked at Abundance Market, overseeing the beer and wine department. To Charlie, she seemed as bored by her job as by her fiancé, the regional manager. The former she knew because Faith repeatedly mentioned how boring her job was, and the latter, because whenever the topic shifted to Michael, Faith changed it to talk about wine or beer instead.

"We should have gotten a few Devil Dogs," Faith said, picking up another mini-dessert.

"Those are so fatten—erm—delicious," Sofie corrected with a bright smile.

"What's a Devil Dog?" Charlie asked.

Faith's eyebrows rose.

The last bite of Sofie's cheesecake hovered an inch from her mouth. "Are you serious?"

"I'm not much of a sweets person."

Faith looked at Charlie like she'd announced she was a white supremacist. "I don't understand."

"The Devil Dog is a chocolate-dipped cake—"

Faith cut Sofie off with a karate chop to the air. "*Two* layers of chocolate cake sandwiched together with cream frosting in the middle, *then* dipped in dark chocolate."

Charlie pressed her lips together to keep from giggling.

"Dark chocolate," Sofie repeated reverently. "Well. We must get one of these Devil Dogs."

"One for each of us," Faith reiterated.

"Not me. I have to work off the extra seven pounds I gained over the winter." She dipped her chin at Faith. "I don't have your height to disguise the gain."

No one did. Faith was hovering around five-ten, several inches over both Sofie and Charlie.

"Eat." Charlie pushed the tray toward Sofie.

"One's my limit."

"*Sofie*," came Faith's scolding tone. "I'll eat them all if you don't help."

"I'll help." Charlie popped another cheesecake into her mouth, this one dripping with a sugary cherry drizzle.

"*Fine*," Sofie acquiesced, reaching for another.

"There isn't a part of your body you should be ashamed of." Charlie licked a drop of cherry drizzle off her thumb. "At least you don't look like a porn star in a bikini."

Sofie choked back a laugh.

"It's true! I'd kill for a normal size pair of boobs instead of a pair of double-Ds sitting distractedly on my chest."

"I'd love to have your rack, Charlotte." This from Faith,

who gestured to her own small breasts. "If I wear a strap-less dress, I have to have it tailored so tight I can hardly breathe or it'll fall to my waist."

"Yeah but your legs are nine miles long," Sofie pointed out. "And so are yours, Charlie. I've seen you in a bikini."

"So did my new neighbor," she admitted with a wince. When she'd strolled down to the dock, she hadn't thought a single thing about laying out in her favorite bathing suit and relaxing...until Evan appeared on the dock.

"Ohhh, now we're getting somewhere." Faith smiled.

"It's not like that." Though, maybe it was a bit like that. Because the moment Evan showed up on the dock, Char-lie had to play it extra cool to not react to his presence. Under his turquoise gaze yesterday, her tasteful, cute bathing suit felt like it was covering a hell of a lot less.

"How are they adjusting?" Sofie asked, meaning Evan and Lyon. Charlie had filled them in on him moving here, on how Lyon was like the nephew she'd never had. Which was not technically true. She did have a nephew, but her sister was distant, both geographically and emotionally, and Charlie rarely saw Theo.

"Good. Settling nicely," she answered, careful to keep any hint of a lilt out of her voice. "Lyon loves it here."

"That's great," Sofie said sincerely.

Faith clucked her tongue. "Must be horrible to find the love of your life and then have to live the rest of your life without her."

"Yeah," Charlie agreed. "Rae was one of a kind."

Rae and Charlie may not have lived close to one another, but it didn't stop Rae from being the most con-sistent person in her life. Charlie's sister lived on the other side of the country—Texas last she'd heard—and their father...their father made it clear to his girls that they were on their own when their mother died. Charlie was seventeen at the time and graduated from high school. She had needed him then more than ever, but unable to deal with his grief over losing her mother, he just...left.

"She died right around when we met, right?" Sofie asked.

It took Charlie a second to realize she was asking about Rae and not her mom.

"Four years." Four long years since Rae dropped to her knees in her hallway, taken by her weak heart, a condition doctors never knew she had until it was too late. "She was twenty-six."

"Wow." This from both girls. That one word said what they were all thinking: *Too young.*

A rap on the wall drew their attention to the doorway where the Evergreen Club's manager stood. "About done, ladies? We have to set up for a bar mitzvah."

"On our way out," Charlie assured the manager, who left with a nod of his head. She turned to Sofie. "He's cute."

"Eh."

"Come on," Faith pressed.

"Yeah." Charlie unscrewed the lens from her camera. "He's fairly tall, has a nice...um...tie."

Faith laughed and stood to fetch the padded camera bag.

"He's so cute, why don't *you* go out with him?" Sofie asked Charlie.

"Because I'm very busy and important." And because she had no interest in diving back into the dating pool after Russell had dragged her to the deep end and left her there with an anchor tied around her neck.

"Not your type?" Faith craned a light eyebrow.

At the mention of "type," a vision of dark hair, blue eyes, and a tilted smile popped into her head.

Well. That was…unexpected. Then again, who could help eyeing Evan Downey in a semi-tight white tee outlining his firmly muscled chest, revealing enough of those delicious tattoos to cause her heart to flutter? Not to mention the brash way he'd pointed out her, uh, assets. All while sporting a smile both lethal and charming.

He didn't mince words, blurting out exactly what he thought. And he'd mentioned a grown man, a cold shower, something about a hot chick he'd come down to ask out on a date.

There was only one way to take that conversation.

He thought she looked hot.

She really didn't know what to do with that.

"Um…"

"Mm-hmm." Sofie, who eerily possessed the ability to read Charlie's mind, hummed. Thankfully, she let her off the hook. "When will you have my brochure designed?"

Charlie shrugged. "A few days."

"Friday?" she asked, lifting the case she had helped pack. "Your place?"

"Over wine," Faith added. "My treat."

"Friday," Charlie confirmed to her friends. "Over *lots* of wine."

* * *

The airport was bustling this afternoon, travelers moving through the crowds with tired looks on their faces, or studying the luggage carousel with far too much concentration.

Evan found himself relieved, as he had multiple times

in his life, that he wasn't a suit-wearing man outfitted with a briefcase and a tie around his neck. His cousin, Shane, and oldest brother, Landon, were those guys, but Evan had always been more like his dad and his brother, Aiden.

To him, the classes didn't matter. Upper, middle, everyone had problems of a different scale regardless of how much money they hauled in. It was more the idea of how he wanted to live. Like Aiden wanted to spend time on a bike or under it—which was the very reason he'd purchased five motorcycle shops in Ohio—Evan had always wanted to make art.

Tattooing had chosen him, a form of art involving blood and surgical gloves, though most people only saw that he inflicted pain rather than relieved his clients of it. Beyond that, the artistry had always come first. The body was a more challenging canvas than paper, which he liked. He also appreciated the permanence of his art. A tat was carried wherever its owner went.

"The flight's on time," his agent, Glo, called out as she approached from the direction of the schedule board. She was Asher's literary agent, too. For better or worse. "Where is he?"

"You know Ash. Probably christening a new stewardess into the Mile High club."

"Gross." Her brow dented over catlike blue eyes.

Evan let out a dry laugh. Like he could offend Gloria Shields. She could match any man shot-for-shot at a bar, and had a mouth like a sailor, which he admired the hell out of.

Plus, Glo was a knockout. A woman worthy of pinup status with a healthy curve to her hips and tits she put on a shelf for the world to admire. He admired that about her, too.

"Since when are you grossed out by airplane sex?" he asked.

She flipped her shiny black hair over her shoulder, lips dropping open in feigned offense. "What are you insinuating, Downey?"

"That you have sex on airplanes," he deadpanned.

She sneered at him but didn't deny it, he noticed before turning to watch the direction of the passengers filing toward them. "I really need him not to have any bad press this week."

"Asher is a rock star, babe. He comes with bad press."

At this, her lips pursed, a certain spark lighting her eyes. He'd seen the look on her face before. The night in Chicago they went out for drinks with the rest of her clients. She had treated, but the other four women and one man who'd joined them bailed before midnight. He and Glo had stayed to order another round. After that round, he took her to the dance floor and they danced slowly, and given the number of whiskey shots they'd done, probably badly. He'd kissed her. Under the pulsating lights and the fluctuating beat, he laid his hands on her hips and tasted those full, pouting lips for himself.

Sobriety never happened so fast.

She pulled her head away and he had done the same. And there, under the smoke and filtered light, they blinked at each other and laughed.

"Eww," she'd said.

"That . . . wasn't good," he'd agreed.

They went back to drinking, shared a cab back to the hotel where he'd been rooming, and never, ever went there again. Gloria felt more like a sister, or a cousin, and he guessed she saw him the same way.

But that sparkle in her eyes since he mentioned Asher by name...no, that was something else. One dot connected to another in his head.

"You and Ash?"

"You're high."

"You're dodging."

They faced each other and her eyelids narrowed. "Didn't we determine it's a bad idea for me to get involved with my clients?"

"We determined it was a bad idea for you to get involved with *me*."

She wrinkled her nose. "Talk to your brother Landon lately?" she asked, forcing a subject change.

He let her. "Yeah, why?"

"Kimber mentioned your new nephew has him wrapped in one tight little fist. Made me think of you and Lyon."

Kimber, Landon's wife, was Glo's best friend, and if anyone asked Evan, the very thing that saved his brother from living life as a robot. Glo was right about Caleb, though. Landon and Kimber's son had Landon under his pudgy thumb.

Evan had been like that with Lyon. He remembered how overwhelming and joyous those first months with a baby could be. His kid almost never slept and he and Rae were up a lot. When Rae took the night shift at the hospital, sometimes Evan didn't sleep at all. Come to think of it, that was when he'd started painting at night. Lyon's sleeplessness the perfect excuse for him to go to the empty back room, turn on some Aerosmith, and sing to his son while amusing him with bright colors on canvas.

"There he is. *Finally*," Glo said.

Asher Knight emerged from a cluster of girls young

and old, all smiles as he walked by. A duffel bag slung over his shoulder, Asher swaggered toward them wearing the required rock star attire of a threadbare black T-shirt, black jeans, and his signature black cowboy boots.

"I keep a close watch on this heart of mine…" Evan started singing.

Gloria chuckled.

"Because you're mine," he finished in a low baritone, "I walk the line."

But Glo was no longer paying him any attention, eyes on Asher as she adjusted her low-cut top to be *lower* cut.

"Glo, babe, hold it together." Evan earned a punch in the arm, but she put on a huge smile when Ash reached them.

Asher ran a hand through his shaggy dark hair, then pulled it down his weary face.

"Hey, Ash." Her voice went breathy.

Good God. Can she pick 'em, or can she pick 'em?

"Hey, Sarge," Asher returned. Her nickname since she'd signed him and began—as Ash put it—"barking orders" at him. Evan suspected he liked being "barked" at. The nickname was in no way an insult, seconded by Glo, who blushed.

Actually blushed. Unbelievable.

"You look like you need a massage and a good night's sleep," she observed, and Evan wondered if she was offering one or both.

"I need Jack Daniel's and a bag of gummy bears," he answered, his voice scratchy.

He jerked his chin at Evan. "Good to see you, brother."

"Took you long enough to get here," Evan said.

Asher popped him in the arm, the friendly tap five

times harder than Glo's full-on punch. "Layover was a bitch."

She held up a hand. "If that's a euphemism of some sort, I don't want to know. I picked up the keys to your skank-free cabin and did a walk-through. See if you can keep it that way."

Ash straightened and gave her a lazy salute. "Yes, sir."

She lifted a black eyebrow, then turned for the exit. "Come on, boys."

"We're men," Asher argued as he and Evan fell in line behind her out the door.

"Whatever," she said without turning.

To Evan, he said, "Skank-free?"

"Yeah, didn't you hear? Evergreen Cove has a ban on skanks."

"What about babes?"

"Open season, man. Especially the feisty ones."

"Yeah," Ash agreed, his eyes on Gloria. "I see that."

CHAPTER FIVE

$\mathcal{A}$sher pushed a bar napkin across the table and gestured to the hopeless doodle scrawled on the tearing paper. "See what I mean?"

Evan studied the napkin, then gave him a bland look.

Asher grinned. "Hey, I'm better at singing than I am at drawing."

"God, I hope so." He spun the napkin so it was right side up...he thought. And tried to make out what he was pretty sure was Swine Flew's superhero costume. "Is this a...cape?"

Asher tapped the napkin. "It's his tail."

Gloria reached over Evan's arm and turned the napkin again. In unison, they both said, "Ohhhh."

"You guys are assholes," Asher pointed out, but his grin was locked on his face. Probably thanks to the Jack and Coke in front of him.

Evan folded the napkin, stood, and shoved it into his pocket. "I'm out. I have to pick up Lyon."

"Where is he, anyway?" Asher asked. "School?"

"It's July, dumbass," he pointed out. Asher flipped him off. "He's hanging out with Charlie."

"Charlie." Ash's voice dipped. "I remember her."

"You do not."

He lifted his glass and shrugged. "I remember you talking about her."

"You have a very skewed memory of our teenage years."

"He has a skewed memory of his current ones as well," Glo put in.

"You'd better be glad my memory is skewed, Sarge."

Didn't sound like something Evan wanted to hear about *at all*. He lifted a hand in farewell, leaving them to their bicker-flirting. "Bye, kids."

He drove to Charlie's, grateful she'd offered to watch Lyon while he had a powwow. He needed to find a long-term babysitter. Her being nearby wasn't good enough reason to dump his kid on her lap whenever he had stuff to do. Willing or no, *she* had things to do, and Evan had always prided himself on his independence.

* * *

"That's so coooool," Lyon said through a fit of laughter.

Charlie couldn't help laughing, too. She'd taken photos of him in her studio while they hung out today, which hadn't impressed him, but when she'd opened Photoshop and started manipulating his facial features, he became rapt.

"I want fangs."

"Fangs?" She laughed but acquiesced, using the mouse to drag one of the program's tools over the tip of his canine tooth to make it pointed. After two "fangs" were in place, he erupted again.

"All right, Lestat, enough play. I'm going to print some for your dad. You pick." She shut down Photoshop and was about to open the folder full of pictures when a different folder caught her eye.

It was labeled, simply, RAE.

"Look here," she said quietly, double clicking the folder. Thumbnail images filled the screen. Rae smiling, Rae being sassy. Rae in a wedding gown. Rae in her prom dress. Rae in Evan's arms on New Year's Eve. Rae holding a newborn baby Lyon in a hospital bed.

He pointed. "That's me."

"Yep. That's you. All eight pounds, seven ounces of you. You were a big baby!"

"No, I wasn't." He wrinkled his adorable nose.

"Your mom would have argued differently. She was in labor with you for eighteen hours."

Charlie could still hear Rae's voice as she mopped the sweat from her brow. *Never doing this again. Mark my words.* Evan had chuckled. Rae had shot him a death glare. Such a good memory.

Then Charlie's smile faded. Rae was right. She'd never done it again.

Before tears could cloud her vision, she closed the photo and opened the pictures of Lyon she'd taken today. Handing over the mouse to him, she gestured to the screen. "See those boxes?" She pointed out the small check box in the right hand corner of each photo.

"Yeah."

"Click the box." He did. "See how there's a green checkmark there now? That's how you can pick."

"How many can I pick?"

She'd taken at least a hundred shots. "As many as you like." She nudged his shoulder. "I have to clean up the mess we made."

Leaving him to his task, she went to her "studio," really the room in her house that should serve as the master bedroom. Instead of sleeping in here, she'd installed room-darkening blinds over both windows and packed the walk-in closet with screens, lights, and other photography equipment. She told herself she'd use the room all the time, which would justify her taking the smaller bedroom across the hall barely holding her queen-size bed, dresser, and vanity. Truth was, she used her studio sometimes, but mostly found herself where Lyon sat now: at the computer, poring over photos or Photoshopping images.

When she had dreamed of having a photography career, her dream hadn't included airbrushing an ill-timed pimple off a bride's nose in three hundred wedding photos.

She scooted the stool aside and rolled up the screen depicting a bright blue, sunny day. Today, the lake was cloudy, the sky gray-green, and the light not ample enough for a shoot. She'd have to get some shots of Lyon on the beach on a nicer day.

"Charlie! Ready!"

She shut off the light in the closet and tracked back to the front room where she kept her desk.

"I picked a lot."

"That's okay, sweetie." His face could eat every drop of her printer's ink and she couldn't care less. "Let's see."

One by one, they reviewed them, and when he paused on one of the black-and-whites of him looking to the side, a look of consternation on his face, she gasped.

"What's wrong?" he asked.

His brows were drawn, his eyes catching light, and the angle of his face...

"Nothing. You look like your dad in this one." He did. Just like Evan, a sharp, but contemplative expression—buried in puffy little boy cheeks, but still. So much like Evan. She'd always thought Lyon looked more like Rae, but now that he was getting older..."Handsome," she murmured.

"I didn't know you were taking that one."

"I know. Those are always the best ones." This one in particular needed to be matted and hung on the tallest wall opposite Evan's dining room. Against the pale pine walls, it would look great with a white matte and thick black frame. "Do you like it?"

He thought for a moment, then nodded. "Yeah." Then the moment was over.

"I have to check Clashing Clans."

"Go ahead, honey, I'll print these off for you."

Evan had informed her not to let him play the game on the iPad all day long, but she'd kept him occupied with the photography for two hours, and she considered that a win. She'd have to tell Evan his son had an interest in art after all.

The printer whined to life, pulling paper in and beginning to print. She scooted away from the desk, her mind on Evan when he'd dropped off Lyon. More specifically, on Gloria, who'd arrived with them.

Charlie had never met the raven-haired literary agent, and when she saw her—long, silken hair, sexy but professional style of dress, tall shoes, red lips, and blue eyes—she felt a pang of jealousy so strong, she could hardly breathe.

In a weird way, Glo reminded her of Rae. All vivacious beauty and fiery attitude wrapped up in quick wit and brains. Charlie, her light hair and simple dress, plain shoes and quieter voice, paled in comparison. That thought led to Russell, and Darian, the spunky redhead he'd married instead of Charlie. Before she could follow that thought into a downward spiral of inadequacy, she heard her front door pop open.

"Honey, I'm home!"

She reached the room to see Evan standing in her doorway, the gray sky behind him, soft lamplight highlighting the angles and planes of his face. He was dark and almost beautiful, one hand casually resting on the doorknob, a slow smile creeping onto his mouth. She wanted to tell him not to move a single muscle so she could grab her camera.

But that would be weird.

"Hey, how'd it go?" she asked as he came into her house and shut the door.

He strolled over to her, no closer than he'd ever stood to her, but somehow it felt *too* close. She thought of the moment he helped her stand when they were on the dock yesterday. He'd been too close then as well. She could smell his skin, hear him breathing.

Too close.

Stepping a foot away from him, she pointed to the dining room–turned-office at the back of her house. "I took some pictures I want you to see."

In the kitchen, Lyon didn't bother looking up from his electronic device. "Hey, Dad."

Evan shot her a look.

"He hasn't been playing long. Come on."

She gestured to the printer. It happened to be printing her favorite photo. When the sheet slipped onto the tray, she lifted it carefully.

"Isn't it great?" She admired the photo again, pointing to the set of Lyon's mouth, the mood in his eyes, the way she'd captured a thought frozen in time. "He looks like you in this, don't you think?" she asked, then became suddenly nervous when she realized she'd gushed over how handsome Lyon looked in the photo. By default, she'd also confirmed she found Evan handsome as well.

"He looks sad." Evan's brows pulled as he studied the picture, not sharing her neurosis.

He did? She looked again. "I thought he looked contemplative."

"I don't like to see him look grown up," he murmured quietly. A penetrating sigh, then, "Rae's missing it."

She was. Missing everything.

Charlie's heart sank. She'd overlooked an obvious factor, seeing the photo as a work of art, a beautiful piece. To Evan, it served as more evidence his son was growing up too fast, and Lyon's mother wasn't here to see it.

"I didn't think of it that way," she said. "I'm so sorry." She bit her lip and regarded the still-printing pile of photos, worried there were more like it.

A warm hand slid up her back, coming to rest between her shoulder blades. Her skin tingled where he touched, a tingle that raced down her limbs. She clutched the photo, wrinkling one edge.

"Sorry, Ace." She caught a hint of spice on his skin, the radiating attraction growing in circumference. His lips were next to her ear when he spoke again. "Didn't mean to hurt your feelings."

There went the heart-flutter. The one she worried would turn into a flap. She swallowed thickly as he straightened away from her, keeping his hand on her back. He sneaked a glance over at Lyon who was ignoring them both, then Evan's turquoise eyes turned back to her, traveling her face before he spoke again.

"I saw him sad. At *age three*. Because his mom was gone."

At the inference of them grieving over Rae, the flutter dissolved into an ache.

"Don't wanna see that sadness again. No kid should lose his mom that young."

"Neither should her husband."

His eyes met hers. "Neither should her best friend."

She gave him a weak smile of agreement. They'd all lost her, and it'd been as unfair as Rae missing out on every moment since. She grasped his arm with one hand, running her fingers lightly over the sparrow tattoo on his arm. Rae's tattoo.

"For what it's worth, I think you're an amazing father."

She felt him lean in the tiniest bit closer. "Think so?"

When she lifted her eyes from the ink, she found him watching her mouth. At that moment, a moment of mutual comfort turned into something…more. Something unexpected. His arm was wrapped around her on one side, his palm high on her back, and her hand was squeezing his forearm. They were holding one another. And now she was admiring his lips, too.

So wrong.

Sorry, Rae.

"Dad!" Lyon's raised voice made her jerk. "Swimming!"

She yanked her arm away, but Evan moved until his palm rested on the back of her neck.

"Okay, bud. Get your stuff." When he turned back to her, his eyelashes were narrowed over his blue eyes, a hint of a smile playing on his mouth. "Ace."

Fluttering. So much fluttering.

"Hmm?"

A gentle squeeze to her neck and then, "We'll continue this later."

With that cryptic promise, he gathered up Lyon and left her house.

* * *

The next morning, Charlie was hunkered over her computer working on Sofie's promotional brochure. The lighting in the photos of Sofie needed a few touch-ups thanks to the darker corner where they'd shot them, but Faith's needed none. Helping the cause were her enviable bone structure, straight back, and flawless skin. She decided to ask Faith to be on standby in case she needed a model.

A knock on her sliding door made her turn her head, where she saw Evan, a mug in each hand, and Lyon, hands cupped on either side of his face, peering through the glass.

She grinned, stood, and opened the back door. Then took in Evan's stunned expression and realized belatedly she didn't look her best. She went to work straight out of bed and was still wearing pajamas. Striped cotton shorts and a thin cotton shirt... and she hadn't brushed her hair.

"Oh, my hair." She lifted her hand to her head in apology. It must be a rat's nest.

Lyon walked past her, paying her no attention, but Evan's dark brows were near his hairline.

"I'll go brush it." She backed away to let him in. "I woke early and got so wrapped up in what I was doing…" She spied the mugs he was holding. "You brought me coffee? Thank you so much. What time is it, anyway?"

He didn't answer, simply abandoned both mugs on her kitchen table, then startled her by gripping her arms and pulling her to him, so tightly her breasts smashed into his chest. That's when she realized something else: she wasn't wearing a bra.

"Don't move," he instructed, his voice rumbling along her rib cage, which happened to be butting up against the hard muscle of his chest and torso. "Buddy," he told Lyon, "wait outside while Charlie gets ready, yeah?"

From the refrigerator, he argued, "But I want juice."

"I'll bring it out."

Lyon lurched to the door, giving a preemptive *Geez, Dad,* before he slid the door shut behind him. He forgot his anger the moment his feet hit the porch, jumping down the three steps and running along the edge of where the grass met the beach.

She dragged her gaze from the sliding door to Evan. "I'm so sorry," she whispered, her hands clutching the sides of his T-shirt. "I didn't think."

He looked down at her face, then lower, to her thin-and-getting-thinner T-shirt, something in his eyes she didn't quite recognize.

"Don't apologize, Ace. We barged in on you. But you're going to have to start thinking, babe, because my kid won't be seven forever."

She cringed. "Oh, and I look—"

"Amazing," he said on a low growl.

She felt her eyes blink, then widen, and angled her chin

in a way that if he leaned a few inches closer, their lips would touch. Not in a friendly, hello-how-are-you kiss, but in a real, pliant-lipped, slightly open-mouthed kiss.

Oh. Oh, she'd like that.

"Sorry?" She was pretty sure he'd accused her of looking amazing. That couldn't be right.

"If I'm alone next time," he rumbled again, "feel free to answer the door just as you are." He shrugged one eyebrow. "Or wearing less."

She blinked. Was he...kidding? Maybe he'd suffered a head injury this morning. Maybe she had. Maybe she was unconscious, in an ambulance on her way to the ER instead of in her kitchen pressed against Evan's body, his tattooed, corded forearms locked around her.

Yes. Well. She should...do something else with herself.

"I...um...I'll get Lyon some juice."

When she attempted to push away from him, his grip tightened on her lower back.

"Don't move." He pressed her closer. "This time for my sake."

That's when she noticed the hardness between them was more than his torso and arms, but also his—*oh.* Oh boy.

As quickly as he'd pulled her to him, the corner of his lips turned up and he let her loose. She scuttled to the refrigerator.

"Get juice," he instructed softly. "I'll take my own advice and wait outside. Get dressed, grab your coffee, and after we drink it on your deck, we're going to the farmer's market."

"We are?" She turned, a carton of orange juice in hand, fridge door open.

His eyes flickered down her body and back up. "Killing me, Ace."

That's when she looked down and saw her nipples pressed against the pale yellow fabric of her shirt and covered herself with her free arm. "Sorry," she muttered quickly.

"I'm not."

He threw a smirk in her direction, then took his coffee and went outside.

CHAPTER SIX

Brown hair mussed, short shorts and shirt wrinkled, the girl stumbling into the sunlight—and out of Asher's rented cabin—was most certainly doing the walk of shame.

Evan rested his wrist on the steering wheel of his SUV and watched as she wobbled up the gravel driveway in short, high-heeled boots, then angled her way onto a path pointing to another group of rental cabins up the hill.

Damn. Ash didn't waste any time.

Evan got out of the truck and knocked on the front door three times before a shout came from the side of the house.

Ash approached, robe open, wearing only a pair of boxers underneath, his face boasting a scraggly start of a beard, hair sticking up all over the place.

"You look like shit."

"Rode hard, man." Ash sipped from his coffee mug

and glanced up the hill where the petite girl had disappeared into the trees.

"Geez, dude. You could have at least walked her home."

"She didn't want to be walked home. You want coffee?"

"Nah."

Evan followed Ash to the backside of the house, where a sprawling, covered deck overlooked a steep hill. Treetops filled with skittering squirrels and chirping birds made up his view, the thick forest blocking the other houses.

A porch swing sat adjacent to a pair of wicker chairs. He moved to the chair and addressed Ash, who leaned a hip on the railing. "Gloria know you're entertaining the locals?"

Ash shook his head. "The less she knows. She's like my mother sometimes."

"Or something else," Evan put in. He tipped his head toward the hills. "Where'd you find her, anyway?"

"Jordan? Salty Dog."

A bar. What a surprise. Evan rested his elbow on the arm of the chair. "And just how old is *Jordan*?"

"Twenty...something." Asher's brow crinkled. "I'm not sure." His buddy looked older than his thirty-two years at the moment. "We drank a lot of Jack, came back here, played a lot of strip poker."

"Explains a lot."

Asher abandoned his mug and reached into his pocket for a cigarette.

"Thought you quit."

"Now you're my mother?" he mumbled, the cigarette waggling in between his lips. He lit it, sucked in a long drag. "I'm down to half a pack a day." He blew out a long stream of smoke and glanced around at the scenery. "It's nice here. I can see why you moved."

Evan took in the leaves rustling in the breeze. "Yeah, it is."

"I gotta rent a boat while I'm here. Fill it with babes." He flashed a tired smile. "Know any?"

Just one.

Again, Charlie had struck him dumb. The sight of her in that tiny cotton getup this morning—her legs on display, the outline of her breasts visible through her shirt. The only thing more intriguing than the way he'd reached for her was the way she'd clung to him when he did.

That wayward attraction he'd noticed on the dock? Not a one-way street.

Changing topic, Evan said, "Glo told me to come find you. Said she couldn't reach you on your cell."

Ash paused, cigarette to his lips, and shot him a look. "What'd she want?"

"The library wants to do a big book signing at the Starving Artists Festival this year."

"Ah, the poor man's carnival. I remember it well. Crafts, auctions, and a fleet of roach coaches with exotic fried foods."

"She thought it'd be good publicity to donate a copy of *Mad Cow* and an original painting for the auction. Wants us to sign and sell copies while we're there, too."

His eyebrows raised and he gestured to himself, cigarette scissored between two fingers. "*Us?*"

"Wants you to sing."

A trail of smoke blew from his nose and he crushed the cigarette into an ashtray on a small table overflowing with butts. "I don't know, man."

"An acoustic ballad by *the* Asher Knight? That'll fill your babe boat right up."

Asher folded his lanky body into the chair next to Evan. "Yeah. Seriously though, you and Lyon should come out with me. Maybe invite your sexy neighbor."

Evan iced Ash with a glare and straightened from his lean. The hand that'd been casually resting on the wooden arm of the chair curled around it in warning.

It was a warning Asher didn't heed. "Gloria told me she met her." Contented to throw kerosene on the brush fire, he pursed his lips and slowly mimed an hourglass figure.

Evan's blood pressure skyrocketed at the idea of Ash sniffing around Charlie. Teeth clenched so hard he swore he heard a filling crack, he growled, "Charlie's off the table."

Unfazed, Ash stoked the flames. "Don't want her on the table, Ev. Want her in my bed."

He pushed himself to standing and Asher rose, put up both fists, bounced on the balls of his feet, and grinned.

Evan continued advancing. "I'm not kidding." He wasn't sure he'd hit his friend, but pushed, he might.

"Bring it, bro." Asher's fists rose higher. "Déjà vu all over again."

Evan stopped walking. He knew exactly what his buddy referred to.

Ash lowered his fists, his grin fading slightly. "The summer you met Rae. You got that same gleam in your eye when Donny and I agreed she was hot."

He remembered. Rae Lynn Mosley had stepped onto that beach and into his life, a towel rolled under one arm and a huge floppy hat hiding her curls. He'd been so distracted by her that Donny had gotten him into a headlock and dragged him underwater. When he sputtered to the surface, Ash had joked he was going to go flirt with her and Evan had dunked him.

"You nearly drowned me," Asher reminded him now.

Hell yeah he did. A small smile found his face, then faded as a new memory cozied up behind the old one.

"Charlie was there that day," Evan said aloud. "Next to Rae." She'd been there other days, too. Year after year. Off to the side the entire time.

"Donny and I stayed away from her, too. You staked your claim in a pretty wide arc back then."

In an instant, Evan was completely gone for Rae. It'd taken him two more summers skirting around her to finally ask for her phone number. It took him two more to use it and call her. To him, at the time, Rae Lynn had been this unattainable beauty. A fantasy mirage he only caught glimpses of one week out of every summer. When he finally got her, he couldn't believe it. When he lost her, he couldn't believe that more.

"Some things never change," Ash said, lifting his fists again. "You go soft, Downey? Or you gonna fight me for Charlie?"

Evan was being baited, and he'd be damned if he'd give into his half-wit friend and fight him over something that wasn't gonna happen. He dropped his guard, crossing his arms over his chest instead. "You wouldn't have a prayer with her."

"True story." Asher was quiet for a moment, then his fists dropped again, and his expression turned somewhat serious. "Sucks she's not here."

"Charlie?"

"Rae."

Evan nodded his agreement as he walked past Asher, planks on the wooden porch creaking underfoot. Maybe not as half-witted as Evan had thought, because his buddy was right. It did suck she wasn't here.

"Where you headed?"

"Got shit to do," Evan answered, stepping off the porch into the gravel and dirt making up the worn driveway. "And hey, keep it in your pants. Glo doesn't want any bad press while you're here."

Ash waved a hand. "There's no such thing as bad press."

Evan had heard that a time or three. When he was half-way around the house, Asher called out, "Tell Charlie I say hi."

Evan lifted his middle finger in the air without turning. Asher responded with a hearty laugh. He should have hit him after all, he thought with a smile.

The asshole.

* * *

Faith lined up three bottles on the kitchen counter and described each one with so much detail, Charlie's head spun.

"Which one?" Faith prompted.

Sofie, thankfully, seemed to have grasped onto more description than Charlie because she said, "The one with the cherry-chocolate finish."

Faith lifted the bottle in the middle, the label a sepia tone with a cartoon cat, its tail wrapped around a wine-glass. Her slim brows rose in question.

"Sounds great." Not that Charlie's palate was all that refined. Three-dollar wine? Thirty-dollar wine? Couldn't tell the difference.

Wineglasses in hand, the girls went to the back deck.
The sky had grown dark, and to keep bugs away, Charlie lit the citronella candles lined along her porch railing.
She'd set the round glass table with dainty plates and cloth
napkins, and dressed the four wicker chairs in cornflower-
and-white seat cushions. Three flavors of hummus and a
pile of blue corn chips sat in the center of the table and
a plate of gourmet chocolates shaped like seashells and
filled with white cream sat off to the side. Sofie dove into
the chips.

"I love your house." Faith reached for a piece of chocolate. "Beats apartment living."

"No kidding. I'd love a place near the water. Or at
least away from my neighbors," Sofie agreed. "They're
so close. I hear everything they're doing." She hoisted an
eyebrow. "And the couple in 2B"—she shuddered—"you
do *not* want to know what they're doing."

Faith started to laugh, but then the laugh faded into
a contemplative *hmm*. "Although, being close to your
neighbors wouldn't be all bad..."

Charlie looked over at her, then followed to where her
eyes were glued.

"...If your neighbor looks like that," she finished.

"*Hello,*" Sofie purred. Then to Charlie, she said, "Oh
my gosh, is that him?"

"Him, who?" Faith asked. Then turned her eyes back
to Evan. "Oh. *Him.*"

Wearing tennis shoes and running shorts, a T-shirt
dangling from his waistband, a shirtless Evan Downey
jogged off his deck and onto the beach. He turned his
head left, then right, as if trying to decide which direction
to run. When he spotted the three of them, and Charlie

hoped it wasn't because they were all staring with their tongues hanging from their mouths, he started in their direction.

"Looks like we'll get an introduction," Sofie said.

Oh boy. Okay. Okay. She could do this. "Be cool," she said, more to herself than her friends.

"Like Fonzie," Faith said.

Sofie laughed. Faith laughed. Charlie couldn't make a sound. Her eyes were too busy traveling the expanse of Evan's bare chest, tattooed round shoulders, and strong arms, all the way down to his confident stride as he approached the porch.

Then he was there. Standing in front of them, his mouth quirked just so.

"Good evening, ladies."

Faith muttered, "Wow" under her breath, and Sofie sucked in a shallow breath.

Charlie managed a, "Hey," but heard the catch in her voice.

Also, she should tear her eyes off his naked-from-the-waist-up body. *Should* being the operative word. He rested a hand on the square white pillar at the foot of her porch—the arm with the evergreen trees—and propped a foot on the bottom step, his grin both sexy and confident, and she couldn't look away.

"I'm Sofie Martin."

Right. Introductions.

Charlie blinked out of her stupor. "Evan, these are my friends, Sofie and Faith."

His grin widened to a distracting degree. He nodded at each of them. "Looks like you're up to no good."

"Hummus?" Faith offered.

He scrunched his face. "Gonna go with *no* on that one."

Sofie laughed. Faith laughed. Charlie swallowed a mouthful of wine. After—how about that, it did finish on a cherry-chocolate note—she blew out a low exhale, and glanced back in the direction of his house. "Where's Lyon?"

"Sitter. Librarian's great-niece."

"You could have dropped him by here while you ran." Both her friends' gazes snapped to her.

"GNO is no place for a seven-year-old, Ace." The nickname drew more curiosity from her friends.

"You know the acronym for Girls' Night Out," Sofie observed. "You're a keeper."

"I had a wife. I know my stuff," he said with an easy smile. "Okay, I'll let you get back to your *hummus.*" With a pat of palm to pillar, he turned his back on them and took off jogging down the water's edge.

Charlie watched until he became a grainy shadow in the distance, then dragged her gaze away from his ass. On the way, she came eye-to-eye with Faith, whose lips lifted impishly. "He is smokin' hot."

"Seriously," Sofie concurred. "*And* he likes Charlie."

"Of course he likes me. He was married to my best friend," she said, reaching for her wine.

"That's not the kind of *like* she means," Faith said, her smile evident.

"You," she pointed at Sofie, "are reading too much into this. And you," she gestured to Faith, "are engaged to be married."

"And you"—Sofie poked Charlie in the arm—"are changing the subject. Admit it. He's ridiculously hot and you'd love to know what's under those running shorts."

"Sofie!" Charlie said in a harsh whisper.

"We *all* want to see what's under those running shorts," Faith said through a laugh.

The sip of wine turned into a gulp. Okay, her friends had a point. His body was beautiful and mostly bare and she did want to see what the rest of it looked like. Which was awful. And made her a horrible best friend.

Sorry, Rae.

"Ace?" Sofie prompted.

Charlie opened her eyes, relieved to talk about something other than if Evan was a boxer-or-briefs guy—if he wore them at all.

Oh boy.

"I've never had a nickname," Faith said.

Charlie cleared her throat, and her mind of Evan's... everything. "It's a funny story." She couldn't keep from smiling. The memory was a good one. "The four of us used to have poker nights when I lived in Columbus. Russell, me, Evan, and Rae. We usually played for Oreos or gummy bears, but this night in particular, we played for change. With real coin on the line, I decided to sneak an Ace of hearts out of my sleeve for the win. Evan busted me."

Sofie gasped. "You? She who does everything right?"

Charlie's jaw dropped. "I do not do everything right!"

"You do. You're the goodest girl I know."

She was? A frown pulled her lips. "Good" sounded synonymous with "bland."

"Hey," Faith spoke up, "I resent that."

Sofie lifted a tortilla chip. "Sorry. I knew you back when we waitressed and you used to do keg stands."

"Did not!"

"Did too!"

"You weren't as sweet then as you pretend to be now, my friend," Faith said to Sofie.

"I was so."

"Don't make me say his name." Faith dipped a chip and munched.

When they quietly chewed for a few more moments, Charlie swiveled her head between the two of them. "Okay, now I have to know."

Sofie drank, then drank a little more. Faith fell silent, craning an eyebrow in challenge.

"Seriously?" Charlie looked from one to the other. "No one's going to tell me?"

"Sofe?" Faith asked, her face showing mild concern. "Should I not have brought it up?"

Sofie waved a hand. "Don't be silly. Donny was forever ago, like, *years* ago."

"Donny?" What were the odds? "As in Donny Pate?"

Sofie's brow crinkled. "Yeah."

"I knew him. Er, knew of him. He was one of the bad boys who hung out with Evan and Asher Knight years ago when we used to visit the Cove."

"Bad boys?" Faith asked in an amused lilt.

"Yeah, or so Rae called them." Donny was taller than Evan and Asher, had long, black hair, and was the quieter, more intense one of the three. She turned to Sofie. "He was cute. When he was seventeen, anyway."

"Yeah, well, he was cute when he was twenty-four, too." She drained her glass, then held it out for a refill. "Garçon?"

Faith tipped the bottle and emptied it into Sofie's glass, her engagement ring glinting in the candlelight. "I have a surprise for you both."

"You've set a date?" Sofie guessed.

Charlie sputtered into her glass. Faith had been pro-crastinating everything about her upcoming nuptials. Setting a date, picking a venue, anything and everything having to do with the planning.

Sofie had shared she thought this was a bad sign and Charlie agreed. Maybe because a version of Rae's warn-ing about Russell still rang in her ears. In Faith's case, Charlie wondered if a man who didn't push for marriage two years after he'd popped the question was also a man who'd walk away. For her friend's sake, she hoped not.

"You wish," Faith said with a smile.

Sofie held up a palm. "I don't do weddings."

It was true. Sofe handled corporate events, charity din-ners, even anniversary parties, but never weddings. She said they were too big and complicated, but Charlie some-times wondered if her reasoning ran deeper.

"I know, I know. No weddings. Now for my surprise." Faith reached under the table and came up with a white bakery box.

Sugar Hi's logo was the cutest. Confection-pink, swirly lettering designed around a frosting-laden cupcake with a cherry on top made up the word "Sugar" and "hi!" was in a little comic-strip-style speech balloon off to the right. Beneath the whimsical logo, in type almost serious by comparison, was the claim "Evergreen Cove's Finest." The claim was true. Hoity-toity Abundance Market and homegrown-style Cup of Joe's could not compare to the epic sweets served up at Sugar Hi.

"It's not." Charlie leaned closer, drawn by the smell of sugar as Faith lifted the lid.

"It is." Faith tilted the box, displaying the desserts as

if she would rare and precious gems. "Soon-to-be-world-famous Devil Dogs."

"Oh, no, you got one for each of us," Sofie said, shoulders dropping in defeat. "Evil."

"Yes. And you're going to eat every bite. Calories don't count on girls' night."

"Besides, when you cut the cake in half, the fat grams fall out," Charlie joked.

Sofie acquiesced with an eye roll. "*Fine.*"

They lifted their chocolate-dipped cakes out of the box and Faith raised hers in a cheers. "To the bad boys of Evergreen Cove." She smiled. "And the good girls smart enough to stay away from them."

Rather than chime in on that proclamation, Charlie took a bite of the most amazing, moist, crème-filled, chocolate-dipped cake she'd ever tasted in her life, and tried desperately not to think of bad boys.

Like the sinful, rich chocolate and bad-for-her sugar causing her entire body to buzz and her taste buds to tingle, thoughts of Evan crashed into her brain front and center. Thoughts about his body, his tempting mouth, and the way those long, long eyelashes swept over eyes that'd seen more darkness than light.

CHAPTER SEVEN

*Th*ree a.m.

Three. *Fucking*. a.m.

Evan glared down at the black, gray, and navy-blue paint covering the canvas in front of him, hating it. Hating the proof of the darkness that covered him during sleepless hours. Hating that *this* lived inside him while on the outside he struggled to be the best father possible. A father like his own.

He wanted to turn over the easel, smash the painting, knock everything off his desk. But he didn't want to wake his son; have him come down here and find Evan in the throes of ... whatever he was going through.

He'd moved here to find the light. Not get darker.

He snapped the graphite pencil in his hand into two pieces and threw it across the room. It plinked off the walls and rolled across the wooden floors. Too tame a reaction for what he was feeling. He paced across the room to the wide windows, feeling like a caged animal. Rather than seeing the nighttime lakeside landscape, he focused on his wavy, angry reflection in the glass.

After his run, he'd paid Lorraine to stay another two hours so he could come in here and get some work done undisturbed. He'd pulled out the tattered napkin with Ash's pathetic sketch and attempted to get Swine Flew down. By midnight, Lyon was in bed, Lorraine's curfew past due, and Evan had drawn three pages of sketches he couldn't use.

He'd gone to bed shortly after only to wake from another nightmare-slash-memory, his head filled with thoughts of Rae, his big bed making a mockery of the idea of restful sleep. An hour ago, he trekked in here, his skin crawling, needing to let loose, let go.

Forget.

Needing the hit that paint on canvas promised. Needing the release of freeing himself from space and time and the life partner he'd never again see on this earth.

Shutting off the studio lights, he snatched the video baby monitor Landon had sent him as a housewarming gift, glad he had a way to watch his boy when he was in the bowels of the studio being tortured by repressed demons. A look at the screen showed Lyon asleep, limbs splayed, mouth open.

Evan needed to move. Walk off the building pressure, get a whiff of air not piped through the AC vents. He would bet the fancy monitor worked away from the house, as well.

Say . . . two doors down from the house.

Charlie.

Suddenly, he needed to see her. The painting hadn't

cleansed him, hadn't exorcised this twitchy energy radiating across his back and twanging down both arms. If
nothing else, the walk would do him good.

Monitor deep in one pocket of his cargo shorts, he
locked his door behind him. Humid air hit him in the
face, blowing the longer strands against his forehead. He
sucked in a deep breath, listened to frogs and bugs chirping in the night, then broke into a jog for the destination of
Charlie's wide, white, and welcome back porch.

When he arrived, he felt less desperate, a tad less
crazy. The house was dark, no sign of her staying up late
to work. Just as well.

At least one of them was getting some sleep.

Hand on the pillar by the steps, he stared blankly at
the swing on the porch, his fingers drumming, his mind a
zillion miles away. After a minute, he turned back toward
his house, figuring he'd save Charlie the trial of dealing
with his shit, when he heard her speak.

"Evan?"

She sounded slightly groggy, and damn adorable,
and he turned to find her looking the same. Her mass of
honey-blond waves hung out of the small screenless window upstairs, her huge eyes heavy.

He tilted his head to take her in, then put a hand over
his heart. "Juliet."

A sleepy smile pulled her lips, and the tension choking him loosened its stranglehold. In a raspy chuckle, she
asked, "What are you doing?"

Great question. What was he doing? Freaking out?
Walking off frustration? And now that he'd laid eyes on
Charlie, he considered a chunk of that frustration was
sexual.

"Coming to see you," he answered honestly.

Her smile faded. "Something wrong?"

Nothing she needed to know about.

"Nope. Couldn't sleep. Figured you'd be up."

"Well, I'm up." Once again her full lips parted into a smile and something curled around in his chest and tugged.

She closed her window and he glanced at the monitor again. Lyon hadn't moved. Not surprising. Where he'd suffered sleepless nights a year ago, now his kid was a rock. Evan had been relieved for the end of that phase.

The kitchen light snapped on and he stood on the other side of her sliding glass door watching as she entered the room. Short shorts edged in lace coasted along her ample thighs, a matching, tiny sleeveless top bared her delicate shoulders and stretched across her incredible tits. He refocused his gaze to her face when she pulled a long, thin, silky robe over those bare shoulders and closed it, hiding the pale pink pj's—and the promise of what lay beneath them—from view.

"Don't be a horndog," he warned himself as the door slid aside. What neither of them needed was for him to bury this...this bizarre need in her—have some sort of displaced lust at three in the morning ruin the easy friendship they had going.

"Hey."

"Hey," he returned, his voice rocky.

"Wine?"

"Gonna take the same plea as I did with the hummus, Ace."

"Want to come in?" She bit her bottom lip and he watched as her white teeth scraped the plump flesh.

Yes.

"You gonna keep that robe on?"

Her brows curved in confusion. "Yes."

"Then, no." So much for not being a horndog. Man, he needed some sleep.

"Um..."

Before she could respond to that, he said, "Come outside."

"Okay. Give me a second."

Turning, she darted into the kitchen and moved for the fridge. He watched her fluid movements for a beat longer than he should have, then lowered himself to the top porch step and faced the silent, dark lake. The quiet was new. On East Level, the semi-busy street provided plenty of background noise to sleep by, and a few gray hairs when Lyon had become a wandering toddler.

He heard the door slide closed and a moment later, a bottle of water appeared in front of him. Accepting it, he watched as Charlie padded barefoot down a step, arranged the robe over her long legs, and sat next to him, a light, pleasant scent lifting off her hair or skin.

Lid off, he guzzled down half the bottle.

She took a dainty sip of her own water bottle, then eyed him. "Studio time not working out?"

One could say that. He shook his head.

"Can't sleep?"

"Not tonight." He'd be up until morning, which ensured a rough start to his day. Nothing he could do about it now. His eyes left her face and wandered over her robe, covered in bright yellow and pink daisies. "You like flowers."

"You noticed."

He had. He'd never noticed before. But nearly everything he'd seen her in since he got here—dress, pj's, her beach towel—had flowers on it. "Real ones or just wearing them?"

"Both. But I do not have a green thumb. I finally hired a guy to come out and do my beds this year." She gestured at the colorful plants decorating the side of her house. "I have to call him, though, because I think the lavender bushes he planted are dying."

"Yeah?" he asked, having no idea which plant to look at.

She pointed past him to a scraggly brown bushy-looking thing. "It bloomed earlier this year, but now it looks like something from *The Legend of Sleepy Hollow*. This is his signature plant. He's not going to like that I killed it."

"The hell is a *signature plant*?" Evan had never been much of a toil-in-the-soil kind of guy. He loved the outdoors: running, swimming, and he was looking forward to boating and trying his hand at waterskiing for the first time in years, but plants? Not his gig.

"He patented a plant."

"Nerdy."

"Science-y," she corrected, elbowing him gently.

"There a difference?" The plant guy sounded like Poindexter, with a pocket protector full of garden spades. "Whatever makes you happy, Ace."

"So, why couldn't you sleep?" She dropped a foot to the bottom step. The silky material of her robe slid aside, revealing her leg all the way up to her thigh.

He looked—how could he not?—and took another drink of his water as he tried to decide how much to share.

After a beat, he said, "Rae."

The air changed between them, her silence saying more than if she'd filled the space with chatter. She was waiting for him to share more, but he didn't want to share the memory of his late wife's stillness after her last breath, or the memory of her sheet-covered body being loaded into a silent ambulance.

Turned out he didn't need to say more.

Charlie's free hand rested on his forearm and he looked down at her slim, delicate fingers over his inked skin. Her thumb brushed over the hair on his arm, and attraction he couldn't categorize washed over him. He lifted his chin and met her seeking, hazel eyes.

Charlie.

In his peripheral for years, now front and center.

"Painting didn't help?" she asked, her tone cautious.

She was right to be cautious. Whatever lingered between them was downright dangerous. He didn't answer, tearing his eyes from her sympathy-filled, moonlit face and focusing on the reflective surface of the lake instead.

There was a boat in the distance, lights swinging, the distinct sound of laughing and shouting followed by loud splashes. Kids on vacation, he imagined, diving where they weren't supposed to, drinking where they weren't supposed to. Like Evan, Donny, and Asher used to do shit they weren't supposed to.

"Ah, to be young," she commented.

"Yeah," he commented back, but the only sensation in his body was her palm warming his arm.

"You miss those days?"

"Sometimes." Things sure as hell were easier back then. The memory that hit him made him smile. "When we were sixteen, Donny stole a bottle of booze from his dad's liquor cabinet and we got plowed."

"Sixteen? Bet it didn't take much."

"It didn't." They'd all puked, rallied, then headed straight for the library. "That was the night Ash and I decided to leave permanent marks on Evergreen Cove."

"Donny didn't go?"

"He was our lookout. And by 'lookout' I mean he camped out on a park bench and finished the booze."

"Oh boy." Her laughter did a lot to ease his earlier tension. "Not THE night?"

He leaned a shoulder into hers in a playful bump. "The one and only."

"The rise of the Penis Bandits."

A laugh, his, took him by surprise. "Ace. Really."

Her cheeks stained pink as she closed her eyes and shook her head. "I did not mean to say that. I just meant"—she pulled her hand from his arm while he continued to laugh, then put it to her flushed face. "All I meant was that was the start of you breaking hearts and taking names." Her teeth scraped her bottom lip. "I mean rules. Breaking rules," she finished quietly.

He studied her for a second, watching as she watched him back. Tension crackled between them. Tension having nothing to do with Rae or the nightmare that woke him. Tension that made him wonder whose heart he'd broken.

Pushing a stray strand of her honeyed hair off her face, he allowed the back of his hand to graze her cheek. "Ace," he whispered.

She swallowed before she quietly answered, "Yeah?"

He didn't know what to make of any of this, if it was real, or the stuff that didn't feel real in the middle of the night when his mind walked the line between escaping reality and facing it. "I'll let you get some sleep."

"Oh." She looked disappointed...or sleepy. "Okay."

That he couldn't tell which one solidified his decision to leave.

"Lyon," he said in way of explanation.

"Oh. Oh, of course." She pulled her stretched leg in and started to stand. Before she did, he drew the parted robe over her legs, brushing his knuckles along the inside of her knee.

Like the moment he helped her stand at the dock, and the other morning when he'd shielded her peaked nipples from his son's view, Evan recognized her reaction for what it was. *Attraction.*

A whole hell of a lot of it.

His eyes went to her parted lips as she sucked in a breath.

Then she stood and backed up her porch steps so abruptly, his hand still hovered in midair, no longer on her skin. He shot a look over his shoulder in time to see her slide the patio door open and step inside.

"Good night." She slid the door to, but just before it closed, he heard her mutter, "Sorry, Rae."

A second later, the kitchen was dark and Charlie was nowhere to be seen.

* * *

In a horrible Forrest Gump impression, Asher pointed to *Deelightful* and said, "That's my boat."

Evan snorted.

"You can be Lieutenant Dan." Ash elbowed him, then stepped onto the dock and leaned in to check out the mode of transportation Evan couldn't believe he'd been allowed to rent.

"More like I'll be Skipper to your Gilligan after you wreck this thing into the rocks."

"Who's Gilligan?" Lyon asked, snapping his lifejacket crooked.

Evan fixed the straps. "Uncle Asher's long-lost cousin."

Asher did a good job driving, surrendering the vessel to Evan after cracking open a beer he'd smuggled on board. They dropped anchor for an hour to swim. Lyon had been learning to hold his breath underwater in class, and he insisted on showing off by putting his face in the water while he kicked. Evan had to smile at the image of his son clumsily moving through the water, the bright orange floating vest inhibiting more than helping him.

Despite her dislike for the water, Rae would have been proud.

On the deck, he opened the cooler and passed out lunch. Cheetos, ham sandwiches, Pringles for himself, another Miller for Asher, and one of those disgusting Go-Gurt things for Lyon.

Evan had taken a huge bite of his sandwich when Ash spoke.

"Find any babes for the boat yet?"

"You're the rock star. You flush 'em out."

"Charlie's a babe," Lyon chimed in with a grin.

Evan looked at Ash but gestured at his son. "See what you did to him?"

Ash smiled. "Atta boy, Lionel. Call 'em like you see 'em." Then to Evan, he said, "Need to take the boat out for a night trip. Call your sitter for little man there, and come out with me."

He found himself smiling in spite of himself. Sure, Ash was dancing with immature, but Ash was also Ash.

He had no need to bury who he was, at his core. Somehow, who Ash used to be and who he was now blended together seamlessly.

Then again, he had no wife, no kid. Minimal responsibilities.

Like Ash had always been a musician, Evan had always been an artist. And not only one-half of the "Penis Bandits." He remembered losing hours poring over comic books and attempting to draw the characters, or entering art contests but never hearing back. He'd once painted the inside of his closet solid black and then in white painted a pair of eyes and the outline of a figure that made his mother shriek the next time she'd opened the door to hang up his clothes.

When puberty hit, his focus shifted from art to art *and* girls. Then Rae entered the picture...and, man. There'd been no going back. He was twenty-three to her twenty-one when they got married, which was crazy young, and they'd behaved like it. Fighting over stupid shit all the time. But the makeup sex, ah, the makeup sex with her had always been worth it.

The Achilles' heel in their otherwise picture-perfect marriage had always been the fact that he painted late at night. Back then he'd spent countless hours on new tattoo designs. Rae would be up breastfeeding Lyon, and unable to go back to sleep, Evan would wander to the freezing-cold utility room, crank on the space heater, and start drawing.

So into it, he often didn't notice how much time had passed until Rae interrupted him at five a.m., dressed in her scrubs, ready for work.

Those arguments never ended well. And never ended with makeup sex.

"And then what?" Ash was saying, and Evan tuned in to see his friend talking to an animated Lyon.

He described a battle from his favorite iPad game—Evan had refused to let him bring the five-hundred-dollar electronic on the boat, much to Lyon's chagrin—his cheeks lifted, a dimple denting one of them, his smile broad and genuine.

Passion for a video game. Evan didn't get it.

He started to apologize and tell Lyon not everyone wanted to hear about Clashing Clans, when Asher asked, "What are you battling for in this game?"

"The queen," Lyon answered.

"Man after my own heart," Ash said.

"I think she looks like Mom."

Evan felt his face go numb. He and Asher exchanged glances.

"Aunt Charlie gave me a picture of her in a long, white dress wearing a crown."

Wedding photo.

"The queen has a dress like that," Lyon said, then took a bite out of the middle of his sandwich.

Asher reached into his bag and pulled out a cell phone. "Well, this I have to see," he said, followed by, "After I download it, will you show me how to play?"

Lyon's eyes lit, happiness evident in everything from his posture to his animated voice. "Yeah! And then you can join my clan!"

To which Asher uttered a flattered-sounding, "Really? Me?"

Evan watched the exchange, and Asher connect with his flesh and blood, and realized that he'd shrugged off his son's passion much like Rae had ignored his—

overlooking the fact that Lyon's borderline obsession for that game had something to do with his mom.

Evan's fault for burying the pictures of Rae in the first place.

Fuck.

He watched, with a hint of jealousy, badass, rock god Asher Knight and his kid lean over Asher's cell phone as Lyon described the rules of the game.

Dedicated badass *and* good with his kid.

Two things Evan had yet to pull off simultaneously.

CHAPTER EIGHT

"Can Charlie come swimming with us, Dad?"

He debated his son's request, unsure how to answer. On the one hand, she might like a chance to take a break and swim with them, and he certainly wouldn't mind seeing her in a bikini. On the other, after the night he'd wandered onto her porch, inviting her was playing with fire.

"Who's she talking to?" Lyon had his beach towel around his neck and his hand wrapped around the strap of the packed beach bag resting on the floor by his feet.

"Buddy, get your sunglasses. And put on your flip-flops." What he didn't need was Lyon forgetting something and having to come back to the house to get it. Granted, the dock wasn't that far away considering it was between his house and Charlie's, but it was a long way to go when he could just get his shit together now—

"I don't know that guy."

"It doesn't matter who it—" he stopped himself as

his son's words sank in. *Guy?* He walked to the window where Lyon stood peeking out. "What guy?"

"That guy." Lyon tapped the glass.

Sure enough, there was "a guy" standing at Charlie's back porch, gesturing at what, he couldn't tell.

"Should we still ask her to swim?"

Normally, he would have answered "no" and given Lyon a lesson in privacy. Instead, and now that he'd seen the pair of arms on the man standing way too close to Charlie for comfort, he said, "Yeah. Let's ask her."

As they drew closer, he was able to see more and more of Charlie's guest. And the more he saw, the less he liked. The guy was probably around Evan's six feet tall, his chest and arms massive. He wore shorts and a tank top, a tribal tattoo wrapping around his upper right arm. It was a good one, too. Despite already not liking the guy based on principle and proximity to Charlie alone, Evan appreciated quality artistry when he saw it.

"Aunt Charlie!" Lyon burst onto the scene, and for once Evan was grateful for his son's lack of couth. That little burst did exactly what he'd hoped for: it turned the guy's head away from Charlie. His narrowed eyes assessed Lyon, then moved to Evan.

He stood taller, mentally vowing to do more curls tonight. The other guy's arms were tanks.

Lyon invited Charlie to go swimming, and she bent at the waist, pulled her hair out of her face, and promised she would—God, Charlie. Such good people.

The guy held out a hand in greeting. "Connor McClain. You must be the famous illustrator she was telling me about." He smiled. Nodded toward Evan's house. "Did all kinds of repairs at your house before the Millers moved out of there, so if something starts acting up, let me know."

He gripped Connor's hand briefly, then let go, propping his hands on his hips. "Repairs?"

"Connor works for his father's handyman company," Charlie put in, stepping closer, her long, beachy—and flowered, he noticed—dress blowing in the breeze.

"Part-time," Connor was quick to add. "I'm recently out of the service, but I help out some."

Ex-military, too. Shit. Probably was a decent guy.

He gestured to the fresh dirt and Evan recognized the scraggly brown plant was gone, a fresh green one with pale purple buds in its place. "This is my real gig."

"Right. The lavender." He and Charlie were both wrong. Connor McClain didn't strike him as nerdy or science-y.

"Landscaping," he clarified. "Library Park's my most recent design."

He'd noticed how nice the park looked, mainly because Mrs. Anderson had pointed out what was new while showing Evan and Gloria where the setup would be for the Starving Artists Festival. He didn't know a lot about landscaping, but he noticed the place was highly manicured with plenty of small fruit trees and a line of hedges along the back of the library.

"Yeah, I saw that. Looks good." Evan threw Charlie a glance and she gave him a demure smile.

"The three of us have childhood friends in common," she said.

Evan frowned. How? The sandy-blondish-haired guy in front of him had to be at least five years his junior. "Yeah?"

"Donny Pate was my roommate and drinking buddy." He shrugged massive shoulders. "I was underage. He was my supplier."

"Sounds like Donny." Evan had kept in touch with him over the years. He'd left the Cove a few years back, making his home, and finding his calling, in New York. Evan had flown out to the Hamptons for a party thrown by one of Donovan's crazy-rich clients. They'd hung out near an outdoor fireplace Donovan had built with his own two hands, while Evan had noted things: one, Donny had morphed into more of a loner, but less of a fighter, and two, in spite of that loner status, he seemed a hell of a lot happier there than when he'd lived in the Cove.

Connor reached in his wallet and extracted his card. "My cell number."

The card was white with black block lettering and Evan's first thought was that an aspiring landscaper needed something much more artsy than this snooze fest of a business card.

"Repairs, landscaping, or if you want to sell me a signed book for my nephew"—Connor smiled and though he'd been trying not to, Evan decided he already liked the guy—"gimme a buzz."

He left Charlie with a few more instructions for her new lavender plant, bent at the waist to high-five Lyon, and ambled out to the driveway before climbing into a huge white Ram truck.

Damn. Nice truck, too. Made Evan's family-guy SUV look tame.

"He's super nice," Charlie said from beside him.

"Seems okay."

"Can you believe he knew Donny? Used to work with

him, Faith, and Sofie at that seafood restaurant on Fifth.
Small world right?"

"Very," he agreed. *And getting smaller by the minute.*

"Daaaad," Lyon said, proving his impatience had
reached Code Red.

"Meet you at the dock, okay, buddy?" she said to him.
"I'll get my suit."

With the promise of getting to see Charlie in a bathing
suit, the rest of Evan's day instantly got better.

                         * * *

It didn't fit well, but she'd decided the black one-piece
bathing suit and printed sarong looped around her hips
were far more appropriate than her hot pink bikini around
Evan and his seven-year-old son.

But mostly Evan.

After the night he arrived unexpectedly, and the
bizarre yet permeable air of sexual tension between them,
she understood that this Evan-living-next-door thing had
come with a certain set of challenges. She was sure she'd
get used to seeing him shirtless eventually—and get used
to him being in her space more often than not. But for
now, she seemed to be reverting back to when she crushed
on him at fifteen.

Though that night had nothing to do with crushes or
when she was fifteen.

There'd been something else there. Something other than
sexual tension. A connection, almost. Artist-to-artist, or
maybe it was their shared grief for Rae, or the fact that Evan
wasn't sleeping and Charlie cared why he wasn't sleeping.

That's why she'd chosen the black bathing suit. Because

that connection was as dangerous as the heart flutter. That connection could turn their friendship into something it shouldn't be. Something she couldn't allow it to be.

She made her place on a towel on the dock, lathered up with sunscreen, and soaked in the rays. Evan stood in water up to his chest, Lyon paddling a few feet away from him. She considered unlooping the sarong over her legs so her tan wouldn't be uneven, but opted for safety disguised as modesty.

Last night, after Evan had grazed his hand along her cheek and brushed his knuckles against the inside of her knee, she'd run inside in a panic, shut off all the lights, and hid. Not exactly the most mature of reactions.

Maybe she was fifteen years old.

Upstairs, she peeped out her bedroom window and watched as he swaggered down the beach back to his house. Not able to help herself, she'd stared—admiring the fluid yet masculine way he moved, every intentional footfall, and the sharp lines and curved planes of his body.

She hadn't been able to help it. She was single bordering on spinsterhood, and he was an incredibly attractive guy. Sue her.

But.

She couldn't keep objectifying him if they planned on being neighbors for years to come. He was still her friend, still Rae's husband, and still completely and entirely out of the realm of "available bachelors" for herself.

Despite her inner speech, her eyes traced the lion tattoo on his shoulder now, its mane curling over one chiseled bicep. And when Lyon commanded to be thrown into "deep" water and Evan turned to placate him, she got a view of the roses on his other shoulder: two big blooms, and a swirl shaped like an infinity sign closing in around them. Beautiful artistry. Designed by his own hand, executed by another, but—Evan had told her—under his watchful eye and instruction. They had to be perfect. Because what they represented was too important to be anything less.

And what they represented was family. A lion for his son, and roses for his mom and his aunt. Then there was the sparrow on his forearm for Rae. His body had been etched with ink honoring his favorite people. Which said so much about who he was and how deeply he loved.

How wonderful to be a part of the artwork on his skin— to be carefully chosen, drawn with precision by his own hand, and permanently showcased on his amazing body. Not on a whim or because he was a tattoo artist, but because those people mattered enough to him to earn the privilege.

Against her will, her lips lifted into a sad smile. She hoped one day to matter that much to someone.

Lyon splashed underwater and popped back up, giggling. Evan, wide smile on his face, scooped up a handful of water and wet his dark brown hair, sweeping it off his forehead. She studied the newest bit of ink on his body— the evergreens—and allowed herself to imagine that it'd had something to do with her.

Then she chastised herself for being selfish. He'd made Rae's dreams come true. And since her life was cut so very short, that mattered more than any silly fantasies Charlie entertained now.

She hadn't realized Evan was so close until her sighed exhalation drew his attention. He turned his head in her direction and caught her staring. She tried to stop, honest to God, but how could she turn away from what was near perfection in the flesh?

The long ends of his wet hair curled and dripped down his neck, beading his wide shoulders with water. His sunglasses were perched on his nose, his eyes scrunched at the sides. Crow's feet fanned out from each corner, far more attractive than she cared to admit. The sunglasses on her own nose hid her perusal of his fine body, and for that, she was glad. Especially when he approached, his powerful arms slicing through the water, tattoos flexing with each step.

Sorry, R—

"Ace."

"Yeah?" she said a little too quickly, a little too loudly, and maybe a little guiltily.

"Don't you swim? I had no idea you were such a princess."

"Yes, I swim," she said—this time defensively. "I just washed my hair."

Lyon and Evan gave her twin, confused expressions.

"Why are you wearin' a dress?" This question came from Lyon, who scrunched his equally perplexed face up at her.

"It's not a dress," she started. "It's—"

"Ace. It's a dress. Lose it."

What…had she been about to say? She had no idea. She had nothing. Nothing at all, not after Evan said the words of her daydreams.

Ace, lose the dress.

"No, that's okay, I'm going to—*eee*!" The squeal was due to two very cold-with-wet-lake-water hands on her ankles. The squeal died in her throat when he yanked the sarong open and exposed her bare legs, water dripping from his forearms onto her warm skin.

A small smirk sat on his mouth.

Lyon burst out laughing. "Don't be a baby, Aunt Charlie! It's not that cold."

"Yeah, Aunt Charlie," Evan said, a certain teasing tone in his low voice. He took off his sunglasses and dropped them on the dock. His amazing blue eyes were on her as his hands grasped her legs a few inches above her knees. "I'll keep you warm."

This was said under his breath while Lyon happily doggie paddled back and forth a short distance away.

Aunt Charlie.

You're Rae's best friend. Lyon's aunt. Evan's friend. Start acting like it.

Shaking off her inappropriate reaction, she forced a wide smile and, recent hair washing be damned, stood and dove off the dock and into the lake. When she resurfaced, she shrieked again.

Because it was freaking *cold*.

"You lie!" she accused Lyon between shallow breaths. "It's freezing in here!"

Lyon found this hilarious, so she swam out to him as he tried to swim away, his laughter high and completely infectious. This kid. His heart, his big beautiful heart, was such a perfect split between Rae and Evan. And his joyful, rambunctious spirit reminded her so much of Rae, it caused a dart of pain in her chest.

Before she could get caught up in memories and melancholy, Evan joined them and tossed Lyon twice before turning to her. "You're next."

She paddled away from him. "No, no, no."

"Yes," he insisted, dark intent in his eyes.

"Do it, Dad!"

"Evan—"

Too late. Evan had a hold of her ankle and was tugging her. Her backward strokes did no good, and water nearly went up her nose as he dragged her toward him. Then his hand went from her ankle to higher on her leg while she treaded water with her arms.

"Don't you dare." She made a feeble attempt to escape again.

"Do it, Dad," Lyon repeated, each word choked with laughter.

"You heard my boy." His voice was low and sexy as his hands slipped to her waist.

"Evan..." she started.

He had her out of the water before she finished and, despite her expelled *noooooo!*, tossed her a few feet, where she landed with an inelegant splash.

When she came up out of the water, a huge hunk of her hair was slapped over her face like a clinging octopus. She moved it away to see Evan's smile as wide as she'd seen it in forever, followed by a belly laugh that'd been missing from his repertoire for much too long.

Lyon joined in, and she lost her anger when a huge smile found her face, followed by reluctant laughter of her own.

Dipping her head in the water, she smoothed her hair back and gave Lyon the bad news. "Gonna pay for that, buddy," she told Lyon, swimming to him as he attempted to get away. Before she dunked him, she gave him a second to hold his nose, then pushed him under. Both he and his safety-orange vest popped to the surface, his smile intact, his dimple denting one cheek. Then he started his own game— spinning in circles attempting to start his own whirlpool.

Evan swam out and put first one hand, then the other

around her waist, grasping her with flexed fingers. Shocked at the feel of his hands on her, she turned to dunk him first, putting her cold fingers on his solid shoulders and pushing. She hadn't expected it to work, and for a moment, it didn't. Putting all her weight on her arms required her to leap out of the water a bit, so she was there, hovering, her breasts kind of in his face, her arms straight, her hands on his shoulders.

Keeping his eyes on hers, and the sly, barely-there smile on his lips, he finally let her push him under. In a move she should have seen coming, he took her with him, pressing on her shoulders and sending her down. Once submerged in the murky water, those hands moved to her waist and he tugged her against him. While she couldn't see him, she could *feel* him. Hard, wet muscle slid against her Lycra front, causing her skin to erupt in goose bumps that weren't caused by the cold lake.

Her hands covered his and she moved her leg to kick to the surface, her thigh brushing against something else. Something . . . hard. And she was sure it wasn't biceps or a triceps or any other sort of -ceps.

He gave her a slight boost and she popped to the surface and swept her hair off her forehead. "Sorry," she sputtered when he came up.

He pulled a hand down his face and then back through his hair. "You should be." A salacious smile graced his mouth. "That's your fault."

Before she could react to that naughty comment, Lyon's voice cut in.

"Dad, I'm hungry."

He jerked his chin toward the dock. "Paddle in, kiddo. Charlie and I are right behind you."

Relieved to escape Evan—and Nessie hiding below the water there—she started to wade to the dock.

He stopped her with a hand on her wrist, pulling her to him again. "What are you wearing?"

Since this was the last thing she expected him to say, she blinked at him.

Twice.

"What?"

He glanced down. "This suit." He gestured to the dock. "The dress-wrap thing. What happened to the hot pink one? I liked it better."

She couldn't think of a single response. Not one reasonable response came to mind while his hand rested on her waist, his feet on the lake floor, and her arms treading—needlessly, she might add, since he was holding her above the water.

Okay, she could think of one response. Her eyes moved to his mouth, those firm-looking lips, the way they were slightly quirked, the shallow lines around them from where he'd once smiled often.

She wanted to kiss him. Just lean forward a scant inch or two and lay one on him. The lake had ceased being cold. Her pulse had kicked up a notch. And Evan's eyes trickled from her eyes to her mouth.

Therefore she blurted, "Rae."

Yep. That's what she said.

His eyebrows slammed down, his half-smile gone like a rogue wave had washed it from his face.

"What about Rae?" he rumbled.

"She..."

Something. Words would be helpful.

"Um. She hated the water," she continued, desperate

to change the subject, to remind both of them—mainly herself—who he belonged to.

And who he didn't.

What Charlie needed—more than anything—was for them to both remember she was Rae's best friend, or used to be anyway... but that kind of thing didn't really have an expiration date, did it?

She couldn't just float here, enjoy the feel of his hands anchoring her to him, and think inappropriate, sexy thoughts about his mouth and what she'd like him to do with it... Another tingle shot through her and she gave her head a small shake to realign her thoughts.

Inappropriate.

Her gaze went to the dock where Lyon was climbing up the ladder.

"Lyon does well in the water," she said. "I think Rae would like that, in spite of the fact she never liked it." Charlie heard how uncomfortable she sounded, which made her notice Evan noticing she was uncomfortable.

His reaction was the opposite of what she'd hoped. Rather than let her loose and swim away, his hold tightened and he tugged her an inch closer. "Thought the same thing recently. She would be proud," he answered, too close to her, his confused-slash-incensed expression in a holding pattern.

Aware he was staring at her, his face frozen into a look she was pretty sure _wasn't_ happy, she pressed on.

"Rae would have liked it here. She hated to swim, which, I assure you, was more for cosmetic reasons." She let out an uncomfortable, brief laugh. "Getting in the lake after her hair was done, or getting brushed up against by a fish—the great outdoors wasn't her thing, you know?"

He shook his head, but whether it was in agreement or

in disagreement, or in wonder at her never-ending mono-
logue, she wasn't sure.

"You probably already know that." She cleared her
throat. "Since you were married to her."

His hold tightened and he dragged her even *closer*.
Their noses were practically touching. "You making a
point, Ace?"

Maybe. But she hadn't yet figured out what it was. But,
hey, she could talk her way to it.

"She liked the attention she got from the boys whenever
she fussed over getting in the water," Charlie continued
blathering. "She preferred never to be this close to wild-
life. Squirrels terrified her. She was a true city girl who—"

"Dad! Phone!"

She used the interruption as an excuse to pull away from
Evan and give herself some much-needed breathing room.

Lyon stood on the dock, cell phone to his ear, holding a
towel around his body with one hand.

Evan hadn't looked away from her so she pointed to the
dock and said, "Your phone."

"I heard." He continued staring at her, brow furrowed.

"Dad!"

"Yeah, bud," he called out. Then he turned back to
Charlie and erased the space she'd created, so close, her
breasts grazed his bare chest. Then he just ... watched her.

She held her breath and listened to her heart pound
relentlessly.

His eyes narrowed.

Water lapped around them.

In the distance, a gull cried.

Abruptly, he let her go, forcing her to kick her legs to
keep from going under. Swimming for the dock, he cut

through the water with powerful strokes. She watched as he hauled himself up the ladder on the side. Watched water rush off his chiseled body and long trunks and run down his legs. Watched as he accepted the phone as sun glistened off the water droplets clinging to his wet body.

Wow.

Just...

Wow.

She moved her arms through the water, her pace intentionally slow, both to give herself time to recuperate from his hands on her body as well as not to horn in on his conversation. Not that he cared. About her recuperation or privacy. Openly, he watched her while squeegeeing the water from his hair. When she reached the ladder, he bent to pick up her towel and, with barely a glance in her direction, he offered it to her when she stepped on the dock.

Pressing the terry cloth against her body, she dried quickly, and then just as quickly tied her sarong back into place. Sunglasses once again hiding her face, she wound her hair into a ponytail and squeezed the water out, leaving a puddle that could've accommodated a small family of ducks if it hadn't run through the slats of the dock.

"Yeah, burgers sound good. *Turkey* burgers? You shittin' me?" Evan was saying into the phone. He frowned at her. "You know how to cook a *turkey burger*?"

He asked this as if burgers made from turkey required some fancy preparation like frog's legs or foie gras.

"Of course," she replied with a shrug.

"Charlie'll take care of that," he told the caller. Then to her, he said, "Wine or beer?"

"Um... either?"

"She likes wine," he said to the phone. "I like beer." A

pause and then, "Yep. No problem." He ended the call and dropped the phone into the beach bag Lyon had hauled onto one narrow shoulder. "Bud, will you plug that into the charger for me?"

"Sure," he said, lugging the bag up the dock toward the stairs that led to the beach.

"Glo and Ash are coming for dinner."

"And I'm invited?" she asked, noting he hadn't asked.

"Ace. Turkey burgers."

Like that was an answer.

He watched her for a beat, looking unhappy, and she wasn't sure if he was unhappy because of her not-so-grace-ful segue into talking about Rae in the lake, or if he was unhappy because she seemed to be pushing him on this whole dinner-with-Glo-and-Asher thing.

She decided to be agreeable. "Turkey burgers."

With a curt nod, he grabbed his towel from the rail-ing, wrapped it around his waist, and headed up the dock. When he reached Lyon, he took the bag from his son's shoulder and transferred it to his own.

"What time?" she called after him.

"Five."

That one word, and a stellar view of his backside, was all the answer she got.

She spent the rest of the afternoon wondering if she shouldn't show up after all, because she didn't want to have another conversation that might involve him asking her what her point was about bringing up Rae. But then she'd sort of promised to cook the turkey burgers, so she decided she'd better show.

$\mathcal{C}$HAPTER NINE

"$\mathcal{T}$he mood," as Charlie had come to think of it, remained when she arrived at Evan's place at four instead of five. She wasn't sure when Gloria and Asher were coming by, nor was she sure if she was supposed to help with dinner *prep* to be served at five, or if everyone would arrive at five and make dinner together.

Then again, maybe she was being slightly obsessive. Since their odd parting in the water, she'd been slightly obsessive about a lot of things, including the fact that she wasn't ready to discuss what had happened.

What *hadn't* happened...

After dissecting it every which way, there were only tiny, barely discernible pieces left before she'd had to toss the whole mess aside, get dressed in her favorite short, pink-with-white-flowers sundress, and walk to Evan's house from her own.

Now she was here and worried that if they were alone,

she might have to talk about it after all. Maybe she should go.

"Hi, Aunt Charlie."

Too late.

She turned to find Lyon, eyes on his iPad, back on the sofa, heel propped up on one knee with his other bare foot on the couch's cushion.

"Hey, honey."

"Dad's in the studio," he said without looking up from his game.

"Okay." No escape.

She walked to the opposite side of the house, through the laundry room in the direction of the studio, and past a wall of windows facing her place but obstructed by Laney Edwards's house standing between them. Not that Laney was ever in it. Save for the few weeks in May she and her husband, Hank, came to the Cove, they mostly stayed home in Michigan.

Charlie heard rustling and, since the door was open in the studio, couldn't resist poking her head into the private lair. As a photographer, she understood the sacred space where the magic happened. And this space was most certainly, where Evan, the artist, made the magic happen.

He sat, back to her, hunkered over large sheets of drawing paper littering the floor. He'd changed into a worn, gray tee with some sort of black pattern on it, baggy cargo shorts, and sneakers. From the backless stool, he shifted his weight, wheeled over to a drawing, then picked it up and wheeled it over to another pile of drawings and dropped it on top.

She was aware she was intruding but couldn't look away, or keep from admiring the strong arch of one arm resting on his knee, or the way he scratched his scruffy chin while debating on what to do with any one of the various drawings of cartoon pigs.

Not having noticed her yet, he shifted another paper, this one with not only the pig on it, but also Mad Cow. The pig, it seemed, was the character in progress. Every rendering showed a varying degree of features—from oversized versus dainty snouts, to big, floppy ears versus tiny pointy ones. One boasted a Mohawk. Another had a wooden leg.

She was studying the one with a bandanna over its head when Evan noticed her. "Hey."

"Hi. Sorry to barge in," she said, suddenly feeling as if she *was* barging in. Depending on the level of concentration, she knew interrupting an artist mid-creation was much like interrupting a churchgoer mid-prayer.

"You're not." He lifted the drawings off the floor and walked them to the desk against the wall.

Taking that as an invitation, she stepped into the room, liking the light, liking the space, liking that he'd set up a tattoo base camp in one corner. At the desk, she peeked around his wide back. "I like the one with the hair."

"Yeah?" He picked up the paper and examined it before adding, "I'll put it in the *maybe* pile."

Figuring it'd come up sooner than later, she dredged up her courage to say what was on her mind. "I'm sorry about earlier."

He was standing over his desk, knuckles resting on the surface. When she spoke, he turned his head to the side, his thick, dark lashes narrowing over his blue, blue eyes. His longish hair was dry, and sticking out at every angle in a style she'd come to think of as his "perfect bedhead."

"Not sure what you're apologizing for."

Her cheeks heated, but she'd committed to this path, so she continued. "You seemed mad in the lake earlier. I guess I'm apologizing for...whatever it is I did to upset you."

His brow crinkled like it had earlier. "You do that with Russell a lot?"

She felt her head shake side-to-side, not to answer in the negative but because his question was not computing. "Sorry?"

"There you go again."

She had to bite her lip not to repeat herself. "What do you mean?"

"Noticed you do that a lot. Apologize and don't know why," then in a slightly louder, more demanding tone, he tacked on, "Russell teach you that?"

"What does that have to do—"

He pushed off his fists and moved to stand in front of her—way, way too close. "Don't apologize to me, Ace, unless you know what it is you did wrong."

With that command, he started for the door.

Angry, she opened her mouth, speaking before she knew what she would say. "Well, maybe you should apologize to me."

He halted in the doorway, his hands curling into fists. He didn't turn around right away. She waited, her heart thrashing against her ribs. He hadn't faced her, which was probably why she was brave enough to say, "All you've done is frown at me today. And now you're being rude. I came over here to help you cook for *Gloria*"—oops, she hadn't meant to put peeved emphasis on her name—"and Asher," she added quickly. "Not get the third degree from you."

His shoulders raised and lowered with a deep breath

and she crossed her arms, feeling half-satisfied she'd stood up for herself, and half-nervous he'd turn around. He did, a second later, and the same scowl resided on his chiseled face. He stalked back to her and it took every bit of her wherewithal to hold her spot on the floor and not back away from him.

Especially when he lowered his face so that his eyes were level with hers.

Eep!

"All I've done is frown at you today?" he repeated. "What about when I had my hands on your hips, Ace?" The soft but rough tone of his voice undid her convictions. "When I tore off your skirt?"

Her heart had made it to her throat and when she swallowed, she did so around her hammering pulse.

"Was I frowning then?"

He hadn't been frowning. He'd been smiling—and eyeing her with a heat that . . . well, a heat that resembled the heat in his eyes now.

His brows rose. "Was I?"

"Uh—"

"We're here early!" came a female voice from the direction of the kitchen.

Saved by the bell!

"Gloria and Asher are here," she pointed out, stepping to the side and attempting to dart around him.

He stopped her by wrapping a hand around her arm. Warm fingers, and a warmer gaze, pulled her in.

"Answer me," came his soft command.

A whispered "Evan" was all she managed. The hand around her arm tugged her closer. His eyes were unmistakably glued to her mouth.

"Hey! There you guys are—oh, sorry, am I... interrupting?"

He didn't move, but she jerked at the sound of Gloria's voice. Glo stood in the doorway, looking at the male hand most definitely wrapped around Charlie's arm, her red lips poised in curiosity.

Charlie patted the hand and untangled herself from his grip. "Arguing over the pig drawings." She added an exaggerated eye roll. "You know artists," she said, hoping Gloria *did* know artists because it was a throwaway statement she had no follow-up for. She stepped past Evan, this time because he let her, and said, "I think he should have hair, Evan is strictly no hair. You can settle it for us. Wine?"

There. Talking ninety miles a minute ought to get her out of this pickle.

"Uh... sure, thanks." Gloria approached the drawings while Evan faced her, doing a dead-on impression of the statue in the city square. "Still struggling with Swine Flew, I see," Glo said. "Can I help?"

Charlie left them and hustled through the hallway and toward the kitchen, so relieved to be out of the studio's oppressive air she literally sucked in a huge breath the moment she entered the living room.

"They fighting already?" Asher Knight asked as she stumbled to a stop at the kitchen island. This was as close to a real rock star as she'd ever been. She hadn't met Asher yet and now that she was seeing the singer of the swoony ballad "Unchained" in the flesh leaning on Evan's breakfast bar, she'd admit to being a touch starstruck.

"Fighting? No, um... no, I don't think so."

He leaned his arms on the bar, his lips curving, the stubble prevalent on his chin and cheeks. His hair was a mess, but the style was purposeful, caused by hair products unlike Evan's, whose style was less of a "style" and more a result of nervous fingers and lack of knowledge *about* hair products.

It was a good look for Knight, though. In a designer black tee with pale gray angel's wings on the front, several braided hemp bracelets tracking up one of his wrists, and the array of chunky silver rings decorating his fingers, the man standing before her was not merely a sexy rock god. He was King of the Sexy Rock Gods.

"Do they fight often?" She crossed to the counter and peeked inside a few reusable grocery sacks.

He blew out a breath. "Like they're fuckin' married." Then was quick to add, "'Scuse my French."

"That's not French," Lyon pointed out from his perch on the couch.

"Hey, don't say anything I say. Ever. Okay, bud?"

"Why not?"

"Because your dad will throttle me."

Lyon grinned like he might not mind seeing that.

Charlie grabbed the grocery sacks and pulled out foam, plastic-wrapped packages of ground turkey, beef, and bottles and jars of various burger fixings, then began arranging them on the counter.

Ash moved to her side. "What can I do?"

She searched a drawer, then another before finding a knife and a cutting board. "What's your specialty?"

He leaned a hand on the counter and hovered over her, a devilish smile on his devilish face. "My specialty . . . lies outside of the kitchen."

She took in his hooded dark eyes, the practiced smile affixed to his face, and the lack of space between them, and laughed. Honest to God, threw her head back and laughed.

He straightened away from her—literally taken aback. "Somethin' funny?"

"You." She shook her head as she rinsed a tomato under the tap. "Coming onto me."

"Was not," he lied with a smile.

"Were so." She smiled back.

"So you do recognize when it happens." Evan's voice cut in as he entered the kitchen. Gloria trailed behind him, her sharp blue eyes snapping from Asher to Charlie and back again.

Charlie occupied herself by angling the knife and slicing the tomato into thick slices. "I hope you don't mind I started without you," she said to Gloria, suddenly worried she'd stepped on the other woman's toes.

"It's fine." But Gloria didn't sound sincere. Her gaze fettered to Ash again as she casually positioned herself between him and Charlie. "I'll make the patties. Evan, you have any seasonings in this house?"

"Salt and pepper," he answered.

"Chili powder?" she asked. "Cumin? Granulated onion? Thyme? Any of these things sounding familiar?"

"Off my back, lady." He moved to a cabinet.

Asher gestured to them while they were preoccupied and mouthed the word "married" to Charlie.

Which she didn't like at all. Because if Glo and Evan acted like this in front of everyone, maybe there was more going on between them than she'd originally thought.

Subconsciously, or maybe very consciously, she moved to the cabinet and helped Evan locate the spices Gloria requested, as well as a few of her own choosing.

* * *

Dinner was informal. Evan ran the grill while Ash mostly tried to tell him *how* to run the grill. Charlie and Gloria had divided the work on the burgers—turkey was Charlie territory and Glo was on beef. And while he wasn't a fan of turkey, and because the girls had formed some kind of competition with their seasoning skills, Evan ended up eating one of each. The poultry patty wasn't half-bad.

The girls cleaned up while Ash palmed two beers and stated that "the deck beckoned." After the first cold sip, Evan found himself in agreement.

Leaning on the railing, they watched the dark lake for a while. The party boat from the other night had either migrated to a different area, or the guys had gone home already. Hard to tell.

"How's Jordan doing?" Evan asked, not bothering to hide his smirk.

"Asshole."

Evan tapped the bottom of his beer bottle against the top of the neck of Asher's, pleased when the *pop* rang true and foam spilled out over the edge in a virtual cascade.

Ash tipped his bottle, drinking down what hadn't ended up on his T-shirt. When he lifted the edge to wipe his chin, he pointed at Evan. "You're lucky the library signing is around the corner, or you'd pay dearly for that."

"That I'd like to see."

Ash let him have the jab, leaning on the railing and going quiet for a moment. Then he muttered, "Your girl's somethin' else."

He was talking about Charlie, and probably talking about her because he'd hit on her. "Cozy up to Ace and library signing be damned, there'll be hell to pay," Evan said, watching the water.

Ash turned so his back was on the railing. "Yeah, yeah. You already threatened me."

"Not me. Gloria." Evan turned his back to the railing, too, and both of their attention went to Glo and Charlie in the kitchen.

"Gloria," Ash repeated.

"Watches you like a hawk."

"Charlie watches *her*," he added. "Especially whenever Glo is talking to *you*."

The girls did dishes side by side amicably. No sign that one of them might pull a two-pronged fork or drown the other in the dishwater.

Ash swirled the beer left in his bottle. "I may have helped that along by telling her you and Glo fight like you're married."

"Siblings."

"Siamese twins," Asher joked.

"Accurate." Evan chuckled. "Terrifying, but accurate."

"She didn't like it, Ev." His tone was so serious, Evan turned to face him. "She didn't like it when I cozied up to her in your kitchen."

Neither had he.

"And you didn't like it, either. She's into you, man. All I'm sayin'." That statement hung on the air until Ash said, "You touchin' me up while I'm here or what?"

Shit. He nearly forgot.

"Yeah, let's do it."

Evan led the way to the corner of his studio where he'd set up his chair beneath ample overhead lighting, and a few lamps in case he needed more.

Asher pulled off his T-shirt and revealed his tattoo-covered chest and the cross on his left arm. Evan pulled out a pair of surgical gloves and arranged the still-in-plastic needles, eyeing the uneven lines on the edge of the cross.

"What'd I tell you about going to these new guys who open shops and go out of business a year later?" Evan asked.

"Hey, I was drunk."

"Any respectable guy will not tattoo clients while they're hammered."

Asher gestured to himself. "Celebrity."

Evan shook his head as he selected which color ink to use. "Shut up and hold still."

A few hours later, artwork done and his arm wrapped in plastic, Asher sat on the patio next to Evan, who had a pad of drawing paper open on his lap.

While he'd done his ink, Ash had brought up Swine Flew and they'd talked over a few ideas that had Evan's muse sitting up and begging. Never one to lose the moment when the bitch started to obey, he snagged the first sketchbook he'd laid eyes on and a few graphite pencils, and darted outside.

In the background, he was vaguely aware of Charlie and Gloria going in and out of the house, opening wine, and chatting about something or the other. Asher had commented back once or twice. Not Evan; he was in a zone.

The lighting was shit out here, but the night was clear and the wind light enough not to blow the paper. Since relocating might mean breaking the flow, Evan worked with what he had. The flicker from a citronella candle on the small side table, and Ash hovering over the sketchpad putting in his two cents.

Evan had drawn several different incarnations of Swine's outfit, headgear, and expressions. At last his buddy pointed to his most recent one and said, "That."

"Fucking finally, man." And that wasn't an understatement.

"I'm going," Glo announced out of nowhere.

After hyper-focusing on the cartoon superhero on the page before him, Evan had to blink her into focus. "What time is it?"

Asher lifted his phone. "One."

"Lyon." He'd zoned out drawing and had no clue where his kid was. *Way to go, Downey.*

"I tucked him in," Charlie said.

All the air left his lungs in a rush. She'd saved his ass again.

"He came out, man, didn't you hear him say good night?" Asher palmed Evan's shoulder and shot him a quizzical look.

"Yeah," Evan lied. Because he hadn't. His imagination had hooked onto a cloud of thought and dragged him away from this world and into another. *This one's the only one that matters, baby,* he heard Rae say in his head.

An old, and not fond, memory hit him front and center.

> *"Why are you awake—gosh dang, baby."* Rae's voice had faded into a soft note of concern, her eyebrows bowed, her hands clutching her robe tight around her pajamas.
>
> The utility room had been cold, but Evan had turned on the space heater. Maybe it was the hum coming from the unit at his feet, or the headset he pulled from his ears

and hooked around his neck that had him detaching from the real world so efficiently.

Her arms crossed, her brows rising in challenge. Shit. He was screwed.

"This *is what you're doing while I'm breastfeeding our son?*"

He felt his own brows lower. Not this again. "Don't know if you noticed, but I lack the equipment to perform that function." *They'd argued about this before—how she wasn't the only parent in the house, always stressing the words* "our son" *as if he'd forgotten Lyon was half his.*

"I have an idea." *But it wasn't a solution she was speaking of, he could tell by her tone. It was a finger-snap away from an all-out turf war.* "Why don't I carry the baby, give birth to the baby"—*she was ticking each item off on her fingers to annoy him—*"and why don't you just come out here and play."

"Play?" *He hated when she referred to his paintings—tonight a few new tattoo designs to add to the board at work—as play. Lyon had already woken them both, and Evan hadn't been able to get back to sleep.* "You think this is play?" *He gestured to the paintings of the tattoos, this one a series of dragons.* "Knowing my life's work—"

"Evan Alexander," *she snorted, her tone sounding so much like her mother, he narrowly avoided asking her when Patricia Mosley had entered the building.*

"Let me guess." He threw down the
paintbrush and faced her before she conde-
scended further. *"Your work is more important than mine."* Another theme of another
repetitive argument. They were on a loop.

"You ruin people's skin, baby," she said
in the same calm tone while his blood began
to boil. *"If I have a needle in my hand, I'm
saving lives."*

"You able to show up tomorrow?"

Evan snapped out of the memory to see Gloria standing over him. "Library, yeah," he confirmed.

"Two o'clock." She turned to Charlie. "Awesome turkey burgers by the way."

Charlie smiled, but it looked forced. "Thanks."

"Come on, big boy." Glo hauled Ash out of the chair.
When he stood, he wrapped an arm around her and Evan
watched as she melted into him like a snow cone on a hot
sidewalk.

"To my cabin, wench," he joked—*maybe*. "Thanks for
having us, Ev. Charlie, a pleasure." Asher added a hand kiss.

Evan refused to react.

When they'd gone, he turned for the house to look in
on his boy.

"I checked on him a few minutes ago," Charlie said.
"Teeth brushed, pajamas on, television set on a twenty-
minute timer." Lyon liked to fall asleep to noise, something she must have picked up on when she'd stayed with
them in the past.

He nodded his thanks, feeling a wave of shame for not
getting his kid ready for bed.

Picking up on his mood, she shrugged and said, "You were busy."

Busy ignoring his son. Though that could be Rae's voice haunting him.

"I'm heading home," Charlie said. "Thanks for dinner."

"No." He grabbed her hand before she walked off his porch. "You're having a drink with me."

Her eyes strayed in the direction of her house with a look that was almost longing. "I don't know..."

"I do. Haven't had a chance to talk to you all evening, Ace."

"Evan."

He took two full steps toward her until he stood so close she had to crane her neck to look up at him. "One drink."

They had things to talk about. He wasn't letting her run from him again.

CHAPTER TEN

The wind blowing off the water had turned cold, and since she'd had about enough of sitting out in the dark, cool air in a short, sleeveless sundress, Charlie poured a glass of wine and pointed to the studio.

"Do you mind if we have our drinks in there?"

Evan had cracked open a bottle of beer and chucked the lid into the trash. "Whatever's clever, Ace."

She walked into his studio, but once she was in there, the big space felt claustrophobic. And dark. She looked for an overhead switch but didn't find one. A side lamp clicked on, followed by a reading lamp on the desk where he'd stacked his drawings when she was in here earlier.

"You need better lighting in here if you hope to work at night." She nodded to the large shadows yawning over his papers.

He pointed to the track lighting on the ceiling running the length of all four walls. "Don't need light for drinks."

True, but *she* might need it for drinks with him. She'd managed to keep her distance from him this evening, avoiding the awkward tension choking this very room earlier. Come to think of it...

"On second thought, why don't we go out on the deck? You can throw a few logs in your fire pit and—"

"Ace."

She fell silent and tried to think of something to say. She didn't think of a darn thing the entire time he sauntered, one foot in front of the other, to the desk, forcing her steps back until the backs of her knees collided with the chair. She sat with a rather ungraceful *whump!* and gripped the wooden arms. He abandoned his beer bottle, backed his butt against the desktop, and stood sentry over her, arms crossed.

Forcing her eyes from his long, strong legs encased in cargo shorts to the drawings on the surface next to them, she finally thought of something to say. "What did Gloria say about your new character?"

"You snarl her name when you say it."

Crap. She did. She knew it. She played dumb anyway. "What do you mean?"

He remained silent, statue still.

"I like Gloria," she argued, with herself apparently, but her voice was a little too high, making her sound like she was lying. To be fair, she wasn't exactly *lying*, but Glo was sort of...blunt. Charlie didn't do well with bluntness, preferring to smooth over the tops of subjects rather than plumb too deep.

"What is it about her that rubs you the wrong way?" His body choked the air between them, and she felt like he was looming. He wasn't. Not really, but he was near. Too near for her to think.

I don't like the way she rubs against you, she thought. But after an appreciative look at the man before her, what woman wouldn't get as close to him as humanly possible?

His T-shirt ringed defined upper arms where the mane of the lion on one arm, and the broad rose petals on the other, poked out from beneath the hem of the short sleeves. His shorts were loose, but there was no mistaking the muscular thighs beneath them, or his visible and, oddly enough, attractive knees (who had attractive knees, anyway?). The whole of him was tanned from his time at the lake, his brown hair starting to lighten the slightest bit on the ends from being in the sun. His blue eyes were bright and eagle-sharp.

In short, Evan Downey was a tall, sexy, ridiculously attractive hunk of man. And having that gaze settled on one-self was enough to make any woman swoon, and enough to make Charlie, who'd known him for years and should be immune, forget what he'd asked her a second ago...

"Ace."

Right. She remembered.

"The truth?" she offered, feeling sweat prickle her underarms.

He didn't move an inch.

"Okay, well. Gloria's ... uh." How to say this? "Do you think she's a good role model for Lyon? Do you think him seeing you two..." She waved a hand while she thought of a way to say this delicately. "...Carry on the way you do is healthy for a seven-year-old?"

"*Carry on*? I don't have a problem with it, no." He watched her for a seemingly infinite amount of time. Continents could have shifted in the millennia that passed before he finally asked, "Do you?"

She reached for her glass and took a sip of peppery red.

It did little to wet her throat. "No, of course not," she lied to her wine.

Then the glass was gone, taken from her hand and placed on the desk next to his beer. She tucked her elbows into her sides and clasped her hands together. He dropped a hand on one of the chair's arms and repeated the motion with his other hand. He was straight-armed and this time, yes, *looming* over her.

"Know what I think?" It was a question, but his question sounded like a command and not a question.

It was a question she had no interest in answering.

Digging around in her head, she nabbed the first topic she thought of—a topic that happened to be the one she'd brought up earlier. "I was thinking of Rae when you were cooking burgers on the grill. Do you remember the time we all—"

"That's not how this is gonna go, Ace."

His blue stare was so intense, she had to swallow twice before she eked out the word, "Sorry?"

But he was gone, had straightened from his *loom* and moved to the opposite side of the room where an easel with a huge, blank pad of paper waited for the touch of a talented hand.

He dragged a wheeled stool from there to the front of her chair. Like, *right* in front of her chair and sat. Then he grabbed her chair and rolled her until one of her bare knees was between two of his.

Her grip tightened on the chair's arms when he reached past her to hold the rungs at the seat like a man in prison might hold the bars. He had her caged, his arms brushing her arms, his face inches from her face.

Her heart ratcheted up about a thousand notches.

With zero chance of escape, she could do nothing but stare wide-eyed at him and wish she had something to hold on to besides her crumbling resolve.

Words. She could hold on to words. Opening her mouth, she tried again to change the subject. "Is Asher going to play at the Starving Artists Festival? Because I have a friend who—"

"Not the way this is gonna go, either, Ace." His intense gaze was on her like *Blue* on *Bayou*.

But she had to say something, because this was… unnerving.

Because it's turning you on.

Especially for that reason.

"I'm sorry. I don't think Gloria is good for you."

His face morphed from intense to almost relaxed. Well, not relaxed, but the concrete set of his mouth had softened enough that she believed he might almost laugh. "Hell, I know that."

His comment stunned her.

"Glo and I didn't fit in Chicago. Tested it out, didn't work."

She cringed. Tested it out? So they had slept together. She'd known it, on some intuitive female level, but to hear it…

"Ugh, I don't want to know. Let me up, please."

His arms tightened around hers, his body warming her to the point her face heated. And so did the leg trapped between two of his.

"Not gonna let you bolt when something's happening between us."

At this, she didn't blink. She stared. Something was happening between them? Not only her but *them*?

"Good," he said as if she'd spoken aloud. "Like when

you pay attention. Keep paying attention. Gloria and I kissed. One drunken kiss that did nothing for either of us. She is one of the guys. Gorgeous as all hell, but make no mistake, she can match any dude whiskey shot for whiskey shot." His eyes went to the side as he thought. "Except for Asher. He has a titanium liver."

He was joking. She felt her mouth lift in a smile of relief. Some of the tension had ebbed from the minimal space between them, enough to allow room for her to inhale some oxygen. Then there was the iota of relief that all he'd done with Gloria was kiss her. Followed by the truckload of relief because he hadn't liked it.

"Next subject."

Oh, great. He wasn't through yet. Her smile fell.

"Why do you bring up Rae whenever I'm close to you?"

"I don't," she was quick to say.

"You do."

She did. It's just that she didn't want to tell him *why* she did it. Because it would involve her admitting she was bringing up Rae as a defense mechanism. A way to keep her new, confusing, and delicious sexual fantasies about him at bay.

Gosh, it was hard to think with him this close.

"Ace," he prompted.

"Maybe you shouldn't be close to me." This came out in a whisper. He heard. There was no way he couldn't have heard. He was *right there.*

"I disagree," he whispered back. He smelled like suntan lotion. His hair was beachy and mussed, his body heat radiating around her. Unfair. The steadiness of his eyes made her gaze flutter around the room like a moth bouncing off a lightbulb.

Unbelievably, he leaned *closer.* She pulled back until

she realized she likely had a double chin, then settled her head on her neck in a more reasonable position.

Gosh. He was making her crazy.

"Know why I moved here?" he asked, keeping his voice low.

She wrenched her eyes from his and focused on a spot over his shoulder.

"Because you didn't want to live in Columbus anymore." That's what he'd told her. That he wanted a change. That he and Lyon had outgrown the house. And, she imagined it'd be hard to live in the house where Rae had passed.

"But why here?"

"Um…"

His fingers grazed her jaw and turned her head, his palm moving to her neck where he cupped her nape and forced her eyes to his.

Reluctantly, she met them.

"Rae's more alive when you're around, Ace."

Her heart, oh her heart. Kicking against her chest in a confusing, hectic rhythm.

"You bring her to life for Lyon—more than anyone else. I need him to remember her because he can't remember her alive." His hold stayed, his palm warming her neck, his gaze unwavering.

She tried to separate the two feelings she was having—one, she was now talking about Rae with Evan, and two, he was touching her while talking about Rae.

Before she could, his lips closed over hers.

Her thoughts short-circuited.

This wasn't anything like a soft peck hello. This was his lips moving over hers, slanting over hers, warm and firm and then his mouth opened and—

Oh my gosh!

His wet, warm tongue slid along the seam of her lips. She stopped being passive and started kissing him back. When she would have touched her tongue to his, he relocated it, running along her bottom lip instead and tugging with his teeth.

If she'd been standing, her knees would have given out and dropped her right on her butt.

The palm on her neck speared through her hair and clutched on to a handful of it. He held her captive, his hand fisting her hair as he angled his mouth again. In response to the whimper escaping her throat, he swept his tongue into her mouth. He tangled his tongue with hers once, twice, then released her.

When he pulled his mouth away, a long, satisfied sigh escaped her lips. Because *that* was a kiss. A kiss to rival all other kisses.

She opened her eyes to realize (a) she'd closed her eyes, (b) she'd at some point wrapped both hands around his forearms where she was holding tight, and (c) Evan looked as pleased as she felt.

"God *damn*, Ace. Your mouth." His eyes flicked to her lips. Lips still tingling from the rough scrape of the stubble surrounding his.

She concurred with his sentiment. Not that she said anything. She'd gone dumb, completely mute.

He backed away but held on to her chin and tweaked it lightly with the rough pad of one thumb. "*That's* the way this is gonna go from now on."

Her breathing went shallow, her thoughts went muzzy, and her head blurred as her heart palpated to the point of panic attack.

"Sorry, Rae."

She didn't mean to say it, and it had only been a whisper, but by the look twisting Evan's face—the *angry look* twisting his face—he heard. And he hadn't liked what he heard.

"Sorry," she said to him this time. "I should go."

Surprisingly, he gave her space. She used that space to stand, push the chair back under the desk, and dart for the door. Not surprisingly, before she escaped, his hand wrapped around her wrist.

She ground to a halt and lifted her eyes to his.

His face was utterly unreadable. When he finally spoke, it was the last three words in the English language she'd expected.

"Watch Lyon tomorrow?"

"Uh...sure." Whatever it took to get away from the man who had slid his tongue along hers seconds ago and was loosely gripping her wrist now. Because both the kiss and the grip were distracting to the nth degree. She needed to get back home and sort out her thoughts. Not like she could do that here. Around Evan, her thoughts were thoroughly unsorted. Obviously. Since she kissed him.

Oh no.

He gave her hand back. "Tomorrow, Ace," he called as he crossed the room. Back to her, he brushed a hand over the blank page leaning against the easel.

Without a word, she left the studio, grabbed her purse, and dashed across the beach to her house.

* * *

Charlie examined the Make It an Event! brochure on her breakfast bar for the third time. "I don't know. Do you think I should have lightened up this one a bit?" She tapped a fingernail on the photo of Faith's stunning smile.

"No nitpicking!" Sofie closed the brochure and stuffed it into her purse. "I think they look great. You're a great photographer. Now come with me. I have shoe shopping to do, and so do you, because I'm treating you to a pair as your bonus for the amazing photos you took for me."

"You don't have to do that."

She grabbed her arm. "I know."

Cobbler's Cove had not only the best shoe shopping in town but the best shoe shopping—according to Sofie—on the planet. Sofie had a penchant for heels and boots and slides . . . and just about every other kind of footwear.

She slipped on a pair of short cowgirl boots and twisted her ankle to admire them. "Gah. I'm going to have to get these, too!" Kicking off her shit-kickers, she dropped them in a box and stacked it atop four others.

Four.

Charlie had found a cute pair of beach sandals, which Sofie claimed were identical to her other pairs of beach sandals, but she knew better. The color of these was clearly stated as *fawn*, and her others were beige, camel, and sand.

Hmm. Maybe Sofie had a point.

After shoe shopping—Sofie had racked up so many points at the shoe store because of her frequent purchases, not only were Charlie's pair free but the boots as well—they swung by Cup of Jo's for an afternoon caffeine hit.

Jo was behind the counter, a spunky forty-something with streaked blond hair, not a hint of gray showing, and a deep voice like she was a smoker or maybe used to be. Jo had been an Evergreen Cove staple for as long as Charlie could remember. Sofie walked in and Jo shouted, "The usual?" proving Sofie was a frequent flyer.

"And for you, gorgeous?" Jo smiled at Charlie, pleasant lines crinkling her eyes.

"Oh, um. I have to care for a very rambunctious seven-year-old in an hour, any suggestions?"

"Double caramel mocha latte, with whipped cream and a drizzle of chocolate syrup." Jo snapped her fingers and went to work without waiting for her to confirm.

When Sofie reached for her purse, Charlie beat her to the punch and paid the young girl working the cash register. "You bought me shoes, let me at least buy you coffee."

Cups in hand, they took to the sidewalk, sipping their drinks. Despite the warm day and warm breeze, the hot coffee tasted amazing, and the sugar-slash-caffeine dump had Charlie's adrenal glands rolling around like a feline in catnip.

"How's your hot neighbor doing?" Sofie asked as they turned the corner to walk down to the furniture store, Cozy Home. Without her previous employee discount, Charlie couldn't afford anything in the place, but it was fun to look.

"He's . . ."

Hot. Kisses like a dream. Making me have lusty, sinful thoughts I should run to church to pray about.

". . . Fine."

"I saw Asher Knight the other day at Salty Dog. That man is the embodiment of *fine*."

"I hung out with him last night. He's a handful."

"Look at you, surrounded by all the hot guys in the Cove. And here I keep going on dates and having nothing to show for them."

Outside Cozy Home, they admired a white leather sofa set covered in brightly colored retro-print pillows.

Charlie took a breath and blew out the words that'd been gnawing at her insides since this morning. "Evan kissed me last night and I feel so guilty, I can hardly breathe."

Since she didn't go to church, Sofie was going to have to be her confessional.

Sofie's hand went to Charlie's back. "Honey, why? Why guilty?"

"Because of Rae." Her reflection in the store's glass showed how guilty she felt. It was written in every distraught line on her face.

Sofie rubbed Charlie's back and watched her in the window. "He kissed you, or you kissed him?"

"He kissed me."

"And you think that's wrong?"

She didn't know what she thought. "I don't know. I think if Rae were here, I—"

"You never would have kissed your best friend's husband if she were here. And I hope Evan never would have kissed you."

She turned to face Sofie. "He wouldn't have. He loved Rae. Loved her with every bone in his body."

Sofie flipped her long brown hair off one shoulder. "Listen, from what you've told me about Russell, I get that you aren't used to being pursued. Sounds like Evan is pursuing you."

"Russell pursued me," she argued, but it was a weak argument. "He picked me up at a wedding."

"After he caught you..." Her eyebrows lifted as if she was waiting for Charlie to finish the sentence. When she didn't, Sofie added quietly, "The pursuit stops when they get what they want." Her mouth twisted. "Believe me. It does." Then she snapped out of whatever memory she was having. "Evan pursuing you probably feels very foreign. New. And that's okay."

"But if we start this…If it doesn't work out…If I lose him completely…"

Charlie couldn't think it. The thought of losing someone else she loved nearly paralyzed her.

She wasn't close to her family. Her sister lived far away and preferred the distance. Her mother died of cancer when Charlie was in high school, and her father…Her father had made it clear to his girls they were on their own after Mom died. Last she'd heard, he was living in Maine with a woman named Becky.

Charlie, Russell, Evan, and Rae had been close. As close as she'd been with anyone. Then Rae died, Russell left her, and she found herself keeping people at arm's length.

Including Sofie, she realized now. Her best friend in the Cove, and Charlie had just learned at wine night they had an acquaintance in common. Charlie had shared the basics about her life, but had she *really* let Sofie in? No. Since Rae, since Russell, she hadn't let anyone else in.

Charlie used to travel to Rae's parents with her. They'd visit, have dinner, catch up. Patricia and Cliff had been like a second set of parents—or a first set when hers were no longer around. But after Rae was gone, Charlie let that tie break, too.

So far, Charlie had lost her father, her sister, Rae, Pat and Cliff…

What she had in the present was Evan. Lyon. Sofie

and Faith. She'd do well not to mess up those hard-won relationships.

Hating how she'd kept Sofie in the dark, she confessed, "If Evan and I tried and didn't work out, I could lose him and Lyon for good." Losing Evan and Lyon was *not* an option, she decided firmly.

Gently, Sofie smiled. "But what if you did work out?"

She returned her friend's smile, but it was a weak one. "That might be worse. Because then I'd have to face his family. Face *Rae's* family." And explain to them how she'd had the audacity to steal away her best friend's family and claim it for herself.

It was selfish and wrong on so many levels.

"A day at a time, Charlie. You don't know what the future will bring."

Charlie's phone sounded three quick beeps. "That's my alarm. I have to get back." She kissed Sofie on the cheek, thanked her again for the shoes, and insisted on walking back to her house by herself. Charlie wanted some time alone to solidify the decision she'd made outside of the furniture store.

She couldn't afford to be with Evan Downey.

Not unless she wanted to lose it all.

CHAPTER ELEVEN

$\mathcal{M}$rs. Anderson puckered her lips, crossed her arms, and clamped her false teeth together. Evan and Asher exchanged glances, and Evan noticed Gloria had actually *hidden* behind them both.

Despite the clear and undeniable fact that Asher and Evan were adults, Evergreen Cove's oldest, and only, librarian scolded them like children.

"I know you two have grown into nice young men now," she said, sending a scathing gaze over first Evan's tattooed arms, then Asher's, "but I can't have the Penis Bandits at my library. Charity or no."

Gloria stifled a snort, likely because hearing Mrs. Anderson say the word "penis" was the funniest thing any of them had heard in a while.

Ash coughed into his hand to cover a laugh.

Evan, now a parent, saw her point. He wouldn't want his kid to deface public property, either. "You're right,

Mrs. Anderson, it was wrong of us to redecorate your library."

Another cough from Asher had Evan elbowing him.

"Hmm." Mrs. Anderson considered them both, then poked her head around Ash. "Ms. Shields?" They gave her up, stepping aside. Glo had one arm looped around her stomach and the other over her mouth, telltale tears of laughter shining in her eyes. "You think this is funny, Ms. Shields?"

She straightened and shook her head, reining it in. "I don't, ma'am. I just . . . I really want these boys to atone for what they did to your lovely building all those years ago."

Evan whipped around and pegged her with a warning look. *Oh, hell no.*

"That's why Asher has agreed to do an acoustic ballad at the festival. Evan will create a piece of artwork of your choosing to donate to the library, in addition to the donated books, the signing, and the autographed painting of Mad Cow."

"Sarge." This from Asher, whose eyebrows lowered into the same *Oh, hell no* expression on Evan's face.

"No." She lifted a palm and physically moved to stand next to Mrs. Anderson. A united front. "I don't want to hear your excuses. You owe this town a debt, and now that you've gone and made something of yourselves"— her mouth twitched with buried laughter and Evan felt his eyelids narrow—"you need to make up for what you did."

"Ms. Shields is right. I'll agree to those terms. That and a public apology for putting penises on my building," Mrs. Anderson spat.

Glo lifted a hand and put it on the librarian's shoulder. "But maybe not that because there will be children present at the Starving Artists Festival. We wouldn't give them any ideas, you know."

Mrs. Anderson's jaw slackened at the thought. Then she uncrossed her arms and said, "I suppose you're right. But I want a written apology." She pointed one bony finger at Evan and then turned the digit on Asher. "From each of you."

"Yes, ma'am," Ash said. "But the ballad..."

"You'll do it," Mrs. Anderson stated. "I love that song. Only one you sing where I can make out the words because you're not screaming them."

With that, Mrs. Anderson started talking specifics—table setup and whatnot now that she'd allowed Evan and Asher back into the Starving Artists Festival. They tagged back several yards, letting Glo work her magic on the older woman.

"Glo sold us out," Evan muttered.

"Mrs. Anderson loves my song." Ash pulled a cigarette out of his pack, but the moment he lifted it to his mouth, the librarian turned around. He palmed it and tucked it to his side. Once her attention returned to Gloria, he tucked the cigarette behind his ear. "Damn. Sharp old lady."

"At least you don't have to write her a *new* song." But Evan was asked to paint something at her behest. And, wild guess, she wanted something other than broody, moody nightmares on canvas.

"You and Charlie hang out last night?" Asher asked.

"She left shortly after Glo left with you."

Ash made a face.

"What? What's that for?"

"I wasn't going to tell you, but I feel like I should. I tried to kiss her, man."

"*Charlie*?" Evan took a step closer to the friend he was now going to beat the hell out of in Library Park.

"Gloria!"

"I'm busy, Ash! Gimme a second," Glo responded, thinking he'd summoned her.

He waved. "My fault."

When her attention was with Mrs. Anderson again, he and Evan trekked over to a fountain in the middle of the park.

"And?" A leftover surge of jealousy over thinking Ash meant Charlie at first moved through his limbs.

"And she let me."

"Because she likes you, dumbass."

Ash palmed the back of his neck and rubbed, looking nauseous. "Gloria, she's . . . smart. Sexy."

"Smart and sexy new territory for you?" Evan knew better. Ash could fill a tour bus with chicks meeting those qualifications.

"I sleep with women who dress sexy and look sexy. Gloria . . . she pulls you in with all that sass, then hits you with the smarts. And, Ev, man, she's *smart*."

Evan laughed. "Intimidated, old boy?"

Ash didn't laugh; he only looked more worried. "Yeah. Kinda."

Evan knew what he meant. Because of her looks, Gloria was easy to marginalize at first glance. Low-cut shirts and high-cut skirts advertising her tits and ass, added to makeup and fuck-me heels broadcasting her femininity in high-def. But her outer appearance wasn't all she was. Gloria was smart, didn't put up with bullshit, and could flay a man in two with one sharp turn of a phrase.

Asher, on the other hand, had gotten through life on charm and jokes and a career that allowed him to behave like a big kid. This time, Evan's surge of jealousy was paired with admiration.

"What, you're not intimidated by Charlie?" Ash asked.

"No." Intimidated wasn't the word. Frustrated. Now there was a word.

"No, I guess you're not."

"Meaning?"

Asher dug in his pocket and pulled out a handful of change, a condom, and a guitar pick. He put the pick and the condom back into his pocket. Evan took a few coins and they each plunked one in the fountain wordlessly before Ash finally answered him.

"You and Charlie are friends. I've never been friends with a woman."

They *were* friends. But after last night, Evan wanted more. "I kissed her."

Ash tossed a nickel into the fountain with a *bloop*. "Hell yes, bro." He raised his hand to high-five. Evan glared until he lowered his palm. "You're such a drag."

"She said 'sorry, Rae' after. Apologized to my late wife the moment my lips left hers. The fuck is that about?" He asked this question to himself, but Ash answered anyway.

"Guilt."

He didn't like that.

"Charlie and Rae grew up together," Ash said. "They were best friends for ten years before Rae passed. And now, she's into you, and you have Rae's kid, and in her mind, you're Rae's. She's made it her life's habit not to look at you any other way than as 'Rae's husband.'"

His frown deepened. He could feel it. He looked at the four coins in his palm. If what Ash said was true, and it sure sounded logical, then Charlie was really, *really* messed up. Evan had vowed to be with Rae until death, through sickness and health. He had loved her, *still* loved her, without fail until she took her last breath on that carpeted hallway on East Level Road.

When he had to care for his three-year-old, motherless son on his own, he had done that as well. It wasn't easy telling a young kid his mother had gone to heaven, explaining why they couldn't see her in this world ever again, but Evan had done that, too. It hadn't been easy working and finding care for his son while running his tattoo shop—a vocation that drew judgment from the other school moms on PTA night—but he'd done it. And it sure as hell hadn't been easy dating again when he was ready, knowing how some people looked at him—namely Rae's friends, who one-by-one wandered away—like he should be ashamed for going out on Rae who'd been gone nearly two years.

And now Charlie? Who *he thought* understood him and Lyon and what they'd endured. But, no, she was judging him in much the same way as Rae's "friends." Keeping vigil for Rae instead of exploring what he knew she felt for him. Denying herself, denying him what they could have if she responded to that kiss instead of painting a red A on her chest and running home in shame.

He tossed the coins into the fountain in a series of plops and splashes, then turned for his SUV parked on the side of the road.

"Where're you going?" Asher called.

"Charlie's. Let Gloria know I'll call her later."

* * *

Charlie and Lyon walked across the beach, Lyon toting his iPad and the photos she'd printed that he'd taken today. Turned out he was a natural—yes, he was seven, but he'd taken some decent shots by any standard. And seeing the world through his eyes fascinated her; a totally fresh perspective on the surroundings she looked at every day.

He was proud of his photographs, and she loved sharing that pride with him. He'd taken some really honest shots and she couldn't help being excited for Evan to see them—proof he'd passed down some of his artistic talent after all.

At the back door, Lyon let himself in and dumped his stuff on the kitchen counter. She was certain Evan wouldn't let this fly, but since he wasn't in the kitchen, she did what he'd warned her not to and took care of it. *Yes*, Lyon should put his things away, but he was also on summer break and she knew one only got so many summer breaks before growing up and having to work year-round.

After hanging his bag on a hook by the door and draping Lyon's damp trunks and towel over the railing on the deck, she heard the side door open. Evan strode out, cell phone to his ear, looking smoking hot in very thin, worn jeans and a navy tee. He finished his call with "sounds good" and pocketed the cell, stuffing both hands in his pockets. She took an unashamedly long gander at his biceps.

Yummy.

His eyebrows were down as he squinted into the distance.

"Everything okay?" she asked, sensing it wasn't. Or he could be in need of a pair of sunglasses. It was hard to tell with him sometimes.

"That was Patricia."

Rae's mom.

"How is she?"

"Good. She and Cliff want Lyon to visit. I invited them to the Starving Artists Festival. They're going to come and take him home with them after."

"Oh, that's great. I haven't seen them in ages." Too long. Guilt speared her. She saw the occasional post on Facebook, but other than a "like" or a brief comment, hadn't truly connected with them in a while.

"She asked about you," he said, his face softening.

She knotted her fingers together. "That makes me feel bad."

Untangling her fingers, he took her hand in his and stepped closer. "I'm getting that about you, Ace."

He kissed her hand and stroked her thumb with his. She watched with a sort of out-of-body amazement. Except when his lips touched her hand and her thighs tingled. That was very *in body*.

And so was when he tilted his head toward hers. But when she thought she'd get a kiss, or maybe *hoped* was the right word, he stopped short of her lips and said, "I'm pissed at you."

The words were an electric shock, shooting through her fingers and her toes. She felt the sting in her face like her cheeks were reddening...or like she was having a stroke.

"Sorry?"

He kept hold of her hand. "I thought we were friends."

"We...we are." Her heart pounded harder. What had she done wrong? Was it the photos? Did he see Lyon's work and not like it? Did he not like that she'd let him have the camera—or maybe Evan would have liked to teach him instead?

"You don't get to judge me, Charlie, because of some

messed-up ideas you have knocking around in that head of yours."

Heart pounding faster, she could do nothing but blink at him for a few silent seconds.

"I don't know what you mean." The words came out in a whisper because she could not find the voice to give to them. When did she ever judge anyone? And why would he think he wasn't her friend?

"Dad, I'm hungry." Lyon stepped outside, shutting the door with a *bang*!

She tried to pull her arm away, equally relieved to get space from Evan as she was disappointed for the interruption.

Undeterred, and confusing her further, he not only kept hold of her hand but tugged her to his side and wrapped an arm around her waist. "You think we should ask Charlie to lunch?"

He leaned a hip against the railing, his fingers rubbing the material on her dress like he hadn't accused her of not being his friend or being judgmental five seconds ago. And that question...

You think we should ask Charlie to lunch?

Wasn't that like a king casually asking if he should pardon a criminal or hang him? And here she waited, on tenterhooks, for the younger Downey to accuse her.

Lyon took in the two of them, her standing in his father's arms, and quirked his mouth. "You look like Aunt Sadie and Uncle Aiden."

Evan's brother and his wife. Married. Very much in love. She wanted badly to force a laugh and make this situation okay, but she couldn't shake what Evan had said to her. How had she failed him?

Maybe it was the kiss. She knew she shouldn't kiss him. That was a rule she'd made with herself. Then again, he'd *kissed her*, so how much of the kiss was her fault anyway?

"Bud?"

"Yeah! Lunch!"

At least she had Lyon on her side, who was smiling and clearly not "pissed" at her. This little boy had no doubts they were still friends.

She pulled away from Evan and hugged Lyon. "Where to?" She'd go anywhere for this kid. So when he exclaimed "Reggie's Subs!" and his father agreed, she went. Despite sharing a meal with a man who was angry with her for reasons she'd yet to figure out.

CHAPTER TWELVE

*C*harlie pulled out the pan of blueberry muffins, turned off the oven, and tossed her potholder aside. Lunch had been agonizing and involved the impossible task of sitting across from Evan and attempting to ignore him completely. She'd taken her seat next to Lyon, feigned interest in his iPad game, and laughed too often, too loudly, her discomfort showcased in every awkward gesture.

Meanwhile, Evan had silently glowered at her nearly the entire time he ate. He'd kept silent on the ride home, too—they'd opted not to walk downtown since dark clouds had been pooling in the sky since midday. Once again, she'd filled the air with too many questions to Lyon so she could avoid conversation with his father.

Now it was nearly midnight, and not being able to sleep, or stop turning the conversation from earlier over and over in her head, she'd resorted to baking. She'd started with apple-cinnamon muffins, moved to peach cobbler, and lastly, blueberry muffins. Evan liked baked anything, so it wasn't a picky palate she was trying to please, but more the need to delay the not-so-long walk across the beach to his house.

She peeked out her kitchen window hoping to see his windows dark, but as her luck would have it, his studio lights burned bright. He was still awake, painting.

Bummer.

Carrying a plate piled high with muffins, she took her time walking across her yard, past her neighbor's yard. On Evan's deck, she hesitated yet again, peering into the dark kitchen before finally walking to the side of the deck and trying the door.

Unlocked.

Bummer, again.

She clucked her tongue. An unlocked door was slightly dangerous. Yes, they were in the Cove, but anyone could walk in. Anyone at all. Like his guilt-ridden neighbor who had wandered over way too late.

Though, she could flick the lock and shut the door and walk back home. Or flick the lock, leave the baked goods inside, shut the door, and walk back home.

But then what?

She hadn't been able to work, hadn't been able to sleep, hadn't been able to do anything but worry and wonder why he was angry with her. Instead she had baked an entire plate of "sucking up" as an apology for what, she had no idea. Her neurosis was such that she knew turning around and going back would only result in more baking and pacing.

Facing Evan, as much as she didn't want to, was better.

Inside, she followed the dim light through the hallway,

through the laundry room, and to his studio door. The entire wall to her right was made up of windows, framing a nighttime sky dotted with stars. The moon hid behind clouds, barely visible through the fuzzy sheen of mist. She sort of felt like that now. Fuzzy. Barely visible.

At the doorway, she lifted a fist to the door, but dropped her arm without knocking. Evan, one earbud in, one out, stood in front of his easel shaking his fine ass to music she couldn't hear.

On the canvas before him, he painted a patch of color, halting his smooth moves long enough to dip the brush into a smear of color and carefully paint again. Bright cyan made up the background color for a portrait of the comically badass Mad Cow: pierced, tatted-up, gauged, and by the look of his overly thick, frowning brows, indeed very mad.

Evan's creation graced the pages of Asher Knight's debut novel, launching the friends into semi-stardom, and bringing him to her. Proof that once a passion was embraced, success was inevitable. She wanted to believe that.

She could see it. Passion poured from his brush, echoed in the sway of his hips, confirmed in the bob of his head, lost in the music as well as the art. He was in the zone—a zone she'd admired, had yearned for, but had never quite captured for herself.

Watching him do what he was best at doing, seeing the brilliance on the canvas before him, filled her with longing. Had she ever done work that imbibed her very being with that kind of passion?

Sadly, the answer was no.

She didn't love portraits. She didn't love weddings.

She didn't love newspaper photography or shooting land-scapes. What she loved was people—capturing that rare moment where they were themselves and didn't know it.

She wished she had her camera now. Because she'd never seen Evan more himself than she did in this moment. It was a rare, cherished glimpse, an honor to wit-ness. And almost enough to make her forget he was upset with her. Until he caught her in his peripheral and lowered his brush.

In a blink, he yanked his earbuds out of his ears and crossed the room, his eyebrows a pair of angry slashes over blue, blue eyes reminding her of the cartoon cow looming behind him.

"What's wrong?" He lifted a baby monitor standing on a nearby stool, studied the video screen, and frowned at her again. "Is he okay? What time is it?"

He looked so worried, she raised the plate in her hand to assure him everything was dandy by showing him the pile of homemade proof. "Nothing's wrong. I couldn't sleep, so I baked. Your door was open and I came in. That's it."

"Lyon didn't get up? Call you? Come get you?" Per-plexed, his eyes returned to the screen on the monitor again. Lyon was sprawled on top of his sheets, looking like he was—and had been for some time—fast asleep.

"No. He looks wiped."

"Yeah, we swam." He watched the monitor for another long, silent minute and for some reason it bothered her.

"He'd come get you first," she told him. "You know that."

"Not if I didn't hear him."

"He'd come in and slap your arm if you didn't hear him."

He nodded but looked unconvinced. "Be back," he said, leaving her and her muffins to check in on Lyon.

Charlie rested the plate on the desk, her eyes tracking to the stack of canvases leaning against the wall behind the easel.

Shades of deep blue, black, brown, gray, and green covered the canvases. Clouds of billowing smoke on some, smudges on the other. As she flipped through them, she noticed there was another stack wedged between the shelf and wall to her left. These were nothing like the colorful, fun paintings of cartoon characters Evan painted for a living. These were dark. Unhappy. These made her heart squeeze, made her feel. And the feeling was not a good one.

Before Evan caught her snooping, she left the paintings alone, but when she went back to studying his most recent artwork, the feeling from before hadn't left her.

Sad.

Those paintings were sad.

And it saddened her those emotions lived inside of him.

Evan stepped back into the room a minute later.

"Yep. Out," he said, talking about Lyon.

"The monitor does not lie." When he came closer, she loosened the cellophane covering the plate on the desk and handed him a muffin.

He accepted, taking a huge bite. "Mmph. Good."

She smiled. At least that was something. His eyes went to the painting he'd been working on. Hers followed. It was also good. So very good.

"Mad Cow has your eyes," she told him when he joined her.

"Lyon's," he corrected, polishing off the muffin in one big bite.

She studied the surly expression on the cow, the human way he stood on his hindquarters. Facing Evan, she said, "Lyon has your eyes, too."

Turquoise blue. Stunning, honest eyes.

"Probably why everyone can relate to Mad Cow," she told him. "He's a bad cow with a big heart."

"And four stomachs," he quipped.

She laughed, but she laughed alone. When she turned he was frowning again, staring not at his painting but more through it.

"Been a while since I've painted anything good."

Briefly, her eyes went to the paintings leaning against the wall.

"Thought if I went back to what I knew," he said, and she turned her attention back to him, "the rest of the book would flow from there."

"Is it working?"

"Dunno."

Okay, enough small talk. She had to get the real reason for her being here off her conscience. "I came over to apologize."

Turquoise eyes moved to her. Arms crossed over his paint-dotted black tee. She focused on a smudge of red on his bare arm rather than look at him.

"I'm really sorry."

"Why?"

She'd asked herself this question over and over again tonight. And had arrived at only one conclusion. A conclusion she didn't look forward to sharing with him. Not at all.

"I'm sorry I kissed you," she said.

"I kissed you."

"I'm sorry you did."

He uncrossed his arms and stepped close, tipping her chin upward. When she met the ferocity of his expression, every last part of her wanted to cower. "Why?" It was a demand.

She swallowed. Girded her loins. She could do this. "It's not fair to Rae. Or Lyon. Or you."

"Rae," he growled.

She pulled in a breath, keeping her eyes locked on his. "Yeah."

"What about you?"

Not understanding, she shook her head, her chin brushing where his fingers rested. "What about me, what?"

He clenched his jaw and his brows lowered over his eyes. Anger radiated off him like a kerosene furnace. She could feel it. She could practically *hear it*. His fingers left her chin, slid along the sensitive skin of her neck, and into her hair, sending a drove of gooseflesh down both arms. The palm on the back of her neck tightened, forcing her to tilt her head in order to meet his gaze.

Slowly, he reiterated his earlier question, this time in the form of a statement. "Is it fair. To you."

Fair? To her? "Fair to her" didn't come into play. Yes, in a way she had lost Rae, too, but Rae wasn't her spouse, the mother of her child, or her soul mate. Losing Rae had devastated her, but it couldn't compare to *Evan* losing Rae. To Lyon losing his mother.

"I . . . don't understand."

"I know."

His hand squeezed her neck, then released. His eyes went to her mouth for such a long time, she got light-headed and then realized it was because she hadn't taken a breath since he touched her.

"I'm going to kiss you. Better stop me if you don't want me to."

It was like she'd been injected with venom that paralyzed her body but left her brain aware. She wanted to say stop, to bring up Rae again, but only intellectually. Her body—and every last cell in it—wanted to feel Evan's mouth on hers.

So she said nothing.

And he kissed her, as promised.

When his lips lowered, she lifted hers and met him in the middle. The pressure increased on her neck as he adjusted the angle, and she lifted a palm and laid it on his firm chest, feeling his heart pound, feeling the earth shake, and tingling and fluttering everywhere capable of tingling and fluttering.

She lost track of hands and feet, the whole world. Everything but their mating mouths fell away as he tasted her. Their tongues speared, her head swam, and the pulse throbbing low in her belly relocated to in between her thighs.

He held her steady—and it was a good thing because she might teeter if it wasn't for the strong hand gripping her waist. The thought came to her, though she had no idea how the thought-making part of her brain was functioning at the moment, that no one had kissed her like Evan was kissing her now. Like he needed her mouth on his. Like the air they shared was paramount to survival. Like their hands, skimming and sliding over clothes, and exploring planes and curves, were as necessary as if neither of them had sight.

The same passion he'd poured onto the canvas behind them, he poured onto her lips now. It dripped like honey, the sweetness too much for her to deny.

He pulled away from her mouth and she came down hard. And when she did, she found one of her hands had wound itself into his hair while the other one clenched on to his T-shirt. That her breasts had mashed against his solid frame, that the whole of her, from thighs to knees to shins, had leaned into him so far that if he moved, she'd fall to the ground. She appropriated her weight so that she was supporting herself, then loosened her grip on his hair. She didn't let go right away, testing the strands. Soft. Thick. Just like she'd imagined.

Evan didn't seem to mind that she'd buried her fingers in it. Russell had very carefully arranged hair but never let her touch it. Evan had not only let her touch it, he'd let her *mangle* it.

Ungripping the hand fisted in his T-shirt, she attempted to peel away her body pressed to his like cellophane stuck to itself. He clutched her closer, not letting her back away, and most of her—the throbbing, fluttering, tingling parts— was glad. Because she didn't want to back away yet.

The hand on her waist moved to splay across her back. "Do you paint?" he asked, his voice low and rumbly and far too sexy for such a weird question.

"Finger-paint," she joked. "But that was a long time ago." His smile turned wicked.

Her heart kicked against her rib cage.

The hand left her back and grabbed hers, and she had to remind herself how to use her knees as he led her in three wide strides across the studio. In front of the easel and small table covered in, and with, paint, he stopped and positioned her much in the way she had been standing on the other side of the room. Facing him, very close, one of his hands once again splayed across her back.

She watched his face, then his hand as it lowered to the palette on the table. His finger lifted, and when it did, she saw a dab of bright blue paint on the tip. He dragged it down her cheek to her jaw, the cool sensation of the paint causing her flesh to pucker with raised goose bumps.

She sucked in a breath as he lowered his hand again. Then he returned, this time with red, and dragged another chilly line down her neck.

"How come you never asked me to tattoo you?" he murmured.

The bizarre line of questioning kept coming.

"Um…"

The truth was Charlie had wanted Evan to tattoo her. He was amazingly talented and she wanted something on her body that had meaning. She'd picked out what she wanted a long time ago but lacked the courage to approach him.

For one, Rae hadn't been tatted at all, and Charlie felt weird asking Rae's husband to ink her skin when his own wife wouldn't let him do it. For another, Charlie wanted the tattoo very close to a…um…private place, and the idea of Evan Downey's face that close to her boob was, well…it wasn't right.

Then Rae had died and any idea of entering his intimate space and asking him to tat her in an intimate place went right out the window. Getting someone else to do it was out of the question. Evan was the best.

None of which she could tell him, so she said, "Never got around to it."

Another dab of blue, but this time, he ran his finger along the V-neck of her shirt. "Where."

"Um…"

The finger dipped past her shirt, skimming along the top of one breast.

"Here," she breathed, moving her left hand and resting it high on her right rib cage.

He lifted the hem of her shirt, grazing her bare stomach with his knuckles. Then his hand replaced hers under her shirt, dangerously close to her breast—that was, as it turned out, *not* encased in a bra.

His eyes continued burning into hers, much the way the palm of his hand burned into her skin. "What."

She sucked in a breath, her thoughts scattering to the wind. Closing her eyes, she saw the image she'd long wanted immortalized on her skin. "A camera."

"Lift your arms."

"Evan." A whisper. "I'm not wearing a bra."

That smile grew more insidious. "Perfect."

She laughed his name a second time, but not out of humor, out of terror. And lust. Lusty terror. Was that a thing?

"Let me see." He spoke with intensity, and while looking right at her.

As if entranced, she lifted her arms to do as he asked, squeezing her eyes closed as she felt the material lift, the room's cool air hit her breasts, and finally the sweep of her long hair as it swished between her shoulder blades.

She'd sensed he wasn't near, and when she popped her eyes open, she saw him drawing the blinds on the three windows in the room. Then he closed the studio door.

They were alone. Her throat constricted as she realized there had been a fantasy in the back of her head since he'd moved here, and it involved this very scenario. Them alone. Her naked. His hands on her body.

He approached, his eyes flitting over her, and she had

to resist the urge to cup her large breasts to hide them. What was she doing?

What are *you doing?*

"You're beautiful, Ace." He dipped his fingers into the paint—all four fingers—and traced them down her body, slicking multiple colors in long lines between her breasts, down to her belly button, and over her waist.

Her breathing went shallow. "Evan."

"Gonna help me out?" he asked, mischievous glint in his eye.

"Sorry?"

He shook his head. Slowly. "No apologizing." He took her hand, kissed her palm, then directed her to the palette dotted with paint colors. She stroked her finger through the yellow and lifted it to his face. He shook his head again, grabbing her wrist. "Not me. You."

"Me?"

He pushed her fingertip to her nipple and drew a cool circle around the tightened bud. "*You*," he repeated.

She gasped at the contact. The sensations of cool paint, mixed with the fire in his eyes as he watched her touch herself, filled her with longing. Rational thought was a faraway thing, her only focus on this moment, and the man who was using his talented hands to seduce her.

He dipped his finger back into the blue, tracing slow circles around her other nipple until it pebbled.

"A camera like yours?" he asked. More paint, another circle.

She knew this answer...her Nikon, or a drawing of it anyway, but her brain wouldn't send the words to her mouth.

Finally, she managed a breathy, "Yeah."

"I can do that, Ace."

No doubt. She'd bet he could do anything.

He took her hand, re-dipping into the yellow, then returned her finger to her nipple. Knowing what he wanted, she stroked on the paint in circles while he watched. The slickness of the paint against the hardened bud lit a spark within. Her mouth fell open, and he smiled.

"Rae hated this side of me," he whispered, leaning in to kiss her lips lightly.

Her finger stilled. She blinked. How could anyone hate this side of him? Let alone Rae. Did that mean . . . did that mean they'd never . . . done this before?

Before she could let that neurotic thought take root, he took hold of her, making her hand his brush and he the painter. Her eyes closed, her thighs clenched.

"She didn't like when I got lost in the art."

Charlie relaxed her hand, gave him full control, and focused on what he was saying.

"She didn't like when I took time away from her, away from Lyon, to paint for hours."

The admission surprised and confused her. "I thought you didn't like when I talked about Rae."

He dipped her finger into the red this time and moved it to her other nipple. Eyes on his work, he said, "We didn't have the perfect marriage."

Another circle had her struggling between listening and ignoring his words. Every part of her wanted to give into the sensations cascading over her skin, not feel the pain and guilt that would surely come over talking about Rae.

"Someone passes away, everyone idealizes them. Including me. Including you. That's not always the true side of things. We disagreed. We fought. We didn't see eye to eye on a lot of issues."

Letting go of her hand, he mixed his fingers through three different colors until he came up with an orangey-yellow and then pulled another four-fingered line straight down her torso. When he got to her jean skirt, he flipped the stud.

Her hand automatically covered his.

He leaned close, breath sifting over her lips as he whispered, "Let me."

Breasts heaving, heart thumping, she moved her hand from his. She wasn't sure what he was doing, but she didn't want to stop him. Right or wrong, she wanted this man, had been mesmerized by him. Too mesmerized to argue further.

He unzipped her skirt and tugged, and she wiggled her hips until the denim fell in a puddle at her feet. She stepped out of the circle of material, kicking off the new fawn sandals Sofie had gifted her. He brushed the pile of clothes aside with his foot.

Fingers returned to paint, and this time he raked them along the swell of her hips and down to her thighs while he spoke, smearing greenish-blue with one hand and creating orange-yellow swirls with the other.

"I loved Rae. Loved her half my life."

When guilt would have stabbed her, he fisted her panties and stripped them off her legs. On his knees before her, he admired where her thighs came together, a long look that made her want to cover herself. Something about his rapt attention, and the way his rough palms moved along the skin on her legs, kept her from it.

"Beautiful." He stood, going no further, and she couldn't decide if she was disappointed or relieved. Kind of felt like a dab of both.

He raised her unpainted hand to his lips, kissing her fingers one by one.

"I miss her, Charlie." He placed a soft kiss to the inside of her thumb.

"I know," she whispered, the emotions in her heart rising to her face. "I do, too."

"Been grieving for years." He stroked his tongue along her index finger, kissed her fingertip. "Four years," he whispered.

Tears stung the back of her eyelids but she refused to let them come forth.

"I know." How she must look now...naked, half-covered in paint, Evan's attention on her body while he talked about his late wife. She tried to imagine an outsider looking in, tried to cast judgment, but she couldn't. She was too into this moment. The here and now of him turning her on and on, of being under his unwavering attention and focus.

"We deserve to be free."

His words stunned her.

"Sorry?"

He sucked her middle finger into his mouth, letting it out in one, long, slow pull. Then he positioned her finger between her legs, slid into her folds, and directed her to stroke herself.

"We deserve it, Charlie. It would have killed Rae all over again if the two people she loved most in this world died right alongside her."

He was right, but her thoughts didn't get any further as he increased the pressure of her fingers.

A fractured, keening sound escaped her lips as he continued guiding her fingers over her clit. Once he was satisfied with her speed, he left her to it, dipping his fingers back into the paint and returning to her breasts. Pinching and pulling through the sticky, wet paint, he plucked her while she thrust against her own hand.

"You don't have to feel sorry, Ace." Another slick pull on her nipples had her bucking against her own fingers.

He tugged his shirt off and she opened her eyes to see all his exposed, inked flesh, the dark, detailed lines etched along each shoulder, curving down the ample biceps to his bare chest, taut abs, and defined obliques.

Beautiful.

Every inch she'd seen so far.

Grasping her hips, he tugged her close and rubbed his body against her, painting himself with her breasts as he kissed her hard on the mouth. A hand came around and palmed her butt, then the other, squeezing and lifting, pressing her closer and tighter against his form. When his tongue entered her mouth to clash with hers, her head vanished from this plane altogether.

There was only the feel of the slide of her finger, her building release, the hot insistence of his tongue and body.

He ended the kiss long enough to say, "Let go, Ace."

Her moan almost a whimper, she watched him from beneath hooded eyes, loving the heat she saw there, loving that heat was for her.

He kissed her again, then grinned against her lips. "So fucking sexy. Let go, baby." His hand reached between their bodies to clasp her wrist and increase her speed and pressure, and she felt herself going over.

"Evan." She tried to speak, but it was more of a high-pitched squeak. "Evan."

"I know, Ace. You need it. Take it." He kissed her

again, guiding her arm with one hand while the other clasped her butt and his chest rubbed against her sensitized nipples. "Take it. You deserve it."

"For you," she heard herself say, cresting, the wave nearly rolling over and drowning her beneath.

"For me, baby," he agreed.

With a broken sob, she came, and his mouth closed over hers, kissing her deeply, mercilessly, swallowing her cries. As she wound down, her body pulsing, her thighs wet, her body damp with drying paint, she lost the ability to hold her head up and dropped her forehead on his chest. Vaguely, she registered his body moving, him cleaning his hands on a nearby cloth, before sliding his fingers into her hair.

"How much better does that feel?" he asked, kissing her temple.

"Mmff," was all she managed.

His deep, rumbling chuckle bobbed her head and echoed around the room, making her heart swell. "You're a good finger painter, Ace."

Somehow, she lifted her head and smiled.

Still holding her, he stepped away and showed her his chest. Two round smudges of mixed paint from her breasts, and mirroring lines streaked his torso and marked his jeans.

"One of a kind," he said. "You'll never find another creation like this one. And if we tried it again"—he winked—"and we will, it wouldn't come out the same way twice."

"Amazing," she said.

The whole thing was amazing. She'd never let go so thoroughly. She had paint in her hair, on her clothes. She'd pleasured herself in front of someone—all things she'd never done before. Speaking of...

"You've never done this before?" She wanted to add "with Rae," but it seemed wrong to bring her up.

"Never." He saw through her anyway. She registered in his expression that he knew what she was thinking. "Nothing's perfect, Ace."

But when he kissed her again, an argument hatched in her head. Because this entire thing had been pretty perfect. Raw and wrong and daring.

And perfect.

So perfect.

* * *

He'd known it on some deeper level. Had known Charlie saw him differently—saw these moments of creativity in a different way than Rae had. Charlie was an artist by her own right, and it came as no surprise that she'd gotten swept up in the room's energy.

And it was some incredible energy. The kind only found when the world was asleep and the phones were quiet and children were sleeping. The kind of wild energy that, when harnessed, created the best art. Germinated amazing ideas.

So it came as no surprise to him that in his sexual frustration, he'd managed to find Swine Flew after nude finger painting Charlie and watching her make herself climax.

She sat on his lap now, where he'd insisted she sit. He allowed her to get dressed again, which almost killed him, but he counted himself lucky as it was. While she nestled against him, he sketched and painted and asked for her opinion on colors. She liked Swine with hair, but he argued Swine was too Miss Piggy with cascading blond locks, and she agreed she'd been remiss to overlook the resemblance.

He had an arm wrapped around her waist and his paintbrush on the canvas when she spoke. "Would you tattoo me?"

He sifted his hand into her shirt and palmed her ribs where she'd said she wanted ink, and gave her a squeeze. Unable to stop himself, he felt his way north until he brushed the underside of one breast, his thumb flicking her nipple. Her head dropped back on his shoulder.

Against her ear, he licked, then breathed, "I'd do all sorts of things to you."

"How did this happen?" she asked quietly, and he wasn't sure to which of them she'd directed the question. He dropped his paintbrush and moved her hair aside. They needed a shower. They were covered in dried paint, and he only hoped she could get the blue out of her blond hair.

She turned her head so her cheek was on his shoulder and sought him out with earnest eyes. So he told her the truth.

"Want you to be free. Great place to be."

He was. Some days.

"There are always consequences to getting what you want." A worry line bisected her forehead.

He shifted her so he could focus on her face. "There are consequences to everything, Ace."

Consequences to marrying young and having a child. Consequences to doing things the right way. Consequences to living honest, loving honest, to committing to one person.

Sometimes those consequences were fair. And sometimes they weren't.

Losing Rae hadn't been fair. Lyon did nothing to deserve his mother being taken away from him as a toddler.

"I feel ba—"

He kissed her. "Don't say it." He regarded her and she watched him. "Don't you dare say it. First off, I know it's a lie. Can tell by your loose limbs, you feel great, baby." He cupped her breast again and she sighed. "Imagine when *I* touch you there."

Her mouth dropped open long enough to pull in a breath, then she closed it.

"You . . . we didn't take care of you."

Fact.

The proof was stretching his shorts and pressing against the side of Charlie's ass. Much as he wanted more, he knew she'd had enough for one night.

"No more time, Ace. Sun's coming up."

She blinked around the room as if noticing the natural light through the drawn blinds for the first time, stiffening against him. "Oh my gosh, Lyon. And I'm . . . And you're . . ."

"Relax."

"I have to shower."

He tightened the arm around her waist and kissed her again, whispering against her lips, "If Lyon wasn't here, I'd take you up to my shower, soap you from head to toe. Lick you from head to toe." He licked her top lip and kissed it, then gave a long, slow pull, showing her how he'd take his time. No doubt she tasted this amazing everywhere; he'd find out soon. "I'd lap you like a dish of cream. Until you came for me, Ace."

She shuddered and he kissed her bottom lip this time before tracing it with his tongue.

"I'd make you scream my name. *Scream it*." He nipped her lip and let go to find her eyes wide. He grinned, unable to keep from it. "And you will."

"Evan." Her voice was a whisper and her hand had clutched his hair again. He loved her fingers there, tugging, pulling, stroking. He'd like her fingers doing that elsewhere, too, he thought, lifting his hips and grinding against her.

But tonight hadn't been about him. It'd been about making her see what they could be. If she let go. If they let go together.

And it'd been more amazing than he'd allowed himself to believe.

Powerful.

He wanted more.

CHAPTER THIRTEEN

The white painted banner strung over the entrance of Library Park read: EVERGREEN COVE'S STARVING ARTISTS FESTIVAL, CELEBRATING 25 YEARS!

Every year, local artists came together to donate their works to a silent auction from which the library directly profited. Charlie donated a photo of the lake at sunrise. She'd taken the shot earlier this year from her back porch, dock and pines in the distance, and decided then it would be the one she donated.

When she'd dropped off the photo, Mrs. Anderson mentioned how some of this year's funds would go for new shelving while a portion of it would be put aside for repair of the east foundation wall. As she'd put it, "before the whole dang building topples over."

Viewing the stately old brick building now, Charlie doubted "the whole dang building" was going anywhere. A study in good old-fashioned craftsmanship, the place was likely as sturdy as it looked.

Not that she'd dare argue with the intimidating librarian. Mrs. Anderson was a spitfire force to be reckoned with. No one knew her exact age or remembered a time when a different librarian had been in charge of the Cove's loaned-out books.

Rare as it was for her to take a day for herself, Charlie had blocked the entire weekend off when she'd learned Evan and Lyon were moving here. It would give her an excuse to take Lyon to the festival and introduce him to the bizarre food offerings from the questionably sanitary food trucks lining the blocked-off street.

Hey, it was tradition.

She leaned against the aluminum railing surrounding the teacup ride in the center of the festival. This, another spinning ride called "The Scrambler," and one that looked like a giant roulette wheel turned on its side were the only three rides at the festival.

The carnies in charge weren't carnies at all, but Evergreeners Tom Anderson, Mrs. Anderson's long-suffering husband, and his two grown sons, Willie and Kyle. The three men organized the entertainment for the fair every year, guaranteeing both safety and fun. Though Willie, when she'd purchased Lyon's two-dollar ticket, informed her he'd "tuned the ride myself" but regrettably "can't guarantee against puking."

Evan had given her that guarantee, claiming Lyon had a solid stomach. She certainly hoped so considering the array of deep-fried foods they'd shared before he climbed aboard the cup-and-saucer.

After he stopped waving at her at every pass, she

allowed herself to take in the perfect eighty-something-degree weather, cloudless blue sky, and full, thick maple, oak, and pine trees dotting the park. 'Greeners flocked to the festival every year, and she wished Sofie or Faith hadn't worked today so she had someone to hang with.

Evan and Asher were at a signing table under a huge white tent, their own painted banner promising visitors could *Meet the creators of Mad Cow!* Next to their seats was the painting of the cow himself propped on an easel, the same one she'd watched him paint the other night.

At the thought, a secret smile curled her lips and she put her hand to her face. That'd been . . . something else.

She blinked him into focus now and watched him lean forward to shake the hand of a very small boy, coming half off his metal chair, pretending to crumple underneath the kid's grip. When the boy laughed and let go, Evan shook his arm out, his face an exaggerated wince.

It was so adorable, her heart gave a little tug. He had an ease with children she shared, except where his came from was no mystery. He had a big, boisterous, loving family, and though they were scattered in Ohio, Tennessee, and Illinois, he claimed getting together with them was an easy reunion.

Oh, to be so lucky.

She felt a squeeze of envy for not having that kind of relationship with her father and sister. They preferred distance. Charlie had decided years ago to let them have their space and stop trying to create a reunion that would, most likely, be unsuccessful.

They hadn't fought her on the decision, which made her feel equal parts hurt and relieved.

She took a deep breath, caught another glimpse of

Evan's smiling face, and her thoughts returned to the night in his studio. Now other parts of her gave a squeeze, simultaneously more pleasant, and less welcome than the one before.

She'd tried to figure out her brazen reaction—the mysterious "thing" possessing her to strip *nude* for Evan Downey for cripe's sake—and had come to only one conclusion. The conclusion? Well. The answer was right there in the question. *Evan Downey.*

The man could talk a nun out of her habit. And a good girl into a series of bad ones.

That realization led to her thinking of how he'd behaved since the afternoon on the dock, when the air snapped between them palpably—and she thought about it *a lot*, both while pretending to work and fervently avoiding being alone with her sexy neighbor.

If she wasn't mistaken, Sofie was right. Evan *had* been pursuing her.

It didn't assuage her guilt—guilt over Rae as well as a bigger guilt than Rae, which wasn't something she understood yet—pricking her like one of Evan's tattoo needles. Although on second thought, maybe that bigger "guilt" wasn't guilt at all, but something else entirely.

Yearning.

So much of it built up during the years after Rae died. Charlie lost her best friend, Rae's parents, and Evan and Lyon for a while. And in the last two years since Russell left her, she'd found herself wishing she had someone to yearn *for.* And now, she did. After bottling that longing, Evan had come along and shaken her up.

No wonder she'd exploded, all the *want* flooding over her like an erupting soda. Now, imaginary, effervescent bubbles popped along the surface of her skin whenever she thought of him. It was a great feeling; one her body wanted more of.

That kind of longing could easily become her new pastime. Pastimes took up too much time. And, as the saying went, *Ain't* nobody *got time for* that.

The ride wound to a halt and Lyon stepped off, pretending to stagger, his tongue hanging out.

"I know you're okay. You must be missing a dizzy gene," she joked.

"Can I feed the goats?"

The fattest goats she'd ever seen. Poor things. They'd been fed fistfuls of sweaty, cracked corn throughout the day by kids young and old, and were going to have to go on a goat diet, or perhaps to the goat gym, if they had a prayer of making it through the summer with a modicum of self-worth.

"Um." She looked for a less cruel distraction, spotting a booth that would do the trick. "What if you try and win a fish instead?"

His green-blue eyes lit like a cool flame. "Really? Dad will let me keep a fish?"

There was so much excitement in his tone, she worried, albeit belatedly, that she'd overstepped a line. "Um…"

Too late. Lyon was off, and all she could do was follow, secretly praying he didn't win a fish she'd then have to explain to his dad.

Charlie gave the older woman running the booth a ten-dollar bill, figuring Lyon would keep busy for a long while since the Ping-Pong balls he was attempting to land in the almost-too-small fishbowls were five for a dollar. He had just tossed his first ball when Evan's agent approached.

Gloria's long black hair cascaded down her back, straight and smooth-as-silk. Charlie opted to pull hers into a clip today and avoid sweating her fool head off. Besides, if she'd let her honey-colored locks free in this humidity, she'd look like a Fraggle. And not a cute one.

"Hey, *sistah*," Glo said, coming to a stop next to her. She wore a tasteful pink skirt and delicate silver jewelry on her neck and ears, but her black top was all rock and roll... especially since it literally read ROCK 'N' ROLL in pink glitter across the front. The collar of her T-shirt had been cut and her cleavage was on display, and practically in Charlie's face thanks to the other woman's tall, spiked black heels.

Charlie had worn flats considering the grass was soft and there was straw over the muddier parts of the Library Park lawn. It both fascinated and perplexed her how Glo wasn't sinking into the ground.

"Hey." She forced a smile, but it felt false. Normally, she wasn't one to be fake to anyone, but this was the girl who Evan had kissed, and for reasons unbeknown to her, that fact continued to fester jealousy. Maybe because Glo had been bold enough to lay one on him at some point in time, but Charlie had to be marauded into a kiss she now felt super guilty over.

They watched Lyon throw another ball. It bounced off the rim of a glass bowl, and the woman running the booth caught it and encouraged him to try again.

Glo chuckled. "He wins one of those, Evan will freak."

A new flare of jealousy pinged her insides. Likely because Glo knew things about him and Charlie didn't, and she didn't like that. Not at all.

"Okay, enough." A sharp clap made Charlie flinch before giving over her full attention. Glo smiled and rubbed her hands together a few times before she spoke. "You probably know by now I'm pretty direct."

Uh-oh.

Her heart rate increased to dangerous proportions. She didn't like confrontation. She didn't like it from anyone, let alone a woman as no-nonsense as Gloria Shields. With no way to run away from this situation—thus leaving Lyon—Charlie was trapped. It took every ounce of her self-control to not slap her hands over her ears, shut her eyes, and hum in order to avoid hearing whatever Gloria had to say.

"I'm just going to say it." Gloria was smiling.

Charlie was pretty sure she was grimacing. She felt her body chill, then heat with worried anticipation.

"Sweetie"—Glo reached out and put a palm on Charlie's shoulder—"Evan's your man. You don't have to worry about him and me."

The statement startled her so much, she blurted out, almost defensively, "He's not mine." But her defense lacked authority, not to mention her shoulder was now sweating where Gloria's hand rested.

"Our feelings for one another are platonic and mutual," Glo continued. "We kissed." She pulled her hand away to hold up a finger. "Once. I promise you, it was like kissing one of those fish over there." She gestured to Lyon, who threw a ball and (*phew!*) missed again.

Well.

Charlie had kissed Evan, too. *More* than once. She knew full well he was better than kissing a fish. He was better at kissing than any man she'd kissed, like, *ever*.

"Nah, he wasn't that bad." Glo laughed.

The feeling of ease swept away like ebbing tide.

"We knew on contact it was the wrong move."

"Okay." Despite the fact this was almost verbatim what Evan said, Charlie couldn't say she felt better. But, at least she knew Glo wasn't pursuing him in any way...which, now that she thought about it, did make her feel better.

"You're wrong, by the way," Glo stated, making Charlie go rigid again. "Evan *is* yours, doll." She turned to watch Lyon. "I don't know if you want him or not, but they're both yours." Her cell rang and she answered it with a cheery, "Roger, hi. Did you have time to review my e-mail?" She wandered a few feet away to take her call while Charlie stared at Lyon, feeling...*Gosh.*

What *was* she feeling?

Her entire body buzzed like she'd just finished a really hard workout. Her heart stuttered in her chest. Her mouth was dry.

They're both yours.

Both of them. Lyon and Evan.

She blinked a few times in quick succession, turning the phrase over and over in her mind.

Both yours.

She wanted them both. She loved Lyon in the way she imagined a mother loved her son. She loved Evan in a different way...sure, as a friend, but now...in a lusty way. A way any woman would recognize as sexual, and never, ever mistake a kiss from him as fishlike *or* platonic.

What did *that* mean?

Should she allow herself to have what he was offering? Not that he'd offered a relationship, per se. But he'd certainly promised a few other things: painting involving orgasms, showers involving his lips on every inch of her body, and a tattoo for her. She could accept, *if* she let go of the guilt, let go of the worry of taking Rae's family for herself.

Could she fill the role her best friend had filled before her? Would Lyon resent her? Would Evan compare her?

Her mind swam, her thoughts too confusing and too many to sort. This was not a decision she could make under the blazing sun while standing next to a woman Evan had kissed a year ago. There were other, more pressing problems to deal with.

Three seconds later, Lyon added to those problems by one.

"Aunt Charlie!" He bounded over to her, plastic bag in hand, shaking the tiny brown fish inside. "I won! I won, I won, I won!"

"Easy, buddy. Let's not give him brain damage." She stilled the bag and looked inside. The fish's mouth was moving at an alarmingly fast rate, his eyes bugging out, though she supposed, since fish had no eyelids, they always looked like their eyes were bugging out. He was pretty, though she was unsure if he was a "he" at all. Unlike the others waiting to be won, he wasn't orange, but goldish-brown in color with long, flowing fins.

"I got to pick him," he said proudly.

"He's beautiful."

"That lady said we can get everything for him over there." He pointed to a strategically placed booth next to the one with the fish game where a vendor was selling everything from bowls and tanks, to filters, food, and decorations.

"Yeah." She walked with him to the booth. "I bet she did."

* * *

"Ah, hell," Evan said under his breath as he watched Charlie and Lyon—with a fish in a bag—approach a vendor who was happily gesticulating to a million accessories she could buy for the miniature carp he guessed he'd be flushing down the toilet within forty-eight hours.

"The little lady got you a pet." Ash elbowed him.

"Laugh it up, dickhead."

Mrs. Anderson cleared her throat from nearby and angled a glare at them. Evan lifted a palm in apology.

"No swearing, Mr. Downey," Ash said, his impression of Mrs. Anderson as bad as his Forrest Gump.

"Looks like your girlfriend's talking to mine," Evan told him. He was sure Ash would jump to argue that Gloria was not his girlfriend. "Girlfriends" made Asher Knight as nervous as a long-tailed cat in a room full of rocking chairs. Commitment wasn't his thing, or so it was written in his rock 'n' roll credo somewhere.

"Oh-ho! Charlie's your girlfriend?"

Evan speared him with a silent glare.

Ash grinned.

He shook his head as he looked around the park. Almost every kid here carried a signed and personalized-to-them copy of *The Adventures of Mad Cow*—and girls of all ages who'd accepted the book when Ash, under the reproachful gaze of Mrs. Anderson, refused to sign their tits—which meant he and Ash were almost off the clock. Good thing, too.

"I'm starving. You want a"—Evan squinted at the booth across from them—"deep fried apple fritter hot dog?"

God. What the hell was that?

"Sounds like a dare."

The booth to their right displayed a menu boasting its claim to fame was something called a "pork rind peanut butter burger."

"No." Evan nodded toward the booth. "I think that blue ribbon goes to Jack's Shack."

"I say we get both," Asher said. "So. You get laid?"

Evan felt a grin come on, tried to stop it, and failed miserably.

Better than laid. He and Charlie had painted one another's bodies while he kissed the breath out of her. She made herself come while he watched, holding her close, and listening to the sounds she made when she did. Listened to the way she said his name, all high and tight because her moment of pleasure was mixed in the paint imprints on their bodies. And he'd taken her there—she'd arrived there because he was guiding her arm and tasting her mouth and encouraging her with his words.

Erotic as hell, and like nothing he'd ever experienced. Tapping into her, and into a moment in the *middle of a moment* where he'd been so filled with artistic vibes and creation. It'd happened right in the middle of a "zone" and on the canvases of their bodies. The smell of paint in the air would forever have a sensual smell after they'd—

"You son of a bitch. You did get laid."

Ash shoved his shoulder and Evan snapped out of what Rae would have classified as a midday "zone out," only he hadn't been painting, he'd been remembering painting Charlie.

Speaking of, he turned his head to see her carrying a miniature tank—a freaking fish tank—loaded with supplies and things that looked like they plugged into the wall. Lyon cradled his new pet to his chest like he'd won a puppy instead.

"I can't believe it, man."

"Yeah, a fish," Evan grumbled.

"Not what I meant," Asher said, a smile clear in his voice.

Luckily, he didn't have a chance to expound on that statement because Mrs. Anderson stepped in front of them.

She eyed a tiny gold watch—how could she see the face well enough to tell the time?—and proclaimed, "Mr. Knight, your ballad starts in thirty minutes if you'd like to tune up your guitar."

"Shit," Ash grumbled. "Shoot, I mean," he corrected when she gave him the evil eye. "Yes ma'am. I'll go uh, tune up." He slapped Evan's arm and said, "Drinks at Salty after."

Salty Dog was located on the main drag in town, but they'd also set up a temporary dwelling. The tiki-hut-like structure sat apart from the rest of the festival with a sign overhead that read 21 AND OLDER, colored Japanese lanterns hanging from ropes looped around the perimeter.

"Mr. Downey, I've decided what I'd like for the library's main room."

She had, had she? He lifted his eyebrows at the petite older woman standing over him.

She blinked at him through a thick pair of trifocals. "An abstract painting."

"Abstract," he repeated.

"Ms. Shields said you'd paint whatever I requested."

Yeah, well *Ms. Shields* tended to overpromise on occasion. He stood and smiled, palming Mrs. Anderson's petite shoulder. To his surprise, she didn't feel the least bit frail. There was muscle, strength under that peach blouse, making him wonder if she did bench presses when she retired for the evening.

He gestured to the painting of Mad Cow. "I don't do

abstracts, ma'am." Unless they were done at three in the morning while he was mid-nervous-breakdown over his deceased wife. He gestured at the easel next to him. "But if Mad Cow is too...unrefined for you"—and he was—"I can paint you an owl, or maybe a fox reading a book? Foxes are trendy."

She glared up at him, the force of her glare so much he removed his hand from her shoulder.

"I want a piece of art, not a cartoon, Mr. Downey." She checked her tiny watch again and snapped her fingers at two young guys whose faces looked as miserable as if they were serving time rather than volunteering. "Joel and Micah. Break down this tent and put Mr. Downey's cow painting in the silent auction section." Then to Evan, she dipped her chin. "Art," she said.

"Art," he confirmed with a sigh.

CHAPTER FOURTEEN

*O*h boy.

Charlie watched Evan leave the tent as two teenagers went to work dismantling it. Her hand curled around the five-gallon aquarium, her steps deliberately slowed, which meant Lyon had run ahead of her with Terror—the name he'd chosen for the fish—displayed prominently in front of him.

When she got close, she heard him saying, "...a few fish flakes twice a day or he won't eat it and the tank will get too dirty and he'll die."

"Okay, bud, we'll stick to that so that Terror won't die." Evan cut his eyes to Charlie, then mouthed the word "Terror?" and she knew he wasn't upset over the whole fish thing.

"Hey, Ace," he said when he'd ambled within arm's reach. He relieved her of Terror's new home, his eyes going to her mouth like he wanted to kiss her.

She wanted him to. But her eyes deliberately went to Lyon, then back to Evan in silent communication. Evan leaned close anyway and whispered, "He's gonna see me kiss you a hundred times, Ace." Then he brushed his lips over hers in a way that made her anticipate the next hundred times to follow. The kiss was slower and sexier than their last kiss, and she didn't know if that was because he'd kissed her deeper and with more meaning the night in the studio, or if the kiss now was deeper and more meaningful.

She didn't have time to figure out the answer to the quandary because Lyon shouted, "Nonna and Poppa!"

Her blood chilled.

Evan must have seen her reaction because next he said, "Relax, Charlie." Then to Rae's parents, he called out, "Hey, guys."

She turned to see Patricia Mosley fawning over her grandson, wearing a flowing floral dress and flat sandals, her curves prominent but controlled. Patricia and Rae had the same light brown skin color, the same curvy, sexy, and enviable build.

Cliff's wide hands tenderly lifted Terror to get a better look. "That is one fine fish."

Charlie smiled at the same time her chest clutched.

She'd seen them once since Rae's funeral. Once in four years.

After Lyon was done telling the tale of how he'd saved Terror with his Ping-Pong ball prowess, Patricia and Cliff both looked to Charlie. She felt the longing from earlier bubble over again, this time for the people who had been more like a family to her over the years than her own.

"Charlotte." Patricia, who looked close to tears, approached, arms out, and pulled her into one of those mom hugs. The kind of hugs she used to get before her mother grew ill and too weak to tighten her arms around her.

It felt so good to be nestled against her, Charlie let the hug linger. Pat let her.

When she pulled away, they both wiped their eyes and Cliff clucked at his wife. "Don't make my baby girl cry, Patty." He embraced Charlie next, giving her several swift pats on the back, his laughter rumbling against the cheek she'd rested on his barrel chest. Then he wiped the stray tears tracking down her face with his big, big hands.

"Baby girl," he said with a huge, genuine white-toothed smile. The sparkle in his eyes reminded her of Rae, and made her aware of Evan and her feelings for Evan, and that sent another jolt of guilt surging through her bloodstream.

Rae's parents. If they only knew.

Evan got a handshake from Cliff and a kiss on the cheek from Patricia, not because they loved him less than Charlie, but because he'd obviously seen them multiple times since Rae died. That, too, made her feel guilty.

Ugh.

"Thanks for picking him up. I'll come get him when you're sick of him," Evan joked. He kicked Lyon's tennis shoe. "Probably be ready to send you home by tonight."

"Ha-ha," Lyon said, taking the teasing in good turn.

"Your dad says you've been taking swimming lessons," Patricia said.

"Yeah!" Lyon explained the lake, the life vest, and a twenty-foot slide going into the deepest part of the lake nicknamed the Slide of Insanity, followed by mentioning he'd watched kids go down it but hadn't tried yet himself. "Dad won't let me."

"Your dad's smart." Pat winked at Evan. "We have a surprise for you, Lionel."

Lyon grinned. "What is it?"

"Don't tell him," Cliff teased.

"Poppa!" Lyon's eyebrows frowned.

His grandfather laughed. "I'll give you a hint. It's big and filled with water."

Lyon's eyes widened before he guessed, "A swimming pool?" Then jumped up and down, jarring poor Terror some more. "Dad!"

"I heard." Evan took the fish from his exuberant son and slid the bag into the tank nestled in the crook of one arm.

"And not one of those blow-up pools, or kiddie pools, either." Cliff threw his arms out. "It's huge! It even has a diving board."

"A diving board!" Lyon practically shouted.

Pat stayed her husband with a hand. "You're not ready for the diving board, yet, dear, but you can definitely swim in the pool." To Evan, she said, "We also bought water wings and floatation devices. He'll be totally safe."

"I know he will, Mom," he answered easily.

Hearing him refer to Pat as "Mom" made Charlie's heart squeeze. Evan had lost his mother a few years back—cancer, also. Cancer was a bitch. It was good to see he'd gotten a second chance at a mom. Of course, Pat had been like her mom at one point, too, but Charlie had let herself grow apart from both Pat and Cliff. Maybe her distant family was to blame for that, too, but she thought it was probably the lack of knowing what to say after Rae passed.

She still didn't know what to say.

"Lyon's bags are at the house," Evan said. "I'll grab 'em if you guys want to hang here."

"Can I bring Terror to your house?" Lyon asked his Nonna.

"No, bud," Evan answered. "Terror has had a rough day. You can't ask him to make a ninety-minute car ride on top of everything else."

Lyon looked worried but pragmatic when he looked from the fish to Charlie. "Will you make sure Dad doesn't feed him too much so he won't die?"

She dropped her hand on Lyon's head. "Yeah, buddy. I'll make sure he doesn't die."

Evan shot her a look that said she may be making a promise she couldn't keep, and she realized she might be. If she had to replace Terror because he went to the big fishbowl in the sky, she'd have a heck of a time finding a goldish-brown, long-finned fish roughly the length of her thumb. Maybe once the Mosleys took Lyon, she'd go and see if the lady running the booth had Terror's twin just in case.

"All right. I'll be back."

"Dad." Lyon held his hands in front of him, the look on his face stunningly serious. "I have to set up Terror's tank. You don't know what you're doing."

Charlie stifled a giggle by covering her mouth.

"Don't you want to stay with Nonna and Poppa and show them the festival?"

"No."

Patricia laughed, the musical sound reminiscent of Rae's contagious laugh. Charlie thought that might be the reason she'd avoided the Mosleys. Everything about them reminded her of Rae. How did Evan do it? Be around

them, around Lyon, without letting grief for Rae overtake
him? Then she thought back to what he'd said to her in the
studio.

We deserve to be free. He'd embraced freedom for
himself . . . could she?

"Why don't we come with you, help you set up Terror's
new home, and get your things?" Pat asked Lyon.

"Okay!"

"Charlie? Want to come with?" Evan tilted his head
toward the cars parked along the street.

She did. So much. But this was Rae's family, and there
was something intimate about the four of them doing the
whole aquarium-setup thing together. "Can't," she white-
lied. "I promised Gloria I'd meet up with her for a few. I
should go find her."

He looked suspicious but she plastered the smile on
her face, hoping to convince him she and Glo had become
besties this afternoon. The lie was harmless, but necessary. She knew if she gave a plausible reason why she
wasn't going with him, he'd go without her.

She was right.

With kisses for both Pat and Cliff, Charlie promised
to visit soon—and meant it this time. Then she hugged
Lyon and told him to be careful and have fun. She nodded at Evan, but didn't hug him—his hands were full of
fish tank so it was a no-brainer as well as a relief. Showing him affection in front of his deceased wife's parents
would have been awkward.

After they left, she set off by herself to peruse the artwork on display for the bid, admiring again the photo
she'd donated and hoping it fetched a handsome price.
Then she visited a few local vendors and meandered over

to try the wine Jell-O shots she'd heard so much about. She didn't drive herself here, and wasn't planning to drive herself home, so she figured a few wine Jell-O shots wouldn't be a bad idea.

Until she ordered and ate one. Then she determined wine Jell-O shots were, in fact, a very bad idea. A very *bad-tasting* bad idea. As she was making a face and choking down the bitter, boozy shot—it was either swallow it or attempt to spit it into a public trash can buzzing with yellow jackets and flies—she heard Gloria call her name.

Wiping her fingers over her mouth to make sure she didn't have Jell-O on her face, she waved rather than spoke.

"Where're your boys?" Glo asked as she approached.

Her boys. She really did like that. More than she should.

"Setting up the tank for Lyon's fish. Rae's parents followed him over to help. They're taking Lyon to their house for a few days."

"That's wonderful. The Mosleys are great people."

Dang. She'd met the Mosleys, too?

Gloria looped her arm in Charlie's. "Relax. I was in Columbus, dropped in on Evan when they were there to see Lyon. You really need to stop seeing me as 'the other woman.' You have no one to compare yourself to, sweetie."

Except for Rae. The woman Evan fell in love with, chased, married, and created a baby with. Just her. No big deal.

"Ash finished his acoustic version of 'Unchained' a few minutes ago." This, Gloria said on a soft sigh. Her voice going gentle and funny in a way it definitely didn't do when she talked about Evan.

"I missed it."

"Well, I bet if you tell him, he'd play it for you at Salty Dog."

"Does he have a gig there?"

"No. He has an appointment with a couple of guys named Jose and Cuervo." Gloria started for the other side of the park. "And since you are unchaperoned, my dear, so do you."

* * *

The sky was darkening, and the streetlamps had come on, along with the lights tied to strings that draped the festival in glowing garland. A few kids were meandering around with their folks, but from the look of most of it, families had given way to adults who had come out to party.

Evan ambled past the stage where Asher had performed his solos earlier, and he paused for a minute to appreciate the foot-stomping, jig-dancing band playing what sounded like a cross between bluegrass and rock. Cool mixture.

He'd stick around and listen longer, but he needed to find Charlie.

Terror's fish tank setup wasn't difficult, but it required a lot of reading and, under Lyon's close supervision, it required a lot of specific steps. He didn't get his kid sometimes. Lyon could be a wild child full of energy, one who sometimes loved superheroes and other times loved football and soccer and anything with a ball, but also had a very precise, all-business side of him reminding Evan more of his cousin Shane or his brother Landon.

Power to his kid if Lyon grew up to be like his uncle or

cousin. If Lyon evolved into a million- or billionaire, he could retire his old man to the good life. Evan was more a thousand-aire, like his other brother Aiden and his sister, Angel, but Evan could definitely afford a good life, if not *the* good life, and that was enough for him.

After Terror was happily hiding behind his hot pink (really, Charlie?) castle, and the little blue air stone was bubbling away in a corner, Lyon watched him for a few minutes, tried to feed him—he'd been too traumatized to eat—and then Rae's parents talked Lyon into getting his things and loaded him into the car.

Lyon got a brief, wide-eyed look of worry the moment he was about to part. This was new. Normally, whenever he went to stay with anyone—Angel, Landon, or their dad, Mike—he'd eagerly load up, sometimes forgetting to tell Evan good-bye. Moving to Evergreen Cove affected both him and Lyon more than Evan had anticipated.

Evan had simply smiled and buckled Lyon in. "You got this, buddy." He hoped that was encouraging. He figured Lyon was nervous, but wasn't about to cripple him by allowing him to super-glue himself to Evan's side. He'd get used to being here, to having a new home. He'd adjust to school. Evan knew kids—Lyon's school friends—who were wrapped in cotton batting and bubble wrap, and for good measure crammed into a giant plastic hamster ball, so if they bonked into the real world they wouldn't get hurt.

That kind of parenting was bullshit.

Evan was raised with a firm word from Dad and gentle coaxing from Mom, and that was the way to go. He couldn't fill the "mom" role alone, however, and he needed backup for that. Thank God for Patricia and Charlie. And

Aiden and Landon, for that matter, who bent to Lyon's will whenever he shot his uncles a dimpled grin.

The thought made Evan grin. Lyon was in good hands. Patricia would give him too much sugar, and Cliff would let him sit up too late and watch TV when he shouldn't, and he figured that was okay, too. They were Lyon's Nonna and Poppa, and Evan was looking forward to having a beer with his buddies, and Charlie, and taking his first deep breath since he'd moved here.

Music at Salty Dog was a far cry from the band on stage. Jimmy Buffett faded into a Bob Marley song and that faded into raucous laughter and the chatter of many drunken townsfolk. And it was still early.

He weaved around picnic tables and waitresses and then spotted the back of Gloria's sleek, black head and angled toward them. Glo, Ash, and Charlie sat at one of four high-top tables under the tiki-style roof, having garnered one of the best seats in the house—hell, at the entire festival.

He figured Ash had used his smile and celeb status to get both the table, and permission to smoke, which he wasn't doing at the moment but likely had been. Ash always smoked when he drank.

Ash leaned over the table, pressed an index finger into it, and said something that made Charlie throw her head back and laugh. Evan stopped advancing and, for he didn't know how long, simply watched her. Watched her toss her honey-blond hair, bat those huge hazel eyes, and part bee-stung lips into a soft smile he wanted to taste.

Damn. She was gorgeous.

Conversely, Glo sat ramrod straight, watching the exchange between the other two—and Ash's attention locked on Charlie—with visible disdain. Glo's red lips were twisted, her hand encircling a shot glass filled with golden liquor.

Glo didn't know Ash like he did. She didn't realize that for Ash, Charlie was nothing more than a new set of attentive eyes and ears, eager to hear his stories for the first time, and ready to laugh loudly and generously when he told them. Glo didn't have to worry about Ash moving in on Charlie any more than she had to worry about Evan moving in on her.

It was clear she didn't understand that.

He put a hand on her back and stroked, greeting every-one with a collective, "Hey, guys."

"I was hearing more tales of the Penis Bandits," Char-lie said with great effort, and a slur. Ho, boy. What'd Asher do to his good girl?

"Charlie Harris, are you drunk?" Evan teased.

She laughed again, and he could see now from close up that yes, she was. Didn't make her any less attractive. In fact, it made her more attractive. She wasn't holding herself in check, instead lazily leaning on the tabletop, one hand propping up her chin, her eyes glazed, while Asher took advantage of her attention and told another tale of teenage debauchery from his and Evan's "Penis Bandit" days.

Evan used the lack of attention on him to lean in and speak to Gloria. "Just Ash being Ash, babe."

She turned and blinked at him, then lifted her drink. "Tequila?"

"I'm driving. Better stick to beer." He waved to a wait-ress, ordered a Bud, and slid onto the stool next to Gloria. He faced her, keeping his side to Charlie and Ash, though neither of them seemed to notice.

Ash was animatedly telling the tale of how he'd stolen a boat from the marina, and Charlie's big eyes got bigger than usual as she listened to the completely embellished tale. He claimed there was a joyride, but Evan knew the truth—he'd never made it farther than starting the boat before he was caught, and anyway, it'd been tied to the dock, so he wouldn't have ridden anywhere except straight to juvie in the back of a cop car.

The waitress handed off the bottle and Evan paid, tipped the beer to his lips, and downed several long drinks. "Ahhhh."

"You needed that?" Glo asked, her smile faint but present.

"More than air."

"Kids. Exhausting." She said this with a wrinkled nose, but she forgot he'd seen her with Landon's and Kimber's son—his nephew—and what he'd seen shocked him to no end. Despite her grumbling openly about children, Gloria was good with Caleb, and talked in a gushy, motherly, sweet tone he hadn't known until that point she was capable of emitting.

He took another drink of his beer and leaned in. "Hear you kissed."

She snapped her head to Ash, then Evan. Then her lips curved. "What's it to you?"

He shrugged with his shoulders and mouth. "Good?"

The glance she sent Ash this time was so full of longing, it made Evan want to punch him in the throat. His friend was clueless. So clueless.

"Really good." She lifted her tequila and downed it.

"And now?" He pretended to look around the bar, hoping Ash and Charlie wouldn't notice this exchange happening a foot away from them. So far they hadn't.

"I'm waiting."

"Not like you, Glo."

She craned an eyebrow and it disappeared into her black bangs. "Right?"

"Another Mad Cow Tini," Charlie ordered.

"Ace."

She blinked at him like she forgot he was there, which he didn't like. "What?"

She'd had too much already. He could see it. And there was an empty martini glass in front of her. Had she only had one? Rather than lecture her, he asked, "What's a 'Mad Cow Tini'?"

She gestured sloppily at Asher. "Ash made it up. It's blue curaçao, pineapple juice, tequila…" She ticked off each ingredient on her fingers.

"Vodka," Ash spoke up.

"Vodka." She ticked off that, too, then pointed at Ash and confirmed, "A splash of sprite, and a maraschino cherry."

Evan frowned at his friend. "Ash—"

"I learned how to tie the stem into a knot with my tongue," Charlie interrupted to announce proudly.

His mind promptly entered the gutter. He turned toward the table to face her fully. Then his lowered brows went to Asher. Then he thought about punching him in the throat again as he envisioned a scene where Ash was in Charlie's space, teaching her how to use her tongue to tie a cherry stem in a knot.

"I taught her," Glo said, and he felt his shoulders relax at the same time he saw Asher's grin turn sinister.

"That was quite a show, brother," he told him. "You should be sorry you missed it."

Over the next two hours, Evan nursed another beer, then switched to water. Charlie, meanwhile, had one more tequila shot and two Mad Cow Tinis, which, Glo informed him by her count, was four total.

"I never puke," Charlie stammered, then hiccupped. Then laughed. "But tonight, I might."

"You won't puke," Ash said. Glo and Evan had traded seats an hour or so ago and now, Ash threw his arm over Glo's shoulder and rubbed. Glo, looking sober and like a kitten about to close its eyes and purr, leaned into Ash solidly.

Evan felt his head shake. He really needed to have a talk with his buddy. What he was putting her through was hard to watch. If he didn't like her, he shouldn't lead her on. If he did, then he should lead her right out of this bar.

Which was exactly Evan's plan for Charlie. "She better not. Not in my car."

"I'm just sleepy." Charlie hiccupped again. Then she smiled at him warmly...at least he hoped she was smiling at him. Her gaze fettered to the left and then back to him.

"You're a mess, Ace." He chuckled.

"I am?" Her face turned innocent and he could swear her concern sobered her some.

"No, baby, you're good. I'm teasing."

"Aww, you never call me baby," Asher said. The ass. "Is it because we've never—"

Glo stopped the stream of words with her fingertips when Evan had decided to make good on the mental throat-punch he'd entertained all evening. "Get her home," she said. "I'll take care of Asher."

"You bet you will, honey." Ash moved her hand and kissed her fingertips.

Evan took Charlie's hand. "Purse, Ace." His hand linked in hers, he pointed at the bag on one of the seats.

"Oh, got it." She held it to her chest and walked with him. She wasn't staggering, but she wasn't exactly walking a straight line. He dropped her hand and wound his arm around her waist instead, pulling her close enough to support her but giving her enough room to maneuver.

The ride was short, and as Ash predicted, Charlie did not puke.

"Did you lock up your house when you left, Ace?"

They entered his kitchen, the only light coming from the range, which he'd left on. Terror's tank was dark and the fish hovered in the center of the tank, his fins twitching, shockingly alive and well, as he watched from his watery home.

"Yeah, I always lock up," she said. Then she frowned. "I don't know if I can walk back. Can you drive me?"

"Drive you?"

"I know it's only two doors down but I'm so sleepy." She yawned.

"Ace, you're not sleeping alone when you're hammered."

This seemed to sober her up. Her eyes went big. "Why not?" Evidently, her brain never shut off.

"Because you'll wake up feeling like crap and I don't want you waking up alone with no one to take care of you."

"You don't?" She curled her hands around the back of one of the stools resting at the base of the island.

"No, I don't."

"But I have to brush my teeth."

"I have an extra toothbrush, Ace."

"Why?"

"*Why?*"

"Yes, Evan. *Why* do you have an extra toothbrush?"

"Because they were buy two get one free and you never know when you need a spare."

"For girls?" Something cut into her expression. Something that looked a lot like pain.

He came closer. "Yeah. Drunk girls who come home with me and ask a zillion questions."

She tilted her head back to take him in, then licked her bottom lip.

He liked her tilting her chin up to take him in.

"I liked what we did in your studio," she said.

A jolt of awareness he couldn't act on radiated from the back of his neck to his balls. Because she was drunk. Too drunk.

Too *damn* drunk.

Shit.

"Yeah, Ace, I know," he told her. Because he did know. He'd watched how much she liked it. It had been written all over her gorgeous, orgasmic face. Drunk or not, she was telling the truth about liking it.

"But we can't do it again and that makes me sad." She placed one hand on his shirt and rested her other palm on his neck, her fingers playing with the longer hair there.

Both hands on her waist, he tugged her until she pressed against him. "Why not?"

Now was not the time for a repeat performance of the other night, but when she was sober, hell. He was all over her.

"Because," she whispered, her eyes heavy.

Leaning down, he got close enough to her mouth to kiss her, but didn't. "That's not a reason, Ace."

She kissed him instead, moved her mouth on his in a series of soft, warm kisses he returned while drawing her closer and clutching her harder. He slanted her jaw and deepened their connection. She took it. He pressed his body against her curves, the liquor on her tongue tasting sweet, tangy from the cherry—

Wake up, man.

Hands on her hips, he pushed her back and tore his mouth from hers before he could talk himself out of it. They were not on the same page.

She slid her hands to his jeans, specifically, to the *stud* of his jeans, and had it undone and the zipper halfway down before he once again forced his body into action and took a step away from her.

"Oh, no you don't, gorgeous." If he didn't say it now, there'd be no saying it.

Promptly, he turned her around, pointed her to the stairs, and walked behind her as he angled her to the bedroom. Charlie, drunk and loose and accommodating, was incredibly tempting. In spite of her mouth saying things her body instantly contradicted. Or maybe not in spite of it, but *because* of it.

He wanted her. She was dead wrong in her assumption earlier. That studio thing? Definitely happening again. But he wanted her present, aware—not feeling displaced guilt over a decision she made while simmering in Mad Cow Tinis.

Without letting her try to de-pants him again, and with his pants partially open to accommodate the growing erection she was responsible for, he wrangled her to the bathroom where he gave her a fresh toothbrush. While she brushed, he fluffed the pillows—snagging one for himself for the couch downstairs—turned down the white comforter, and put a glass of water on the nightstand. Then he tucked her into his bed and went to his studio to paint and pace off his sexual frustration.

Or, as it turned out, a bit of both. Simultaneously.

CHAPTER FIFTEEN

*T*equila was the devil's drink.

Since waking up in Evan's bed, the sun peeking through a crack in the floor-length dark gray curtains, Charlie had downed a glass of water, refilled and drank another, then brushed her teeth.

And she still felt as if she had a mouth full of sand.

Bleh.

Head pounding, she crawled back under his fluffy, white comforter, hoping her throbbing head and dry mouth might distract her from how amazing his sheets smelled.

But no. The part of her brain logging every detail about the man she was harboring lusty thoughts for didn't miss the chance to soak in the fresh ocean air scent of either his fabric softener—did he use that stuff?—or his cologne, or a mix of the two.

Her brain also didn't give her a reprieve from remembering, with agonizing clarity, the way she'd attempted to seduce him last night. Drunk as a skunk, she could only imagine what a hot mess she must've looked. This morning, she'd refilled her water glass and found her eyes caked with yesterday's mascara. Then found it on the pillowcase. The *white* pillowcase.

With a groan, she pulled the other pillow over her ratty hair and wondered if she could sleep until, say, Lyon went to college. By then she might live down the embarrassment wrought by throwing herself at Evan Downey while slurring, stumbling, and slovenly drunk.

Ugh.

"Aspirin, Ace."

The muffled voice in the room grew more muffled as she crammed the pillow over her head. Suffocation. That was a good idea.

Her host thwarted her plan, tugging the pillow off her face and dropping it to the other side of the bed.

"You've been awake for a while," he stated.

The scent of coffee curled into her nostrils, luring her out from behind her hair. She swept the length of it off her face and leaned on one elbow.

Evan sat beside her. "Hey, beautiful."

She replied with an inelegant grunt of disbelief.

"Aspirin." He held up his fingers, between which were two small tablets that she swallowed with a gulp of water. Then she sat up and lifted the coffee mug to her lips. It was red with white block lettering that read: CARPE BEANAM: SEIZE THE COFFEE.

The brew was hot, and delicious, and had so much milk, it was almost more cream than coffee. Just the way she liked it. That he remembered made her heart tug. She gave herself a mental poke. After last night, he'd probably check her into Betty Ford.

"Hangover Hash."

She blinked at him, coffee mug held to her lips. "Hangover Hash?"

"Yep. My specialty," he answered with a small smile.

Oh, he looked good today. His hair was wet on the ends, from his shower, she figured. The lake was way too cold in the morning for a swim. His T-shirt was tight and white, made to look old, but was new, with faded gray lettering in a banner reading: AXLE'S: FEAR NO ROAD. The banner looped stylishly around a faded gray drawing of what she guessed was a Harley Davidson. And she further guessed, since his brother had recently purchased several motorcycle shops in Osborn, Ohio, and because she knew Evan didn't ride, this shirt was from Aiden's shop.

"I have another hangover specialty if you're interested, Ace."

The sultry heat in his words disrupted her thoughts. She dragged her attention from the shirt molded to his body to find a pair of turquoise eyes dancing in the light eking through the closed curtains.

Something in those dancing eyes told her by "specialty" he meant something sexual. And that idea started pounding away in her heart, her stomach, and then traveled lower.

She clutched her mug. "I'm okay," she said, anything but.

"Guaranteed to get your mind off your headache." The side of his lips tipped.

Her hips shifted. Definitely something sexual.

He tugged the blankets aside and ran a gaze down her

clothes—actually *his* clothes. She didn't want to know how he'd gotten her out of her cute yellow dress and into the black shirt pooling around her thighs.

He planted a fist on either side of her body, his weight depressing the bed. She held the mug of hot coffee between them and stared at him over the rim.

"Put the mug down."

"I'm okay."

"Want you trembling, barely able to speak, Ace, not 'okay.'"

Oh. Well, when he put it that way . . . wait, no. She was a hungover mess. And they had no parameters yet for their relationship. And she needed to brush her hair.

Plus her coffee would get cold.

"Put the mug down," he repeated, proving how little he cared about the temperature of her coffee.

"Shouldn't we talk about—"

Carefully, he removed the mug from her hand, put it on the nightstand, and scooted up the bed until he practically lay on top of her. She backed her head into the pillow as he lowered his face to hers.

"Kiss me."

She lifted her head an inch, smacked her puckered lips against his, and dropped her head onto the pillow again.

He righted a brow—the right one—and pulled his mouth into a look of pure dissatisfaction. "My kid's gone. The curtains are closed. We are in bed together."

Her heart knocked against her chest as he reminded her of the things she already knew. "We haven't talked."

"Nope."

"I—I need to," she stated.

His eyes went to the side in thought, then snapped back to hers. "Okay, Ace. You talk. I'll be down here."

He moved so fast, she didn't have the opportunity to brace herself, but she should have because one minute she was looking at his face inches away from hers, and the next, Evan Downey was underneath the covers, tugging the T-shirt she wore up to reveal her stomach, and darting his tongue into her belly button.

"Evan!" She palmed the top of his head over the covers and pushed, but he didn't move, continuing to run his tongue around her belly button as his fists found the edges of her panties.

No, no. This couldn't be happening.

But it was.

"Evan, come out of there." Her words drifted out on a sigh. A soft sigh, the longing so evident, they both heard what she *really* wanted. And what she wanted was for him *not* to come out of there.

His chuckle and muffled reply confirmed he, too, wanted that. "When I'm done."

"I'm serious." She scooted herself up the bed to get away. The move had the opposite of the desired effect, placing his face directly between her thighs. When he muttered the word "perfect," she felt the rumble of his voice *there*. Between her thighs. The *very spot* where he'd had her touch herself in the studio.

Oh my.

And now he was—

Oh. Oh, that's very nice.

The warm slide of his tongue played along the edge of her panties and then dipped beneath the material. His mouth was warm and wet and, again, before she knew what had happened, he'd tugged her panties away and kissed her thigh as he swept them down her legs.

Then she came to her senses.

Clamping her legs together, she trapped the cotton panties between her knees and whipped the blanket off. His messy bedhead was now messier, his lips damp, and his brows lowered.

"What are you doing?" That was supposed to be a demand, but she sounded breathy. Or, more accurately, out of breath.

"You want to watch." He shrugged briefly. "Fine by me." He tugged at her panties again.

She held her knees together. "Evan." That came out a little whiny, but she pressed on. "I need to know what you're doing."

This made him lift his head and sigh. "Charlie, if you don't know what I'm doing, your sex life has been a sad, limited experience." He grinned. "Let me enlighten you, baby."

What he'd said hadn't been far from the truth. She and Russell used to have sex she'd qualify as "good," but not earth shattering. The few boyfriends before him were okay, but nothing noteworthy. Especially since she was sixteen when she lost her virginity (stupid) and twenty-two when she dated Josh (inexperienced). Not to mention the guy after Josh who was annoying and moronic and she refused to even think his name. With her limited experience, she'd thought Russell and she had found their rhythm. The way a couple builds habits and learns to maneuver around one another. They'd discovered a way to satisfy one another that, yes, was basically a trade of services, but fulfilled a need. What they each needed. Sexually. But getting Russell to do what Evan was eagerly offering... Well, that was always something she had to barter for with quite a bit of... um... artillery.

"I'm not ready," she whispered. "To do that to you."

She winced, hating to admit that she wasn't, but she wasn't. She'd lusted after Evan, yes, and had enjoyed his company in the studio without reciprocation, which in her mind meant one thing. This time, he'd expect her to reciprocate.

And in no way was she ready to just... just... *dive in* like he was.

He released her panties and climbed her body, his face scrunching. *Angry.*

She recognized that face. Russell used to have that face when she refused to go down on him after he'd, as he called it, "rewarded her" with fellatio. *One for one, Charlotte. I did you. You do me. You love me, I love you. See how this works?*

"I'm sorry, Evan. I think we should talk about—"

"Who said anything about me?"

She focused on his face, which was, indeed, angry.

"Sorry?"

"You think I'm going down on you to get you to return the favor?"

She did think that. That was the way these things worked. Right? Sensing this was not the correct answer, she said, "No. Uh, I um... I realize it'd be wrong of me not to do it to you after you took the time to—"

She stopped talking to gasp, and the reason she gasped was because he'd taken advantage of her distraction and ripped her underpants off her legs and dropped them to the floor.

He slid his hand up her calf, over her knee, and stroked the inside of her thigh. "Is that what you think?"

She answered with an expelled breath.

Keeping his eyes on hers, he swirled his fingers higher. "You think you have to do whatever I do to you? Is that how Russell worked things, Ace?"

She felt her cheeks heat from embarrassment. Her hips lifted involuntarily toward his attentive fingers tracing the sensitive skin on her inner thighs.

"Answer me." This command was paired with his fingertips touching her intimately.

"We . . . um, I don't know," she hedged.

"Ace." He dipped a finger inside her, then out.

She shuddered. "I—Evan, please."

He brought his face close to hers, his fingers continuing their delicious strokes. "Charlie, answer me. *Now.*"

When he pulled his fingers away, she blew out the answer on three hectic, short breaths. "Yes. We . . . traded. Stuff."

"You traded stuff," he repeated, his hand going still between her legs, his face severe. "He never did something to you without expecting something in return?"

"Um . . ."

Had he? She thought back to the years they'd spent together. The things they'd done together. Russell had always been one-for-one. He set dollar limits on gifts so they spent the same amount. He insisted on picking the next movie if she'd picked the last. He would slide the black book at the restaurant to her across the table and say, *I paid last time, Charlotte. Remember?*

And yes, in bed, if he offered a sexual favor, it was presented as a trade-off for what she'd do for him afterward.

Evan's angry face softened and his eyes roamed her face for a solid minute—or maybe a month—looking for what, she had no idea. He seemed to find it, placed a gentle kiss on her lips, and muttered just as gently, "Hang on, baby."

She blinked at his unexpected words. "What?"

His smile tipped in the charming, crooked way she loved. He bent his head and said to her T-shirt. "My hair. Hang on."

She put a hand in his hair and he lifted his face and kissed her again. Against her lips, he said, "Tight. Tug when I do something you like."

Without waiting for her response, he pulled the blanket over his head and dove between her legs. Charlie hung on as instructed.

And she tugged a lot.

* * *

Evan's "guaranteed to make you feel better" Hangover Hash was good. Not as good as what preceded it, but good all the same. They shared breakfast and he did the dishes, insisting she sit and sip another cup of coffee.

She let him do the chore where normally she'd have butted him out of the way. But she was too relaxed and stuffed full of seared red potatoes, perfectly over-easy eggs, and sharp cheddar cheese.

A contented sigh left her lips.

"Glad to hear that." He dried the last plate and put it into the cabinet.

"I'm sorry I didn't help."

The tiny frown denting his brow was offset by the smirk on his lips. "Ace."

"What?"

"Gonna have to think of a consequence for you, you keep using that word with me."

She tried to think what she'd said. "What word?"

"*Sorry.*"

"Most people think it's polite to apologize," she argued, her throat clogging as he strutted over.

He tossed the dishtowel over one shoulder and leaned in close. "I'm not most people." Pushing her hair away from her face, he kissed her tenderly. "Don't want you to be sorry."

When he pulled away, she turned her eyes up to his. "What if I do something horrible?"

"Not possible."

"What if I...um...tell you your latest painting is awful?"

He blew a short laugh from his nose. "Grateful you were honest."

"What if I told you I didn't like your Hangover Hash?"

"You'd be lying. Bet the neighbors heard you moaning from across the beach."

Her face grew warm as she thought of the other kind of moaning she'd done this morning. He noticed. And pointed it out.

Brushing his knuckles along her cheeks, he said, "Never forget that sound, Ace. Stained my brain in the best way possible." Not the gentlemanly type, he also pointed out, "Your face is red. Don't want that, either."

She palmed her cheeks with her hands to cool them, which didn't help because her hands were warm from the hot coffee mug.

He took hold of her wrists and hooked them around his neck, turned her on her chair, and positioned himself between her parted legs. Her fingers were in his hair and her thighs were clamping his, and her heart was racing against his torso.

Tipping her jaw with his thumbs, he brushed her lips with his before the long, slow slide of his tongue entered her mouth. She melted into him, tasting coffee, tasting *him*, and never wanting the kiss to end. How long had she wanted to kiss Evan Downey? How jealous had she been the night she watched his son and he came home from a date with a girl who didn't deserve him?

Not that Charlie deserved him. But this was a fantasy.

A fantasy...

That ended too soon.

He finished her off with a few soft, damp presses of his lips. "Get a shower and get dressed. We're leaving for the Starving Artists Festival in an hour."

Her eyes went to the wall clock though she didn't register the time. "Do you and Asher have something today?"

"Yeah."

"I can...I mean, you can go without me."

He pegged her with a look she interpreted as one part confusion, one part unhappiness.

"No, Ace, we're hanging out this week."

" 'Hanging out'?"

He turned toward her again. "Yeah."

What did that mean? "I have to work this week."

"We'll hang out when you're not working." He crossed the kitchen and started down the hallway. "I have to get a few things together for the festival. You have an hour."

CHAPTER SIXTEEN

$\mathcal{A}$ slightly cool breeze blew in gray clouds that looked like they might bring rain. Luckily for Evan, he and Asher were under a tent, and the library had provided them with plastic bags so the kids wouldn't have to subject their freshly signed copy of *The Adventures of Mad Cow* to the elements.

Asher was uncharacteristically quiet today. Evan thought at first he was hungover. After the signing wrapped and Mrs. Anderson's two teenage lackeys were breaking down the tables, he asked him what was up.

"Nothing," Ash grunted. He reached for a cigarette and lit it, pulling in a drag and sifting his gaze across the crowd. Evan watched, and because he'd been watching, he noted the very second Ash's mouth went flat and his eyes went hard. He followed his buddy's gaze across the park where Mrs. Anderson stood talking to Gloria.

He'd bet a million dollars it wasn't the elderly librarian who'd caused Asher's scowl.

"Shit, man," Evan said.

"Shut up."

"What happened?"

He crushed his cigarette under his boot heel and then picked up the butt and dropped it into a not-nearby trash can. Evan waited, arms crossed, but Ash didn't come back. Instead, he walked across the festival and straight toward Salty Dog.

Looked like today, beer-thirty started at two p.m.

* * *

Evan had had about as much time with his friends as he could stand.

When Gloria showed up at Salty Dog, it was obvious she'd come with a chip on her shoulder. Charlie sat next to him and they each sipped their drinks while watching Ash and Glo passive-aggressively snipe at each other.

When they parted, it was awkward, not that those two noticed. Asher was ignoring Gloria, spinning his glass in one hand, and Gloria was examining her nails.

"Well," Charlie said from the passenger seat of Evan's SUV now. "That was fun."

"Whatever you say, Ace."

"Sarcasm," she pointed out.

He pulled into his driveway and she hopped out of the car and took off down the edge of the street for her house.

"Where're you going?"

"Home." She walked backward toward her house. Away from him.

Dammit. This hadn't been the plan.

He started after her, ready to toss her over his shoulder and take her into the house. Then he'd command her to take off her clothes and show her what she'd nearly missed out on with this duck-and-run maneuver.

"Come over in twenty minutes?" she called to him.

He stopped advancing and studied her grainy figure in the dark, unsure he'd heard her correctly. "Yeah?"

She nodded. "Yeah."

The word was quiet, but affirmative. He'd take it. He turned on his heel and walked to the house. Before she got too far to hear him, he called out, "Fifteen!"

In *ten* minutes he showed, unsure what to expect, but with a condom or three in his pocket.

Hopeful? Yeah. *Hell, yeah.*

At her sliding door, she was sitting at the desk, lamp lit, robe on, clicking something on her computer. Her face glowed in the soft light emitting from the screen. Instead of knocking, he lowered his arm and watched her.

Watched her delicate fingers work the mouse, the way she licked her bottom lip and dragged her teeth over it as her hazel eyes tracked the screen. His chest tightened, in a different way than usual. Sure, he noticed her physical attributes each and every time he saw her. But this...

This was new.

This was *want* in a different way. Want that combined their old relationship with the new. He wanted to be her friend. To sit on the couch with her and watch a show like when she came to stay with him and Lyon in the past. To laugh over a card or board game like when she and her jagoff ex used to come and visit when Rae was alive. To hold her hand and walk with her down the shoreline. And make love to her. Not please her until she didn't feel badly about him touching her, but have her willing and ready and wanting him back. Calling his name on a high cry with him inside her.

That's what he wanted.

He hadn't been sure how to get it, so he'd been trying what he thought might work. But tonight...if she invited him over to talk, he'd be back at square one. Maybe the best tactic was to be her friend until she came around.

Then she lifted her chin and met his eyes, and he felt the impish smile curl his lips.

Nah, screw that. He was seducing her.

She swished to the door in her flowery robe, pulling the belt tight. There were no other lights on anywhere in the house, only the glow of the computer screen.

"Hi," she said as he stepped inside.

"Hi." He looked around. No lit candles. No soft music. No sign she'd invited him over for anything other than hanging out. He lifted the belt on her robe and dropped it. "You look ready for bed."

Her eyes slid to half-mast, her lashes sweeping low over her cheeks, then up as she flashed him with—God help him—bedroom eyes. "I am." The most sultry, sexy smile twitched her lips as she tugged the belt, opened the robe, and let it puddle at her bare feet.

He nearly dropped to his knees in praise of what lay before him.

Black lace. A lot of it. Her bra was the tiniest bits of fabric cupping the bottom half of each of her breasts— the top half bursting from the cups as if on display. Her panties were not like panties at all, but a tiny triangle hiding...not much of anything. True, he'd seen every inch of Charlie naked, but this...this was different.

Because she was ready.

He came to her in two steps, tipped her jaw with both hands, and kissed her hard.

* * *

It was happening.

She was doing it.

Finally taking what she wanted.

What she wanted... was Evan.

Charlie knew this in her bones, in her heart, in her head. She was ready and the reason she was ready was in thanks to the lesson taught to her tonight. Taught by the most unlikely person to give one.

Asher Knight: *A cautionary tale.*

Tension had run high at Salty Dog. Asher had some sort of minor self-destruction when Gloria went to the ladies' room and Evan went to pay the check.

Ash had angled his head to Charlie and rolled his eyes. "She's pissed at me."

She was sure of this, but to be polite asked, "How can you tell?"

"I can tell."

"What happened?"

"You don't wanna know."

"I do."

Asher had watched her for a second before opening his mouth. "She's not a girl you sleep with one time, Ace."

She'd raised her eyebrows in surprise at that comment. First, because Ash never called her "Ace," and second, because she wondered if he meant he didn't want to sleep with Gloria only once, or if he meant he had slept with her and wanted to sleep with her again. Seemed rude to ask, so she hadn't.

"You're not, either," he pointed out.

Torn between offended and flattered, she'd bitten her lip.

"You're a keeper," Ash continued. "Evan'll want to keep you. He'll fight to keep you." He jerked a thumb in the direction of the bar. "He'll pay the tab."

"You paid Glo's tab."

"Evan will be paying your tab for a long time, sweetheart. I know him."

"I'm not … we're not …"

She hadn't been able to finish her sentence truthfully. She *was* and they *had*. Maybe not "all the way" but they'd done plenty together that crossed the invisible, but very real, line between friends to lovers.

"I'm not good at it like Evan is."

She'd bitten the other side of her lip, unsure what "it" was until Asher spoke again.

"The keeping part. The fighting for someone part." He'd pulled the cigarette out from behind his ear and gestured to his tattered jeans and tight black T-shirt. "Not a catch, Charlie." With the cigarette between his lips, he muttered, "A mess," then lit it and dragged in a breath.

"You're not a mess," she'd said, though he kind of was. But he wasn't an unsalvageable mess like he'd suggested. "Just because you've never succeeded at keeping someone before doesn't mean you can't."

His voice gravelly, he asked, "What about you, Charlie? You embracing this thing between you and Ev?"

"I didn't … I wasn't talking about me."

"You sure as hell were." She shook her head again but he leaned close. "You're scared as shitless as I am. Don't pretend different." His voice had dropped low, then lower, as Gloria strode up behind him and took her seat.

His mouth widened into a false grin. "You look dead sexy tonight, Charlie."

She'd blinked at Glo, who shot Ash a glare. Charlie thought for a second the other woman would stand and leave. Instead, she hooked her purse over the chair and snapped her fingers for the waitress. "Two shots of Jack," she ordered, then grabbed the young girl's arm before she left and corrected, "Hell, just bring us the whole bottle."

Charlie's eyes had gone to the glass of wine she hadn't finished. Evan's beer bottle was half full.

"Drinking to forget, sweetheart?" Ash had prodded Gloria.

"Yeah," she'd answered. The waitress arrived with a bottle and two glasses. Glo poured the shots and slid one to Asher. "And so are you."

Charlie considered the scene the entire ride home, finally admitting to herself that while it wasn't fun, it sure was educational.

She wasn't a mess like Asher, and she wasn't as stubborn as Gloria. And she refused to advance blindly, ignoring signs that clearly read: BRIDGE OUT.

Although with Evan, it was more of a YIELD sign. But Charlie would no longer hold up the STOP.

So when she'd invited him over, she'd done so with a clear, sober head, and a willing spirit.

Now that his hands were sliding along her waist and pulling her close, his tongue diving into her mouth, she was a million percent sure she'd chosen *wisely*.

He tasted like toothpaste, and she liked that he'd cleaned up to come over here, that he'd anticipated seeing her, kissing her. Though from the look on his face when she stripped, he hadn't anticipated seeing her in the skimpiest undies she owned.

She'd found the lingerie stuffed into the back of her sock drawer, purchased long ago and since forgotten. Shoved aside for sturdy, but pretty, cotton—the most practical choice for a woman not currently having *sexy-times* with anyone.

"Ace," he muttered almost reverently against her neck. He swept her hair off her shoulder and kissed it, giving her a full-body shudder. "You steal my breath away."

Another kiss. More shuddering.

The warmth of his palms slid the chill aside. The only sounds his firm, suctioning lips as they moved over her skin, and her own erratic heartbeat. She swallowed thickly, nervous for reasons she didn't quite understand. He had seen her naked before. *More* naked than she was now.

When he pulled his head up to look at her, a few strands of her hair stuck to the stubble surrounding his lips. He tugged them away. Those lips grinned. A salacious, sexy grin revealing his dark intent as clearly as if he'd said it.

Then he did.

"This time, Ace, you come with me inside you."

She gulped.

He pulled her close, brushed the tip of her nose with his. "Foreplay later, yeah?"

Oh yeah. She nodded.

"Say it," he whispered.

"Foreplay later."

"The other part," he demanded.

Gathering every ounce of courage she had, she whispered, "I'll come with you inside me."

That must have been what he wanted to hear. He lit her up with another deep kiss, slanting his mouth and digging his hand into her hair. At the same time, his other hand traveled to the small of her back, moved to her ass, and squeezed.

"You're ridiculously sexy." He tongued her neck.

So was he. She clung to him, afraid she might lose it before they got to the bedroom. Her breathing had become so quick and hectic, she worried she might have to employ a paper bag soon. She hoped she could relax enough to enjoy herself—that he enjoyed himself.

Oh no.

What if he *didn't* enjoy himself?

New worries shut her body down like a nuclear power plant on high alert. Sirens blared in her head. The low buzz that had fanned through her limbs began to ebb.

Evan sensed this. His head came up. "Ace?"

"Um..."

Come on, pull it together!

"Charlie?"

"I need a drink," she whispered, pushing his shoulders away.

He tightened his hold on her waist.

"No, Ace," he stated firmly.

Too late. The panic was already creeping in. The worry over her performance...or lack of *good* performance, taking over her thoughts.

"Just a little something..." She continued pushing against him. "Wine. A shot of rum..."

"No."

Russell hadn't always been satisfied after. Sometimes he hadn't been able to keep it up during. If losing interest in the middle of sex wasn't a testament to how poorly she performed in bed, she didn't know what was.

Granted, Evan wasn't Russell, but—

"Ace, dammit, look at me."

She did. A muscle in his jaw flickered, at the same time his turquoise eyes went soft. Soft and warm and accommodating.

"Want you sober as a nun." A whisper, followed by a gentle kiss. "Hands in my hair, gorgeous."

She pointed toward the cabinet that held at least one bottle of wine. Blessed wine.

"Don't want anything between us."

"No?" she asked quietly. But was that really possible considering there was at least one unspoken entity between them?

He hugged his arms around her. "Hands in my hair."

She did as he said, winding her fingers into his thick, dark strands.

"Hold on."

She held on.

"Now, kiss me."

She closed in on him, stiffly. She had to forcibly loosen her limbs to lift to her tiptoes and do as he requested. When she placed her lips on his, she waited for him to take over. He didn't. So she kissed him lightly again. He held her to him and kissed her back, but only returned the same amount of pressure she gave.

She waited, her lips over his.

He waited, too. Waited for her to take control.

She went for it. Sliding her tongue along his bottom lip, she gripped his head and closed her mouth over his. He opened for her and she dipped into his mouth, savoring the taste of him, and liking how he held back enough to give her free rein.

When she deepened the kiss, his hold on her body tightened. His hands went to her bra, unhooked it. She briefly took her hands from his hair to allow him to drop it to the ground, but returned her fingers instantly to the silky strands giving her purchase where she had none.

She was afloat. Bobbing in the low tide of her imagination, the place where the sandbar dropped off between fantasy and reality. His thumbs went to her nipples and brushed them until they pebbled, then one of his hands dipped past the flimsy lace barrier of her panties and into her wetness.

A low groan of approval sounded in his throat. The next sound that left her lips was a returning groan of her own.

Eyes and hands still on her body, he wheeled her backward into her office, past the desk and the bookshelves littered with photography books and various papers, and to the couch against the wall.

"My bedroom's—" she started to say.

"Too far," he finished, coming down on top of her on the couch. Fusing their mouths, he tasted her, sending her brain into the clouds. Somehow through the veil of lust shrouding her, she registered the scratch of the lace as her panties slid down her legs, the cool press of his fingers at her center.

He dropped his forehead on hers. "Ace, my God, you're fucking killing me."

Though her eyes widened with shock at his words, she secretly loved that he'd said that. Or maybe she loved how he slipped along her folds while he'd said that. Her eyes fluttered shut.

"Pants, Ace."

It took a second to reroute her thoughts.

"Unbutton my pants," he reiterated.

Crap! She was already screwing this up. Ignoring the burn of embarrassment in her face, she unbuttoned and unzipped his jeans. He left her briefly to discard them and pull off his shirt.

She tried not to read too much meaning into the tats, tried not to remember his entire family had been permanently inked into his body. Tried to ignore the feeling of disloyalty, like she was being silently watched and/or judged. Instead, she focused on the arm with the evergreen trees. Let her eyes wander up his arm and over his muscular chest, before skimming down his firm abdomen. She followed the line of her eyes with her fingers, savoring the feel of his hot skin while his fingers danced over her body: plucking a nipple, dipping into her well of desire, coating her brain in lust-addled confusion.

When she reached his black briefs, tenting impressively, she cupped his length in her hand and stroked. He filled her palm, and her mind flashed a pleasant vision of him filling her elsewhere.

But... she hadn't planned on doing this on the couch.

She stopped stroking him to deliver the bad news. "Condoms are in my bedroom."

His sly smile clicked into place. He put his hand on hers and encouraged her to stroke him some more, which she did. Happily.

"I have condoms."

He came down over her, kissing her mouth hard as his cock grew harder against her. By then, all rational thought had leaked out her ears, and by the time he stood to pull the condom from his jeans, strip his briefs off, and roll the protection on, she was damn near panting.

Evan half-naked was worthy of a photograph.

Evan all-the-way-naked was worth casting in bronze.

He laid over her, his body covering her cooling skin. When she thought he would have nudged her entrance, he paused, the length of him resting against her thigh instead.

"Ace."

"What?" she asked, alarmed. What had she done wrong?

He grinned. "You want this?"

"Yes," she breathed. No hesitation.

His grin widened.

"You want me?"

"I want you."

"Say it."

"I want you."

"Say my name."

She met his eyes, unerring in their quest to see right through to her soul. "Evan." The tip of his cock entered her. On a breath, she said, "I want you," then gasped when he slid inside. What was most definitely a moan pulled from her lips like taffy. Long and loose, and oh-so-sweet.

"Almost there, sweetheart. You okay?" he asked with what sounded like painstaking effort.

Wait.

Almost?

"There's more?" she breathed.

He chuckled and she learned a second later there was, indeed, more. She accepted every inch, wrapping her legs around his back and tilting her hips to meet him. He eased into her the rest of the way as she clung to his solid back with both hands.

"Charlie." Her whispered name against her lips filled her heart as much as he'd filled her body. "Okay, baby?"

"Yes." She closed her eyes as he came to her, chest to chest, hips to hips. "I'm *so* good."

He began moving, his strokes long and slow. Her desire built with each thrust, her body winding tighter and tighter.

Unbelievably tighter.

She said his name on a sigh and held on.

"Have you ever come like this, Ace?" he panted, sliding into her again.

"I...I don't think so."

"Open your eyes."

She did, seeing the unmistakably cocksure tilt gracing his lips. He lowered onto an elbow, sifted his fingers into her hair, and anchored his other palm onto the arm of the couch. "Hang on, sweetheart. 'Cause you're about to."

She didn't have to be told twice. Feeding her fingers into his hair, she hung on as he ratcheted his speed up, up, up, until the friction and sweat from their bodies had her eyes shutting in ecstasy.

Every long, wet pound hit her deep in her core. This was going to be a big one, she could tell.

Harder and faster, he slammed into her while she squirmed beneath him, her voice strained and tight as she made a series of nonsensical sounds.

"That's it, Ace," he said between expelled breaths. "Let go, baby."

She obeyed, exploding on a cry of release, her hands clawing at his scalp as he continued thrusting—mercilessly, and without pausing to give her a prayer of recovering. Her orgasm stretched out on waves, coming at her until her shouts had waned to nothing more than exhausted, muffled mewls.

Sweat tracked down her temple, her body damp with it, and he continued moving. Finally, he claimed his own release on a long, low breath. He dropped down on top of her and blew out an *Uhhh*, followed by a wheezy laugh.

A laugh? Oh, no.

She felt her entire body grow rigid as she snapped out of whatever post-coital bliss she'd been about to slip into. Taking her hands from his hair, she tried to pull them to her body but he let her do no such thing.

He was in the way. Inside her, pinning her down with his weight. There was no way to curl away from him. To curl into herself.

"Enjoy it. Stop fussing."

She ignored him and fussed.

He frowned. "What's wrong?"

Since she figured this discussion would continue until she told him anyway, she told him. "You laughed. Was it...not okay for you?"

The frown eased into a look of satisfaction, his eyebrows returning to their neutral, unconcerned homes. "Charlie," he said gently. Too gently.

Oh no.

"It's okay if it wasn't...okay...for you." *Ugh*. There was no easy way to say this. She'd just have to say it. "If you want me to do something differently next time, I want to know so I can please you."

"Ace."

"For however long this lasts."

"*Ace.*"

The firmness in his voice made her clamp her lips together and listen.

"I swear to you, I'm going to find Russell and put one

dent in his fancy-ass car for every wrong thing he said to you to make you this insecure."

She winced. Not for worry over Russell's stupid Escalade, but because she didn't like Evan seeing her insecurity so clearly.

"I'm sweating," he said. "Out of breath. Damn near cracked a tooth trying to hold on 'til you stopped coming."

She blinked at him.

With a kiss to her lips, and a forward thrust that had him pushing deep inside her again, he kept talking. "Wanna know what it feels like to be embedded deep inside you, Ace?"

The breath leaving her lips stuttered out, uneven.

"It's hot." He licked her ear and nipped.

She squirmed.

Another thrust. "It's wet."

Her arms loosened, one hand returning lazily to his hair.

"You pumping around me, clamping down over and over and over. So tight, had to concentrate to hold off."

She curled her fingers into his hair. "But you did."

"Yeah, Ace. I did," he whispered.

He kissed her for a long time, before pulling out of her body. When he did, he stood, held out a hand, and tugged her down the hallway.

In the bathroom, he disposed of the condom and turned on the shower. Sticking a hand through the gap in the curtain, he tested the water temperature while watching her. She'd leaned against the sink, naked as the day was long, trying really, *really* hard not to cover herself.

He grinned.

"What?" She wasn't the least bit miffed but pretended to be.

"You said 'next time.'"

She felt her cheeks go warm.

"Gotta tell you, glad there's going to be a next time."

Her cheeks went warmer. She was glad, too. Especially now that she knew she'd pleased him.

He shook his head gently.

"What now?" she asked with a smile of her own.

"Gonna show you."

She had to incline her head to look at his face, since she'd been taking a long gander at his nude body. "Show me what?"

Wolfish was the only way to describe his expression.

"Everything you let me. *Repeatedly*. Until you know, without a doubt, how amazing you are."

Before she could recover from that coherent and completely flustering statement, he took her hand, kissed her palm, and shoved them both under the spray. After they made out for many luxurious minutes under the hot water, he pressed his body to hers.

"Spread your legs."

"Evan. You don't have to—"

"Ace. Legs," he said, not willing to hear her argument. In fact, he was already lowering himself to the tub floor. "Want to taste you."

And here, in the alternate realm of her reality, she leaned back against the shower wall and watched the man of her fantasies work to prove to her she was amazing.

Funny thing was, she'd started to believe him.

CHAPTER SEVENTEEN

*C*harlie woke in the morning to the smoky smell of bacon. The alarm clock then informed her it was not morning. It wasn't even *late* morning.

"Twelve oh-five?" She bolted up, muscles she hadn't used in too long sore. She'd slept in nothing, apparently. Nothing but her lotion-covered skin. Evan had insisted on applying it after her shower and she'd insisted he didn't have to.

He listened as well as he had earlier. Not at all.

He'd guided her into her too-small bedroom and too-small bed and tossed her down onto it. "Lotion, Ace."

"Too tired."

"Lotion."

Bossy. Too tired to argue, she pointed to the coconut-vanilla fragrance she'd chosen for summer sitting on her dresser. He picked it up, shook it, and put a knee on the bed, dipping the mattress significantly under his weight.

It'd been a long time since a man significantly dipped the mattress with his weight. She decided she liked it. And liked that it was Evan, who had a healthy amount of lotion on his hand, tossed the bottle aside, and rubbed his palms together.

Seeing him naked wasn't a sight she had yet gotten used to—maybe never would get used to. All that still-damp, tousled dark hair, thick, dark brows, the fan of thicker, darker eyelashes. And then there was his chest, the hair curling over his pecs, swirling around his belly button, and tapering off in a trail into his shorts. Only now, there were no shorts. It tapered into the length of his semi-hard penis, and that, she decided, was a beautiful, beautiful sight.

Warmed, slick lotion hit her thigh as he worked it into her muscles, half-massaging, half-copping a feel before running both hands down the length of her leg. She closed her eyes, moaning long and low and enjoying lying in bed, her body warm, his rough, talented hands sliding over her skin.

Yes. She could get used to this.

After an epic foot massage, he put a hand on the bed, leaned over her, and grabbed the bottle of lotion. While there, he turned his head to suckle her nipple for a few hot seconds before returning his attention to her other thigh.

Air cooled her damp flesh, her hips lifting involuntarily as her fists tightened around the sheets.

"Be patient." He rubbed his hands to warm the lotion and started on her other thigh. "You'll get more." The devilish smile quirking his lips could cause an orgasm on its own.

"Who said I want more?" she dared.

His smile dropped. "That a challenge?"

Yes, please.

"Yeah."

Tossing the bottle aside, he'd positioned himself over top of her and brushed her belly with his erection. He lowered his mouth and tongued her breast, encircling the nipple until it hardened. She began squirming all over again.

"You want more," he stated.

He was right.

Rather than say he was right, she whispered, "Ev."

He'd hesitated over her other nipple, his warm breath cascading over her skin.

That's when she realized what she'd said. She'd never called him "Ev" before. And the reason she'd never called him that before was because *Ev* was Rae's nickname for him.

Sacred ground.

His mouth returned to her nipple where he took his time laving her. When her eyes had closed, and her hips had canted, and her mind had erased, he let her go with a soft *pop* and said, "Like that."

She liked it very much, so she answered, "Yes."

He moved to her lips. She opened her eyes as he kissed her and then he spoke against them. "Like when you call me Ev."

She blinked at him, taking in all of him—the bright, heated blue eyes, sexy bedhead, strong, inked arms, and thick, muscled chest. "You do?"

Nose nuzzling hers, he said simply, "Yeah."

And maybe it was simple. Maybe she'd been complicating everything.

"Want more?"

She nodded.

"What do you say?"

"Um...please?"

He kissed her bottom lip and spoke in a low, rumbling, sensual voice that chilled her overheated body. "Please what?"

"Please, Ev," she whispered. This earned her another kiss, a longer, wetter, deeper one than before. He followed his tongue down her neck and to her breasts again, a rippling orgasm building between her legs despite the fact he hadn't touched her there.

"Ev," she panted again. "Now, please. *Now.*"

He didn't leave her breasts right away, settling in to torture her in the sweetest way possible for several minutes. Then when she'd nearly torn his hair out by the root, brought the walls down with her loud wails, he left her, rolled on a condom, and came back to her.

When his lips closed over her breast, and she'd tipped her chin back to moan, he entered her. No warning, no nudge, just one long, deep slide until he was encased to the hilt.

Her hands returned to his hair, where she held tight while he continued torturing her with his talented mouth and drove into her slowly, ever-so-slowly, until she was writhing, shaking, and practically crying from her powerful release.

She'd collapsed with a happy, exhausted smile on her face, her muscles thoroughly worn out. Evan continued applying lotion to every inch of her skin he'd missed— paying way too much attention to her breasts, not that she complained—and tucked himself into bed behind her, his arm locked around her waist.

Shortly thereafter, with his front warming her back, she'd conked out.

And slept until midday.

"Crap!" She hustled to the bathroom, brushing her hair and teeth simultaneously. There was an appointment on her calendar for today, she was sure of it. What was it? She needed to get to her phone but wasn't willing to go past the kitchen—where he was cooking—and retrieve her cell from the desk until she looked halfway presentable.

Five minutes later, satisfied she'd achieved at least halfway, she slowed her rushed pace and attempted to amble into her living room. She shot a glance over at the stove, a prepared casual "good morning" on the tip of her tongue.

The words wouldn't leave her mouth.

Evan stood at the stove, nothing but a pair of black boxer briefs cupping his fabulous ass. Bare feet, bare calves, bare thighs. Naked back and shoulders. She studied the hand braced on the countertop, followed the evergreen tattoos up his arm to the shoulder featuring the regal profile of a lion, and up to his hair she doubted he'd bothered to brush.

Every inch of him so delightful to look at, she stared, phone forgotten, calendar forgotten . . .

"Ouch! Dammit!" He jumped away from the burner and flipped the stovetop off, turning to swipe at his stomach with a dishtowel. When he saw her watching, his lips kicked into a wry grin.

"Never fry bacon naked," he said.

"Oh, I don't know. It makes for a fun show."

Tossing her blue-and-white-checkered dishtowel over his shoulder, he pulled her to him, delivering a very long, very slow, very deep good-morning kiss.

It ended too soon.

Eyes closed, she murmured, "Hmm."

"Hmm?" he asked.

She looked up at him. "I have to work today."

"Hmm." He frowned, then winked. "BLT?"

"Coffee."

"And BLT," he answered, moving away from her to plate her breakfast.

Unapologetically, she watched his butt as he moved around her kitchen, getting the coffee on, putting bread in the toaster. She tried not to admire how at home he looked there, or how much she liked him taking up a portion of her space.

She turned away and unplugged her charging phone to check her calendar.

Phew.

The only "appointment" she had today was to touch up the Johnson reunion photos and e-mail them to Tami. It would take all day, but at least she didn't have to physically go anywhere.

He delivered her breakfast to her desk five minutes later while munching on a piece of bacon. "What'cha got?"

She looked up from her phone, having begun scrolling through e-mails. "A day full of Photoshop." She wrinkled her nose.

He gestured to himself. "Swine Flew sketches."

"Can you draw in the daylight?" she teased.

He angled his head. "You continue to keep me up all night, Ace, I'm going to have to make it work."

Flattered, she smiled and put a palm to her reddening cheek.

A thought about how this situation would *so* not work once Lyon was back home infiltrated her mind, but she hid from it. When she'd come home last night and changed into her lingerie, she'd made a promise to herself to have some fun. To be brave. This thing between her and Evan may only last until Lyon came home, and after, only exist in sneaky rendezvous when Lyon was at school, but she was willing to do a bit of circumventing to get what she wanted.

But when she glanced over and caught the flash of the sparrow etched onto Evan's inner forearm, she thought of Rae. Rae, maybe only in memory if not in spirit. She was always with them. *Always.* Charlie imagined he'd compartmentalized Rae for the time being. She could do that, too. Forget her guilt for a few days. It'd be worth it.

Evan was worth it.

If they never became more than what happened on the couch and in the shower and on her bed, she knew she'd never regret spending this time with him. Memories to keep for a lifetime, no matter what happened after. She wouldn't let it come between them—ruin their friendship, or her relationship with Lyon.

She *couldn't.*

Simple as that.

Evan and Lyon were as good as family. Charlie wasn't willing to lose them. Not ever.

Disconnecting her heart from her body was the only way to pull this off. Evan didn't need to know he was fulfilling a dozen different fantasies for her. If he could compartmentalize, so could she.

A cup of coffee appeared by her sandwich.

"Get to work," he said, then vanished down her hallway.

* * *

Charlie rubbed her eyes and blinked at the screen. Her back hurt, her head hurt, her neck hurt. She had no idea how many hours had passed, but the sun was bright in the sky, telling her there were plenty more hours in the day. And she still wasn't done. She stood and stretched, tilting her head left then right, and noticed someone coming her way.

Evan cut across the sandy grass to her house, sunglasses over his eyes, hair blowing in the wind, and a very large pad of paper and a black bag she'd bet held an array of artist's instruments inside. Seeing him perked her up, made her heart flutter. In a very *not* temporary way.

A flutter of love, the real kind. Not the lusty kind, though it was there, too. The I've-known-you-for-years-and-respect-and-adore-you kind of flutter. It was a flutter that, if she allowed it, could transform into a flap with big, sweeping wings. The kind of flutter she'd seen in brides at the weddings she'd shot, or on occasion while in town and walking behind a hand-holding couple on a date.

It was the kind of flutter she had to keep in check. Or else she could lose everything.

He let himself in. He'd been whistling and he segued into a wolf-whistle when he saw her. She rolled her eyes, but playfully. He flattered her constantly.

There went the flutter again.

"Thought you were stuck inside all day," he said as she stood. "Why the dress?"

She ran a hand down the huge red flower on one side of her short, white dress. The brushstroke-style poppy's petals blanketed both the front and back of the dress, its black center at her hip, where she rested a hand. "I have to get dressed or I can't work properly."

His eyes tracked down to her sandals and up her body again in an appreciative sweep. "That theory needs testing."

He dropped his pad of paper and bag onto her couch.

"What are you doing?"

"Working with you."

She studied her tiny office-slash-rec-room. "Wouldn't you have more space in your studio?"

"Yeah." He ambled over and clutched her hips. "But my studio doesn't have you."

Her next breath came out shallow. "Won't it be hard to concentrate?"

She didn't know if she could concentrate with him here. She couldn't concentrate now. Wrapping his arms around her waist, he leaned down and kissed her, and when the kiss was over she knew for sure. She definitely couldn't concentrate with him here.

"I have a deadline."

He shifted his glance left, then right, then back to her. "Me too."

She gave him a patient smile.

He returned it. "You'll never know I'm here," he lied.

* * *

On the large pad of paper resting on his knees, Evan sketched various poses for Mad Cow and Swine Flew's adventures. Swine's character attributes were solid. Now to set Asher's words to pictures.

Evan took a look at the eight drafts he'd drawn, satis-fied at least two of them would become large paintings ultimately used in the book, and became aware of the soft clicking of the mouse across the room.

Charlie sat forward, her posture abysmal—back curved, neck jutted forward like a chicken—and stared, no, *squinted*, at the screen.

"Need glasses, Ace?"

She jerked as if his voice had surprised her. It may have. They'd been working without a word for a while.

"Sorry?"

He gave her a slight headshake. One day, he swore on everything he loved dearly, Charlotte Harris would stop apologizing for her actions. Instead of engaging her in conversation, he set aside the pad and strolled over to her. She sat straighter, big eyes growing bigger as she tilted her head to look up at him. His girl. So damn gorgeous.

She'd pulled her thick hair into a ponytail. He reached for the band and slid it from her hair. It whispered free. Fingers in her strands, he arranged it over her back and then dug a thumb into the muscles in her shoulder.

She moaned.

He smiled. "Your posture's a chiropractor's wet dream, honey."

Her top lip curled in amusement. "I won't say anything about how you were hunkered over your drawings for the last hour, Igor."

"Good," he teased. Taking her hands, he tugged and she stood. He sat on her chair and pulled her down onto his lap. He wrapped his arms around her sexy white dress with the red flower on it when she was settled.

He moved her hair to one shoulder and settled his chin on her other.

"If you didn't want my hair in your way, you shouldn't have taken it down."

"Like it down," he told her, peering over her at the photo she was retouching. He turned his face and pressed a kiss behind her ear. "That's good."

She hummed in the back of her throat but kept her attention on the screen. "Thanks."

Another kiss to her neck, his arms gave her a squeeze. "Show me more."

"Okay." Breathy, she maintained her position at the mouse, minimized the window, and brought up another, this one displaying multiple images. She scrolled through, commenting on which photos she preferred, on which the family preferred.

He continued moving his hands over the material of her dress, up her ribs, along the sides of her breasts.

Somehow she stayed focused. *The Force is strong in this one*, he thought with a small grin.

"We agree on this one." She maximized a portrait of the entire family. Not a single one of them looked at the camera. Several kids ranging in age were scattered at the elders' feet, some playing in the grass, some crying, and two boys he guessed around Lyon's age appeared to be mid-fistfight. The parents were in various poses—each reprimanding their own misbehaving children. The oldest couple in the center of the photo Evan would bet were the grandparents leaned close to one another, watching the melee and sharing a secret laugh.

Charlie's finger brushed the corner of his mouth. "See? It makes you smile."

"It does." He moved his palms to her shoulders and began to knead. "You done?"

Where she'd begun to relax against him, now she stiffened and blew out a breath. "No. I have to retouch five more photos, e-mail Tami, and order matte boards since I'm out of stock."

"Custom framing, too, Ace?"

She shrugged. "Not really. But when I have one I like, I like to matte it for the buyer. A little something extra."

"That's sweet."

She ducked her head and watched him over her shoulder. He took the opportunity to kiss her jaw, then move his lips down and nuzzle her neck. She squirmed.

Another good sign.

"Keep doing what you do," he told her. "I'll be here, making sure you don't pull your spine out of alignment."

A soft chuckle emitted from her throat. Too bad he wasn't kidding. He reached for the zipper at her neck and lowered it while she wiggled her ass on his lap. When he had unzipped to her waist, he slipped a hand inside and cupped her breast over her bra.

"Like I'm not even here," he said against her neck, thrilled to hear her laughter ebb into a soft "mmm" sound.

He thumbed her nipple and she wiggled again.

"Ev."

Rae's nickname should sound wrong coming from her, but it didn't. It sounded scary-right. So right, he was getting hard.

He licked the sensitive skin behind her ear again. "Yeah, baby."

"I can't"—her hand covered his tweaking fingers on her breast through the material of her dress—"I can't concentrate on the Johnsons with you doing that."

"Doing what?" He pinched her nipple, then let up.

She gasped, her head falling back. "That."

"Seems fair," he said. "I can't concentrate on anything *but* my johnson while I'm doing this."

Clucking her tongue, she breathed, "Crude."

"What else am I supposed to call it?"

"Um...I don't know."

"Bet you do." He continued kissing her neck, slipping his other hand into her dress and massaging her other breast as well. She tilted her head to give him more access. He took it, exploring the length of her neck with his tongue.

"You prefer cock?" he whispered when he got to her ear.

"Every chance I get," came her sultry reply, followed by laughter letting him know dirty talk wasn't something his sweet girl was normally into.

He nipped her neck. "Know what I like?"

Her breaths shortened as he took one hand from the inside of her dress, spread her legs, and slid his fingers along the inside of her right thigh.

Licking her ear, he whispered in his quietest voice, "Your sweet pussy."

Her head snapped up. "Evan!" But the scolding came in the form of a hot, expelled breath. Yeah. She liked that, too.

"Would you prefer..." He glanced around as if he was thinking. "Love mitten?"

"Love mitten?" That sultry laugh again. He loved that laugh.

He brushed his fingers over her panties. Her laugh died.

"I prefer you didn't talk about it lewdly."

"I wasn't being lewd." He breeched the barrier of the cotton underwear and stroked her folds, only to feel her wet and warm against his fingers. She turned her face and kissed him.

"That's a term of endearment," he muttered against her lips.

Her mouth dropped open, her breath rolling over his lips. "Yeah?"

"Yeah, Ace. I have more. Want to hear them?"

She shook her head. With absolutely zero conviction.

He continued touching her, leaned into her ear and whispered a litany of descriptions for the part of her he was currently worshipping, pleased when she squirmed against his hand and turned halfway in her seat to hold his head to her ear. She came shortly after, spasming around his fingers, her cries wrapping around him, filling his ears.

Not wanting to waste any time, he pushed her to standing. She bent over the desk, giving him a helluva view.

"Ev," came her impatient mewl.

"Gimme a sec, Ace." He wrestled off his jeans while admiring her nude bottom and the glorious part of her he'd complimented seconds ago. Every inch of her—fantastically gorgeous. Condom in place, he sat, grabbed her hips and backed her onto his lap, pulling her down on his length. She accepted him, sinking slowly, impaling herself with a long, low moan. He grunted, a shake working its way across the width of his back, down both legs. He dropped his forehead onto her back.

"Your cock feels good," she said, moving up and down on his shaft.

"*Now*? You tease me now?" His speech was broken, his mind erased.

She sank down twice as slow while he metered his breathing. "So, so good," she said in a seductive purr.

His hands tightened on her perfect ass. "Hang on, Ace."

She looked at him over her shoulder, cheeks flushed, eyes half-mast. "I can't reach your hair from here."

He lifted his hips, thrusting deep, and watched her profile as her eyes closed and her mouth dropped open. "Better hold on to something."

She obeyed, grasping the arms of the chair he prayed would hold them both, and he clutched her hips as hard as he dared, lifting her off his lap and slamming her back down while her cries rang out around him.

Not muffled. Not muzzled. Not controlled. Wild, crazy cries that turned into whimpers of pure satisfaction. When she pulsed around him again, he let himself go.

"Ace," he growled, one arm around her waist the other wrapped around her front and clasping on to one of her shoulders. "Baby." He kissed her bare back and, still encased in her warmth, pulled out and pushed into her a final time. She dropped forward onto the desk, her breaths heavy. He rested his cheek on her back.

"You…" she said, trying to catch her breath. "…have… a…dirty…mouth."

Grinning, he said, "Sorry."

Her body shook gently with laughter, and he lifted his head to see her cheek leaning on her forearm. She peeked at him through tangled hair, smile affixed to her face. "No apologizing."

CHAPTER EIGHTEEN

Charlie had grossly underestimated how much Evan could eat.

For dinner, she'd made grilled cheese sandwiches and soup. He'd devoured the meal—with groans of appreciation reminding her of earlier—then went back to the kitchen and made not one more, but *two* more sandwiches and inhaled those, too. She also learned she'd cut them "wrong."

Triangles, Ace. Lyon would never stand for this kind of shoddy craftsmanship, he'd joked of her "square-cut" sandwiches.

He gave her a bite of the pointy end of one of his halves and she agreed. Henceforth, triangles. They did taste better that way.

More quiet hours passed after the sex on her office chair. She spent them listening to the pencil scratches coming from his talented hands and thinking back on the completely amazing experience of making love to Evan Downey.

Both gruff and sweet, as concerned for her well-being as he was willing to push her limits, she'd never experienced a lover like him. She shouldn't, but while she was at it, she allowed herself to imagine this was really her life. That she and Evan would work quietly side by side every day, and end curled against each other in bed at night.

But that wasn't the case, was it? The thought made her heart hurt.

They were in a bubble. Like a vacation where you eat too much of the wrong thing, drink way too much, and have temporary consequences, then return home where you have to resume a normal, human schedule and eat responsibly.

Reality sucked sometimes.

She thought back to the day they returned from the farmer's market. They'd been chopping vegetables for salad and Evan had been instructing a very uncooperative Lyon to set the table.

> *"I'll do it," she offered.*
>
> *This earned her Evan's frowning eyebrows. "We're not on vacation, Ace."*
>
> *"I know."*
>
> *"I don't think you do."*
>
> *Because he seemed angry, and because she found this unfair, she mirrored his stance, leaning a hip on the counter and crossing her arms.*
>
> *"You're catering to us as if we came to visit," he said. "We're not visiting. This is where we live." He gestured around to the*

> *bright, airy, work of art that was his home.*
> *"He has to do things here same as he did at*
> *home. Go to school. Do his chores."*

His words echoed in her ears now.

We're not on vacation, Ace.

They weren't. Seemed they'd forcibly forgotten that for the meantime.

Finished with her photos, she e-mailed Tami Johnson to let her know her retouches were ready to go, when Evan's voice sounded behind her.

"Hey."

She started to respond until she heard him continue.

"Are you having fun?" His tone had changed, going soft, his voice dipping when he said. "The diving board? Poppa show you how to do that? Yeah? What else?"

She sat, back to him, listening to the exchange between father and son and feeling the recurring ping of longing in her chest. She remembered Rae and Lyon playing together when he was very little, and she remembered Evan and Rae together, exchanging diaper duties, or running to get their crying baby boy when poker night ran late. Charlie had watched them throw rock-paper-scissors to determine who would fetch Lyon. The memory made her smile. Rae only ever wanted her boys to be happy.

Charlie hazarded a glance over her shoulder at Evan, feet kicked up on her sofa, hand in his hair, phone to his ear. He chuckled at something Lyon said on the other end of the phone, and the scene both tugged her heart and her lips into a smile of their own.

Somehow, in spite of Rae's not being here, her boys *were* happy.

"They're okay, Rae," she whispered to the ceiling.

"Brush your teeth, buddy," Evan said, wrapping the call. "Love you, too. 'Night."

Charlie had made a vow to Rae after she passed to look after Evan and Lyon, at the time never intending on replacing her. If Lyon knew she was with his father, would he see her as trying to replace his mommy? Would he reject her right out? Rae's son had no memories of her that weren't soaked in love, Charlie had seen to that. And now here she was, horning in on that relationship by getting close to Evan.

Her chest squeezed in a different way from before. A worried way.

Warm hands slid over her shoulders and massaged. Her eyes closed. "Come on, beautiful. No more work today."

He dug into a very sore muscle in her shoulder and because he'd done that earlier, she immediately thought of the amazing sex they had on this very chair. An answering heat jettisoned to her girl parts.

Pavlov would be proud.

"Don't you have to paint?" she asked.

He sighed.

She put a hand on his. "Go. Get your work done. I need to sleep anyway."

His lips came down to kiss the top of her head. "Don't wanna let you sleep."

Laughter rolled in her chest. It felt so good to be with him like this. Bubble or not, she'd take it. "A few hours of sleep, I beg you." But she needed space for a different reason. To get used to the natural space between them when Lyon came home. She couldn't help adding, "You can harass me tomorrow."

"We can go out on the lake," he said. "Asher's been wanting to spend a day boating. You available?"

That sounded amazing. A day on a boat. Sunbathing, laughing, swimming.

"Your whole body just went pliant," he observed. "That's a yes."

"I have to work."

"Work around it."

She could. Tami Johnson was a lawyer who kept incredibly crazy hours. Tami wouldn't be able to meet her until the weekend anyway—if then. "Okay."

"Gotta get up before noon." He gathered his art supplies and paper. "Leaving the dock at ten sharp."

She turned in her chair and watched him walk to her door.

He winked as he grabbed the knob. "'Night, Ace."

"'Night."

He closed the door behind him and she whispered to the room, "Love you, too."

CHAPTER NINETEEN

Yeah?" he grunted, pushing into her deeper.

"Yeah," she breathed, taking all of him. Her legs were wrapped around his waist and he had her ass in both hands, pulling her to him while she held on to his shoulders.

He thrust deep again, his palm wrapped around her neck, his other fingers resting between her butt cheeks and pushing her in closer.

She gasped. He dropped his mouth to her nipple and thrust again.

"Ev."

"Let go, Ace."

"Ev!"

"Come for me, baby."

"*Ev*. Wait," she laugh-commanded.

He halted, his lust-filled eyes hazy but coming to hers. Smiling, she palmed his face with both hands and kissed his lips. "My calf is cramping." Biting her lip against the pain, she attempted to straighten her leg.

"Damn. I liked that position." He let her go so they could come apart. "Left or right?"

"Left." She sat, grabbing her calf and pulling her knee to her chin.

They'd come back to Evan's studio after boating. Ash and Gloria had gone out on the boat, too, and Sofie and Faith. The girls had a chance to dish while watching water sluice off the muscular, tanned backs of the men who kept cannonballing off the boat's edge.

"Show-offs!" Gloria had called out.

They'd basked in the hot sun and over a hot grill. Evan made burgers—no turkey this time—and corn on the cob dressed in parsley, butter, salt, and pepper. Faith's idea. Best corn on the cob ever.

Asher and Evan then had a contest to see who could chug a can of beer faster. Asher won, but Evan argued it was because Ash spilled half his beer down his chest. Charlie took the opportunity to point out the bad boys of Evergreen Cove were alive and well.

Evan had crossed over to her and kissed her lips—which drew very interested looks from Sofie and Faith—and said, "Nope. Down a musketeer."

Asher had grunted. "Down a stooge."

At which Evan had pointed out, "If one of us is a stooge, it's not Donovan, it's you."

Charlie hadn't missed Sofie sucking in a long, long breath and averting her eyes at the mention of Donny, proving he was missed by more than just the guys.

The moment Charlie and Evan walked into Evan's house, he'd pushed her in the direction of the studio.

Despite the fact she was exhausted, she let him. Within seconds, he had her stripped, laid flat on her back, his tongue visiting every part of her from neck to thighs. He'd allowed her to climb on top, and she produced a condom from the pocket of her discarded jean skirt.

He'd grinned his naughty grin and rolled it on. He'd also pointed out, "Need to keep a stash in here, apparently."

About that, he was right. They did need a stash in here.

Now, he massaged her calf, laying another long, slow, warm kiss on her mouth while he was at it.

Mmm.

Cramp averted, she flopped to her back and realized she'd done so on top of something. A sheet of large, thick paper. "Oh, no, am I on your artwork?"

"Have an idea."

She sat up. The paper was blank.

"Oh, no you don't." She started to stand when he came at her with a variety of colored tubes of paint. "I almost didn't get it out of my hair last time."

"Tie your hair up." He pushed her shoulder until she fell backward. "You always have one of those thingies in your pocket."

She did, indeed, have a hair tie in her pocket. Nevertheless, she argued, "Evan."

Kneeling in front of her, his eyes warmed as they danced over her naked body. "Make art with me, Ace." He lowered his lips and kissed her, and unable to argue with a request like *Make art with me, Ace,* she gave in. Soon her mind went on vacation and her limbs wrapped around him.

They made art. Blue and red and yellow, and where it mixed purple and green, art. After thoroughly enjoying themselves, they rolled to a nearby drop cloth so as not to destroy the fine wood floors in his studio. Evan sat and tucked her against his front. She'd pulled her hair up as instructed, but noticed a strand had come down.

She held it out and groused at the red paint striping her hair. "Man! I knew it!"

A male chuckle vibrated her against her back. They were speckled in paint from the neck down, and it'd taken some very careful planning to not end up with it in (ahem) places that weren't safe, but they'd managed.

He dropped his chin on her shoulder, kissing her neck as he did. "You're sexy and beautiful." Another kiss, then, "I love that you let me do that."

Her heart ka-thumped the moment he got to the "I love..." part. She didn't know what the ka-thump meant—but it felt very similar to hope mixed with fear. She chalked it up to too much sun and paint fumes.

"Now we burn it in the fire pit," she concluded, studying the painting leaning against a few others. She could make out the shape of her breasts when he had been behind her, and his butt cheeks when she'd ridden him.

"Absolutely not."

"Evan!" she scolded. "You can see the sex on that canvas."

His arms squeezed her, painted fingers linking with hers. "I know. It's amazing."

"You can't let Lyon see this! You can't let anyone see this!"

He chuckled again. "Relax, Ace. I'll paint in a few more lines, hide the obvious parts. Like that nipple." He pointed with his free hand.

She gave him a playful slap. "You can't keep it."

"Let me keep it." His soft murmur against the shell

of her ear made her spine melt against his front. "I don't burn art, Ace."

Her thoughts, and her attention, went to the stack of dark art leaning against the wall. The paintings of smoke and billows, smears and smudges. "I see," she murmured.

His head turned as he looked with her. She said nothing, not sure if it was her place to ask.

His arms tightened around her. "I dream of Rae."

Charlie squeezed his fingers. She was right about the paintings. They *were* sad. "This would be an appropriate time to say I'm sorry," she whispered.

He kissed her neck and murmured, "You're sweet, Ace." His soft chuckle tickled her skin. "Outside and in."

Warmth unfurled in her chest, but her eyes hadn't left the paintings. "Why do you keep them?"

"They're the truth. Always been honest."

He was. Evan always told the truth. "You're beautiful, Ev," she returned quietly. "Outside and in."

Turning her, he kissed her mouth, this time long and slow and oh-so-smooth, his arms skimming over her nude body.

When they broke apart, her eyes went to the painting of them they'd just created. "But why keep this one?"

His arms had wrapped around her once again. He gave her a squeeze. "Never want to forget."

Her eyes closed, her heart sliding into her throat and clogging her next breath. His words were sweet, and said while his lips rested against her ear. What she didn't know was if he never wanted to forget because this was the beginning of something that would last forever . . . or if he never wanted to forget because this was something that would soon end.

Well. She would have to avoid reading into it.

She was still trying not to read into it when he helped her up and carried her into the bathroom closest to the studio. And when they showered. And when she pulled on one of his T-shirts and crawled into his bed upstairs.

She especially tried not to read into it when he said, "'Night, Ace," kissed the back of her neck, and crawled in behind her, wrapping his arm around her waist.

The more she tried not to think of it, the more she did. Thought about all of it—every angle, every possibility, every minute breath, utterance, or slide of his turquoise eyes.

Which was likely what kept her awake until the wee hours stretched into dawn and beyond.

Tired was settling in when Evan's phone rang. Letting loose a sleepy groan, he reached to the nightstand and promptly knocked the phone to the floor.

She laughed and he grumbled, but she thought it sounded like a laugh through the grumble, which made her smile despite being epically sleep-deprived.

"Yeah?" he said in a rocky morning voice as he rolled back onto the bed.

She was stroking a hand on his back, admiring the planes of hard muscle with a soft touch, when those muscles grew harder. Taut. Rigid.

"Where?" His voice had gone as rigid as his body. "I'm on my way." He tossed off the blankets and stood, phone resting between shoulder and ear. In a tone sharper than before, he repeated, "Yeah, Pat, I'm on my way."

Pat?

Oh no.

"Lyon?" Charlie guessed, her stomach sinking.

Evan, naked, pulled on jeans and a T-shirt. "Fell on the

diving board. Cracked his head." The cell was still in his hand, and he spun, searching the floor. "Where are my shoes?"

"When?"

"Just now. They're driving to the ER," he said while searching, tossing dirty clothes over his shoulder. Then his voice got loud. "*The fuck* are my shoes?"

Heart hammering, stomach tossing, she scrambled out of bed. "Ev."

Aiming his loud, angry voice at her made her bristle. "Why Pat and Cliff bought a goddamn *pool* with a goddamn *diving board* is beyond me. Too old for that shit."

She had already pulled her sundress over her head. "Is Lyon okay?" He was being irrational, but she understood why.

He spun on her. "He needs stitches. That sound *okay* to you, Ace?"

Pins and needles prickled her from head to toe. Partially for his anger, partially because stitches sewn into the kid she loved more than life itself was . . . scary. Tears of worry burned the backs of her eyes.

He turned and jogged down the stairs, calling behind him, "Lock up when you leave."

Leave?

"Evan! Wait." She heard keys jingle and the door open, catching up to him at the side door. He paused long enough to poke his head back in. "Wait," she repeated. He waited, but his brows were creased, that Downey look of determination etched into his features. "I'm coming with you."

"Charlie, I don't have time—"

"I'm coming with you," she stated more firmly. "Let

me run home and get dressed before we make an hour-
and-a-half drive to Fairport. In the meantime, you can put
on socks and underwear, which you will need later when
we're stuck at the hospital longer than we'd like to be."

His eyes narrowed, but she could tell she was getting
through.

"You're upset. I can drive."

"You're not driving, Ace."

Well. Worth a shot.

"At least grab some granola bars while I'm getting
ready. Pat and Cliff will refuse to leave Lyon's side and
likely be starving when we get there." She knew the Mosleys. That's exactly the way this would play out.

He dropped his keys in his pocket, a sign he was going
to wait for her. But the miserable expression, the worry in
his eyes, intensified.

"Ace."

She reached up and palmed his cheek. "He's in good
hands. We'll get to him as quickly as we can. May want
to pack a change of clothes if we have to stay the night."

Something severe crossed his face. His eyes narrowed
and he reached for her, squeezing her hand and then pulling her into him the rest of the way. She went to him,
allowing him to fold her in as she held him.

"My boy." The two words were spoken roughly, into
her hair, and in a broken tone similar to the night he
called about Rae.

Charlie's stomach flopped.

But she had to be strong and not let that break her.
They had a long drive to make and someone needed to be
levelheaded. She pulled away, looked into his eyes, and
put her hand on his cheek. "I know, baby."

"If—"

"No, Ev." She shook her head. *If* nothing. There was no *if* when it came to Lyon. He was going to be fine. He was going to live a long, healthy life. So was Evan. *So am I,* Charlie decreed, sending a look up to the heavens and silently saying, *Right, Rae?*

To which she'd like to think Rae cocked her head to one side and affirmed, *Damn straight!*

Evan took her hand from his face and squeezed her fingers. "I'll pack. Ten minutes."

"Ten minutes," she confirmed, then grabbed her purse from the sofa, bolted out the side door, and sprinted to her house.

Twelve minutes later, they were on the road. She kept up a constant stream of chatter the entire drive to try and distract him, but it was useless. Plus, she was just about talked out. She'd jabbered on about everything she could think of while he remained mostly quiet, his eyes alert and frowning at the windshield.

The trip was almost over, and she was relieved. She couldn't take much more of his worried silence.

Giving up, she grasped his hand and twined their fingers. He squeezed, a light squeeze, but the action relaxed her. "Here for you, Ev."

He spared her a glance and his lips lifted the slightest bit. "I know, baby."

She sagged back in her seat, feeling more tired thanks to worry piled on top of her sleepless, and active, night. Her eyes closed on their own, but he spoke, making her instantly alert.

"Messed up," he said.

"Sorry?"

"I messed up," he reiterated, louder this time. Untangling their fingers, he put both hands on the wheel. "Acted like a kid—an irresponsible kid while my kid—my only reason for breathing in and out—was bleeding—"

She heard his voice go taut, fighting through what may have been tears.

"Bleeding from his head in Pat and Cliff's swimming pool," he finished.

"That wasn't your fault," she interrupted, unwilling to let him take the blame.

"Wasn't it?" Again, he turned his angry tone on her. "I didn't insist they come take him this week so I could paint? So I could get into your pants?"

She sucked in a breath, telling herself he was worried and didn't mean what he was saying. But, *ouch.*

"Rae was right. I can't be a good father and embrace this other side of me at the same time. Drawing takes everything I have. It takes away from my son. Erases all reason. Sucks every last brain cell out of my head." He banged his palm on the steering wheel, making Charlie jump. "*Damn it*! I should have been looking out for my kid, not fucking around in the studio with Asher." He tossed a hand in her direction. "With other shit that doesn't matter."

Wow. That hurt worse. A physical pain curled up next to the worry and lack of sleep and settled in for the long haul.

He fell silent and Charlie didn't say another word.

* * *

Lyon was crying and hadn't stopped, according to Pat, for the last hour. That was when he'd insisted on a mirror. She finally relented and handed over a small compact from her purse.

It hadn't been the stitches to send him into tears, though Evan was not surprised. Lyon was half Rae. Rae had a stomach of steel and had always been fascinated by blood and guts. Their kid, as it turned out, was like his momma in that way.

No, what had Lyon's bottom lip dragging the top of the hospital sheet was what they'd done to prep him for the stitches, and soon, the MRI.

They'd shorn his hair.

"Poppa has short hair." Cliff gestured to his graying head.

"You have no hair!" Lyon argued, more fat tears rolling down his cheeks.

"It will grow back, sweetheart," Patricia said, running a hand over the part of his head not sewn together. "I think you look handsome."

"I don't want to be handsome. I want to be cool!" This sent him into another slack-jawed crying jag. Evan couldn't take it one more second.

He climbed into bed with his son, scooting him over and wrapping an arm protectively around his small shoulders. He addressed Pat. "Can you get Charlie? She's in the waiting room and would probably like to come back."

"Sure, sweetheart." Her hand left Lyon's head.

"I'll come with you," Cliff said, following her out.

Lyon's tears stopped like a shut-off water main. "Aunt Charlie?"

"Yeah."

"Aunt Charlie came?"

Evan smiled down at his son, feeling like a royal asshole. His kid got it. Got it like that.

"Of course she did," he said, stating what should have been obvious to him over the last two hours. "She loves you. She wants to make sure you're going to be okay."

And she wanted to make sure Evan was going to be okay. Which was why she'd talked for most of the trip and had unwrapped a granola bar and practically fed it to him. *Shit*. He'd been a prick.

"Do you think she'll like my hair?" His eyes had gone wide, tears drying on his cheeks. Evan shook his head at his boy. This kid. Never would he cease to amaze.

"Oh my gosh! Who is that handsome devil in a hospital bed?"

Charlie, a hand to her chest, her mouth open but smiling, said exactly the right thing, proving to be better at handling pressure than Evan was.

"Name's Evan," he teased with a wink, though for all he knew she felt like punching him in the nose for his behavior earlier.

She threw a hand at him. "I'm talking about the very suave younger man with the awesome haircut."

Lyon beamed, his dimple denting his cheek. "I have a hundred stitches!"

"Not that many, bud," Evan corrected.

He frowned. "The doctor said girls think stitches are cool, so I'm going to say I have more of them. Then I'll be more cool."

Charlie lifted her brows. "Can't argue with that logic." She bent and inspected the stitches, only showing her worry when Lyon wasn't able to see her expression. She exchanged a slightly concerned glance with Evan but when Lyon lifted his head, she promptly plastered a smile on her face.

Good at handling pressure, good at easing the tension in the room, good at drying his son's tears. And she hadn't broken a sweat.

"Very cool," she commented after her inspection.

"Did Terror eat today?" Lyon asked.

The fish. Evan had totally forgotten about it.

"He did." Charlie took the chair by the bed. "I put flakes in his tank before we left and he ate every last one."

Saved. Evan sent her a smile of gratitude. He watched her talk, shaking his head at himself. Beneath her faux upbeat chatter, and the happy face she'd put on for Lyon's benefit, his girl looked beat. Not only from the car ride, but from her not sleeping much last night, which she'd mentioned in passing on the trip here.

He hadn't had a chance to consider why she hadn't slept—he'd absolutely crashed, satisfied and beat—and hadn't asked her to elaborate, his thoughts firmly on his son's welfare and not at all on her feelings. His mind went to the mini rant he'd gone on about Rae being right, about how he'd messed up. And, now that he thought back to it, he'd balled Charlie into that group of things he'd regretted doing this week while ignoring his son. The comment about getting into her pants may have been accurate, but wasn't the least bit charming.

No good, he thought with a frown.

The doctor came in a few minutes later to explain the MRI was for peace of mind, but they suspected Lyon hadn't sustained a concussion or any permanent damage.

In the waiting room again, Charlie wrung her hands, and Evan dropped his arm around her shoulders. He noted she shied away from him when the Mosleys returned with cups of coffee for themselves. If he had to guess, he'd say it was thirty percent what he'd said in the car and seventy percent the fact she didn't want Rae's parents privy to the fact he and Charlie were "together."

Both points miffed him.

The scan came back normal, after an ungodly amount of waiting resulting in Lyon eating a terrible hospital lunch Evan helped him finish. Pat, Cliff, and Charlie went to the cafeteria to have what Charlie assured him was an equally terrible lunch there.

When Lyon was finally released, Evan had to remind him not to run and endure an argument about why he couldn't play the iPad for twenty-four hours. "To be safe," the doctor encouraged. "No television, computer, or any electronics."

"It'll be cool," Charlie had said. "We can read."

Lyon did not think this was cool.

Pat and Cliff insisted he stay at their house. Pat, somewhat tearfully, apologized again and Cliff and Evan both assured her that accidents happen. As rambunctious as Lyon was, none of them should come down on themselves for him getting hurt.

This was a lot easier to say now that Lyon was whole and intact, Evan had specific instructions, and his kid was in sight sitting next to him on Patricia and Cliff's deck, chattering about everything under the sun.

After dinner—Pat's pork chops and baked beans and kale salad were legendary—Evan and Charlie stayed on the deck with their drinks and Pat and Cliff excused themselves to go inside. Evan was sure this was to give him and Charlie some time alone. Pat insisted on reading to Lyon and Cliff had bustled off after she'd angled a very pointed glare at her husband.

"They haven't changed a bit," Charlie commented, sipping her iced tea.

Evan was drinking scotch. Cliff and his dad and their damned horrible liquor. He swallowed the end of it and winced.

"Not a big fan of scotch, huh?"

"You had it?" he croaked, throat dry. "Awful. The drink of old men and my oldest brother."

"Landon's a scotch drinker?"

He made a show out of taking a drink of her iced tea and swishing it around his teeth. She laughed. It was good to hear her laugh. Either she'd forgiven him or was pretending to be okay. Unfortunately, he thought it was the latter.

"He is. Landon is a millionaire. He could choose any drink he wants." He gestured to his glass. "And he chooses *this*."

She chuckled again.

They sat in silence, watching the low light of the summer evening bounce off the pool's surface. Lyon had been bummed he couldn't swim anymore. Figures. That kid was fearless sometimes.

A shiver climbed Evan's spine.

Charlie noticed. Turned her head.

"Coulda lost him, Ace."

Her hand closed over his forearm. "But you didn't."

"I lost Rae." He snapped his fingers. "Like that. Five, six minutes later. Gone." There was nothing like the feeling of watching someone lose their hold on life.

He'd witnessed it and to this day didn't grasp it. She looked like her, felt like her, her body warm and still, her face beautiful. But she was gone.

Surreal.

Hot tears burned his eyes, and in a breath, he was back on East Level, frantically shouting into the cell phone on the floor. Shouting at Rae.

Baby, wake up. Dammit, Rae! Breathe!

Those shouts would forever be burned in his head. As would the chest-caving sobs that rendered him unable to stand when the paramedics got there.

Charlie's hand squeezed his arm, bringing him back to present.

He blinked back the tears. "Thank God for Pat and Cliff acting fast. What I said earlier about them having a pool..."

"I know."

"This isn't their fault."

Her grip tightened. "I know."

He turned to her to find her giving him a tender smile, tears trailing down her face.

"Ace." He lifted a hand and brushed her tears aside.

"I remember that phone call, Ev."

She meant the phone call when he'd told her about Rae. He remembered he'd called her, but didn't remember what he'd said. Not even a little.

"You sounded like that today over Lyon," she said in a whisper. "Scared me."

"Baby." He turned his body toward her, moving his hand from her face to her neck, but she backed away before he could get a firm hold, her eyes cutting to the kitchen window.

He clenched his jaw. He *knew* it. She was worried about Rae's parents seeing them together.

Dropping his hand to his lap, he said, "Guess now's not a good time to tell you I didn't mean to be insulting when I said I wanted to get into your—"

"Evan!" She sought the window again, lowered her voice. "It's fine. Everything's fine. The important thing is that Lyon is okay. And that you realize you are not a bad father because you needed a break to paint." Conveniently, she'd left herself out of the equation.

He felt his eyes narrow and steam began to build behind his ears. Everything wasn't *fine*. They had entered some sort of alternate universe where she didn't want him touching her. That was new.

He didn't like it.

"You are capable of being both a talented, amazing artist and an incredibly loving father." She smiled. Her words may be true, but the practiced sentiment was fake. Or, if not fake, at least reined in. He didn't like her reined in. He liked her wild. He liked her honest. Honest and cheeky like she was in his studio. At her computer. On her bed. But this... this pseudo, false friendship bullshit she was peddling wasn't cutting it.

"Ace—"

"You've been through a lot," she continued. "Both of you. I lost my mother when I was young, but it still hurts. I never talk about her. I don't want to. You want to pretend you've moved on, and I so get that."

Pretend? He felt his brows pull. The hell was she talking about?

She stood, taking her glass with her. "It's okay. I know you think you have. You're working on it. You've committed to Evergreen Cove. You got a tattoo of it on your arm, for goodness' sake."

He glanced at the pines climbing his left arm. What the hell was she—

"Grief takes years. A lot of years. I understand the

need to bury it, and to hide behind things because of it. I'll always be your friend, no matter what's happened between us," she said after another perfunctory look to the blank kitchen window. "I'll always be here for Lyon. You don't have to worry about me being strange because of what happened between us. Take your time to grieve and feel those things for Rae. And take your time with your son."

"Ace, you're starting to piss me off."

But this fact didn't erase her soft, patronizing smile. His lip curled.

"Take the time you need, Evan. And don't worry about me at all." She smiled again, turned, and walked inside.

He watched her go, then groused at the pool, thinking. He thought until the sun set, until Patricia poked her head outside to say good night and let him know there were fresh towels in the bathroom for his morning shower. He'd nodded vacantly, growing more and more pissed as he put together what his girl had done.

She'd dumped him.

He stood and stalked to the house, aiming for her bedroom. Little did she know...

Not gonna happen.

CHAPTER TWENTY

That conversation went well.

Kind of.

Charlie felt like her heart had splintered, but quickly shoved the pieces aside and thought of anything but what would happen when she got home. Right now, she was in Rae's old bedroom, decorated in beige with a pale green and soft blue floral print comforter and curtains with wide, vertical stripes in the same colors. The Mosleys hadn't kept the bedroom the same as it was when she moved out and married Evan. They had promptly redecorated, which Rae hadn't liked *at all*. She smiled remembering the conversation between the Mosleys and their only daughter. Charlie had taken the afternoon and driven out with Rae, shortly after Rae's engagement.

"I can't believe you scrubbed me from this house like I never lived here!" Rae had stood in the kitchen, one hand on her hip, and argued.

Patricia had clucked her tongue. "Drama mama!" Pat's nickname for Rae was scarily accurate. "I always wanted a sewing room. You know that."

Charlie's eyes wandered to the compact desk and drawers on the other side of the room where a sewing machine sat. She slid the closet door open to find square cubbies filled with various materials, boxes of organized threads, needles, and a shelf holding craft books. She brushed her fingers along a pile of material—striped beige, cream, soft blue, and pale green. Her eyes went to the curtains.

Patricia had sewn the curtains.

Charlie's smile stayed intact.

Thoughts like this—thoughts *not* on Evan or the way she'd been forced to lay down the way things were with him—would get her through tonight. Tomorrow when she got back home, everything would gradually get better. They were going to be busy in the coming weeks. She had work to do, and Evan would be getting Lyon ready for school, which she assumed involved supplies shopping and buying him some clothes.

Poor kid was going to have to start school with stitches, or at least a scar, and without the haircut he wanted.

Then there were school pictures.

She wished she could make this easier for him. For both of them.

Maybe her staying out of their way was the best way to do that.

A soft knock at the door came and she looked down at her short pair of pink-and-yellow-flowered pajama shorts and a pale pink tank. In case it was Cliff, she opened the door only a fraction. She found Evan through the gap instead.

She pressed her face to the crack and studied the long, dark hallway. The Mosleys' bedroom was on the other end of the house, but Lyon was in the spare room with a pull-out sofa across the hall, and Evan was supposed to be sleeping on the couch in the family room.

He wasn't ready for bed, still in jeans and the T-shirt he'd frantically pulled on this morning.

"What time is it?" she asked.

He answered her question with a question. "Why are you awake?"

Because she'd tried to sleep but her mind was too filled with Evan. So she'd gotten out of bed and clicked on the small bedside lamp and proceeded to distract herself with the contents of Patricia's sewing closet. "Drank too much tea."

"Bullshit." He pushed the door wider, and her out of the way with it, and came inside. Here, in Rae's old bedroom, in a very skimpy pajama outfit with Rae's husband...

Oh Lord.

This was bad.

Like, *bad* bad.

He shut the door until it clicked, making *bad* worse.

Her heart pounded and she covered it, along with her nipples, with crossed arms. "Lyon is across the hall," she pointed out.

"We're not sneaking around behind his back, Ace."

Well. Evidently, he had no intention of wrapping up their affair, or sneaking around once Lyon came home. News to her.

She took a step away from him and tried a new tactic. "Pat and Cliff are light sleepers."

He shook his head, his gaze intent and focused on her.

"Yes, they are," she argued, though she doubted the headshake was Evan denying that factoid.

"You and I are gonna talk."

"Not tonight we aren't." She put her arms down and walked for the door, only to be stopped. He pulled her back to stand in front of him, gripping her upper arms firmly in both hands. She tipped her chin to look up at him. "Let me go. I have to sleep."

"Not until we talk."

"Evan." Suddenly, she was fatigued.

"You think *I* need to grieve, Charlie? You kidding me?"

Uh-oh. This was what he wanted to discuss? She thought he'd come in here to talk about them staying together, which she would have argued against. Then again, it hurt he'd so readily accepted that part, arguing instead about his denial over his grieving Rae. Shifting mental gears, she shrugged out of his grip.

"Fine." She plunked down on the tiny twin bed by the window. "Have a seat." She gestured to the chair at the sewing table.

He ignored her suggestion and sat next to her on the bed.

But of course.

"You need time to yourself to mourn her."

"Mourn her." He sounded as angry as he was this morning—or at least close. "You gotta be kidding me," he said again.

She softened her voice. "I'm not kidding." She put a hand on his arm and offered a gentle smile like she had on the deck. Connected by touch, but her mind disconnected from what he was to her. This was for him, for Lyon. Charlie knew how to console someone who'd lost someone close.

After the loss of her mother, she'd experienced plenty of consolation: grief counselors, pastors, and friends of the family. She'd help him through this. This was what she had mentally promised after Rae passed, wasn't it? She'd vowed to watch out for Rae's boys.

Better late than never.

"You don't take the time to be quiet long enough to miss her," she observed. His brows went from angry to furious. Swallowing back her trepidation, she pressed on. "You've been running the tattoo shop, running a household, playing the role of two parents since she died. You lost your mother a few years back; another woman in Lyon's life. Gone. What did you do? You kept working at the shop, parenting for two, and then you jumped into your artwork with both feet and pursued publication. It's been a wild ride, honey." She patted his arm, hoping he was getting what she was telling him. He needed a break, and now that he lived in Evergreen Cove, she could help him take a break. "You need to take some time to *really feel* this."

His nostrils flared, teeth clenched as he continued seething.

She tore her eyes from his, unable to take that furious gaze locked on hers and regarded the room instead. "This was Rae's room."

His sharp laugh cut into the tension between them. It wasn't jovial or pleasant, just a dry huff of air scratching his throat.

She wasn't sure if this was part of his process or if he was ticked at her.

"I know this was Rae's room, Charlie," he stated. "We made love on this bed." He slapped the mattress.

She felt an ice-cold blade of regret slice into her chest.

"Well, not this one. It was bigger. But it was in this room."

The pain radiated to her limbs.

"Ace."

She didn't want to look at him. Didn't want to hear any more about Rae, her lost best friend and Lyon's mother, or any reminder that she and Evan had been intimate in the past. Silly, she knew, but she was too fragile right now to—

"You're full of crap."

She blinked up at him. Most definitely, he was ticked.

"You don't know what I've done to grieve Rae."

She blinked again, a new sensation fanning across her chest. Still painful, but hot, not cold. A warning she'd overstepped her boundaries. Angered him in a way he wouldn't brush aside.

"You weren't there in bed with me after she was gone," he said. "Didn't see me wake up in the middle of the night, pain like an anvil crushing my chest. A fear so palpable I couldn't breathe. Pain so powerful it kept me from expanding my lungs."

He leaned into her and she froze.

"Know what happens when you don't breathe, Ace?" He didn't wait for her response. "Your body freaks out. Your diaphragm"—he poked her below her rib cage, where, she guessed, her diaphragm was—"seizes up. Adrenaline dumps into your system. Then you hyperventilate; have a panic attack."

He'd had panic attacks? Her heart hammered, feeling like she might have one now.

"I'd wake up, reach for her only to find her side of the

bed empty. Took me two years before I could sleep anywhere but on my half. Replaced two worn-out pillows
because I refused to use hers."

Her chest constricted. Oh, she'd had this so very
wrong. He *had* grieved. And she'd been trying to extricate
herself from the picture, latching on to what she thought
would be the easiest way out...She couldn't have been
more incorrect with her assumption.

"I'm sorry," she whispered, reaching for his arm.

"Cried into that pillow more than once. Latched on to
it with both arms." She felt the muscles in his forearm go
taut where she'd rested her palm. "Pillow wasn't what I
wanted, Ace. Wanted my wife. My living, breathing,
laughing wife."

Her stomach tossed.

"No amount of wailing, praying, yelling, bartering, or
breaking every one of those stupid crystal figurines she
collected brought her back."

She covered her lips with her fingers, feeling the sting
of fresh tears in her nose. He'd told her he had donated
Rae's figurines to charity. But instead he'd...broken them?
Broken them because his heart was breaking for a wife he
couldn't get back no matter how much he wanted to.

She felt a tear stray from one eye and raised her hand to
his face. Hating he'd gone through this. Hating she hadn't
known. "Ev," she said on a broken whisper. When he
pulled away from her touch, she realized she'd used Rae's
nickname for him, and wondered if she shouldn't.

He held her eyes. "Four years, Ace."

"I know." She wound her fingers together and dropped
her hands in her lap.

"Four years of uncertainty. Of pushing through when

I felt like grabbing that anvil and taking it to the river. Of not having the time or luxury for a mental breakdown. Hell, a break, period. Of having an anxiety attack at a PTO meeting, for God's sake, where I knew I didn't fit in. I didn't." He shook his head and mumbled almost to himself. "Rae did that stuff."

She could picture him, nervous, hands in his pockets while he tried to talk with teachers and other moms. How come he'd never told her about any of this before now?

"Whenever Lyon stayed here or with Dad, I didn't know what to do with myself. I worked my fool head off, tried to get ahead, tried to distract myself. Terrified if I let that hold go, I'd lose my mind."

"Honey." More tears streaked down her face. She couldn't fix it. There was a time she could have, but she hadn't known. He'd never told her. Then she thought of Russell and thought, maybe if she had known, it wouldn't have mattered. He wouldn't have liked her taking off to care for Rae's husband. Evan had to go through it for himself.

And he had, she realized suddenly. *All by* himself.

"Tried to bury it, ignore it, blame myself for it." He gestured at nothing with slightly shaking hands, then held his palms up in front of him. "I'm out."

She blinked at his hands, searched his eyes.

His voice got quiet. "For the first time since I lost her on the hallway carpet—carpet she insisted was 'salmon' but I'm telling you as I sit here, Charlie, it was fuckin' pink."

A surprised laugh stuttered from her lips at his ridiculous, and true, statement. The carpet *was* pink. But Rae, knowing Evan would not stand for pink carpet, spent every year she lived there insisting it was "salmon." It so wasn't. And everyone knew it.

He smiled, but now the smile faded. Hers followed.

His voice softened, along with his gaze. "For the first time since I held her in my arms while she died on that salmon-colored carpet"—he grasped Charlie's arms—"I know what I want." One hand moved to cup her jaw. "I'm where I belong."

More tears fell from her eyes.

He swiped her cheek with one thumb and his eyes left hers briefly before returning. Then they didn't move. "You're trying to fix a problem I don't have, Ace. I think that problem's yours."

"Wuh-what?" She pulled away from his palm to blink at him, confused.

"You lost your mom. Your dad bailed. Your sister's distant. Your past is full of unresolved grief."

She felt her head shaking. But she was okay... wasn't she?

"If you'd let yourself get through that—get through the Rae part, at least—you and I just might have a shot at something real."

He pulled his hand away.

"You want to turn what we've been doing into . . . something real?" she asked numbly.

He sighed. "Baby, it *is* something real. You don't see that?"

Her mind was spinning. Her stomach sick. Nauseous and angry and confused. And—

"I want this to be more to you than a handful of orgasms," he whispered, his fingers returning to tip her chin. "Something involving you living in my house, working out of yours, coming on vacation with Lyon and me to Osborn to see Dad and Aiden, or to Tennessee to see Angel, or to Chicago to see Landon."

His family. His entire family. Her mind blurred along with her vision.

"Something that looks a lot like a family when we're home. With you in the role of mom, me in the role of dad, and us sitting Lyon down someday to talk to him about sex, and college, or let him know he's got a brother or sister on the way."

Time stopped.

Had Evan implied he wanted to have a child with her?

And now her head was spinning.

He poked her under the ribs. "Diaphragm, Ace. Breathe."

She breathed.

"Scares you to death, doesn't it?"

Lying, she shook her head. It did. It scared her in a way she couldn't understand. Scared her silly.

When she stood, he stood with her, grasped her upper arms again, and turned her gently toward him. "Can't fix that part for you," he stated. "The scared part, you not dealing with your fears part." He lowered his head and met her again-watering eyes. "But I promise, I'll be here when you come around."

She shook her head again. She wasn't the one who needed to come around. She—she...she'd lost her train of thought. Lost it on all the words he'd spoken since they'd curled up in her heart like a litter of purring kittens.

...you living in my house, working out of yours, coming with Lyon and me on vacation...

...you in the role of mom, me in the role of dad...

...talk to him about sex, and college, or let him know he's got a brother or sister on the way...

"Not going anywhere."

She looked up at Evan, his expression serious.

He shook his head for emphasis. "Not going anywhere, baby. Not giving you a break. Not giving you an out. Including tonight."

"Tonight?"

"Wasn't in your bed one night and I hated it. Not gonna give you a break until you know I'm here for good. Here wanting you, wanting us, wanting *this* every single day."

This... was too much to process.

"Charlie, baby, I'm not letting you hide from this the way you've been hiding from all the things in your life that have hurt you."

"I—"

"Kiss me."

The bedroom door was closed, but she could imagine Pat and Cliff, and Lyon, on the other side of it. Eyes filled with judgment, concern, confusion... "They could find out."

"I know, Ace," he said. *Unbelievably.* "And that's okay."

"But this room—"

"Rae's room. Pat and Cliff's house. Almost too much for you, isn't it? One kiss and I'll take you back to my room."

"You're sleeping on the sofa," she said, pretty sure she'd slipped into a parallel universe, her brain unable to connect incoming thoughts to her current reality.

"I'm sleeping in the bedroom across the hall. Lyon wanted to sleep in the family room."

"Evan—"

"I sat up with him and we read and talked and I tucked him in. He's out. Feelin' no pain."

"Evan."

"Kiss me, Ace."

Squeezing her eyes closed, she said, "I can't."

"You can."

"I *can't*." With weak hands, she shoved him.

He stood firm. Closed his hands over hers. "You *will*."

Hearing his smile, she opened her eyes. Sure enough, a sexy curve sat on his lips.

"All we've been through, you don't trust me? Don't think I'm putting your needs ahead of mine? Can't see that's what I've been doing since I got here?"

She hadn't thought about it that way.

"Wine for Charlie."

"Turkey burgers, Ace."

"Let go, baby. Take it."

"You deserve it."

"I have another remedy, guaranteed to make you feel better."

He was right. Everything he'd done, he put her first. He was the one pulling her along, patiently waiting for her to catch up.

"Ace," he prompted again.

This time she didn't hesitate.

Looping her arms around his neck, she kissed him.

CHAPTER TWENTY-ONE

*A*nd Evan had thought seeing his kid's heart break had broken him.

Watching Charlie realize not only that she hadn't grieved Rae, but also hadn't dealt with the loss of her family, hurt him to watch.

Much as he hated to, there was no way he couldn't point that out. His future with her depended on it.

A future with Charlie was the only future worth considering.

He wasn't sure when he'd decided, but it was there. Cemented in his gut—in his heart—in Lyon's hopeful expression when she'd walked into the hospital room today.

He hadn't been sure he'd get her over this hump—the one where she'd dumped him on the Mosleys' deck—but given the way she moved her lips against his now, he had a pretty good guess she'd let him back in a little.

A little isn't enough.

Hands sifting into her thick, blond hair, he slid a palm to the small of her back and pressed her womanly hips against his. She mewled in the back of her throat and he squeezed her ass and pressed into her again.

Another mewl.

The sounds she made lit him on fire, and if that didn't do it, the way she stroked his tongue with hers, while standing on her tiptoes—practically climbing him like a cat on a tree—*yeah.* That would do it.

About the time her fingers moved to thread into his hair and he cupped her breast, a knock at the door pulled them apart. He turned his head but held her close.

She squirmed. But not in a sexy way, in a nervous way. "Oh no." Her hands pulled from his neck.

"Lyon," he guessed.

"Knocking?" she whispered frantically, attempting to disentangle her arms and legs from around his.

"Probably not." The rap came again, soft knuckles. Patricia. Had to be.

Charlie buried her face in her hands and dropped her forehead to his chest. He let her go, moving her aside to answer the door.

When he pulled it open a crack, Pat was outside the door, one thin eyebrow lifted in suspicion.

* * *

Nightmare.

Charlie was having a waking nightmare. This was like being caught by a parent. Only worse. Because this was Rae's parent.

Patricia had caught Charlie and Evan making out in Rae's old bedroom.

Oh, this was so, so much worse.

Ack! Sorry, Rae.

"I heard crying," Patricia said from the hallway. Evan had one arm braced on the door frame on his right, the other palm holding the door open a crack. A crack he filled with his body.

It was the wrong time and place to appreciate the way his worn jeans cupped his amazing butt, or the way the dark T-shirt, wrinkled from a day's wear, skimmed along his shoulders and back and made her want to peel it up, but Charlie did appreciate it. Until appreciating it was interrupted by Pat speaking again.

"I came to check on Charlotte. Make sure she's all right."

He looked over his shoulder, gave her a wink, then turned back to Pat. "She's good."

Then, to Charlie's mortification, he let go of the door and pushed it open, revealing Patricia in a fuzzy pink bathrobe, a very "Momma is not happy" scowl on her face.

Pat's gaze raked down Charlie's barely dressed body. "I see," she said tonelessly. Charlie promptly covered her breasts with her crossed arms. "I thought I heard crying." Her eyes snapped back to Evan. "Perhaps I was mistaken."

Charlie opened her mouth to say she *was* crying, and further explain why—because they'd been discussing Rae, but he spoke before she could.

"What brings you to this half of the house, Pat?" He crossed his arms, too, but not in a protective gesture, more in a combative one. If he planned on taking on Patricia Mosley, Charlie needed to find a window to climb out of.

"Originally?" Pat crossed her arms now, as well. "Lyon

woke wanting to eat and I wake up and eat this time of night anyway. I came to find you and make sure a midnight snack was okay, when I heard"—her eyes tracked to Charlie—"*something* coming from this room."

"Mom." Evan unlooped his arms. "You don't have to check with me for things like that. I trust you to make the right decisions for my son."

Her face turned from scorning mother to guilty grandmother. "I thought that, too, before the accident. I turned away for two seconds, tops. I never—"

Reaching out, he pulled Pat into his arms. "Come on, Mom, what'd Cliff and I say?"

Pat wasn't crying but she clasped on to Evan tightly enough to make Charlie think she was struggling not to. After holding on a few seconds, she patted his back with both hands, pulled away, and gave him a tight-lipped smile. Keeping it together. "Today frightened me so very much. I was right back to four years ago when you called us about Rae—"

Oh gosh. *Rae.* Evan not only had to call Charlie, he had to call Pat and Cliff that day. There was another thing she'd never considered. She had underestimated what he'd gone through.

Completely underestimated him.

Holding Pat's hands, he listened while she talked about Rae, about Lyon falling, about the frightening trip to the ER. Then Pat directed her gaze to Charlie.

"Sweetheart, there's another robe of mine on the other side of that closet. Feel free to borrow it."

That was it? Pat found Charlie mid-clinch with her son-in-law, her late daughter's husband, and all she had to say was feel free to borrow her robe?

"Are you two hungry?" Pat asked. "Since we're all awake, this calls for eggs."

"Ace?"

She blinked at Evan, the dynamic in the room confusing her.

"Hungry?" he asked.

"Um…"

"Eggs are good," he told Pat. "Meet you out there."

Pat nodded her head and turned down the hallway as he shut the door. Charlie smacked her palms to her face and groaned.

She heard a low chuckle as he grasped her wrists.

"She thinks I'm a horrible person," she whispered. He removed her hands and lowered his face to look at her.

Cupping her jaw in his palms, she watched as a thoroughly amused tilt took over his lips. "You're okay, baby. Let's eat."

"How can you say that?" she whisper-screamed, if that was a thing.

Continuing to look at her with that same immovable smile, he stated simply, "You're a grown-up. I'm a grown-up."

"She caught us…*almost* kissing!" she hissed.

He shook his head, annoyingly amused. "We weren't dry-humping in the hallway, Ace."

The sound she made was sort of a choke and a laugh. He took it for the latter.

"That's my girl. Grab that robe."

She did as instructed, surprised when he took her hand and walked down the hallway with her. At the kitchen table, Lyon was awake and smiling, and Charlie noticed he'd noticed their linked hands.

"Hey, bud."

"Hi, Dad." His eyes went to his father's face, then their hands again. She pulled away.

Evan let her, but then put his hand on her back and pulled out the cushioned, rolling kitchen chair that had been a part of the Mosleys' dining room for as long as she'd known them.

Similar to the outdated dinette set were the flowered curtains over a sheet of lace at the kitchen window. Pat must not have had a chance to sew new ones for out here, yet.

"What's the ruckus?" Cliff, also in a bathrobe, scuttled down the hallway.

He clasped his chest, feigning shock at the gang inhabiting his kitchen, then kissed his wife, who was cracking eggs into a large iron skillet, no doubt laced with pork fat from the chops.

"Eggs, baby?" Pat asked him.

"You know it," he answered.

Charlie smiled at the exchange. She and Rae had often talked of wanting that kind of enduring, forever love. Her smile fell. Evan and Rae had lost their forever.

Evan leaned into Charlie's frame of vision, interrupting her thoughts. One of his hands flattened on the table, the other wrapped around the arm of her chair. "Coffee?"

"It's nearly one o'clock," she said quietly, alarmed by his nearness to her lips.

"I have decaf," Pat called, making it known she could hear and see every last thing happening between them.

Charlie cringed.

"Decaf it is." He winked, leaned closer, and said against her temple, "Relax, Ace."

Then he kissed her. Briefly, but thoroughly, and at the very moment Cliff sat down at the kitchen table.

"Welllll," he said as Charlie tried not to cringe. His large, rough hand came across the table to rest on top of hers. Evan moved away to make coffee. Cliff patted her, gave her a genuine, loving smile, and turned to Lyon. "What will we have for breakfast if we have eggs now?"

Lyon's smile was alert and alive, even this late. "Pancakes!"

Cliff chuckled and slid Charlie a look before patting her hand again. "Pancakes it is."

* * *

"After dinner," Evan repeated for the tenth time.

That's how many times she'd heard Lyon ask to play his iPad game on the drive home. And they weren't home yet.

They'd packed up and left the Mosleys' house late afternoon since they'd been up since two in the morning eating food that should definitely only be eaten at two in the morning if they'd all been on a bender.

Pat made pancakes for breakfast and after, Charlie showered. She'd just finished making the bed when Pat rapped on the door and poked her head in. As it turned out, Charlie didn't go back to Evan's room last night. He'd let Lyon crash on the pullout sofa in the spare bedroom. She'd been relieved. They may be adults, and Evan may not mind everyone knowing about them, but her sleeping in the same bed with him under Rae's parents' roof was a stretch.

Plus, Pat hadn't exactly seemed *happy* upon finding them canoodling in Rae's old bedroom, currently her sewing room or not, and no doubt wouldn't appreciate them turning that canoodling into more canoodling. Especially considering Lyon was a few rooms away.

In the bedroom, Pat had shut the door behind her. Charlie fidgeted, hanging the robe on a hanger and putting it back into the closet.

"Charlotte."

She'd turned to find the older woman wearing a striped blouse and black pants, short-heeled sandals on her feet, her makeup just so. Conversely, Charlie's hair was air-drying into a frizzy mess and she was in a wrinkled T-shirt, skinny jeans, and a pair of Toms.

"Thank you for letting us stay," she said, her smile wilting.

Pat had given her a very slow eye-blink and came to the bed, where she patted the duvet. "Sit, sweetheart."

Heart in her throat, Charlie sat. Last night she'd finally fallen asleep around four. The reason it'd taken so long to fall asleep after being awake was because of Pat. Charlie had lain awake trying to decide if the woman would confront her come morning, then decided she most definitely would, then fretted about it until she couldn't keep her eyes open.

She sat up straight, ready to take the talking-to she knew was coming. It'd be done out of love—this was Patricia Mosley, after all—but Pat would be firm, and likely remind Charlie to be loyal where Rae was concerned, and extra cautious around Lyon at his tender age.

Because this was what she'd expected, guilt pooled in her stomach the second Pat took a breath. But when she spoke, she said not one thing Charlie had anticipated.

"So. You and Evan."

Surprised by Pat's *laissez-faire* tone, Charlie's next word blew out on a soft, stunned breath. "Sorry?"

Pat tilted her head, another slow eye-blink. "Baby. You and Evan. I see it. Poppa can see it. Lyon can see it."

Her stomach flipped, pancakes riding a wave of terror crashing through her torso. "It's not what you think."

"No?" Pat's penciled eyebrows rose. "You haven't snagged my grandson's heart? You haven't snagged Clifford's heart? You haven't snagged my baby girl's husband's heart?"

Her baby girl's husband.

Oh gosh.

Sorry, Rae.

"Rae was my best friend," Charlie had said. "More of a sister than my own was to me. I'd never"—she closed her eyes against the lie and started over—"I didn't mean to infringe."

Charlie had looked to Pat, feeling her own face crumpling, then grasped the older woman's hands. She needed Pat to believe what she had to say. She needed penance, forgiveness...acceptance.

"Pat. This is nothing, I promise. It *was* something. It was. But now, I'm going to make sure it's not. I don't want to jeopardize my relationship with any of you. I'd never dream of hurting you or Cliff or..."

She trailed off when Pat smiled and shook her head.

"Well, I certainly hope that is not true."

She had blinked up at Rae's mother, shocked. "Wuh-what part?"

Pat laughed her musical laugh and Charlie had felt her eyebrows slide to center in confusion. "I hope it's not 'nothing,' Charlotte. Those boys love you. All of them."

She tossed a hand toward the hallway. "Including Clifford. And you know how much I love you."

She did know that. But it was great to hear. "I love you, too," she said, an emotional edge in her voice.

"Rae's not here for Evan, baby." Pat blinked a few times, her eyes not watery, but looking like they might be headed there.

Lord help her, if Pat lost it, so would she.

"I know."

Pat grasped her hand. "You are here. You are *here*. Living and breathing and loving them both. I can see that, too."

She did love them both. More each day.

"I care very much," she said.

"You love Lyon."

"Yes, of course."

"You love Evan."

Charlie had bitten her lip and swallowed thickly before speaking. "He's a very good friend."

Rae's mother tilted her chin and raised her eyebrows. "You *love* him, Charlotte."

Yes. She did. She closed her eyes in a combination of shame and embarrassment.

"I'm glad you have one another."

"You are?" Charlie sought Pat's eyes for a sign she wasn't telling the truth. But Pat always told the truth. That was her way.

"I love you like my own daughter. I have missed you like crazy since you have stayed away. Having you in my home, eating at my table, making my grandson laugh, and putting a smile on the hard face of my son-in-law has made me happier than I've been in a long, long time."

"Pat." She'd felt her own tears welling. Because it was all too much.

"I know, baby." She pulled her close and dropped an arm around her shoulder. "It's hard to imagine us accepting this. Evan was our baby girl's husband, and we miss Rae. We hurt for him and Lyon as much as we hurt for ourselves. We lost her, and it's so unfair."

All this Charlie knew.

"But you lost her, too." Her hand rubbed circles on Charlie's back. "You lost her and you deserve to grieve, deserve to heal, and deserve happiness as much as any other member of this family."

Almost verbatim what Evan had said.

This family. That was nice.

"You make Evan happy," Pat pointed out.

Charlie's chest inflated. She liked the idea of making Evan happy. Seeing him happy made her happy.

"Keep making him happy. And come see us more often." She stood and brushed a hand down her wrinkle-free slacks. "They're waiting for you in the den. Cliff's showing off his racecar collection and boring our boys to death."

Our boys. She liked that, too.

Pat opened the bedroom door and turned before she walked out. "Sandwich for the road?"

"Sure, Pat. Thanks."

She winked. "You got it, sweetheart."

Charlie, Evan, and Lyon had eaten their sandwiches on the trip home—ham and cheese on wheat bread, which Lyon hated but Evan made him eat anyway.

Now, the SUV edged down the long, winding road leading back to their houses on Lakeside Avenue.

"Lyon, bud. When we get in, I'm doing laundry, so bring your bag to the laundry room, yeah?"

"Yeah, Dad."

She wanted to offer to do it for him, but then, they were not on vacation, she reminded herself. And though he had stitches, Lyon was perfectly capable of carrying his backpack into the laundry room.

Evan pulled into her driveway first. "Wait here, bud," he told Lyon, then got out. She followed.

He lifted the back of the SUV, refusing to let her carry her bag, which wasn't big or unmanageable. Then he waited while she unlocked her door and followed her in.

He dropped the bag on the chair in the front room and pulled her into his arms, lighting her on fire with a long, slow, wet kiss.

When she pulled back, she realized her fingers were twined in his hair.

"Missed you, Ace," he growled. "Tonight. Dinner at my place."

"Evan . . ."

"I want you to stay the night, too. So when you unpack your bag, pack another."

She shook her head. "Lyon shouldn't—"

"He shouldn't control what we do," Evan finished for her. "I'll talk to him when I get home." His hand skated down her pants and cupped her bottom. With a soft squeeze, he said, "Dinner."

She nodded her agreement—figuring he wouldn't take no for an answer—and earned another series of kisses on her lips. After he'd curled her toes, he swaggered out to the SUV and left.

Then she stood by the chair staring at her bag for she

didn't know how long, trying to figure how he had talked her into staying the night when the very thing Charlie thought she needed was a night away from him so he and Lyon could have family time together.

Well.

There was no going back, so she'd do the next best thing. Go over for dinner but not with a bag. She wasn't going to shack up with Evan while Lyon was home no matter what Evan said.

CHAPTER TWENTY-TWO

Lyon had had about enough of no electronics and it showed in every whine and wallow on the couch over the last hour. Evan left the kitchen, and the prep for dinner: salmon, asparagus, and baked potatoes, to tend to his son who was flailing in the living room.

He plopped down on the couch and leaned over his kid, tickling him, but careful not to make him move his head too much. Didn't matter. Soon, he was roiling, giggling, and begging through those high-pitched squeals of his, "Stop it, Dad! Stooooop iiiiit!"

He stopped it. "I have to talk to you, buddy."

Lyon recovered, pushing himself up. "Okay."

"About Aunt Charlie."

He picked at a thread hanging from his T-shirt. "'kay."

"Did you like her being at Nonna and Poppa's house with us?"

He nodded. "Yeah."

"Me too. I like having her around." Evan took a breath. "I'd like her in our house more often."

Lyon looked up.

"Would that be okay with you? If Charlie was here more?"

"Like for dinner?"

"Dinner . . . and breakfast."

Lyon's eyebrows pinched. "For pancakes?"

Kids. So simple.

"Yep. Pancakes. She's going to sleep here sometimes. I wanted you to know." He wasn't seeking his son's permission—but he knew Lyon would appreciate a say, and a heads-up.

Evan wanted Charlie in his life more, and in his bed more. And while he knew they had to be careful—she was a moaner during sex, and not a quiet one—he knew the right place for her was curled up next to him.

The right place for her was in his and Lyon's lives.

"Can I play my game now?" Lyon asked, done with this adult conversation.

Evan ruffled his hair—what was left of it—on the side of his head without stitches. They'd get used to it. He and Lyon had been through worse than a short, slightly choppy haircut.

"Did you feed Terror?"

"Yeeeeessss," Lyon said with an eye roll.

Good to see he was back to his old self.

"Yeah, bud." Evan stood and paced to the kitchen. "Have at it."

* * *

Charlie was impressed. Evan cooked the fish to flaky perfection and halved the potatoes to lay them face down on the grill as well. Asparagus was wrapped in foil with lemon—pretty fancy for Evan.

After she teased him about it more than once during the meal, he admitted his sister, Angel, had provided him with the how-to on the semi-elegant dinner. Charlie was touched he'd gone to the trouble.

Lyon was not impressed, so Evan fixed him hot dogs, muttering, *Kids*, but she'd watched him grill himself one as well, eating it while their fancy dinner finished cooking.

Charlie and Evan cleaned up, though Lyon did contribute by loading the silverware in the dishwasher. They settled in to watch *Man of Steel,* since she hadn't seen it yet and Lyon had bragged it was "the best movie in the world." She didn't know about that, but she did enjoy the guy who played Superman. *Yowza*. He was a hottie.

But the handsome blue-eyed man on screen had nothing on the handsome blue-eyed man who was lying flat on his back on the couch, head turned to watch the film. Lyon had settled on the floor with a pillow and blanket.

Having finished wiping down the countertops, she walked into the room and toward an adjacent recliner. Evan gestured to the sliver of sofa next to his prone body. "Ace. Over here."

"I'm okay."

"I'm not," he said.

She tipped her head in a meaningful nod to Lyon, and Evan promptly shook his head and pointed at the very limited space on the couch where she was supposed to wedge her body.

"The chair is fine, really," she tried again.

"It's not fine for me."

"Aunt Charlie, it's starting!"

At Lyon's frustrated pronouncement, she gave in and went to Evan, who smiled when she gave him his way and tugged her down onto the couch. He turned on his side, pulled her butt to his hips, wrapped an arm around her waist, and linked their fingers.

Then she fell asleep.

She stirred slightly when Evan moved, aware of him climbing over her and mumbling for her to stay put. As if she could have moved on her own after two sleepless nights in a row. She stayed put, her eyes closed, hearing rustling and distant conversation: Evan asking Lyon to brush his teeth.

Wiped out, she'd fallen back to sleep by the time Evan returned—and having no idea how long he was gone, was surprised to open her eyes and find the living room completely dark and silent.

"This wasn't what I meant when I asked you to stay the night," he said from somewhere in the dark.

She stretched, warm and cozy in the sofa. He put a knee between hers and came down on top of her, his weight a warm blanket.

"Ace."

"Mmph," she grunted.

"Get in my bed," he whispered, kissing her lips.

"Going home," she said, groggy, not sure how she'd get her limbs to do what her mouth had suggested.

"My bed."

"Home," she whined.

"Ace."

"Shut up."

His weight and warmth left her and a second later she

was lifted into his arms and being carried up the stairs to
his bed. Too tired to argue, she looped her arms around
his neck.

Soft blankets enfolded her and she curled to her side.
"Have to brush my teeth."

"Do it in the morning."

"Yuck," she mumbled, feeling him crawl in beside her,
but it was too late. She'd already faded off to sleep, his
body curled around her back, his arm at her breasts, and
his hips snuggled into her butt.

* * *

This time when Evan jerked awake from pictures flashing in his head, it wasn't only Rae's lifeless eyes and still
body. It was also the image of Lyon, blood pouring from a
head wound while he splashed in the Mosleys' swimming
pool.

Heart racing, sheets damp, his eyes flew open at the
same time his arm lashed out to the other side of the bed.
Instead of encountering cool, empty sheets, his hand
landed on the soft, feminine curve of a hip. In response
to his not-so-gentle touch, Charlie answered with a soft,
feminine hum.

He'd forgotten he wasn't alone.

It'd been a while since his last nightmare. Waking up
to thoughts of Rae typically drove him straight to the studio where he'd paint off his jitters. How could he do that
with Charlie here? He hadn't considered this might happen. Hadn't—

"Ev," her sleepy voice murmured in the dark room. She
rolled over to face him, scooted closer, and threw an arm

over his chest. Palm flat on his sweat-slicked skin, she must have felt his escalated heart rate because she mumbled, still sounding sleepy, "Okay?"

More than four years had passed since he woke up next to a woman. That woman used to be Rae. That woman continued to be Rae, only he woke up to her memory instead. Now, Charlie nestled against him, taking a deep breath and slipping right back into the sleep he'd barely nudged her from, he considered her question.

Was he okay?

The nightmare that jarred him awake had already turned foggy, the memory less terrifying with his eyes open. Flat on his back, he pulled in a deep breath and rubbed his eyes, dropping his hand over Charlie's hand resting on his chest.

His thoughts were organized and rational. His limbs were not tingling with impending doom. Lyon was home safe. Charlie was in his bed, in his arms. The clock in the living room ticked the seconds away.

And remarkably, Evan's eyes slid shut.

Wrapping an arm around Charlie's shoulder, he pulled her closer. She came, throwing a leg over his leg and inching her hand up to his neck.

He gave her another squeeze, finding solace in her presence and the feel of her breath warm against his neck.

He was asleep within minutes.

* * *

Sleep came, or maybe it never left, and it didn't fade off until she heard clattering in the kitchen the next morning. Charlie sat up, stretched, and pulled on her dress from yesterday. What she really needed was a shower, but she settled for brushing her teeth with the toothbrush Evan had given her.

I have a toothbrush at his house, she thought absently as she stared at her foamy-mouthed reflection in his bathroom mirror.

Downstairs, he sat on a stool, flipping through a magazine and sipping a mug of coffee. Oh, he looked good there. Bare feet resting on the bottom rung, tattooed arms leaning on the counter. One bicep flinched impressively as he lifted his mug to his lips...which seemed rather intentional now that she considered how little effort it took to lift a mug.

"Show off," she muttered.

His lips left the edge of the mug and he turned his head to give her a grin, flexing for her again. "Brush your teeth?"

"*Yes*," she said, sounding slightly impatient. He'd goaded her into staying. And she'd stayed. Not her fault. He was too hot, and she was too rested, for her to get any dander up over the situation. Didn't mean he got off easy. Petulantly, she added, "I'm in yesterday's clothes."

His eyes heated as they grazed from her head to her toes. "Got no complaints, Ace."

"Where's the kiddo?"

"Legos."

"So he is seven."

"Seems so."

She tapped the edge of the countertop with nervous fingers. "I have a shoot this afternoon."

Unfazed, he turned back to his magazine. "Dinner."

"Going to be a late one."

He put down his mug, abandoned the periodical, and slipped off the stool. She braced herself for an argument or a kiss. In front of her, he breathed out a sigh, very close to her lips, but she didn't get a kiss.

Bummer.

"You don't want to have dinner with us?"

Us. She liked that. "I don't want you to have to wait on me."

"We can save you a plate."

We. She liked that, too.

"I'll grab a bite at the event." In a nervous gesture, she pushed her hair behind her ear. "Really. It's not a big deal." It wasn't, she didn't think, but his face suggested he didn't agree with that assessment.

"What event?" he asked.

"Policeman's Ball."

"Seriously?"

She nodded. "Mm-hmm. Every year. First time I was asked to do this gig. Could be good. If they like me, they might ask me back next year."

"'Course they'll like you," he said gently, and that made her tip her head the slightest bit closer.

She'd promised Sofie to fill in for a last-minute photographer need, and her desperate-for-a-photographer friend had been over the moon, promising to double her pay (Charlie refused) and take her out for dessert after (Charlie had accepted).

"Stop by when you get in." He dropped a kiss on her lips.

"I might be late."

"I'll wait."

Oh boy, she liked that too, too much. How was she supposed to get things back to normal when he kept insisting on moving the "normal" boundaries closer and closer to himself?

She chewed her lip and shot a glance to the door. "I'd better go get ready."

"Taking Lyon school shopping tomorrow. Interested?"

She shook her head. "Tomorrow's not good for me. I'm sorry."

"Not a big deal." He shrugged and she could tell he meant it.

"Are you going to go...alone?" When her father took them school shopping, he used to hand Charlie and Dani each a wad of money and tell them, "When it's gone, it's gone," then drop them at the mall and tell them to take the bus home.

Not surprisingly, Evan was way more present than her father had been, but men and clothes shopping? In her mind, never the twain shall meet.

He lifted a very sexy dark eyebrow. "Yeah. Why?"

She swept aside the notion that shopping was a woman's job and realized that in Evan and Lyon's world, there had been only them for a while. They were self-sufficient, these Downey boys. Which apparently included laundry, cooking, and school clothes shopping.

"Nothing. Have fun."

"See you tonight," he said.

"It'll be late," she said to his back.

Without turning he confirmed. "Tonight, Ace."

* * *

The ball was a success. There were lots of well-dressed policemen in attendance. Sofie had gone on a blind date with one of them—Officer Brady Hutchins. He was a good-looking guy. Head full of blond hair, full lips, broad shoulders. According to Sofie, their date was "nice," but neither of them had felt the spark.

And didn't Charlie know just what her friend meant by that? Now that Evan had set her panties on fire more than once, she could see the lack of spark in every relationship she'd had in the past.

After the ball, Sofie and Charlie retreated to a nearby, all-night diner to feast on hot fudge sundaes and French fries.

It didn't take long for Charlie to spill about Lyon's stitches, the trip to Rae's parents' house, and the way she'd spent last night curled into Evan.

"You have the blessing from Rae's mom!" Sofie's face had turned to sweet, soft perfection. "Embrace this, Charlie. Embrace the gift of the people who love you most saying it's okay for you to be in love with Evan."

"I'm trying," had been her parting comment.

Full of trans-fats and exhausted, Charlie returned home, kicked off her heels, and flexed her tired feet on the floor.

She filled a glass with water and drank it. Her eyes automatically slid out her kitchen window, past the neighbors' house, and to Evan's studio. The lights were on and she could imagine him perched in front of a large canvas.

"Embrace it," she mumbled to herself.

Those words, and wanting to see him in his element in the calm of two a.m., had her reaching for her camera bag, spinning on her favorite lens, and heading straight to him. If she was lucky, he'd left the door open and she might be able to get a few shots in before he noticed she was there.

Luck was on her side.

The side door was unlocked, so she slipped into the laundry room. And, having left her shoes off, tiptoed barefoot across the hall and to the studio's doorway. He had earbuds in, head bobbing as he mixed paint on a tray in one hand.

Charlie lifted the camera to her eye and peered through it, sweeping the room and adjusting the focus on the canvas she'd requested he burn. The one smeared with paint from their bodies; the one they'd rolled around on while kissing and laughing.

True to his word, he'd kept it, adding more brushstrokes to hide what it actually was. To be fair, it did look more like a work of art and less like impressions of their nude bodies. But she knew what to look for—and could easily see a butt cheek here, a nipple there...oh yeah. The sex was still there.

With a shake of her head, she returned to her viewfinder and zeroed in on the sexiest painter she'd ever seen.

One of his legs was straight out, heel to the floor, the other foot balanced on the wheels of the stool. The canvas in front of him featured Swine Flew, goggles on, cape flapping behind him, wearing a stars and stripes outfit reminiscent of Evel Knievel.

Behind Swine was Mad Cow, chomping on what looked like a stalk of wheat and scowling, obviously trailing at a slow pace rather than follow Swine's frantic jog. She snapped a few photos of Evan, praying he wouldn't see her too soon so she could get a few unplanned shots.

She got five, six if she counted the one when he turned, brows raised, paintbrush elevated, a slightly surprised expression on his handsome face. And she did count it, because she'd bet it was the best one.

She snapped one more when a crooked smile lifted half his mouth, but that one was for her. The smile, and the photo.

"Ace."

Lowering the camera, she found him still smiling, now swaggering toward her in a bad-boy strut similar to his bovine twin behind him.

"You are Mad Cow. It's official."

He scowled at her, his impression of his cartoon. She laughed.

Scooping her up in his arms, he hugged her close.

He felt good. So, so good. She held him.

"Thought you weren't coming," he said into her hair.

"I'm not...yet," said some errant part of her brain.

Normally, when she wasn't around Mr. Never Censors Himself, she didn't talk like that. She liked the reaction it received, however, since she was now being kissed deeply, with tongue, an accompanying growl sounding in the back of his throat.

"That's my girl." His voice was rough, his hold extra tight.

"About staying..." She pushed on his shoulder to step away from him.

He didn't budge.

"Maybe I shouldn't."

Tighter arms. "Yes. You are."

"Lyon—"

"Is asleep."

"Knows we're getting close," she finished.

"So?"

"*So*? You don't think it's confusing for him to see me as your latest girlfriend?"

Evan's arms loosened. His scowl was now his own and not for show. And not nearly as fun as it had been a moment ago. She supposed she could have eased into that observation, but she'd crashed in with it, much like Swine Flew.

"I didn't mean that. I just meant I'm not Rae."

She watched as his *scowl* scowled. "I know you're not Rae. Lyon knows that, too. He loves you because you're *you*."

Her throat closed. Partially because he'd said Lyon loved her for her, and partially because she wondered if Evan was about to tack on that he, himself, might be suffering the similar plight of loving her for her.

Or, she could be blowing things out of proportion. She wondered if she blew things out of proportion more often than she acknowledged. Not in an overreacting kind of way, but in an *underreacting* one. Like the Rae thing. She'd built it so big in her head she'd failed to see any of the reality in front of her face.

The fact that Evan and his in-laws were very close. The fact that Lyon loved her. The fact that the Mosleys loved her and loved Evan and were supportive of her horning in on Rae's family. Except no one saw it that way.

Charlie had gotten so used to getting out of the way, she'd done it without question.

Definitely out of proportion.

Evan palmed her head and forced her gaze to his turquoise eyes, then delivered a blow covered in softness, causing her breath to exit her lips on a disappointed sigh.

"I'd love to make another painting with you, Ace." He stroked his fingertips into the thickness of her hair. "Especially tonight. Hell, you look amazing."

That wasn't what caused the disappointment. The disappointment came next.

"But, next time we throw down, you do the throwing."

She licked her lips and shook her head as she thought about what he said. "Sorry?"

He didn't correct her, didn't scold her for "apologizing," instead he accepted it, which was kind of worse.

"You look hot, Ace."

Not an answer, but the way he'd said the word *hot* reminded her of all the other *hot* things they'd done together, and she forgot she'd asked a question. His hands skimmed the length of her tasteful black dress, over her ribs and back before settling on her hips. The throb between her legs intensified.

"Gonna quit forcing you to fit," he said in a low, sexy murmur. "I made you come here. Glad you did. You think Lyon doesn't want you here, but babe, he and I cleared that up."

They did?

"You did?"

He didn't answer that, either. "But right now, your grief for Rae is talking louder than me. So loud, Ace, you're not hearing me," he finished on a whisper, his hold loosening on her body.

No, not loosening.

Letting go.

Was he done trying?

"I'm here when you're ready," he said, which was less reassuring when she wasn't being held tightly against him. "Go home, sleep in your own bed. Wake up in your own bed. See if you like it better than mine."

She already knew the answer. She wouldn't.

"Ev—"

"No excuses, no apologies. You're not on vacation, either. It'd do me good to remember that. You have a home, work, a life separate from ours. A lot to do."

She did, but that didn't mean the Downeys didn't fit into it.

What. Was. *Happening?*

"I'll walk you home." He turned her toward the studio doorway and swatted her rear end lightly.

"Lyon..." she started.

The video baby monitor appeared in front of her face, showing Lyon, his hair much shorter, sprawled on his bed, arms thrown overhead, sawing logs.

"Got it covered." Evan preceded her to the door and opened it. "You need to worry about you for a while, Ace. Let the rest of us worry about us."

* * *

Evan didn't know if this was the push Charlie needed, but he did know constantly browbeating her into making love with him or sleeping next to him was not gonna be the norm.

So.

He was trying something new, thanks partly to a suggestion from Gloria.

She'd crashed into his house today all atwitter, arms in the air, her sleek black hair falling down her back. She clicked her way through the wood floors on high heels, dressed in a short skirt and ripped tee—her Evergreen Cove wardrobe, he was seeing—and shouted, "*Rolling* freaking *Stone*, baby!"

Then she'd grabbed up Lyon, who had been trying to build a Lego fort, and said, "Dance with me!" He did, giggling. She let him go quickly and studied his stitches, letting him explain there were "one hundred" and that they were "super cool." Glo, being Glo, didn't question any of it, agreeing, "One hundred stitches are *not* only super cool, Lyon. They are chick bait."

"Glo."

"What?"

"He's seven."

"So?" She'd propped her hands on her hips. "He's going to be hot like his daddy. Hot with two Ts. I'm preparing him."

"Hot with…Never mind," he'd said, wisely changing his mind on asking for further clarification. He didn't want to know.

After she calmed down, Evan had made Lyon swear he would never, ever, *ever*, refer to himself as "chick bait" lest he wind up single and alone for the remainder of his days. Glo took a stool at the breakfast bar where Evan was making sandwiches.

"Turkey or ham?" he offered.

"I ate."

"Tell me what you're prattling about." He cut his and Lyon's sandwiches into triangles and added Cheetos to the plates. She accepted the bag and ate several before answering.

Lyon took his food into the living room. Evan let him. If only to allow him to be clear of Gloria's spastic energy for the moment.

"*Rolling Stone*," she said, fanning fingers coated with Day-Glo orange dust.

He took a huge bite out of his sandwich and waved at her to go on. "And?"

"Asher got the cover! They want to interview you both!"

"Ash is going to be on the cover of *Rolling Stone*?"

His friend had wanted that since Knight Time landed their hit song. Ash had been disappointed when success hadn't propelled them to the cover of the mag. The continued popularity of the song, paired with a hit children's book, however...

"No shit." Evan shrugged his eyebrows and took a bite.

"I tried to get you on the cover, too, but it was a no-go."

Chewing his sandwich, he thought about what she'd said. He'd never expected to be on the cover of a magazine, and decided right then he didn't want to be. "I'm good," he commented, eating a handful of Cheetos.

"Okay, good. They're flying out here to do the interview since Ash is staying a while."

"How long are you staying?" he asked.

She hadn't looked at him when she answered. "Probably as long as Asher."

Really.

"You guys fight like two cats in a sack," he pointed out.

"I fight with everyone."

True. But with Asher, Gloria looked hurt by it.

"He's my biggest client right now," she covered, laying it on thick with, "no offense."

He polished off his sandwich and Cheetos while she discussed the details about *Rolling Stone* and glossed *over* any details about her and Asher. Probably wasn't a good topic to launch into with his kid in the room, anyway. Evan didn't need to hear about their *sexcapades*.

In the studio, he showed off his latest illustration. With a shake of her head, Glo bolstered his spirits. "I knew when I saw your work you were talented. I knew it. And then to have Ash step in to pen the books…" She grinned over at him, her blue eyes going soft. "Sometimes things work out even when you don't expect them to."

He suspected she was talking about more than his involvement with Mad Cow and Swine Flew, but kept that to himself.

"How are you and Charlie? How was the trip to Rae's mom and dad's house?"

He filled her in, not leaving out the part where Charlie had tried to dump him on the deck and the way he'd gone to her after. He told Glo about Patricia, who let Charlie know this morning where she and Cliff stood. Evan knew where they stood. Charlie harbored major guilt over Rae's death and over what was developing between them. He'd told Pat and Cliff as much while Charlie showered.

Pat got it right away. Cliff nodded, agreed "we love Charlie," then escaped the emotions in the room with Lyon in tow to wax poetic about his toy car collection.

Glo had chewed her lip while he spoke, looking indecisive.

"Much as I love the two of you together…"

Did she? News to him.

"…I have to say, you need to give the poor girl some time to process. Her ex left her for another woman, and married that woman instantly. As one who understands abandonment," Glo said, pressing her nails to her chest, "I can tell you, she needs time to deal."

"She can *deal* with me close by," he'd argued.

"Maybe. Maybe not." Glo had stepped in close and put

a hand on his upper arm. "I'm a girl who knows what it's like to be alone. I need my space. When you're used to dealing with things by yourself, it's *easier* to deal with them by yourself." She'd dropped her hand, her gentle moment over almost as soon as it began. "Besides, she doesn't need you going all caveman and dragging her back to your house by the hair. You can't fix it for her."

He knew that. Hell, he'd told Charlie that.

Now, walking along the beach next to Charlie, her pace leisurely, her eyes turned upward, he followed her gaze. Stars twinkled in the vast dark sky and the moon sat fat and round, illuminating everything in a bluish glow.

He considered this whole "space" thing and came to the conclusion Glo had a point. He had four years of space to deal with who he'd become after Rae passed. Aside from the times Charlie had visited Columbus, she'd had hardly any time to deal with him.

So. Space.

At her back porch, he stopped short of climbing her stairs. He watched her do it, though, appreciating the tight black dress cupping her ass. Man, he wanted her tonight.

Camera in hand, she spun and snapped another picture of him. He pressed his fingers over his eyes as the flash all but blinded him.

"Warn me, Ace."

"Sorry about—"

"*Ace.*"

"Sorry."

He smiled when she winced. She may get her space, but he wouldn't leave her hanging. "Get your ass back down here and kiss me."

Happily she obliged him, and he waited as she came

down one step, then another, stopping short of coming to ground level where he stood. Her face aligned with his perfectly from the second step and made it extra easy for him to palm her ass as he made out with her long and slow. If she wasn't going to be in his bed, the least he could do is send her to her room distracted and damp.

She wiggled against him and when her hands tightened in his hair, he figured he'd achieved that goal. Leaving her wanting more left him wanting more.

He stepped back and started toward his house. "Got a chubby to walk off."

"Crude," she said, but her grin suggested she liked what she heard.

Too bad it was true. He did, in fact, have a chubby to walk off. He took his time strolling home, and tried to think of something other than Charlie.

$\mathscr{C}$HAPTER TWENTY-THREE

$\mathscr{T}$he knock on Charlie's back patio door came around four a.m.

She bolted out of bed, getting a heck of a dizzy spell as she did, needing to hold on to the wall to anchor herself for a few seconds until her head straightened out.

Her first thought when she heard the knock was of Lyon and her second thought was of Evan. Her third thought was the phone battery had died and that's why she didn't get a call about whatever trouble they were in.

When she slid the door aside and found Gloria on her deck, her head swam for a different reason. Confusion. A lot of it.

"Gloria?"

Not only was Gloria Shields standing on the back deck, but her eyes were red from crying and her makeup was gone, also from the crying, Charlie assumed.

"Is . . . Evan okay? Lyon okay?"

"I think so. I thought you'd be over there." Glo blinked a few times at Evan's house and then back at Charlie. Fat tears rolled down Gloria's cheeks. "Which makes this awkward."

Charlie wasn't completely awake yet, but she was pretty sure Glo's pronouncement didn't make sense. "Why did you knock if you didn't think I was here?"

"Because I secretly hoped you were."

Which didn't make a lot of sense, either. "Want to come in?"

She shook her head. "Can you come out? With coffee?"

"I can do that, sure."

Glo collapsed on the porch swing and crossed her arms as she studied the dark lake. Charlie moved to the coffee-pot, noticing the clock on the stove read 4:15. It was way, way too early to be awake and caffeinated, but this was an emergency.

Obviously, if Gloria, who was more Evan's friend than hers, had come to her house hoping / not hoping she was home.

Well. Glo was in luck. Because if Charlie knew one thing it was how to entertain on her fabulous patio. Two mugs of coffee and a bag of Pepperidge Farm Milanos in her hands, she went outside to deliver them to her guest.

Gloria Shields had yet to stop crying.

"Her name is Jordan."

Charlie blinked. "Jordan?"

"That's how the skank at Asher's house an hour ago introduced herself to me."

Oh gosh. Asher.

Not a catch, Ace. A mess.

He was right. He was a mess.

"I was up late working." Glo swiped her eyes. They filled instantly. "I missed him so I drove to his cabin and knocked on the door." She turned her watery eyes on Charlie. "He didn't answer. But Jordan did. Wearing a skimpy little scrap of silk and looking at me like *I* was the piece of trash."

Charlie's heart lurched. "No."

"That's not why I'm here," Glo blurted.

"It isn't?"

Glo blinked her tears away and slid into that no-nonsense woman Charlie knew her to be. "Nope. I'm here because I am full of shit, and I thought you should know. I give bad advice. I gave Evan bad advice. I give myself bad advice."

"Evan?"

Glo lifted a brow and dug a hand into the Pepperidge Farm bag. "I told him you needed space." She shook her head, took a bite of the Milano. "You don't. You need smothered. You need caveman dragged to his house by the hair."

Maybe it was the early hour, but Charlie wasn't sure what Glo was getting at. Hugging her mug, she repeated, "Caveman...dragged?"

With a nod, Glo said, "Girls like us do. We need to be pursued because our families have already proven we can't win their love. Right?"

Huh. She made an excellent point, actually. Hadn't Charlie's dad proven that years ago when he left Charlie and Dani on their own? Hadn't he continued to prove to them now, by keeping his distance, that he couldn't care less if he had a relationship with either of his daughters?

"You want a guy who will pursue you," Glo said, eating the rest of her cookie. "Not a guy like Asher, who when you give him an inch of space, fills it with *Jordan*."

Having no idea what else to say, Charlie whispered, "I'm sorry."

"Total jerk."

Asher had sabotaged his and Glo's relationship before they even had one.

Charlie reached for Glo, wanting to comfort her in some way, but the other woman stood before she could touch her.

"I have a flight back to Chicago to catch. Take care of your boys." With a wave of her hand, Glo marched around the back of the house and to her car waiting in Charlie's driveway.

After she left, Charlie thought about going over to Asher's cabin, guns blazing, then changed her mind. Asher's self-destruction was his problem. Charlie had problems of her own. Like the fact she'd backslid a bit. Thankfully, Gloria had delivered some of the best news Charlie had ever heard.

Evan hadn't wanted to back off; he'd only done so at his friend's suggestion.

CHAPTER TWENTY-FOUR

Rolling Stone.

Rolling. Freaking. *Stone.*

Charlie could hardly contain herself as she watched the somewhat wrinkled yet pleasant-looking reporter from *Rolling Stone* magazine interview Asher and Evan.

If it'd set in for Evan yet that he was going to be in a nationally distributed, extremely cool magazine, it didn't show. Asher, meanwhile, looked like the kid who found a golden ticket to Willy Wonka's chocolate factory.

He sat on Evan's patio furniture, elbows on his knees, leaning in close to consider the questions. But when the reporter turned away to speak to Evan, Asher's feet began bobbing, or he'd rub his hands together nervously.

Super excited. Charlie's smile faded as her thoughts returned to last night—er, early this morning.

Asher Knight was a mess.

Poor Gloria.

Since Charlie had been busy working before rushing over to watch the interview, she hadn't had a chance to set Evan straight or tell him about Gloria's visit. Or about all the thoughts pinging around her head while she hunkered over her computer this morning.

Despite her misgivings about Rae, Lyon, or her fitting into the family, Charlie was beginning to think this was a gift horse she was most assuredly looking in the mouth.

So, here she was, keeping an eye on Lyon while Tiger Thompson, reporter with Rolling Stone, interviewed Evan and Asher.

Lyon got a big kick out of Tiger due to their similar names—though Charlie doubted "Tiger" was the reporter's real name—but had since retired to the living room to watch a movie. Charlie simultaneously peeked in on him and clicked photos of the guys.

Interview completed, they stood. Tiger shook Asher's and Evan's hands, then walked her direction, a smile on his face. "Ms. Harris. Get any good shots?"

"Oh, I don't know. Maybe."

"May I?" He gestured to the camera.

Slightly embarrassed, Charlie started to turn Tiger down until Evan sidled up next to her and dropped a hand on her lower back. "Show him, Ace."

She tilted her camera to show him the photos she'd snapped of the interview, and at Tiger's encouragement, kept scrolling back, through the photos she'd taken when Asher first got there and he and Evan were chatting and cracking open beers waiting for Tiger's arrival.

"I didn't know you took those," Evan commented.

"Long as I look good," Asher called from across the deck.

"These are great, Charlie," Tiger said with what sounded like genuine appreciation.

She scrolled back a few more, to the ones she'd snapped of Evan painting before he knew she'd entered the studio. "Oh, sorry, too far."

"Whoa, whoa," Tiger said gently. "Wait. That last one."

Her favorite. Evan's paintbrush raised to the canvas, head turned toward the camera, eyebrows slanted, eyes bright and surrounded by a thick shroud of dark lashes. This was the photo when he'd sensed her behind him and turned. In what he called "the zone," she had seen by the look in his eyes that he was half in it, lost in concentration. Wrapped in the passion of his project.

It was her absolute favorite shot. An honest portrait of the man standing with her now, his hand on her back. In short, it was beautiful in a way that made her throat tighten.

"That," Tiger said. "That's what we need."

"Sorry?" she asked at the same time Evan said, "Excuse me?"

"The inset photo of you," he told Evan. "I was going to ask if you had a professional headshot, but your talk of painting and what inspired you and how you and Asher arrived at these characters..." He gestured toward the display on her camera. "Well. There it is. In that shot."

"Thank you," Charlie said, honestly flattered.

"Asher's flying out to do a shoot with us for the cover and a few pages inside, but this is the shot I want for my article." He shot her a huge grin. "Can you e-mail it to me?"

"I—"

"She'll have our agent call and negotiate a sale," Evan returned.

Her jaw dropped. *Our* agent? She didn't have an agent.

Tiger lifted his chin like he might challenge Evan, then his smile curled up on one side. "Fair enough." He offered his hand to Charlie. "Ms. Harris. I'll be in touch."

She shook his hand and watched as he shook Evan's again. Once he'd rounded the deck and she heard his car start, she turned to Evan with wide eyes.

"Negotiate a price?"

"Yes, Ace. You don't e-mail a vulture like Tiger Thompson your work for free."

She looked down at the photo she knew was good, but still... "It took me only a few seconds to line up and snap. How much could it be worth?"

He clasped her neck with both hands and feathered his thumbs along her jaw. "Took you a decade to hone that kind of skill. You deserve a fair price for it."

"Is it okay? It's such a private photo." It was, too. Evan was raw, real, and perfect.

Evan lifted the camera, held out to the side since he'd stepped in so close, and studied the display. "He's right. It's perfect."

"It's you," she said simply.

Something in his eyes changed. They grew soft, then warm. Then downright hot. "Meaning?"

She swallowed thickly and told him the truth. "It's the real you. Passionate, wild, dedicated." On a whisper, she finished, "It's beautiful."

His eyes never left hers and something in them intensified. Then his hands speared into her hair, and he put his lips on hers for a long, slow kiss. Her eyes sank shut as she savored the feel of his mouth.

Until a seven-year-old boy's voice lifted on the air. "Dad, can I have..."

Her eyes popped open. She jerked her head back on her neck and pried her lips away from Evan's. Her heart raced as a thousand thoughts hit her. Lyon saw her kiss his dad. Rae. Evan hadn't let her go yet. Why hadn't he let her go yet?

Charlie tried to twist out of his grip, but he held her fast and palmed her jaw at the same time he turned his head to greet his son.

"Can you have what?"

Lyon's face was scrunched into a combo smile and grimace. "Are you kissing Aunt Charlie?"

Oh. My. Gosh.

"Yeah," Evan answered.

"Gross!"

Evan's fingers slid around to cup her nape. "Better get used to it, buddy."

Her heart hit her throat.

"Remember how we talked about her being around more?" Evan asked his son. "Her staying over sometimes? Well, I'm going to be kissing her more, too."

Oh gosh. He said it. Just blurted it right out. Why not tell the kid I'm replacing his mother?

"Evan," she whispered. "I don't think—"

"Why?" Lyon giggled.

"Because Aunt Charlie is a girl and girls like kisses," Evan supplied.

All true. She chewed on her lip.

"Whatever, Dad!" Lyon was over it, hanging on to the door frame and leaning out of the house.

"Yeah, whatever, Dad," Asher said.

Oh gosh! She forgot all about Asher.

"Can you have what, Lyon?" Evan asked, steering his

son back to the original question he'd interrupted their "gross" kissing to ask.

"Ice cream." He pointed at Asher. "You can get it for me."

"Me? You're lucky you have stitches or I'd throw you over my shoulder, body-slam you on the couch, and tickle you unconscious."

"Whatever!" Lyon yelled back.

Asher turned to Evan. "Dad? Can we have ice cream?"

"Up to Charlie."

"Me?" she gasped, still in shock about…well…about everything.

Asher tipped his head. "Mom? What do you say?"

"She's not a mom!" Lyon said, laughing again.

The entire patio went quiet for a few seconds.

"She could be," Asher replied. "She'd be a good mom, don't you think?"

Oh, Rae.

Charlie's nose stung with impending tears. Evan slid his hands from her neck and wrapped an arm around her shoulders. She lifted a hand to her lips and pressed. Why, oh why, had Asher asked *that* question?

Lyon squinted up at her. "Yeah."

She squeezed her eyes shut to dam the tears as Asher turned Lyon toward the house. "Come on, kid. Ice cream." He sent her a small smile as they disappeared inside.

The moment they were gone, she lost it.

A great *mom*. A boy. A *family*.

Evan pulled her close and she collapsed into his chest and sobbed for a few brief seconds while he shushed her.

"Ace." Hands rubbed her back and she lifted her face and wiped away the tears on her cheeks.

"Sorry, I'm—"

"You're *what*?"

She laughed a watery laugh at the fact that she'd said the "S" word. "Nothing."

With a grin, he let her off the hook. "Want some ice cream?"

"Yeah."

"Yeah." He kissed her lips, took her hand, and led her inside.

* * *

Finally.

Finally, finally, *finally.*

The word echoed in Evan's head, though he was surprised any words could penetrate the canvas of lust covering his brain.

Things had been good between him and Charlie over the last few weeks. Really good. Until this moment, he hadn't thought they could get better. Now, watching her take his cock deep into her mouth, he reconsidered.

Definitely better.

Lyon had started school last week and since then, Charlie joined them each morning for breakfast. Sometimes she was already there, having stayed the night with him; other times she slept at her house but came over.

He accepted this.

He accepted this because of the moment in his studio when he'd stated that if they threw down again, she would do the throwing.

Lately, and more since his son started school and was gone for the day, Charlie had done *a lot* more throwing.

As was the case now.

This morning, she'd walked through his back door, as per her usual. He had poured himself a cup of coffee after dropping Lyon off at school. Prepped for a run before painting—painting had to happen today—he was wearing nothing but a pair of low-slung shorts.

Ideally, nighttime was best for him to work, but deadlines loomed and he and Asher had received a surprise announcement from the publisher requesting a *third* book in the Mad Cow saga. That would keep him busy in the upcoming months, which he was not dreading. The nightmares had all but ceased, and when they did come, he'd go to the studio. But the darkness he used to paint on canvas didn't come. Instead, farm animals in capes and surly cows poured from his brush.

Thanks to Charlie.

He was getting used to the new "normal" settling in around here. Asher was back in LA, Glo was back to selling anything and everything she could. Including some of Charlie's photos she'd relinquished after Glo had forced *Rolling Stone* to pony up the dough for the shot of Evan.

And if this was the new "normal," he thought, watching Charlie's lips take him in again, hell. He was all for it.

She wore some sort of calf-length sheer wrap-thing over her hot pink bikini, blond hair spilling down her back, wide eyes looking up at him. And her tits—God help him. Cleavage for days.

Enough to make his brain check out. He couldn't think.

Thankfully, his dick didn't need his brain to function.

"Ace," he said on a growl.

When she first sank to her knees, his eyes cut to the back door, and he hoped no one in town popped in for an impromptu visit. If so, he wasn't stopping to shoo them

away. It'd take an act of vengeful, abnormal weather—
Sharknado, he decided with a small smile—to get Charlie to stop what she'd started.

If then.

Now, his eyes rolled back as one hand came to rest on
the back of her head. He tightened his fingers in her hair
each time she slid her lips up his shaft, and she let him
press her back down, which he did gently. *Carefully.* She
was exquisite: all cheeks, tongue, and lips. The sensations
rippling over his body built fast, and built hard.

"Ace." He opened his eyes to watch what she was
doing, what she was *enjoying* doing, and promptly closed
them again. Not that he didn't want to see, because *God*,
did he ever want to see . . . But if he kept watching her do
what she was most definitely enjoying nearly as much as
he was, he'd come, and he'd come hard.

"Baby," he tried again, his voice slightly more firm.

"Mmm?" He watched her, his mouth dropped open,
but she wasn't stopping.

His grip tightened on her hair and the countertop, his
eyes welded to hers. He took several short, fast breaths
and tried to think of anything except the woman of his
dreams going down on him in his kitchen.

Shit.

Impossible.

"Ace, I'm going to come." He fisted her hair as he gave
her a warning he hoped sounded sincere.

Her eyes snapped wide and she let him go with a soft
pop. Then she smiled and licked her lips—

Licked.

Her.

Lips.

Then she said, "That's what I'm counting on." And dived back in.

He didn't have to be told twice.

A few more accurately, and lovingly, placed licks and sucks, and he let go. She drank him in, every last drop, drawing a long groan and breath from his chest.

His knees quit holding him up. When he opened his eyes, his entire body was buzzing and his ass was on the floor.

She was on the floor, too, so he pulled her on top of him, all that soft flesh bursting out of her bikini, and held her tight.

He gripped the back of her head. "Got some of that for me?" he asked, amazed he'd found his voice at all.

She kissed him, and when she put her tongue in his mouth, he found new strength, sucking on her tongue, enjoying her amazing mouth. It didn't take long for his cock to stir to life again.

Which she must have liked because next she wrapped her hand around it.

And stroked.

"Couch, Ace."

"Bed?"

"Don't care," he answered. "Couch is closer."

"Mmm," she confirmed. "Couch."

CHAPTER TWENTY-FIVE

Dinner was the no-muss-no-fuss combination of mac and cheese from a box, tater tots from the freezer, and for dessert, Oreos and ice-cold milk.

Charlie had no complaints. She didn't need fancy, and she didn't need healthy. What she needed, she'd discovered over these past weeks, was Evan.

Alarming? Not any longer. She was under no judgment from Rae's parents, or Evan, or, as she learned tonight, Lyon.

"Are you guys getting married?" He carefully spun his Oreo, nose scrunching when the top didn't come off clean, leaving the creamy filling half on each side of the cookie.

She'd been in the middle of licking the cream from her own cookie and realized she was sitting at the breakfast bar, tongue stuck out like the kid from *A Christmas Story* who froze himself to the flagpole.

Evan stopped dunking—the whole cookie, he didn't bother with separating the tops, which was sacrilege in her opinion—and studied his son. Then he popped his cookie in his mouth, chewed, and kept chewing. When he was done chewing, Charlie managed to pull her tongue back into her mouth, but sat, cookie halves in hand, waiting for what she had no idea.

"Dad?"

Evan, done chewing, ran his tongue along his teeth for an agonizing two and a half seconds before answering... with a non-answer.

"Why do you ask, bud?"

Lyon, carefully transferring cream from one side of his cookie to the other, kept his eyes on his task. "Because a boy at school asked about my mom."

Oh, Lyon.

New school. Of course he'd been asked.

"What'd you tell him?" This from Evan.

"What you told me to. Mommy is in heaven."

And like that, her heart went from aching to melting. Evan had prepared his son for this situation. Of course he had. He was an amazing dad.

"I told him my aunt Charlie lived with us sometimes, though."

Her eyes grew wide and met Evan's lifted eyebrow.

"He told me it was illegal for my dad to marry my aunt and I called him a liar."

Oh boy.

"Buddy, calling someone a liar isn't nice."

"I know." Lyon scowled. "I got time-out."

Evan's frown drew down. Clearly, he hadn't known, and clearly, he didn't like that he hadn't known. Charlie felt her face scowling as well. She didn't like it, either.

"It's not illegal for me to marry your aunt Charlie, because she's not really your aunt."

Lyon looked almost hurt. She gave him a wan smile, trusting Evan with this conversation. No way was she skirting the land mines dotted around this talk.

No freaking way.

"Aunt Sadie is your aunt because she married Uncle Aiden. And Aunt Kimber is your aunt because she married Uncle Landon," he explained to Lyon. "Aunt Angel is your aunt because she's my sister by blood."

"By blood?" Lyon said, his lips forming an *eww*.

"That's a way of saying people are related, bud."

"Oh." He looked at Charlie, then his dad. "And you and Aunt Charlie are not related?"

"No."

"And you're not married," he said, puzzling his way through.

"No."

"If you get married, will Aunt Charlie be my mom?"

Oh boy. The cookie halves were getting sweaty. She put them down and brushed the crumbs on her napkin.

Evan didn't miss a beat. "Yes. She'd be your mom. Your second mom."

"A second mom?" Lyon wrinkled his nose in confusion.

"Sure," Evan answered. "You can have two moms."

Lyon's lips pulled. "My friend Rachael has two moms."

Evan tilted a brow at Charlie, giving her a shoulder shrug that said, *See? Easy peasy.*

Meanwhile, she simply shook her head. He'd handled this like a champ, and here she sat trying not to let the moisture in her eyes leak out the sides. She had no idea how this was making her feel. There was an emotion there she couldn't put her finger on.

After Russell and she decided not to marry or have

children, she'd accepted an unmarried, childless future. She didn't need either one to be happy, and for a few years with him, she proved herself right. She didn't have pangs to be a mother, and she didn't do photo shoots at weddings and feel pangs of loss that she wasn't the one in the white dress smiling and posing.

But with Evan, a different possible future laid out before them, she found herself ready to accept an alternate reality. And with the phrase "second mom" bouncing around in her head, Charlie realized it was the perfect term for her. She and Rae. Linked in their pursuit to raise Lyon.

It was kind of beautiful.

"So I would call Aunt Charlie 'Mom'?" Lyon asked.

"Well, bud," Evan said softly. "That's a big deal, isn't it? It's something you'd have to ask Charlie, not something you can decide over Oreos."

Lyon nodded and smiled his cookie-crumbed face at Charlie.

She gave him a watery smile back, losing the battle and the hold on her emotions.

Evan reached for her knee under the table but focused on Lyon. "Yeah?"

Lyon grinned at his dad. "Yeah. Can I play Clashing Clans? I almost rescued the queen yesterday!"

Who reminded him of his mom, Evan had told her.

Oh, her heart.

"Sure, bud."

"Excuse me for a second." Charlie took the opportunity to bolt. Hustling, she moved quickly through the kitchen, down the hall, and paused in the laundry room. Her chest had tightened with an almost panicky feeling. Making a snap decision between the bathroom, the deck, and the studio, she stepped into the bathroom and shut the door.

After several minutes passed, a light knock came on the door, followed by, "Ace?"

She was settled on the edge of the tub, a wad of toilet paper in one hand she had used to quell the stream of tears running down her cheeks. Thankfully, she'd pulled it together before Evan's arrival at the door.

"You decent?" he asked.

She should have known she couldn't avoid him for long. "Yeah."

The door popped open and Evan sat on the closed toilet seat. He took in the tissue in her hand and the way she was slouched—knees pressed together, feet splayed in opposite directions.

"You okay?" he asked.

"Yeah." She shrugged. "Of course."

He reached for her hand, took the tissue, and dropped it into the trash can. Keeping hold of her fingers, he brushed his thumb over her hand. "Sorry about that conversation. That's what having kids is like. They say what they think, drop verbal grenades when you least expect it."

"I was thinking land mines."

Evan's smile did a lot to loosen her tight lungs. "That's a good description, too."

A few more strokes of his thumb on hers and she commented, "You handled that well."

His smile was smaller, but no less handsome. "Thanks."

"I guess we should have explained what we were before we sent him to school with some know-it-all boy who asks highly age-inappropriate questions," she muttered.

Evan laughed again, but it was short-lived. A shadow

of seriousness covered his face as his dark lashes closed over his eyes briefly. He met her gaze with his. "Maybe we should explain what we are to each other first, Ace."

Eep!

She moved to stand and Evan clutched her hand harder. "Too soon?"

Stuck between half up and half down, she sank back onto the edge of the bathtub. It shouldn't be too soon. Evan and she knew each other intimately; had known each other for years. He'd taken her to the pinnacle of her sexual experience—to, up, and over—several times. She was sleeping in his bed, eating dinner with him and his son, who she considered way closer than a nephew.

But somehow talk of family, talk of "mom," talk of permanence and the future had freaked her out.

Freaked her right out.

"It's . . . a lot to think about," she ventured.

"Yes," he agreed. "It is a lot to think about." His eyes redirected to various spots in the room, none of them in the area she was sitting. Then he dropped her hand and stood. As he walked to the hallway, he said, "Lyon's going to watch a movie. You hanging around?"

She nodded.

He gave her a soft smile, followed by a softer, "good," but worry lined his brow. Charlie wanted to ask why, but in a lot of ways she also didn't want to know.

So she didn't ask.

* * *

It occurred to Evan he'd made a lot of assumptions about Charlie.

He thought her rooting herself into their lives since they'd moved here meant she was accepting not only him but also all that came with him. And the things that came with him were Lyon, a deceased wife, a big family spread over three states, and a career that sometimes caused him to keep weird hours.

Evan made the mistake of assuming after he'd warmed her up, loosened her up with a few dozen orgasms, that she'd wedge herself in tightly at his side. What he had learned this afternoon was she wasn't sure where she stood with him.

Or Lyon.

Not that Evan had expected her to propose to him the moment Lyon asked if they were going to get married— because he'd known that was a huge step for her—but he hadn't expected her to dart from the room and hide for the next ten minutes.

When Evan thought about marriage…hell. He was ready.

He married Rae because he loved her and wanted a family. His mom and dad stayed together until cancer took her away, but if she hadn't been ill, he knew his parents would have stayed together forever. His family was full of promising relationships. Shane and Crickitt, Aiden and Sadie, even Landon and Kimber seemed to have their shit together in the marriage *and* kid department.

No, getting married again didn't spook Evan in the least. And getting married to Charlie…He may have had a few relationships with very loose strings since Rae, but he would have never, *ever* started something with Charlie if he didn't think they had staying potential. She was too involved in Lyon's life, in his life.

Now that they were testing the waters, he was sold.

Charlie for good sounded great. She poured herself a
glass of juice and came to the living room where he was
watching...he didn't know what. Some reality show
about moonshine. He hadn't really been paying attention.

She kicked off her shoes and settled on the couch next
to him, curling her feet under her.

He dropped an arm around her and tugged; she molded
to his side. He kissed the top of her head as she sipped
from her glass and emitted a quiet hum of happiness.

Charlie for good. That was exactly what he wanted.
Lyon didn't seem to mind, either.

She was the only one who wasn't all in.

Yet.

* * *

Charlie stayed over at Evan's house the night before last,
but last night opted to sleep in her own bed. Not because
she wanted to but because she needed to get home and
put in some serious hours on the work she'd been avoiding. After a simple dinner of burgers and potato chips,
baked beans and coleslaw from Abundance Market—
Abundance had the best coleslaw—and a Disney movie,
Lyon had gone to bed and she'd followed Evan into his
studio to kiss him good-bye and leave him to his painting.

But after the kiss, he didn't get right to painting.

He did get right to turning her inside out with his
tongue and his hands and a litany of words definitely *not*
for the PG crowd.

She'd escaped—narrowly—but not before he pulled her
onto his lap, slipped his fingers beneath her skirt, and put
her in such a state that she walked back to her house—a

walk she refused to let him accompany her for—on very, very loose knees.

Sometime around two a.m., Evan had come over to extract her from the couch in her office where she'd crashed, but had no such luck getting her to come back to his place. "Letting you have this one, Ace," she remembered him saying before he left, "but this is the last one."

So, last night. Her own bed.

True to his word, the next afternoon, he hadn't let her be.

"Birthday party, Ace," he'd reminded her as she frantically brushed her hair and slipped her feet into a pair of flats.

"I know! Sorry. I got busy."

Busy doing more work on Guy and Mallory Houston's wedding photos. It was the rainiest outdoor wedding Charlie had ever seen. She was able to snap pictures of soggy guests in the outdoor reception tent while it stormed, but the background wasn't pretty. As a result she'd spent most of last night and today in Photoshop, replacing the drab white tent with shots of Evergreen Cove's apple orchard she'd taken last year. To Charlie it seemed a little disingenuous, but Mallory was willing to pay extra for the backdrop swap.

School had started and it hadn't taken long for Lyon to make friends, so when he was invited to a little boy's birthday party, Charlie wasn't surprised. It was an overnight, which Evan had jumped on, telling her, "Good for him to get away. And good for us. Another painting, Ace?"

She'd be lying if she said that suggestion hadn't sent a drove of full-body chills dancing on her skin.

After four and a half hours of piñata-hitting, screaming seven- and eight-year-olds, and chattering with other moms at the party, Evan pulled the SUV to a stop at his house.

He let them inside and once there, reached for Charlie. She lifted her palms to his chest, her eyebrows raising in interest. In a pair of torn, well-worn, very sexy jeans, and a plain gray T-shirt, she'd admit, it was hard to take him to task about anything…except she hadn't liked what she'd seen at the party.

He angled a glance down at her hand on his chest, stopping him from coming closer. "What's this?"

Thoughts of Leslie O'Brian hit her front and center. She was the mom who had adhered herself to Evan's side most of the party. Charlie wouldn't say he'd flirted with the sexy redhead, but he hadn't thwarted her, either.

Charlie knew this because she was very, very good friends with the party planner.

She and Sofie had hovered behind a chocolate-dipped fruit bouquet. Every once in a while Sofie would eat a piece and make a comment, like, "Do you think her boobs are real?" Or, "Evan must have the patience of a saint."

Now, "Saint" Evan leaned in for a kiss. Charlie turned her head.

"Ace."

He palmed her jaw gently, forcing her to acknowledge him. "Not letting you work tonight. We talked about this."

"More like you decreed it."

He grinned, not caring about her attitude. When he pulled her neck and kissed her, she decided to let him. And then she decided kissing him was a lot better than not kissing him. Still, there was the small matter of the woman at the party. Boundaries had definitely been crossed.

Therefore, when his mouth left hers, she said against his lips, "Leslie O'Brian."

His eyebrows met over his nose.

"She spent the day hitting on you like it was her *job*."

"And?"

"*And*?" she asked, her voice sliding a little too close to hysterical for her comfort. "And . . . and . . . I didn't like it."

He smiled again. "No?"

She fisted his T-shirt and stood on her tiptoes, touching her nose to his. "No."

Rather than argue or defend himself, he crushed his lips into hers and thrust his tongue in her mouth.

She'd admit, much better than an argument.

Her hands went into his hair to hold herself up as he backed her through his living room, his chest pressing against her breasts, his hips bumping hers, the hand that had moved to her ass cupping it firmly. He moved his other hand to the back of her head and buried his fingers in her hair as he walked her awkwardly up the stairs to his room.

When his lips left hers, they were at the landing, his big bed behind her. His lips moved to her neck, further preventing her from speaking coherently, then his tongue moved along the sensitive flesh behind her ear. Before she knew it, she'd been stripped of her clothes and dropped on his bed, Evan lowering himself over her.

With his lips wrapped around one nipple and finger and thumb rolling the other, she couldn't think of anywhere else she'd rather be. His tongue delved to her belly button and darted in, then out, and Charlie—thoroughly speechless—held on to his hair and watched through hooded eyes as he settled between her thighs and slicked his tongue along her center.

CHAPTER TWENTY-SIX

Who the hell is Leslie O'Brian?

Evan had no idea.

What he did know is that Charlie was jealous enough to stake a claim on him tonight, thinly veiled as an accusation she hadn't been able to follow through with. And what that meant was, she was close.

What he also knew was she tasted like absolute heaven. From her minty lips and skin smelling of apples, to where he tasted her now—this. *This* was the best taste of all.

Better than the taste of her on his tongue were the sounds she made. Soft mews mixed with breathy pants as she kneaded his head like a content kitten. Better still? He was going to be inside of her in a few short minutes.

She was close. A high-pitched squeak made its way from her throat as she arched her hips and thrust against his face.

A few short seconds, he mentally corrected. Quickening

his pace, he snaked a hand up her torso and reached for a nipple. He squeezed and she bucked. He knew what his girl needed.

Seconds later, she rewarded him with a long, low groan of satisfaction, her ass cheeks tightening on the bed. She came for so long, his tongue started to get tired.

But he was no quitter.

He stopped when her pulling on his hair turned to pushing and she was practically whimpering. He climbed her body and found her still moaning, flat on her back, arm thrown over her eyes, breathing deep and slow.

The room was dark, but he could make out the perfect outline of her large breasts, her flat stomach, smooth, round hips, and her glistening sex.

Didn't take him long to get hard. He pulled off his shirt with one hand at the same time unbuckling his belt.

"Ready, baby?"

"Mmm," came her incoherent response.

"She's ready," he muttered, kicking his shoes to the floor, stripping off his socks. He climbed over her again and removed her arm. "Ace." He kissed her closed eyes. "Wake up, baby. Work to do."

"Sleepy," she whined.

"All you gotta do is hold on."

"Mmph."

Damn. She was out. *Out* out.

He couldn't keep from smiling. He tugged at the covers she laid on top of. "Ass up, Ace."

"No."

"Gotta tuck you in, baby," he said, tugging the covers again.

Then they were yanked from his hand and he faced a

suddenly wide-eyed and very alert Charlie Harris. "What if I want you?"

His lips spread into a grin. "Second wind?"

She nudged him back and slung a leg over his hips. "*Now.*"

Astride him, she positioned him at her entrance before sliding down onto his shaft slowly. Before they made a mistake, he needed to remind her he didn't have a condom on.

"Ace."

"The pill, baby," she said with a grin.

His hands froze on her hips as he allowed himself to savor the feel of being inside her without anything between them. She was on the pill?

"Yeah?" he blew out as she took the rest of him.

She nodded, leaned over him, and kissed his mouth. "*Yeah.*"

His eyes went to her breasts as she started to move. "Fuck yeah," he groaned, enjoying the 3D view of her plush, pink nipples. Her hands on his chest, she moved off him. He caught a nipple in his mouth as she sat down on him again.

His hands went to her lower back. She rose and fell again, this time taking her nipple from his lips. The marked change her breathing told him she was getting off on this as much as he was about to.

Like a wave, she rolled, cresting into him, her belly rubbing into his stomach, her thighs liquid around his. Then she ebbed, pushing back onto his cock and dragging a harsh breath from his lungs with the movement.

He had no idea how long this went on, how long he kept his palms at her back, encouraging her every movement as he wound tight as a spring inside her. Soon, though, her breathing shifted and he knew she was going to come again.

And he wasn't letting her work her way through it.

Holding her close, he rolled with her, staying inside, and laid her on her back. He thrust forward and she let out a sharp "oh!" which he took as encouragement. He thrust again and was awarded with another shout.

Loud. He liked her loud.

"Like that, Ace?"

"Harder," was her reply.

Gladly, he obliged, riding her hard, her nails abrading his back, her shouts of ecstasy in his ear while his own release built to a deafening crescendo.

"Yes!" she cried. "Harder!"

Unbelievably, he went harder, until they were both sliding in the sweat created from their efforts. Her legs were crossed at his back, and she tipped her head back, crying out and clutching him tight. He followed her over, his breath stuttering from his lips.

He dropped his face into her hair, turning his head when it damn near suffocated him. Slowly, he came up from the moment, surfacing with a haze rivaling any alcohol buzz he'd ever experienced.

That's what it was like with Charlie. She was easy to get drunk on, to take in through every form possible. And like an alcoholic, he wanted her night and day, every morning, until he'd binged so much he ached and shook for her again.

She saturated his bloodstream, muddled his mind, and made dealing with life easier in every single way.

At the party today, he'd felt happiness that Lyon, who'd made friends already, was fitting in so well. Happy that Charlie was here to see it.

His next thought was that Rae was missing it.

Normally, Rae was his very first thought. Today, his first thought was Charlie.

It took the twelve-minute car ride home to solidify what he hadn't been able to solidify before. He hadn't decided when—or how—to break the news to Charlie.

Evan pulled out of her pliant body and she made a quick trip to the attached bathroom. When she came in, a sexy smile tipped her lips and she fell into bed. Fell into him. He caught her, propping himself on one elbow to arrange her hair and then tug the blankets so they covered their naked bodies.

She snuggled into him, her butt against his hips, and he wrapped an arm around her waist and cupped one of her breasts in his hand. Nose buried in her neck, he laid and listened to her breathing, until it grew deep and slow. A sound he'd grown to learn was her falling asleep.

When he was sure she'd zonked out, he kissed her neck lightly. She didn't move.

"Love you, Ace," he whispered.

Then he fell asleep, waking in the morning with a numb arm, a breast in his hand, and a smile on his face.

Peace.

After four long years, he'd finally found it.

* * *

"Still okay?"

Charlie sucked in air through her teeth. "Yeah."

The buzzing needle stopped and Evan leaned over her, his turquoise eyes filled with concern. "Ace."

She opened her eyes, her skin tingling. "I'm good. Promise. This hurts more than I thought."

"I can stop."

"No." She clasped the arm holding the needle marking her skin. "I want it finished."

He lowered his warm lips and kissed her before giving her a small, proud smile. "Okay, baby."

This morning, after hangover hash, which as it turned out was just as delicious when she wasn't hungover, Evan led her to the studio for a surprise. Evidently, he'd risen sometime in the night and had drawn an entire page of tattoo ideas for her to choose from.

An entire page of cameras. She'd chosen her favorite and he tweaked it with the changes she requested, then he laid a long, wet kiss on her and led her to the reclined chair in the corner.

The tattoo was relatively small, and only a black-blue outline, but it was perfect. A simple, iconic front-facing camera, the tops of two evergreen trees rising behind it.

He wiped a towel along her tingling, practically numb skin, and the buzzing needle stopped.

"Done, Ace."

Holding her shirt high, she admired the artwork on her body.

His mark on her body.

And he'd enjoyed doing it, she could tell. After instructions on how to care for her new ink, he walked her down the beach toward her house. She rolled up her T-shirt and examined the artwork through the plastic wrap he'd taped to her skin.

"Ace. Sun."

"I know! I had to look one more time."

At her porch, he stopped, pulled her against him, careful not to palm the sensitive and newly tattooed area high on her ribs under her breast, and kissed her. "Picking up Lyon, then we have to run a few errands. The Wharf for dinner?"

Her lips curved into a smile. "Mmm, seafood."

He grinned again, his dark lashes throwing shadows on his cheeks.

Gosh. Had she *ever* been this happy?

"Lotion," he instructed, pointing at her tat. Then he rolled her shirt down and mumbled, "Only time you'll see me pull your shirt *down*."

With a final, but thorough, kiss, he turned toward home. She stood on her porch watching his confident swagger. She watched until he was halfway down the beach, then, under the shade of her porch, first making sure he wasn't looking, she rolled her shirt up, admiring Evan's handiwork again.

The area was a little red and swollen, but so beautiful. Custom. Precisely what she'd asked for.

A man's tall form stepped around the corner of her house. Thinking Evan had come back to warn her of the perils of exposing her tat to the elements too soon, Charlie opened her mouth to promise this was the last time.

It wasn't Evan.

Two years had passed since she'd seen the man. His hair was a touch more gray than she remembered, and if his pronounced gut was any indication, he was carrying at least twenty extra pounds.

Her formerly relaxed, drenched-in-happy body went rigid as she took in his scowl.

Self-consciously, she covered her body with her shirt and addressed her ex-boyfriend with a delayed, but no less surprised, "*Russell*?"

CHAPTER TWENTY-SEVEN

*J*esus, Mary, *and Joseph*, Charlotte."

Russell Hartman. In her backyard.

In shock over that fact, she mumbled, "What are you doing here?"

He turned his head and studied the direction where Evan had disappeared with a shake of his head. "Charlotte," he repeated as if exasperated.

She used to *hate* when he did that—looked down on her. He did it often during the six years they'd dated. Now that they were no longer dating, she didn't like it any more than she used to.

There was a certain amount of ice in her tone when she spoke next. "You could have called."

"I *did* call," he accused. "You didn't pick up, so I drove over."

Right. Her phone was inside.

"Dare, the boys, and I are staying north of the pier,

and I wanted to show my family the dock and the wall of evergreens."

Dare, as in Darian. The boys. *My family.* Each of those words was a shard of glass he had no problem pushing into her skin.

He also could have shown them the "wall of evergreens" from the other side of the lake.

"I was calling to ask if you'd mind if we parked in the drive and walked down there," he said, sounding defensive while encroaching on *her* territory.

She opened her mouth to tell him "no," that he and *his family* could go to non-private property, when his next words struck her speechless.

"Never did I expect to find you with your tongue down Evan Downey's throat." He shook his head as shame cascaded over her like a bucket of icy water. "I always knew you were too close to him, Charlotte. I never liked it, but I kept that to myself."

He hadn't. He'd reminded her every chance he got.

"Evan Downey," he repeated, this time with enough accusation to stir a jury.

Her heart plunged despite her attempt to keep from overreacting. She crossed her arms, not out of defiance but to prevent the quake working its way through her body from visibly shaking her hands.

Russell helped himself onto her porch. He'd never physically hurt her before but it didn't keep her from backing up as he approached. On even ground now, he could literally look down on her. And he did, talking to her with judgment and disgust prevalent in his tone. "How could you, Charlotte? How could you be so cavalier with your *best friend's* husband?"

That was completely unfair. Unfortunately, it was also completely true.

"He has a *son*."

The anxiety flitting through her veins didn't make thinking of a sensible retort easy. "I love Lyon." She hated the defensiveness in her tone. Hated more that she felt tears building in her throat. All her reasons for kissing Evan Downey tumbled in her head, but if she said them out loud, she'd sound more defensive. And would give Russell more ammo for the Shame-O-Matic weapon he'd toted all the way over here.

I love Evan. I love to watch him paint. I love the way he paints me. I love the tattoo he gave me. I love everything about him.

But the words clogged in her throat, her self-confidence ebbing in Russell's presence.

"Lyon loves you, too, Charlotte," Russell confirmed softly. That truth was made harder to hear when he followed it with "Lyon loves you as *Aunt* Charlie, not as a replacement for his mother."

Her blood matched her tone, turning to ice. He'd zinged her with her biggest fear, her biggest worry. "I'm not trying to replace Rae." That was true, too. She straightened her shoulders and found her strength. "You don't have any right to show up here uninvited and cast judgment on something you don't understand."

He was unfazed. "What I *understand* is that rather than put her kids through the heartache of watching their mother *shack up* with a man"—he gestured to himself, then threw an arm wide—"Darian and I got married by a justice of the peace."

How self-righteous was he?

"You shacked up with me," Charlie reminded him.

Tilting his head, he stepped closer, his body blocking out her surroundings. "Charlotte, honey, you didn't have children."

"You didn't want children."

"I didn't want children with you, Charlotte, no."

Ouch.

She put her hand to her chest, the sting of that blow finding its mark.

"I dated Darian for…a while." For the first time, his gaze flitted to the side and he didn't look in her eyes. He looked at his feet. "I never told you this, but those last three and a half months when you and I didn't sleep together…"

She really, really didn't want to hear the rest of that sentence. He let her have it anyway, making sure he looked in her face when he delivered the news.

"I didn't sleep with you because I'd already met and fallen in love with Darian. I wasn't willing to cheat on my future wife."

Charlie's jaw dropped. He'd…cheated on her? For three and a half months while they were dating? She had no idea. None. He'd played her for a fool. And what a fool she'd been.

"You cheated on me?" she asked numbly.

"I didn't, since technically I wasn't sleeping with you at the time. I was sleeping with Dare. I would have been cheating on her if I took you to bed."

Nausea roiled her insides. Amazingly, he shook his head in disgust. *Aimed toward her.* She tried to reroute some at him, refusing to let his self-righteousness go further, but as usual, he said something next that rattled her scrambling brain.

"It's like I don't know who you've become. *My* Charlotte wouldn't move in on her best friend's family and try to take what was once Rae Lynn Downey's. In a church. In front of *God*, Charlotte. You stood witness at her wedding!"

"She's been gone for four years!" It wasn't what she wanted to say, it just sort of popped out. She went with it. "Everyone has moved on. *You've* moved on," she managed to get in. "Evan has moved on."

"Has Lyon moved on?" Manufactured sorrow etched his features. "Forget all about his mom, did he? Did Evan forget about the wife he once pursued doggedly while ignoring your teenage affections?"

Right then, she hated herself for having ever shared that tidbit with him. He'd kept hold of it over the years, waiting for the right moment to hit her with it. He'd loaded a slingshot and aimed for her heart.

"He didn't choose you then. Why now?" Russell continued. "Did he suddenly forget all about the woman he made a child with? Did he forget the first woman he fell in love with? Did he forget the woman who bore his son, Charlotte? No, I don't think he has," he answered himself.

"It's not about forgetting Rae." She grappled on to the statement like a lifeline. She was onto something. A point. *The truth.* Russell had muddied the truth since he'd arrived, but she finally had something concrete to latch on to.

"It's not about forgetting her," he agreed.

Agreed. Which muddied her mind after all.

"Forgetting her is impossible, Charlotte. No one can forget a woman as vivacious and alive as Rae Lynn. And a man does not forget the love of his life for someone...else."

In his own special way, he reminded Charlie she was not as vivacious, or as alive as Rae—even in her death. He solidified what she secretly knew he'd always believed. Charlie was forgettable. And as much as she wanted to rail against it, this, too, sounded true.

Her sister had forgotten her. Her father had forgotten her. And Russell, after he'd met Darian, had most definitely forgotten her.

How long until Evan did the same?

The hold she had on her earlier point slipped. So did her shoulders.

"You're seeing what you want to see. You want Evan, and he's desperate to have a woman in his life again. He's using you, Charlotte." Russell flicked a hand at her body. "Not your fault, darling, you are only using your best assets."

"Get out," she warned, her voice low. A quake rattled her bones, but she refused to break down in front of him. She could crumble inside. In peace. Away from his poison-tipped barbs.

"Not your fault," he repeated. "No man, no matter who he is, can resist those hips."

Her arm moved on its own, pulling back to land a sharp slap across Russell's face. Eyes angry and teeth bared, he snatched up her wrist before she made contact.

"Get out!" she screeched.

He walked into her, shoving her back several feet, bumping her into the porch swing. Before she could become slightly afraid of the man who was a decade older than her, a blur moved behind him.

The blur grabbed him up by the scruff of his golf shirt.

"Son of a bitch!" she heard Evan shout loud and clear. They tumbled down the stairs as she blinked them into focus. He had Russell flat on his back in a manner of seconds. Russell, several inches taller and out-weighing him in the beer-belly department, tried to get up but Evan clasped his shirt again and delivered a hard right across his jaw.

Russell, never a fighter—no need to be when he could wield his tongue like a sharpened sword—held up his hands in front of his face to deflect another blow.

"Evan! Stop! My family!" he begged.

Evan ignored his pleas and pummeled him again. Another right busted open his lip. Another landing on his nose. One to the eye. Charlie covered her mouth with her hands, frozen in a combination of fear and awe.

"You ever touch her again, Hartman, I will put you in the hospital," Evan promised, his hands wrenched in Russell's collar, biceps flexing as he raised Russell's face to his own. "Get me?"

"Let me go!" Russell scrambled again.

Evan tightened his hold. "Say you get me," he said, his voice a low, dark rumble.

"I get you! I get you!" Russell shouted.

Unfortunately, right at the moment Evan loosened his hold on Russell, Darian rounded the side of the house and shrieked, her hands clutching a white purse hooked on one narrow shoulder. "Russy!"

Distracted, Evan looked up and Russell took a cheap shot, punching him square in the face. Charlie propelled down the stairs toward them as Evan rolled to the side and wiped blood from his nose.

"I'm going to kill him," Evan growled, his eyes furious and unfocused as he pushed himself up.

Charlie hung on to Evan's bicep as he stood, almost losing her balance. "Russell! Get the hell out of here," she shouted. "And take that bitch with you!"

Darian gasped. "Don't you talk to me like that. *Whore*."

Oh no she didn't.

Charlie advanced, her eyes on the other woman. "Get off my lawn." Evan's hand wrapped around her upper arm, but there was no need for him to stop her. She wasn't about to fight Darian Hartman. "Before I sue you and *Russy* for trespassing."

"You two deserve each other," Russell said with a finger-point, still managing to play the holier-than-thou card with blood pouring from cuts on his face.

He walked around the house, his sobbing wife behind him, cooing, "Are you okay, sweetie?"

"I'm okay, darling." He wrapped an arm around his wife's shoulders. "Let Evan sort out his trash."

At that comment, Evan tore off after Russell. Charlie lost her balance as he pushed past her and fell into the sand with a soft *oof!* Evan stopped, spun around, and dropped to his knees in front of her.

"Shit, Ace. You okay?"

"I'm fine." But she wasn't fine. She was the trash Russell had referred to. He'd also pointed out she'd been selfish. And that she was attempting to take the place of her best friend.

Russell never had her best interests in mind, but he was also one of the few people who knew Charlie through and through. Who knew Evan and Lyon. Who'd known Rae. In a way, that made him more qualified to assess this situation than anyone else.

"Ace, honey." Evan's hands ran over her arms, brushed the sand from her clothes. "Let me help you up. Are you hurt?"

She ignored his fussing.

Evan Downey.

Her best friend's husband.

Much as she hated to concede, Russell was right. She had stood next to Rae at the wedding. Stood there and witnessed her best friend bind herself for life to Evan Downey.

Her best friend had died tragically, and what had Charlie done? Fallen in love with Evan.

Why? Why him, the least convenient person in the world to fall in love with?

Since he'd moved to Evergreen Cove, she'd been moving in on their lives. As if she had any right to them. As if they'd accept her as a replacement for Rae Lynn. She'd been fooling herself. They'd all been fooling themselves.

Her stomach rolled. She was going to be sick.

"Talk to me, Ace. That asshole hurt you?"

"I'm fine," she repeated, finally allowing him to help her to her feet.

"Did *I* hurt you?" The blood had begun to dry between his nose and lip. His turquoise eyes darkened with concern.

She shook her head. Tears she'd been attempting to dam throughout this entire episode finally spilled over. "No, Evan. You didn't hurt me."

She'd hurt *him*. She'd hurt him and Lyon by confusing her role as Lyon's aunt and Evan's friend with a role she didn't deserve to play. The role of mother and wife. Rae's role.

Family was grown, not encroached upon. And a family like the Downeys was family in its most pure form. There was no abandoning father, no destroyed sibling relationships. Everyone had a clear part and they played it.

Evan's mother had passed away a few years ago. From what he said, his father was contentedly single. Charlie knew why. Because there was no replacement for Kathy Downey.

Like there was no replacement for Lyon's mother.

At seven, Lyon might not see it now, but what about when he was thirteen? Or eighteen? Or twenty-four with a bride of his own? Soon, he'd see Evan's and Charlie's relationship for what it really was.

Friends with benefits. *Convenient* due to geography and attraction. Both things they had pretended were real reasons and let get out of hand.

"Ace." Evan's face invaded her line of vision, his eyebrows drawn. "Talk to me."

"You should clean yourself up." She shook off his palm and walked away from him. "At your house."

He followed her up her porch steps and latched on to her arm again.

She shook free. "I've been manhandled enough for one afternoon, thanks."

Dropping his hand, he narrowed his eyes, his face pure fury. "Sorry?"

She shook her head, hand wrapped around the handle of the sliding glass door to her kitchen. "No, Evan. Like I've been telling you from the start. *I'm* sorry. I'm sorry for one insane second for allowing any of this. I crossed a line with you."

"*You* crossed a line?" The color flashing in his eyes reminding her of the sky when a storm rolled in over the lake. "I came for you, Ace. Repeatedly."

"You're Rae's husband!" she shouted in his face.

He didn't back off but closed in on her. She pressed her back against the door. Lowering his face over hers, he said in a voice that was pure steel. "Rae's dead."

"I won't be a convenient replacement," she whispered.

He drew back like she'd slapped him. Russell wasn't the only one who could deliver a sharp insult. Evan's reeling away from her was proof she'd hit her mark.

"You wanna say that again." It wasn't a question, but it was. She watched a muscle in his cheek jump as he wedged his teeth together and dared her to speak.

So, she did.

"Admit it. I'm the easy choice. You know me. I love your kid. I've had a crush on you since I was fifteen years old, and my best friend won you."

"A crush." His eyes grew more furious. She kept talking.

"I'm a one-stop shop. You get a replacement mom, a woman Lyon trusts to raise him, and someone who supports you when you're painting in 'the zone.' *Convenient*," she repeated, tears spilling from her eyes.

He searched her face as if she'd transformed into a stranger rather than the woman he'd known for seventeen years.

She felt it, the sharp way it cut into her to know things between them would never be the same. And she took it. Because she deserved it.

After an eternity of silence, he finally spoke. "You're lucky."

"Lucky?" she asked, not understanding his meaning.

"Lucky you're a woman," was all he said. Then he stalked off her porch and stormed across the beach toward his house.

CHAPTER TWENTY-EIGHT

Charlie had never been so glad to have so much to do. She spent the evening alternating between crying and fixing Guy and Mallory's wedding photos.

Stupid weddings.

Sniffling, she reached for a tissue to blot her eyes as she saved the picture she'd altered. She was being unfair. Spitting venom at the wrong party.

What she needed was a mirror.

The clock over the stove read nine, and she stood and stretched, her stomach aching from a combination of hunger and fear. She peeked out the kitchen window and over to Evan's house. Earlier when she looked, she'd spied him and Lyon out on the porch, the grill smoking.

She'd gone back to her computer, afraid he'd come invite her to dinner and relieved when he hadn't.

Being faced with Russell, who threw Rae in her face, had challenged her. A challenge she'd failed.

She saw that now.

Filling a glass with water, it hit her front and center. Where she'd screwed up; what she'd done wrong. She should have stood next to Evan. She should have trusted him.

What had she done instead? Pushed him away. After pushing him away repeatedly when he kept coming for her, how could she expect him to continue trying?

At some point, something had to give.

The windows of the Downey house were dark. The studio lights off. She wondered if they were sacked out in the living room, watching *Man of Steel*, or if Lyon was showing Evan proof he'd finally won the queen on his iPad game.

Rae the queen.

Charlie gave her head a sad shake, seeing herself with frightening clarity all of a sudden.

Not only had she *not* infringed on her friend's role, she'd kept Rae's memory alive for Lyon, for all of them. She thought of the stacks of paintings in Evan's studio. Instead of getting up to paint another dark mural, he'd drawn her tattoo designs. "Because of you, Ace," he'd told her while he punctured her skin lovingly.

She'd reached in and pulled Evan out of the darkness he'd been in for years. Charlie, Evan, and Lyon had created a new family. Rae couldn't be here for them. And that wasn't anyone's fault.

Charlie had fallen deeply in love with both Evan and Lyon. And then, when tested, had pulled her heart from their hands. Taken herself away. She tipped her head back and looked at the ceiling, muttering, "Sorry, Rae" for a whole new reason.

Because Charlie had failed them.

She'd failed them both.

Returning to her computer, she clicked the "Rae" file and sifted through photos of her best friend. Beautiful in color or black and white, her smile shined from each image.

Charlie was in a few of these, too, her arms around Rae. This one was the last Christmas Rae was alive. That one, a girls' night out at a sushi bar.

Her heart ached. She'd lost Rae, and now, she'd lost Evan and Lyon.

She'd lost them all.

Finally, she found the one she wanted Lyon to have, selected a size, and clicked print. The printer at her back whirred to life, pulling in a sheet of paper, when there was a knock at her patio door.

Charlie tried to keep her heart from overreacting, but it pounded hard, and harder when the knock came again, because it sounded like a little boy's knock.

And there was only one little boy who knocked on her patio door.

Creeping around the edge of her desk and kitchen counter, she found Lyon peeking through the glass, hands cupped around his face. When she flipped on the outside light, she saw Evan behind him, leaning an elbow against the post at the bottom of the stairs.

Seeing Lyon made her heart hurt.

Seeing Evan obliterated it.

Steeling herself for the confrontation she should have known was coming, she swiped her fingers under her eyes and pulled her hands through her hair, glad she was semi-decent; dressed in her tee and shorts from earlier.

Then she slid the door aside and used every ounce of strength left in her to give Lyon a smile. "Hey, honey."

"Hi, Aunt Charlie. Dad said you were sad so I brought you this."

In his hands was a large yellow envelope. She accepted it. "Thank you." Flat. Likely a sheet of paper.

Or a photo.

"Want me to open it now?"

"Yeah," he said.

She hazarded a glance at Evan, who stood stone still against the pillar, his face a placid mask.

Bending the metal prongs, she carefully lifted the lip of the envelope and reached inside. What she pulled out took her breath away. It was a photo of her and Lyon on Evan's back porch. She remembered he'd taken it with his phone while she and Lyon grinned and said, "*Cheeeeese.*"

He looked like both Rae and Evan in this picture, but it occurred to her as she studied the way he pressed his cheek against hers, that he also looked like he belonged with her.

"It's beautiful," she said, hoping Evan didn't make out the emotion filling her throat. But why did Lyon bring her this photo? To remember him by? She sought Evan's face for answers.

"Tell her what else, bud." Evan's eyes were on her but he spoke to Lyon.

"We're having a bonfire at our house. Can you come over?"

Carefully, she slid the photo back into the envelope, wanting very badly to ask Evan if the invitation was so he could break up with her for good, and if he needed her to take anything out of his house she may have left behind.

How this would work with her being two doors away? Would they remain friends? Would he—

"Ace."

Her scratchy, red eyes found his. She darted them back down to Lyon. Like she could tell this kid "no" to anything. Evan must have known that.

"Sure, honey. Let me grab my shoes."

Lyon bounded down the stairs but Evan remained, warning his son "not to go too far," then rerouting his eyes until they found hers.

"Be over in a few," she mumbled, backing into her house and wanting to stay there. "Need me to bring anything?"

"Yeah. A bag."

A bag? She swallowed thickly, dread pooling in her belly. She was right. He needed her to get her things.

"Did I leave much over there?" Her voice was hollow. But it made the most sense for Evan to let her come over, hang with Lyon, make nice. He was a decent guy; he'd never take his son away from her completely. What he would do was make this an easy transition, because he loved Lyon with all his heart.

Evan pushed off the pillar and turned his head to check on Lyon, who had obeyed, going no farther than the edge of dark beach in the front of her yard.

He took the porch steps without hesitation while she watched in wonder.

One.

Two.

Three.

When he got to her, her fingers wrapped around the edge of sliding door—the only thing holding her up.

"The hell are you talking about?" He sounded as unhappy as he looked.

She lowered her voice even though Lyon was too far

to hear. "I'm assuming I left things there you'd like me to pick up. That's why the bag?"

Without warning, his arm lifted and he palmed the back of her neck. Then he stood way, way too close. He pulled her out of the doorway and into his chest until she was flush against him. Her hands landed on his solid torso, her body flooding with relief, her eyes closing. He was touching her.

It felt way too right to be wrong.

Evan's fingers threaded into her hair. She felt him watching her. "Something you need to get off your chest, Ace?" His voice rumbled through his body and against her palms.

She tipped her head back on her neck to meet his eyes, needing to clear this up. If for no one else but her. "Are you..." She swallowed, then continued, "...ending things?"

Wow. That hurt to say out loud. She had no idea they could, but his eyebrows actually went lower. His thick lashes narrowed, obliterating his eyes.

"What part of 'not going anywhere' is unclear to you?"

Blinking at him, she said, "Sorry? I mean, pardon me?"

The corner of his lips twitched and repeated, "Not going anywhere. Not giving you a break. Not giving you an out." His hand ruffled into the hair at her nape. "Sound familiar?"

It *did* sound familiar. Those were his words to her while they stood in Rae's old bedroom at Patricia and Cliff's house.

"The bag"—he tipped his head closer to hers—"is because I'm not letting you sleep without me tonight."

He'd come for her.

Again.

"Yeah?" she asked, her voice barely a whisper, her heart filling with hope.

"Yeah."

* * *

Lyon had insisted on s'mores followed by hot dogs over the fire. Evan had indulged him. After they'd all eaten that abominable—but no less delicious—late-night snack, Evan left Charlie on the deck to tuck Lyon into bed.

She watched the flames, feeling...something. Foolish? Contented?

Unsure.

What she felt was unsure.

She'd brought a packed bag and put it in the bedroom. Evan had sat close to her while they readied their food for roasting over the fire bowl. But with little ears around they hadn't been able to clear anything up...and there was more to say.

More from her.

She didn't have a speech in queue. Didn't have any idea of an elegant way to explain what a mess she was. Other than to say she was sorry, a word she knew he didn't like to hear from her.

Such was her state when he came back outside after tucking Lyon in: no speech, sorry, and having no clue how to elegantly say it.

He collapsed into the chair next to hers with a sigh. His lip was slightly swollen from Russell's sucker-punch, but the small bump in his nose was not from Russell. That one Evan said he'd had since Donovan had socked him in the face one summer at the Cove.

Boys.

She turned her head. "How's your face?"

Gosh, he was beautiful. Stole the very breath from her lungs. Messy bedhead, honest turquoise eyes, lips she'd kissed over and over and still hadn't had enough of. He hadn't kissed her tonight at all, come to think of it.

Maybe that was why she felt unsure even after his proclamation in her doorway.

But what did he need to say that he hadn't already proven? In the past couple of days, he defended her honor, he came for her, he gave her space when she didn't need it. And here she sat, staring into his beautiful face, head empty, mouth mute.

There was only one thing she could think to say. "I'm sorry."

This earned her a grunt and a slight lift of his lips. "'Course you are." That tiny lift made her heart do a cartwheel. "You're sorry about everything. Especially shit you shouldn't be sorry for."

"I said awful things." She looked at her hands.

"Yeah. So did I." He shook his head. "Seeing that asshole with his hands on you...I couldn't..."

She lifted her eyes and held his.

"You deserve better, Ace."

She filled the air with a nervous laugh. "I deserve something."

His hand covered both of hers. "You deserve me."

Her smile fell and her heart pounded.

"And I deserve to have you. Tonight. Tomorrow. Every day." He squeezed her hands.

Her heart did another cartwheel.

"Know what part of you I love the most?" he asked.

She clasped her fingers together, felt her eyes grow wide.

Did he . . . just say . . . he *loved* her?

Maybe he means as a friend. Don't freak out.

Her heart kicked against her ribs.

Too late.

She was freaking out.

"Do you?" he prompted.

Shocked, she shook her head in answer.

"Every part. All of them." His crooked smile slipped and he focused on her so intently, she couldn't look away. "I love when you get embarrassed when I compliment your body. Love when you gasp when I say something dirty you find secretly sexy. Love that you love my son"— he took his hand from hers and grasped her neck, turning his body toward hers—"especially that part." He gave her a squeeze. "Love that you apologize for absolutely everything."

She was biting her lip so she wouldn't cry, but she felt the tears building in the backs of her eyes, stinging her nose.

"Know why?"

She shook her head again, still speechless. Overwhelmed.

"Because that's who you are. Every giving, loving, amazing part of you. And every last part belongs with me." He paused, pressed his lips together for a second, then said, "I didn't choose you first, Ace. I can't change that."

Finally, she found words, and the voice to give them. "I wouldn't want you to. Without Rae, I wouldn't be me. You wouldn't be you." Quietly, she added, "We wouldn't have Lyon."

"*We.*" His smile widened. "Love that about you, too, Ace." Palming the back of her head, he lowered his lips to hers.

She tipped her lips to catch the kiss, the only thought in her addled brain that he loved her. Loved everything about her.

Oh, her heart. Her pounding, beating, palpating heart.

"I'd ask if you'd have me, Ace..." he whispered against her mouth. "But baby, you already have me."

Grasping his neck, she pulled his lips to hers and crushed into him. When the arm of the chair pushed into her ribs, preventing them from getting closer, he stood and pulled her up by her elbows. Bending, he hooked an arm behind her knees and scooped her up, kissing her again and again while he walked her to the house.

At the doorway, he teased, "Good to see you agree."

"I do."

Something serious crossed his face. "I know you do."

He did know. He *had* known. And he didn't stop in his pursuit of her because he'd known. He'd seen the truth way before she had.

They belonged together. He loved her.

He *loved* her.

Evan Downey was in love with her.

The words pounded like the backbeat of a song on the radio, throbbing through her body with too much bass.

No, not too much.

Just enough.

If he could be bold, so could she. She grinned up at him. "Can I borrow your shower with you in it?"

Still holding her in his arms, he grinned as he pushed open the door. "Hell yes."

*C*HAPTER TWENTY-NINE

That fall...

*L*ibrary Park boasted a banner that read THE COVE'S HARVEST FEST. Pumpkins, haystacks, and scarecrows decorated the park, and the Andersons' home across the street was decorated as well. Tom had turned it into a "haunted house" for the event, but to Charlie, it looked more Scooby-Doo than Amityville Horror.

She shook her head at the skeleton in the yard wearing a pink dress.

A pink dress.

Not that haunted houses were particularly scary before nightfall, anyway, she reasoned.

Evan palmed her ribs and tugged her close as they walked through the crowd. She wanted to release a long sigh as she curled into him, so she did. She pretty much did whatever she was feeling with him since the night he came for her. She'd promised him he'd never have to come for her again, and he told her, "I'll come for you always, Ace."

Was it any wonder she had agreed to marry him?

After dinner tonight, they walked down to the park with Lyon, along with almost every other 'Greener who had braved the slightly chilly air to buy a caramel apple, spiked apple cider, or—yikes—a scoop of sauerkraut ice cream being offered at Jack's Shack.

Evan's fingers gently grazed the tattoo just under her breast. The tattoo he'd added to since, his latest embellishment happening a few days ago.

He'd drawn in a thick stroke of blue around the camera. He'd been adding paint strokes one at a time since he branded her. The first time, she'd come into the studio to tell him good night and he pulled her into his lap, kissed her, and murmured, "Have an idea, Ace."

She thought he meant another roll in paint on a canvas, but instead, he'd laid her on his chair and added watercolor-style brushstrokes of color to her body. She requested more last week, and as any good tattoo artist and man who was happy to brand his woman, he agreed.

She loved it. There was something special about having her passion blended with his. There was something special about them period, she thought with a smile.

This morning, he surprised her again. He'd added another tat to himself a week ago, sneakily keeping it from her. A bandage over his left pec disguised the surprise for an entire week. He fibbed by saying something about a "freak bacon-frying accident" to cover for himself.

Then, while she was getting dressed today, he tore off his T-shirt while she struggled to maintain some semblance of calm. She'd never get over seeing his naked chest. His naked anything.

He stood over her while she sat on the edge of the bed pulling on her socks.

"Gotcha something, Ace."

Then he took the bandage off his skin and showed her that "something." The letter A and a heart inked into his skin. Over his heart.

An Ace of hearts.

She'd made it onto Evan's canvas.

Fingers to her lips, she'd smiled up at him. "Really?"

He brought his forehead to hers. "Really, Ace." Then he pushed her onto the bed, put a knee between her legs, and kissed her.

They were both later getting to work than they'd anticipated.

"Aunt Sofie!" Lyon looked up from his iPad. He was now consumed with some game featuring towers of fruit—and about nine hundred levels of difficulty. He needed a new distraction ever since he saved the queen on Clashing Clans. Charlie had insisted on commemorating the feat by hanging a photo in Lyon's room—a photo of Rae in her wedding dress, wearing her "crown."

Charlie had worried at first how Evan might react, but when he caught sight of it over Lyon's dresser, he pulled her close and kissed her, much like he'd done a moment ago.

Rae's wedding picture hung right next to a photo of Evan, Charlie, and Lyon. They stood on the dock looking very much like a family. When she told Evan as much, he'd corrected her with, *"We* are *a family, Ace."*

Then he'd proposed, and before she could answer, Lyon was shaking her arm shouting, "Say yes, Charlie!"

Sofie Martin, event planner extraordinaire, was all smiles when she stopped in front of Evan, Charlie, and Lyon. She had been asked to plan the festival, so she should be. This was a huge coup for her business.

The "aunt" thing was new for Sofie. Maybe Lyon had needed a replacement aunt since he'd stopped referring to Charlie as "aunt" last month. Not that Evan or Charlie had asked him to stop. It had happened naturally, like a lot of things between them did.

"Hey guys," Sofie said.

"Everything looks great," Charlie told her, gesturing around at the decorations.

"Except for the deep-fried beets." Sofie wrinkled her nose and pointed at a cart across the way. "And thank you. It's been...*interesting* working closely with Mrs. Anderson."

Charlie felt the low rumble of Evan's laughter at her side where she was pressed against him.

Sofie addressed Evan. "The reveal's in ten minutes, you know."

"Right." Evan's eyes slid to Charlie. She hadn't seen the painting he donated yet, but he assured her that Mrs. Anderson was getting what she requested: *art*.

"I have a few minutes on my hands if you want me to take Lyon over to the haunted house," Sofie offered.

"Dad! Can I?" His eyes were wide and his smile huge.

"Nightmares, bud," Evan said.

"Nuh-uh," he argued. "Nonna gives me cookies and milk to keep the nightmares away." Pat and Cliff were due any minute to pick up Lyon for the weekend.

"Lionel—" Evan started.

Charlie squeezed his side. "Oh, come on, babe. This is

the Anderson house we're talking about. How scary could it be?"

He lifted an eyebrow suggesting she might be eating those words. Mrs. Anderson was pretty darn scary on her own.

Lyon dropped his head back on his neck and looked up at her. "Mom. Can I?"

Mom.

Charlie looked into Evan's son's pleading eyes and pressed her lips together. She wondered when it would happen... sooner than she thought.

"I *promise* I won't have nightmares," he added with an eye roll. As if the haunted house was the most pressing issue at hand. As if he didn't absolutely define her world and future with one word.

"*Mom*," Lyon said, stabbing her right in the feels again with the three-letter word. "Is it okay?"

Evan's palm slipped up to Charlie's nape where he gave her a light squeeze. "Yeah, bud. It's okay with your mom and me."

Gosh. She blinked rapidly. She might just lose it.

Sofie placed a hand on Lyon's shoulder and gave Charlie a knowing grin. "We'll meet you after."

When they left, Charlie had a serious, silent discussion with her tear ducts, instructing them not to ruin her makeup.

Evan lowered his lips to her forehead and kissed her, whispering, "Natural progression, Ace."

"I know, I just..."

She looked at the engagement ring on her finger. Thought of Evan's proposal. *"Promise you forever, Ace."*

She'd said yes to him then. Then she'd said yes a dozen more times in their bed that night.

Natural progression.

"Bound to happen," Evan said to her now. "He loves you. I love you."

Her heart fluttered. She looked from her ring to his handsome face. "I love you, too."

"I know, baby." Another gentle squeeze to her neck. "Better go in. We're late."

They crossed the park and entered the library where a small crowd had gathered for the "big reveal" of Mrs. Anderson's penance painting from one-half of the Penis Bandits.

Real art for the library's wall.

Evan and Charlie positioned themselves near the back of the crowd, behind a short bookshelf filled with children's books—Evan's included and proudly displayed face-out. Mrs. Anderson tugged the sheet and the crowd gasped when it piled to the ground, revealing the painting.

Charlie gasped, too.

"Beautiful," someone said.

"Amazing."

"An original," said someone else.

It was original, all right. A touched-up, refinished original she wasn't sure was safe for public consumption.

"*Evan*," she hissed.

His arm wrapped around her shoulders and tugged her close, his low, sexy male chuckle reverberating against her ribs.

She stared at the painting.

Oh boy.

The very painting she'd asked him to *burn*. He'd wanted to hang it in the living room, which had earned another "no" from her.

"You didn't, baby," she breathed.

"Penis Bandit, Ace."

In other words, you can't take the bad out of the boy.

And maybe that's what she loved about him. People continued to murmur their appreciation, nodding with admiration.

Charlie turned her lips to Evan's ear and whispered, "Crude."

He smiled down at her. "You love it."

She did. And she loved him. Which is why he'd known she'd forgive him.

"A huge gratitude to Mr. Evan Downey, commissioned to do this amazing and artful painting," Mrs. Anderson announced with a flourish of her hand.

The crowd clapped and he lifted his hand in a small wave.

Then a voice cut in, "Ava, is that . . . a *nipple*?"

Mrs. Anderson turned to her prized possession, tipping her head to study it closer. Evan's waving hand dropped and pressed into Charlie's lower back.

He tilted his chin at the door. "Ace."

She didn't need to be told twice. She moved for the door.

A second later, Mrs. Anderson's voice rang out, "Is that a *butt cheek*?"

Evan's laugh cut into the air, making Charlie feel overwhelmingly happy.

She'd found what she didn't know she was looking for—a husband, a family, a son.

Finally.

Outside, they spotted Patricia and Cliff Mosley at the cider booth. Pat had a cup of cider, but it looked like Cliff had taken a chance on the sauerkraut ice cream.

On the way over to meet them, Charlie lifted her eyes to the slowly darkening sky, knowing she was where she should be, knowing they were *all* where they should be.

Spotting a star, she smiled and whispered up to her friend, *"I've got this, Rae."*

FROM THE DESK OF JESSICA LEMMON

Dear Reader,

Every good bad boy should have a hangover remedy in his repertoire. Turns out Evan Downey from BRINGING HOME THE BAD BOY has two. One of them is a recipe for seared red potatoes, eggs, and cheese on top, and the other... well, the other one might be heroine Charlie Harris's *favorite*.

But that's another story for another time.

In case you don't happen to have a go-to recipe for when you've had too many "Mad Cow Tinis," I'm going to give you Evan's. It does employ a bit of skill, so if you're severely hungover, you may want to have a friend (a bad boy?) make it for you.

HANGOVER HASH FOR TWO

4–5 new (red) potatoes, scrubbed and rinsed

¼ of a green pepper, cubed

¼ of a sweet Vidalia onion, cubed

olive oil

2 eggs

sharp cheddar cheese

2 slices multigrain bread

1. The trick, Evan would tell you, is getting the potatoes cooked just right. Place potatoes in a pot and cover with cold water. Put a lid on the pot and bring to a boil. Once boiling, remove the lid and continue to cook the potatoes for 12-14 minutes or until you can stick the tip of a knife in a potato and it slips off the edge. That means they're done. Remove from water and place on a cutting board. When they're cool enough for you to handle, cube them.

2. Put a drizzle of olive oil in a large frying pan and toss in cubed potatoes, green pepper, and onions. Cook over medium-high heat, tossing on occasion. Evan employs the fancy flip-into-the-air move, but he also cooks in his boxer briefs, so you do what is right for you. Employing a wooden spoon is perfectly acceptable.

3. Put a drizzle of olive oil in a small frying pan and heat over medium-high. Crack two eggs into the

pan and immediately lower the heat to medium.
You want a runny yoke for this meal, so you don't
want to cook them too fast. Carefully flip so as not
to break the yoke. Evan prefers to utilize a utensil
for this endeavor since the flip move is a bit risky.

4. Make toast. Butter toast. This should need no further explanation.

5. Pile seared-to-perfection red potatoes, onions, and
green peppers onto the center of your plate, sprinkle on sharp cheddar cheese, and lay your over-easy egg on top. Serve with toast, making sure to
cut them into triangles (no shoddy squares, please)
and—this is important—your first bite should be
the one where you cut through the center of the egg
and yoke runs into the potatoes.

6. Enjoy! Oh, and don't forget the coffee. Charlie
takes hers with lots *and lots* of cream.

Happy cooking!

~Jess

Bad boy Donovan Pate has only painful memories of Evergreen Cove. But when he returns home, a beautiful woman from his past may be his second chance at love...

Please see the next page for a preview of

Rescuing the Bad Boy.

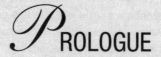PROLOGUE

The mansion ate light. A row of sconces lining the hall-way cast a yellowish glow across the foyer, doing little to illuminate the floor, the thick drapes covering the win-dows, or the staircase leading up to the murky beyond.

One of Donny Pate's hands cradled Sofie Martin's incredible ass as his mouth explored hers, the length of his body pressing her against the heavy wooden door. Her, he could see. Every pliant inch felt as amazing as it looked.

He breathed into her ear, bit her earlobe. She arched her back, rubbing her little black dress against his sweater and jeans. All the blood in his head rushed directly to his pants. He'd kissed her once at the bar, for several minutes in his Jeep when he'd arrived at the mansion, and now this up-against-the-door thing was trying every last ounce of his willpower.

He might die if he didn't get inside her soon.

It'd been a shit week, one he'd rather not think about,

followed by a shit night that was turning out pretty damn good. Tonight's company Christmas party had been boring as hell, but the manager at the Wharf required everyone to be in attendance if they wanted to get their bonus check. And Donny, since he was leaving this godforsaken town the minute the check cleared, needed that bonus.

The Wharf's dining room had been decorated with cheesy decorations, "Rudolph, the Red-Nosed Reindeer" piping through the ancient sound system. Donny had relegated himself to chain-smoking and drinking with his jackass coworkers, making tonight like every Saturday. Until the tip of Sofie's upturned nose poked around the dividing wall. Then his evening had taken a decidedly more interesting turn.

She'd been watching him tonight, sending furtive glances across the room while pretending to sip the same beer she'd ordered the moment she walked in the door. Then she'd caught him watching her watch him and a tiny smile curled her lips.

Sofie looked like a girl bent on making a mistake. She'd come to the right guy. His recently deceased, formerly belligerent old man never let a moment pass where he hadn't reminded Donny he was, in fact, a mistake.

Donny had felt her eyes on him for a few months now—dancing over him as she entered the kitchen for her shift before refocusing on something far less intriguing. In between the clatter of cooking utensils and the tall steel shelves separating the cooks from the waitstaff, there'd been more than a few moments where he'd caught her moss-green eyes on his.

Whenever she'd turn away, he'd let his gaze travel south. Even through the unflattering industrial-wear the

Wharf required for the waitstaff, he'd noticed her body. Donny wasn't an ass man, but Sofie's had a healthy curve to it, and enough cushion to give his imagination plenty of ammo.

A month or so ago, she'd earned a lifelong nickname on a dare. He'd made that night's special for Sofie's tables at least nine times. He'd been in the weeds, sweating over four sauté pans going at once. *"One more shrimp scampi ticket hits my window, Sofie, I'll brand you for life."*

For a change, she hadn't looked at him like she was intimidated or tongue-tied. Her lips had quirked into a completely adorable sideways smile, and she'd marched out to the dining room and sold not one more special, but *three* to her very next table.

Tonight when the same look of determination crossed her face, Donny ignored all the blaring sirens in his head telling him to leave her alone. Good girl or not, he'd have her tonight.

Consider it a farewell present to himself.

"Scampi," he said now against her mouth, tugging her bottom lip with his teeth.

"Donny." He could tell by her breathy response, she liked that. He squeezed her ass again and a small squeak left her lips. She liked that, too.

Against her mouth, he smiled.

Every damn time.

Smiling wasn't really his thing. What did he have to smile about? Nothing, normally. But now, a cute brunette rubbing against his cock, her cheeks warm despite the air leaking through the gap beneath the mansion's door, her lips dropped open in a reverent sigh...hell yeah, he had something to smile about.

He grabbed another handful of her butt, admiring the mess he'd made of her hair when he'd kissed her five, ten...hell-who-knew-how-many minutes ago.

"Library, sweetheart," he said, tipping his head toward the room on his left. The closest room in proximity to the front door held an ugly red velvet couch and a thick white rug. He would happily lay her down on either. He'd even let her choose.

"Okay," she said against his mouth.

He tightened his hold on her—appreciating again what a glorious, cushy ass she had—and lifted her off the ground. He was six four, so he guessed her around five and a half feet. Once he'd slept with a chick who was five nothing; he remembered her being short, but not one other thing about her. He doubted this would be the case with Sofie "Scampi" Martin.

She looped her arms around his neck and in the pale light he saw her grin to beat all. The grin usually reserved for coworkers other than him. The grin he'd wanted turned in his direction for months. Now he had it. Full force. It made him want her more, and he hadn't thought that was possible.

In the library doorway, he paused. "Couch or rug?"

She'd been twirling the back of his long hair with her fingers, but they stopped moving. Her eyes widened. She blinked. Stunned speechless, he'd guess. Scampi wasn't one of the slutty girls he normally took home for a night. And he guessed "making out" had been the extent of her Christmas party plans.

Well, he had other plans. To get her to say yes, he'd have to lay it on thick.

He softened his voice. "Scampi, baby."

Her fingers flinched against his head. In the pale light, her eyes grew warm. There was something about being underneath the gaze of someone who cared that made him simultaneously panicked and horny. He swallowed thickly and asked the question he had to ask if he hoped to get what he wanted tonight.

"Where do you want to make love?" He nearly gagged on the words. *Make love.* Good God.

But it worked. Her entire face melted into an expression that told him he'd broken through her defenses. She was sober, so no worries there. He'd taken her warm, practically full beer bottle away from her at the bar tonight and that'd been an hour ago. Now there was only one thing left. Getting her to agree.

"I dreamed this." She tightened her hold on his neck, lowered her face, and kissed him so softly, so gently, that something in him recoiled.

She's sweet. Too sweet.

As her lips moved on his, he silently argued with himself. He hadn't had a lot of sweet in his life, but maybe he deserved some. Especially after a week that couldn't get any worse. Scampi's own brand of *sweet* was exactly what he needed.

"Your call." The oddest tension strained his voice. He squeezed his hands around her butt to ground himself. *You deserve some sweet.* And she was a whole lot of sweet.

She kissed him again, this time not as soft, her tongue darting into his mouth and stroking his. It startled him so much, he had to tighten his arms so he didn't drop her.

When she pulled away, she clutched onto his head and whispered, "Couch."

Music to his ears.

"Is that a yes?" He felt his lips curve upward. Another smile. Unbelievable.

She smiled back. "Yes."

Angels began to sing.

"That's what I wanted to hear," he said, then wasted no time laying her flat on her back.

* * *

Donny slid inside her *all the way* and Sofie welded her back teeth together and focused on keeping her facial expressions neutral.

Who knew losing her virginity would be so painful?

That's what you get for keeping it sealed up for twenty-one years...

Twenty-one long years of waiting for the right person. Donny Pate, in spite of being the last person she imagined might sleep with her, was the one doing the honors. She'd never, ever felt this sort of attraction to anyone else.

He was incredibly hot.

But hotness wasn't the only thing that drew her to him. It was that darkness he presented to everyone. The scowl that was its own KEEP AWAY sign. Almost everyone at work heeded the warning, save for a few girls who strode right through the barbed wire with eyes wide open. For Sofie, the attraction to Donny had been less about the challenge of bedding a bad boy. It was his darkness, a quiet sadness that drew her in. She remembered vividly when she'd seen him smile for the first time. It transformed his entire face. The flicker of light in his eyes, the curve of his lips above that steely jaw... She'd vowed that day to make him smile more.

"Scampi," he breathed now, stroking into her for the

third time. She unscrunched her eyes to take him in. Long, ink-black hair hung over his cheeks, shadowing beautiful crystalline eyes. She didn't need to see them to know his silver-blue eyes looked like the winter skies. Pale against his skin and dark hair, those eyes trained on her had frozen her where she stood more than once.

Each and every inch of his lean, tall frame was in proportion, sinew and muscle that wasn't bulky, but definitely hard, corded. And tonight she was lucky enough to have every inch of his amazing body against her and quite a few inches nestled inside her.

Like she'd dreamed.

A grunt, followed by muffled curse words she couldn't make out, preceded him blowing out a long breath that ruffled the hair on her forehead. "Okay," he said, his voice rough. Not a question, but he didn't move, almost waiting for her to answer.

Gripping his neck, she lifted her hips, felt the sharp pinch again, the throb of his penis against her inner walls. She moved her palms from his neck to shoulders, then ran them down his hard male chest. God. He was beautiful.

"I'm okay," she said, canting her hips.

His face contorted almost painfully before something flashed in his eyes, and he slid into her again. One smooth, delicious slide that filled her completely. A gasp escaped her lips and as he moved gently, the pain receded. Her eyes fluttered closed.

This. This was like nothing she'd dreamed. It felt a hundred times better than when they'd started and a million times better than she'd imagined. Donny's hands moved to the side of her head where he pushed her long hair away from her face and lowered his lips.

She kissed him while he drove into her again and again. Her stomach coiled, something building...

"That's it," he said against her mouth, pushing into her again, deeper than before. The movement set off another spark—like flint to stone—and she sparked.

Throwing her head back, she gripped his shoulders with the ends of her short nails and let out a raspy, "Donny."

"Come for me, Scampi." He continued to move within her, winding her so tight, she thought she might lift off the sofa. Tingling. She was tingling everywhere.

"I..." She started to argue but she couldn't. She'd never come before... well, not with a partner. Before she could make that admission, he thrust again, and she did. Her body clutched, her hands clasping tightly onto him, her mouth falling open, a ragged moan escaping her throat.

While sparks flashed behind her eyelids and her toes curled, Donny continued moving. Seconds later, he lost himself as well, his groans drowning out hers, his slick-with-sweat chest brushing her sensitive nipples. One of his hands clutched her hip, the other held on to the back of the couch.

Amazing.

Sofie could only hear her thundering heart, Donny's breathing, the blood rushing through her veins. A dream. This was an amazing dream come true. She opened her eyes to take in the man who'd yet to give her his weight. His body barely touched hers, except for where they were still joined. He gripped the couch, lifted off her body. She wanted him to let go, to fall into her. She wanted him closer, wanted to wrap her arms around him. Wanted him to kiss her.

His heavy-lidded eyes had narrowed. Donny didn't look like he'd be interested in cuddling or kissing. He groused down at her, eyebrows drawn together. "Forget to tell me something, Scampi?" he asked between clenched teeth.

Her blood froze. Surely he couldn't know. Could he? There's no way he could know.

"I . . ." She couldn't tell him. Couldn't.

"Scampi," he repeated, this time sternly.

She shook her head. Speechless.

His elbows were locked as he hovered over her, his face growing angrier. A second later, she lost his warmth when he drew out of her abruptly. The dream fell away in fragmented pieces.

As her body cooled in the chilled room, she took in the state of her clothing. The skirt of her dress had been rucked up over her hips, the top taken to her waist, and her underwire bra wedged in the cushions of the couch was poking her in the ribs. Donny stood, shadows slashing across his chest in the moonlit room, and pulled on a T-shirt.

He bent and reached for his jeans. Under his breath, he muttered, "A fucking *virgin*."

Every nerve ending in her body prickled. "How did you know?" she heard herself ask vacantly.

He tugged on his jeans and growled, "You're so tight, I nearly broke it off in there."

She winced, thinking things couldn't get worse. Then they did.

"Get dressed. I'm taking you to your car."

"Can we . . . can we try again?" she asked, tugging the top of her dress up to cover her breasts. She felt so . . . so exposed.

He didn't look at her, instead concentrating on zipping his fly. "I don't do virgins."

Okay. She wasn't going to cry, in spite of the stinging behind her eyes and the lump in her throat. He couldn't do this. She wouldn't *let* him do this. First of all, it wasn't nice. And secondly, this wasn't the way first times were supposed to go. He was supposed to be gentle and accommodating. She was supposed to tell him he'd made her feel like no other man ever had before. She didn't expect perfect. Awkward was acceptable, but this?

This was *awful*.

She'd remember tonight always, and he was in the process of ruining those memories. She owed it to her future self to salvage this night.

Even though she was freezing, she dropped the material of her dress and showed her breasts. Donny's eyes flickered over her skin. "Come on, baby. Let's try again," she purred, forcing a small smile to her lips.

He ripped his eyes away from her, snatched up his discarded sweater, and jammed his arms into it. Leaning over the sofa he'd tenderly laid her on moments ago, he growled, "I'm not anyone's 'baby,' Scampi. There's not going to be a second time." He pulled the sweater over his head and added, "*Ever*. Get dressed."

Wow. That was a solid "no."

Dejected, embarrassed, and pissed off in a way she knew would devolve into her sobbing the moment she shut her bedroom door, Sofie finished dressing. Speechlessly, she grabbed her coat and purse while Donovan shrugged into his leather coat. A minute later, they climbed into his Jeep.

More silence as they drove back to the restaurant. The

restaurant she'd entered for a work party, determined to kiss Donny Pate before night's end. *Mission accomplished*, she thought miserably, unable to dredge up even a humorless smile.

He pulled into the now-empty (save for her compact car parked in the back) parking lot of the Wharf. Snow had started to fall, the light flakes covering the windshield.

She hazarded a look over at the man she'd chosen over all others. He threw the Jeep into Park and looked straight ahead, no expression on his face.

Determined to leave this night with something salvageable—though really, was any of it?—she turned to say good-bye. "Donny, before I go—"

His beautiful mouth formed one word. "Out."

The word was like a stab to the chest. She blinked at his shadowed profile. *Awful*.

Belatedly, she considered she'd made a big mistake trusting her first time, her body, and her feelings to Donny Pate.

He faced her, his gray eyes cold, his face placid. His voice rose, echoing off the interior of the Jeep. "Scampi, get the hell out!"

Instinctively, she reacted, some primal urge lifting her hand before she knew what was happening. Then Sofie delivered the only physical blow she'd ever given another living being. The slap cracked across Donny's angled jaw, turning his head to one side. Appalled by her actions, she widened her eyes as that same hand lifted to her lips.

Through the strands of black hair covering his face, his silver-blue eyes glowed with anger. Before she could get an apology out, his upper lip curled. In a steely voice, he snarled, "Get. The. Fuck. *Out*."

This time she obeyed, feeling a combination of guilt and shame over a combination of things—all of them having to do with Donny Pate.

She was wrong about the sobbing. It didn't start in her bedroom. It started in her car. And continued until morning.

Fall in Love with Forever Romance

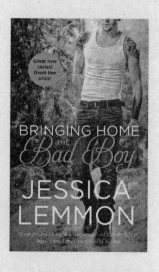

BRINGING HOME THE BAD BOY
by Jessica Lemmon

The boys are back in town! Welcome to Evergreen Cove and the first book in Jessica Lemmon's Second Chance series, sure to appeal to fans of Jaci Burton. These bad boys will leave you weak in the knees and begging for more.

HOT AND BOTHERED
by Kate Meader

Just when you thought it couldn't get any hotter! Best friends Tad and Jules have vowed not to ruin their perfect friendship with romance, but fate has other plans...Fans of Jill Shalvis won't be able to resist the attraction of Kate Meader's Hot in the Kitchen series.

Fall in Love with Forever Romance

FOR KEEPS
by Rachel Lacey

Merry Atwater would do anything to save her dog rescue—even work with the stubborn and sexy TJ Jameson. But can he turn their sparks into something more? Fans of Jill Shalvis and Kristan Higgins will fall in love with the next book in the Love to the Rescue series!

BLIND FAITH
by Rebecca Zanetti

The third book in *New York Times* bestseller Rebecca Zanetti's sexy romantic suspense series features a ruthless, genetically engineered soldier with an expiration date who's determined to save himself and his brothers. But there's only one person who can help them: the very woman who broke his heart years ago...

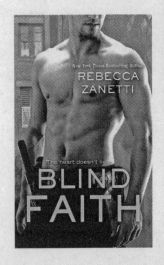

Fall in Love with Forever Romance

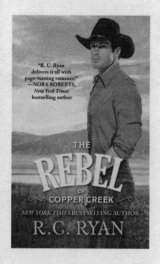

THE REBEL OF COPPER CREEK
by R. C. Ryan

Fans of *New York Times* best-selling authors Linda Lael Miller and Diana Palmer will love this second book in R. C. Ryan's western trilogy about a young widow whose hands are full until she meets a sexy and rebellious cowboy. If there's anything she's learned, it's that love only leads to heartbreak, but can she resist him?

NEVER SURRENDER
TO A SCOUNDREL
by Lily Dalton

Fans of *New York Times* bestsellers Sabrina Jeffries, Nicole Jordan, and Jillian Hunter will want to check out the newest from Lily Dalton, a novel about a lady who has engaged in a reckless indiscretion leaving her with two choices: ruin her family with the scandal of the season, or marry the notorious scoundrel mistaken as her lover.

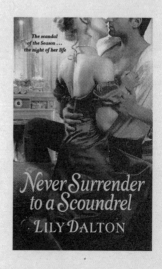